MOSES

By Lester Picker

Dedication

I dedicate this book to my wife, Leslie, my Nefertiti.

Table of Contents

Acknowledgments

I'd be remiss if I did not first acknowledge my father, Martin Picker, for the love he instilled in me for ancient Egypt. On our many trips to the Metropolitan Museum of Art in New York City, we always visited the Ancient Egypt galleries first. I distinctly remember standing at the Pyramids of Giza for the first time and wishing that my father had lived to be there with me.

For my First Dynasty trilogy, I acknowledged the assistance of my historical mentors, Toby Wilkinson of Cambridge University and Gunther Dryer of the German Archaeological Institute. Their influence still continues.

There have been many people over the decades who have suggested that Akhenaten (or one of his devotees) and Moses were one and the same person, including Sigmund Freud. The writings of Ahmed Osman and others carry this forward and propose many links between the Amarna period and Judaism (and, by extension, Christianity and Islam). While I wouldn't agree with all of their conjectures, I am indebted to them for expanding my thinking.

Every writer needs a first draft editor, and I have been blessed with two. First up is my good friend Terry Sexton, who understands story arcs, character development, and structure, as well as anyone. The time he spent reading and commenting on Draft One must have been painful, but I thank him for his persistence. I'd like to blame any errors in this story on him, but he is younger and stronger than I am.

Finally, I thank my wife, Leslie Binder Picker, my second

Draft One editor, for her unswerving support for my creative efforts, be it my writing or my photography. I am indeed a very fortunate man.

As with any work of historical fiction, but especially as regards ancient Egypt, the author must fill gaping holes with a smattering of known facts and an abundance of known fabrications. To that end, I am responsible for any errors in the book… and apologize in advance.

Foreword

For this book, I spent more than seven years researching details of the Amarna period, Akhenaten (or Akhenadon in my telling), Moses, the Exodus, the Old Testament, and myriad aspects of that time period. I was already familiar with Egyptian history from researching and writing my previous three novels about the First Dynasty and from my trips to Egypt. To take the leap from Dynasty One to Dynasty 18, however, required another total immersion.

I fully understand that my interpretation of Akhenadon, Moses, and the Exodus will be controversial and even unacceptable to many. As one who was brought up in a Judeo-Christian world and as one who respects moderate Islam, I felt this story had to be told nonetheless, from the vantage point of archeological findings and sound theological scholarship. The facts are clear: Judaism, and by extension, Christianity and Islam, are all derived directly from Ancient Egypt, its theology, and practices. To deny that is to willfully choose ignorance over knowledge. I have listed in the Afterward a partial sample of Judeo-Christian religious practices that derive directly from ancient Egyptian practices.

I have tried to weave together both historical facts and Biblical storytelling when possible. For example, the Bible says that Moses spent nine years in exile before returning to Egypt. Despite that being unlikely, I folded it into my narrative because it would be plausible for Akhenadon to wait until conditions were right in Egypt before returning.

For those who take on the mantle of Biblical literalists, the plain fact is that there is absolutely no evidence that a mass exodus ever happened. Despite the Egyptians being meticulous record keepers, there are no known accounts of the exodus as told in the Hebrew Bible. Also, despite archaeological research and excavations going back more than 200 years, there has been no evidence uncovered of thousands of people, let alone 600,000, according to the Bible, tramping through the Sinai. If it had taken 40 years to make that comparatively short trip, then the people would have had to camp in various places for extended periods of time. No evidence of this has ever been found, despite intense efforts to do so.

There were also no people known as Hebrews (certainly not known as Jews) until roughly the time of Akhenadon, although the deity Yahveh was worshipped even prior to his time.

We now know that the Old Testament was written by many authors and redacted several times, beginning around 400 years after the time of Akhenaten/Moses. Until then, it was passed from person to person, generation to generation, verbally. There is simply no credible way to treat it as historically accurate. However, it is a compelling tale of creation and the rise of a people committed to monotheism, a strong moral code, and the rule of law. In that, and not for its scientific accuracy, lies its value.

The introduction of the Creation story and its subsequent seven-day week created a problem for me in Book Three of *Moses*. The Egyptians used a ten-day week throughout their history. A month was 30 days, and a year was 360 days. That left a shortfall of five days which were the Heriu-Renpet days of solemnity and which formed the basis of the future Judaism's High Holy Days. In fact, the seven-day week did not come into Judaic practice for several hundred years after the time of the Exodus. However, to provide continuity with the biblical account, I decided to deal with the conflicting calendars within the narrative.

All the poems in the book were actually written by Akhenaten or Nefertiti, although translations may vary slightly from one academic translator to another. I did not change the wording, with the exception that I use Akhenadon rather than Akhenaten for consistency's sake, and changed tenses as needed.

My use of Adon rather than Aten may be confusing. In Ancient Egypt, the "t" was likely pronounced as a "d," much as it is in Arabic today. The "e" sound could have just as well been an "o" since, like Hebrew, the ancient Egyptian written language did not include vowels. If Adon was the actual pronunciation of Aten - and there is at least a better than 50-50 chance that it was -, then one can immediately see the link between the God name of ancient Egypt and Judaism.

Finally, we do not know precisely what the spoken language of ancient Egypt was like. What we do know is that their writing was formal and a bit stiff. Surely the upper classes would have been educated in proper speech and grammar. Therefore, rather than take liberties with their spoken speech, I have preserved what we do know from their abundant writings. **To contact Les, please go to his website: <ins>Lesterpicker.com</ins>**

Praise to the Adon

You are in my heart and none other knows thee
But your son Akhenadon.
You have given him understanding of your designs and
your power.
The people of the world are in your hand
Just as you have created them.
All men since you have made the earth you have raised
for your son
Who came forth from your body,
The King of Egypt who lives in truth,
Lord of Diadems, Akhenadon, whose life is long.
And for his beloved wife
Mistress of Two Lands, Neferneferuadon Nefertiti
May she live and flourish in eternity.

- Akhenadon

Perhaps I am not the right person to write this account. I fear that when it is revealed, it will be a shame cast upon my family and my people. Fathers and sons, priests and adherents, all have difficult relationships. For Akhenadon, who we now call Moses, those relationships were far more perilous. Yet I feel that I must tell his story, for the words fill my soul until I fear I will burst.

I do this quietly in my tent, writing my scrolls in the Egyptian language I have been taught since my youth. It is the season of the desert winds. They howl outside my tent, and every time the gusts are strong enough, handfuls of sand enter the tent from under the loose flaps of coarse woven blankets that cover it. The dust coats our food and mouths and causes the writings on my parchment to be ragged.

I have spoken with or observed all who appear in my telling. I know I am blinded by my love for my brother, but as Chief Priest, I am sworn to truth-telling. So I write this story, this miracle my brother created, a miracle that could only have happened because he lived in the hands of Adon. Yet, even I can no longer say with certainty whether my brother is truly the Son of Adon or mad. I leave it for future generations to decide.

Offered in Love for Adon and my brother

Aharon, Brother of Moses, Chief Priest of Adon, and Royal Scribe

Book One

Pharaoh

Map of Ancient Egypt (18th Dynasty)

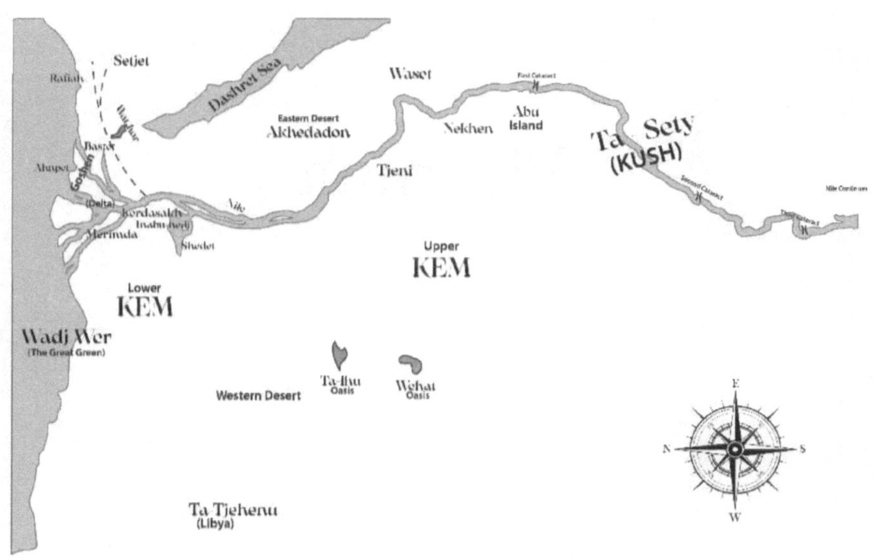

Scroll One

Adon Speaks

I walked quickly through the reception hall of the Great Palace. Despite the urgency of the meeting that Amunhotep the Fourth had indicated, I still had to marvel at the architecture, with its huge columns painted a rare red and each one topped with a green crown. The floor was colorfully tiled, showing scenes of Amunhoterp the Third's reign. The ceiling was a wonder, with scenes of Kem painted over its entire course.

"I do not understand why… why they do not embrace Adon?" Amunhotep the Fourth said in his high-pitched voice as soon as I entered. He paced back and forth in his room, his misshapen body slouched from fatigue. I found the constant noise of his sandals crunching sand against the stone floor annoying to my ears. "They know of Adon's importance to me, even if not yet to themselves." His agitation filled the anteroom, just off the court in his father's magnificent palace. Situated on the banks of Mother Nile, the white palace complex shocked foreign visitors with its splendor.

Once again, I faced repeating the same conversation we had all too many times in the past year or two. "Brother, you have been co-Regent with your father for only four years. Our country has worshipped many other Gods for more than two thousand years. Be patient. They need time to adjust."

Suddenly, Amunhotep turned to me, his finger pointing, his face distorted even more than in its normal state. "Patience!

Patience, you say, Aharon? How patient must I be? I wish my father a long and healthy life, but I will eventually be their King. They must get used to obeying me." Frustrated, he turned once again and leaned against one of the white marble columns. The dark circles under his eyes drooped from lack of sleep, making his long face appear even longer. I walked slowly toward him, speaking softly.

"Amunhotep, we must…"

"Please, dear brother, no pleasantries now. We must find a way to make them comply with my wishes, and soon. They have despised me since my childhood. No, don't try to object, for we both know that is true. But why? Because I look different? I am Adon's creation just as you are and even just like that scoundrel, Maya." I knew my brother well and could see his self-shame reflected in his anger, both of them etched in his deeply creased brow.

Amunhotep turned again and peered out over the royal fields under a blue, cloudless sky. Mother Nile flowed easily, and gardeners were busily caring for the flowers and trees within the walls of the palace. A team of boys steadily filled buckets with water for the gardeners to judiciously irrigate the thirsty plants.

I took full measure of this man, our future ruler, with whom I had grown up since childhood. His elongated skull and fleshy lips, his slanting eyes and prominent jaw, his narrow shoulders, pot belly, wide hips, and ample thighs, as well as his reed-thin legs, had relegated him to a childhood of solitude, hidden from the rest of the Royal Court and the public. But never from me.

I remembered the first time I saw Amunhotep, right after Royal Wife Tiye brought me from Goshen to the palace to be his companion. I was young, but Amunhotep was yet a toddler. As he came toward me, I recalled thinking that I had never seen a child so ugly as he. Yet rather than being repelled, I saw a brightness in his eyes, an eagerness, a desire to connect. He ran to me and hugged me, laughing all the while. From that moment on, we were inseparable.

When Amunhotep was five and I eight, King Amunhotep the Third came to the garden where we played. Thutmose, little Amunhotep's older brother, and future King, stood at a distance, dressed in his army training kilt and a leather belt that crossed his chest, his thirteen-year-old trim body still gleaming with sweat. Tiye stood next to him. They watched as the King brought us close together and nicked our thumbs with a ceremonial dagger, and pressed them together, binding us as sworn blood brothers for all eternity. I have come to suspect that he and Tiye knew even then that their son would need a loyal friend, an advisor, and a protector, for little Amunhotep was as different in heart as he was in appearance. And those differences had only grown greater in our adulthood.

For now, Mother Nile's sparkling waters rolled by swiftly below us, reflecting Ra's light. Fishermen in their reed boats, dressed only in their loincloths, hauled in nets filled with flapping perch and huge catfish. Farmers worked the lush green and brown fields along her banks, and servants carried grains and colorful vegetables up the winding paths that ran along the embankments to waiting carts. Despite what my brother believed at that moment, ma'at seemed strong in the Two Lands.

"We have much to discuss," Amunhotep finally said, looking directly at me. "We must plan for the new city. I can no longer abide Waset and its shameless Amun priests who care about nothing but their riches and power." He resumed his pacing.

"They irk me greatly. They are mere mortals, fleas upon a dog. Adon commands me to build for him a city like Kem has never before seen. I have such visions for it!"

My heart pounded with both excitement and fear, for my brother was often blinded by his own visions, believing its bright light was sent to him alone by his beloved Adon.

"I know you do. Its importance will be clear to all."

"And that is another thing I have been thinking of, Aharon. You call me Amunhotep. Those Amun priests out there," he said pointing, "they revel in calling me Amunhotep, 'Amun is satisfied', then snickering behind my back. Yet that name sears my ka every time I hear it." I did not understand Amunhotep's intent, but as I was about to question his meaning, Vizier Aye walked into the room. I bowed as he passed me. Amunhotep quickly turned to me. "Stop bowing to Aye, Aharon! You are the Chief Priest of Adon. You bow to no mortal but me... and my father, of course." Amunhotep's lisp was more pronounced than usual, and I knew he was anxious.

Aye was visibly taken aback. To his credit, he ignored Amunhotep's statement and bowed elaborately before him, but I could see that his stocky frame made that difficult. The King, however, seemed pleased.

"And what were you saying as I entered?" Aye asked, first looking at Amunhotep and then me. I shrugged my shoulders. "About your name, I believe."

"The name Amunhotep no longer suits me," Amunhotep answered, walking slowly to the table of fruits and nuts laid out against the wall. "I am thinking of changing it." He picked up a bunch of grapes and casually nibbled on one, waiting for Aye's response.

Aye again looked at me with his penetrating, dark eyes, but I kept a straight face. "Are you saying that you are thinking of assuming the throne before your father's passage to the next world?" Aye said with a forced smile due to the absurdity of his question.

Amunhotep leaned against the table. "I have spent much time thinking on this. I have discussed it with Nefertiti. I am considering a Sed festival next year, after Renpet, at the start of my fifth year of co-regency. I will change my name then." With that, he dropped the grape stem on the table and turned his gaze over Mother Nile. No one spoke for a long moment. I detected tension in Aye's shoulders as he tried to compose himself. He took a deep breath.

"You say you spoke with my daughter about this," Aye said deliberately. "May I ask what she thinks of this idea?"

"She said she will support me in whatever I feel is right."

I watched Aye recover his poise, his eyes closed as he proceeded. "But does she feel this is right?"

"Does it m-m-make a difference?" Amunhotep asked. His stutter became even more pronounced.

"Nefertiti has a good heart on these matters," Aye continued. "I have raised her to consider all options when faced with difficult decisions."

"And so you f-f-feel this is a difficult decision?" Amunhotep asked, walking toward a chair. He sat down wearily. "Why?"

Aye turned to face the King. "May I also draw a chair? My poor feet plague me." Amunhotep nodded, and I rested my staff against a wall and dragged two chairs over so that we sat facing one another.

"First, I am sure you realize that a Sed festival upon starting your fifth year, and as co-regent at that, would be highly unusual and…."

"Unusual, yes, but I am told it has been done before," Amunhotep interrupted. "Aharon consulted the scrolls."

"Yes, it has, under unusual circumstances, such as before a King has gone off to war. But before I go on with why I believe this to be a difficult decision, may I ask why you wish to change your name?"

At this, Amunhotep's brows knit in confusion. "Why? You must know by now how I resent being identified with those rabble that we call Amun priests. The priesthood owns more property than the Royal family. Did you know that? Of course, you did. And they enrich themselves behind their false God."

"False God? That is a very strong term to use, Amunhotep. I advise you to be wary of that language."

"I have known Amunhotep since he was a babe learning to walk," I said as I joined the conversation. "We have talked many times of Amunhotep's rejection at the hands of the Amun priests going back to his childhood."

"Perhaps you are being too sensitive," Aye objected, waving his hand and sitting back in his chair.

"No, I think not, dear Vizier. I have seen the disdain they hold for my brother. I have witnessed this and the pain it caused him. They cannot accept the fact that his appearance differs from theirs or that his beliefs are contrary to theirs. You have surely seen this with your own eyes."

At this, I saw surrender in Aye's manner. He even smiled. "You two make a formidable pair," he acknowledged. "Yet what you may not realize is that many arguments went on behind these palace walls to name you co-regent. Are you aware of that?"

"I wondered," Amunhotep responded. "Neither my father nor mother told me the full story, but I thought it was to prepare me for the throne."

"That, too, my future King. But your father and I knew that Chief Priest Maya would object to your eventual ascension. You were also too obstinate if you will pardon my speaking so bluntly, in your insistence to marry my daughter. She does not give you a maternal claim to the throne. We urged you to marry your sister, but you refused. So the only way we could place you in line for succession was to have your father name you co-regent."

"But…"

"And even then," Aye continued, "we had to threaten Maya with the withdrawal of treasure and other measures to get him not to protest too loudly. And we agreed to build him new temples. It was a very unsettled time."

"Maya is a disgrace to their entire priesthood!" Amunhotep raged.

"He may very well be, my King, but he is powerful and a worthy opponent, and if you do not keep that in mind, it will be to your detriment." With that, he swept his hands over his kilt as if to smooth it, then looked up at Amunhotep.

"And what would you suggest I do?" Amunhotep asked. Aye rose and collected his thoughts.

"I would advise you to consider the Sed festival premature and ill-advised. I feel you need to promote some things that would be seen favorably by the Amun priesthood before you consider such drastic action. It is better to sweeten the tea with honey before drinking it." Aye paced now, back and forth before Amunhotep, his kilt and fine linen shoulder cape falling loosely over his stocky frame.

"And as far as changing your name, I have some suspicion as to why you are doing so and what you might want that name to reflect. I urge you to think deeply about this, Amunhotep. King names carry much power. They summon up all manner of thoughts in your enemies, your allies, and your subjects. A king's name portends visions of both good and evil, and those have consequences. But if you feel you must act on this, then do so only after you have thrown a bone or two towards the Amun priests, and I mean bones with meat on them."

"A bone? I have already granted them permission to build a temple downstream near Inabu-hedj."

"Yes, and that calmed matters… for a while. But then you built the Gempaadon near the Temple of Amun, here in Waset no less, which I warned you at the time they would perceive as a direct challenge to their…."

"The Gempaadon is but a small temple devoted to Re-Herakhti."

"Who happens to be the light disk of Adon? Maya is no fool, Amunhotep. He already suspects more changes will be forthcoming."

This banter went on far too long, with neither side giving a finger's width of compromise. Finally, Aye left, and Amunhotep and I sat in silence for many moments. My eyes were closed, my mind tormented, and I began to tap my staff on the stone floor.

"What plagues your heart?" Amunhotep asked.

"Aye is a master administrator. He also possesses much wisdom, and I respect that. We have yet much to learn from him, brother, and we would be wise to listen to him and to abide by his counsel when it advances your vision."

"Listen, yes. But surely I need not follow all his dictates."

"Not all, no. But in this matter, I fear he is right."

"I cannot abide this, Aharon. I feel as if my heart will burst from my chest with anger and frustration. I must act!"

Although I was but a mere three years older than Amunhotep, my ba was always a calmer one than his. Yet his passionate ba was ever contagious, and I had long ago succumbed to its power. But now, my settled ba was what was needed.

I stood and began my own pacing, thinking as quickly as I could. "What I am thinking, what I am about to suggest is action, and action that I think you should begin immediately, today even. Here is my plan, then."

Midway through the afternoon, Ineni, the famed architect of all of Amunhotep the Third's immense building projects, walked into the Great Hall, where a large table had been set for three. His draftsmen waited quietly out in the long corridor, sitting cross-legged, their papyrus scrolls, leather pouches of reed pens, and baskets of inks neatly placed at the ready beside them.

Amunhotep looked at me and smiled as Ineni bowed low before him. He turned to Ineni and held up his hands. "Ineni, architect, a magician of stone, greetings."

"Thank you, Amunhotep, the future of Kem. Praise be to you, Aharon. I came as soon as you called. How may I serve you, my King?"

"Let us eat first and then to business. Aharon, make sure Ineni's charges are fed." I left to arrange for their food. When I returned, the King's servants were scurrying about with plates of figs, dates, fruits, cheeses, and freshly baked bread served with fine barley beer. The King's fan bearer kept away the flies. For a man as slight as Ineni, he ate prodigious amounts, and when he had his fill, long after we did, he sat back satisfied.

As the servants cleared the table, Amunhotep nodded to me. "Ineni, the King wishes to begin planning for a wondrous city that he wishes built, devoted to The Adon."

"Oh, yes, the God that Amunhotep favors." From the corner of my eye, I saw Amunhotep wince.

"Ineni, The Adon is not his favored God, he is the only God, the supreme ruler of all the universe."

Ineni stole a look at Amunhotep. "Oh, oh, I see. Please, my King, excuse my error. It's just that...."

"There is no need for an apology, Ineni," Amunhotep graciously offered. "I am certain there shall not be further mistakes."

"Oh, no, of course. I, uh, I mean, of course not."

"So, then, to continue," I said as one of the servants swept crumbs from the table with a colorful ostrich feather. "This city must be like no other anyone has seen, whether in Kem or any other land. It will be grand, as I said, a wondrous tribute to the One and Only, Adon, our God."

"It sounds exciting, most exciting. More, tell me more!" He looked toward the corridor, then turned to the King. "Where will it be built? How many people will live there? Would you mind if I ask in my lead draftsman so that he may take notes?"

"Not just yet, Ineni, for there is yet another project which must take precedence."

"Oh. I see I see."

"Amunhotep wishes for you to design and build a glorious addition for the Temple of Amun."

"The Temple... the Temple of Amun, you say?" Ineni looked from me to Amunhotep and back again. "But... I... I have not heard from Chief Priest Maya that...."

"It is a surprise, Ineni," I added, "and one that must be guarded with utmost secrecy until we say it is advisable to share it. Understood?"

"Oh, of course, of course. A secret. Of course, it will remain a secret. Yes, yes, of course." By now, I found his repetitious cackling irritating.

"You may not share this secret plan with anyone else. Pick your most trusted draftsman, but no others, as you work on the addition to the Temple of Amun, and if word of it becomes known to Maya, we will hold you responsible." Ineni sat, absorbing what I had just said.

"Of course, you may also begin plans for the new city, which will not be secret. That will allow you some room to hide the Temple of Amun plans. Is that clear?" Ineni's eyes were wide open, his body rigid.

"Ineni, if you have questions or concerns, now is the time to speak," Amunhotep added. Ineni sat with his hands on the table, not moving. He turned slowly toward Amunhotep.

"I never have… I mean, what will Chief Priest Maya say when he eventually learns of this… that… that we have kept these plans secret from him?"

"Maya is not King!" Amunhotep said, slapping his hand on the table.

"No, no, I understand… yes, of course, but…." Ineni countered, staring at the King, his hand shaking.

"There are no 'buts'," Amunhotep said, standing quickly, his chair toppling. He turned and left Ineni shaking.

Scroll Two

Our Kas Unite

I strolled with them from the palace to the banks of Mother Nile. It was a beautiful day, the blue sky showing only the slightest wisp of a cloud high above us. We were still in the season of Shemu, and all around the palace grounds, crops were being harvested. Golden stalks of emmer wheat, flax, and barley waved in the gentle breezes before being cut down, bound together, and brought to the threshing huts. Neat rows of green plants bearing all manner of fresh vegetables were carefully picked and placed into reed baskets, then carried away by servants, destined for markets throughout the nome. Farmers hurried their servants so that grains could be stored before they spoiled or were eaten by rodents, and fruits could be brought to market fresh. It was a busy time, indeed, for we had been blessed with a good inundation during Akhet.

Nefertiti was in high spirits. Having this short time away from their three daughters, knowing she would soon be alone with her husband, was a rare treat. She looked radiant in her sheer, gold-trimmed white linen gown, her makeup expertly applied by her handmaids, her body still trim even after birthing thrice. Even I pledged to celibacy, found it hard not to gaze upon her face and body, so perfect was every aspect of her being. Even her perfume, blended uniquely for her, tantalizing in its subtle fragrance, left an indelible mark on the senses. The softness of her ba projected from her mannerisms so that the common people believed she was Isis reincarnated.

The King's guards kept watch both in front and behind the three of us as we strolled the stone path, but anyone allowed on the Royal grounds who saw the King and Queen walking would kneel before them and give their blessings to the couple. I, in turn, would raise my staff and bless the supplicants.

As we walked, we spoke of matters that faced Kem and that Amunhotep felt the Queen should understand, much as his father confided in Tiye, the Great Royal Wife. I doubted that Nefertiti desired to be part of court intrigue, with its many problems and woeful deceit, but I knew that Tiye influenced her son greatly and felt it would benefit Nefertiti to be knowledgeable so that she could provide counsel when needed. I knew that Aye, Vizier, and counsel to both Amunhotep the Third and my brother, had advocated for this arrangement. Despite my initial reservations, for Nefertiti was also Aye's daughter, I had to bow to Aye's greater wisdom in matters of state.

"I leave you now. I must attend to business with my priests," I said, smiling at the two.

"Is it something of which I need to be informed?" Amunhotep asked. Nefertiti stood calmly next to her husband, her arm intertwined with his.

"No, it's just that I am not entirely satisfied with the way their training proceeds. I must meet with the leaders and make sure they are immersing our recruits in the way of the living Adon."

"Thank you, brother. My patience would wear thin confronting details such as you face every day. I sing your praises." I walked away content, despite the mundane meeting I now faced.

"Enjoy your walk," I called back to them, knowing that they would, for I could see in the loving way they looked at one another that their marital bonds were strong in body and spirit. As I walked, my mind wandered to the time when they first met as children in the palace nursery.

Nefertiti's kindness toward Amunhotep was evident from the very beginning. At the end of their first few months playing together, Amunhotep confided in me that he would marry Nefertiti. I recalled trying to dissuade him, for even then, I knew that he would be married to his sister, Sitamun.

I was wrong, of course. My brother's devotion to Nefertiti was absolute, and no manner of explanation or pleading by priests, nobles, or our father deterred him. They were pledged to one another upon Nefertiti's eleventh birthday and married when she was fifteen.

I learned later what transpired between them on their walk. There were few things that Amunhotep kept from me, for I was not only his brother but his spiritual support. The love that bound us was as strong as the one he shared with Nefertiti. So it was that I learned that Amunhotep shared with Nefertiti, and not for the first time, his frustrations with the priests of Amun.

"It is not just the corrupt priesthood, but the fact that my father defends them! I find this the most difficult part of it."

"Your father, may Adon bless him, is of the old order, my love," Nefertiti said. "He does not yet understand the power of Adon. He has served many Gods throughout his long life. It is hard for someone of his age to change. But I believe he will."

Amunhotep considered Nefertiti's words. "That is true, and I accept that, even though I have tried many times to persuade him to the love and power of Adon. Yet, I always feel that the barriers in our relationship get in the way."

"In what way?"

Amunhotep stopped at a rocky outcrop and sat down, patting the rock to his side for Nefertiti. "I believe my father still grieves for the loss of my brother, Thutmose."

"As he should. We all still pray for him."

"Yes, of course, as do I, but it is more than about grief, far more. My brother was groomed from birth for kingship. He was an excellent athlete, a valorous warrior, a charioteer who could put an arrow through a man's heart at full gallop. Perhaps you were too young to remember those competitions."

"Yes, I think I was playing with Mutnodjmet during those

boring competitions," she said, laughing.

"My father never recovered from Thutmose's chariot accident. It is not about grief alone." Amunhotep paused, his thick lips trembling. He sought to control himself. "It is… it is about the loss of his hopes and dreams. It is about his disappointment in me." Amunhotep nervously fidgeted with his kingship successor ring, the one given to him the day his brother died, a day etched in his memory.

"Why do you say that? He cares for you. I have seen that myself."

"Cares? Yes, he does that, for I am also of his seed and the future of his lineage. But…"

"But, what? Can you not just accept that?"

"He has never accepted who I am. I am so different from Thutmose, from… from all that my father expected of a son. My face is too long, my lips too full, my body too thin, too tall, too twisted. He made my maidservants hide me when foreigners visited. And my lisp, my stutter, and my voice all grate on him. Even today, I see him wince when I try to judge a dispute in the Great Hall."

"I recall crying at night seeing the look on your face when you were whisked away." Tears welled in Nefertiti's eyes. "And, yet, what does any of that matter in the eyes of Adon, who created you in his image? You have said plainly that you are as much the son of Adon as the seed of your father. And I love you for your inner beauty, for the softness that Adon placed in your heart. So what if you are not a warrior? Is not peace better than war? Is not ma'at better than chaos?"

Amunhotep took her hand in his. For a while, they sat in silence, gazing out at Mother Nile and the gifts that emanated from her glorious presence. The water sparkled in the morning light, and they watched as fishermen threw their nets in near perfect circles, pulling in fat catfish with almost every throw. Ducks and geese noisily flew in and out of the reedy marshes.

"It is truly wondrous, is it not, that Adon has given us

Mother Nile and all her bounty? Her floods cover the land, and Adon sends us warmth through His yellow disk to make our crops grow. It is all part of His plan, yet the Amun priests think otherwise. The only reason they tolerate the worship of the other Gods that our people foolishly believe in is because they do not wish to create enemies. They are the largest landowners in the Two Lands. Even the temples of the lesser Gods must pay rent to the Amun priests. Did you know that?"

"I did not know that, but I will say that my father is correct in his assessment. You must be patient. Have a plan for the next year, but also have a plan for ten years and for your entire life. And if one must be changed, let it be the one-year plans."

At this, Amunhotep put his arm around Nefertiti and hugged her to him. "You are right. I will try to be more patient. But this I must tell you before you hear of it from your father or Aharon. I plan to change my name soon, for I can no longer tolerate being known as Amunhotep, Amun is satisfied. Oh, yes, if he were truly a God, he would be satisfied as I do nothing to eliminate his corrupt priests. But that will all change soon enough."

"Change your name? To what?" Nefertiti asked, surprised.

"I cannot say it aloud now. I do not wish to tempt fate. But shortly after the addition to the Temple of Amun is completed, I will order a Sed festival, at which I will announce my name change before Adon."

"And the new city we are planning?"

"And that, too."

"Whatever it is that Adon tells you to do, you must know that I will always support you, for I believe in you to do what is right in your heart. I believe Adon guides you."

The next day, as I reported to Amunhotep the results of my meeting with the leaders of the Adon priesthood, I noted that he looked away, hardly listening. I shortened my report and sat waiting for his reaction. Instead, he sat silently. We were in his private chambers as servants came to empty his chamber pot and also fill his bathing tub. Others brought in food for the first meal.

"And?"

"I'm sorry, Aharon, but my heart is elsewhere."

"Would it ease your burden to share it with your brother?" He looked at me for a brief moment, then looked away. I waved at the servants to leave.

"This is most strange. I feel as if I understand the dark heart of Maya," he began, "yet there are times I truly believe I do not understand the heart of my loving wife." I was taken aback by that comment.

"What causes you such consternation? Did Nefertiti and you not have a pleasant walk yesterday?"

"Oh, we had a most wonderful walk. We both felt our kas so united that after the children were asleep, that is, after I played a game of Senet with them and told them at least three tales of our ancestors as they insisted, Nefertiti and I retired to our chamber and made very passionate love. We were both satisfied." He briefly smiled, then leaned forward, resting his head in his hands.

"What can be wrong with that?" I asked.

"It is not that, Aharon, for I love the feel of her body and the thrill she brings to mine. But after we made love, we lay together, and I acknowledged Adon's gifts of the pleasure of our bodies, and I sang a poem to him, and all the while...."

"She became distant from you. She was cold to you this morning."

"Yes, how did you know that?"

"Oh, my dear, dear brother. You are the son of Adon, married to the most beautiful woman in the Two Lands, and with her, you have fathered three sweet girls. And yet you are still a fool when it comes to women. Maybe you should give up your throne and spend the rest of your days praying to Adon to enlighten you about their mysteries."

"You mock me, Aharon. I should have you tortured and thrown to the crocodiles. The only reason I do not do this is that I suspect you will give me the advice I need." His smile betrayed his words.

"Well, since your alternative does not appeal to me, I will try to enlighten you. Never, and I mean never, link your romantic activity with your fervor for Adon. In your mind, you may. But no woman wants to be told that your mutual sexual enjoyment was Adon's gift when she has just gifted you her loving body! That is the only gift you must acknowledge. In those moments, she, and only she, should be the object of your poetry."

"But I…"

"There are no buts to this, brother. This is as plain as Adon's disk rising each morning. Heed me well, for I have counseled many couples and have studied relations between too many of them to count. There is no mystery here. Keep Adon out of your bed chambers. Praise your wife. Leave Adon's praise for later."

Scroll Three

An Unholy Pact

I walked through the old city of Waset, marveling at all the new building that was going on everywhere I looked. In the wealthier neighborhoods, workers stooped from their labors and carried stones to the masons who mortared them in place under the watchful eyes of architects. In less fortunate areas, families worked together to enlarge mud-brick homes or build new ones.

Businesses were thriving, streets were laid out straight and true, and new ones were added every year. Ma'at felt strong, and I breathed in deeply with pride. Before me, the immense Amun temple complex was still expanding.

The streets were teeming with people. Many of them stopped me as my gold Royal armband, robe and staff announced my presence. People requested a blessing for a newborn or for a sick elder or to help their crops.

Every street seemed to have a market, each with its own smell. Even a blind man could not mistake the fish market, but soon enough, one turn down another street brought the sweet fragrance of fresh-cut flowers and herbs. People raucously bargained for fresh fruits, vegetables, jewelry, and even good Babylonian wine. Cats were everywhere to keep vermin in check and to comfort their masters. Children ran freely, chasing each other, giggling, and sometimes grabbed by the scruff of their necks and admonished if they crashed into unsuspecting adults. In buildings with a second floor, elderly women peered out, watching the commotion, shaking their heads in disapproval at the commotion, or just talking to one another from their perches.

As I approached from the south, I marveled at Nesut-Towi, the Throne of the Two Lands. Here was the entrance to the Temple of Amun, a glorious structure that was the centerpiece of the entire Nesut-Towi. I could understand why this rankled my brother, for the Amun priests, over past generations, had schemed to make their Temple the throne of all Kem. It was an audacious but also a rapacious vision, and one had to admire the resolve of the Amun priesthood for achieving it over decades, if not centuries, and through weak as well as strong Kings. It did not help my mood that I was about to have a meeting with Maya, Chief Priest of Amun.

"Welcome, brother priest," Maya greeted me as he approached. He grabbed my shoulders and kissed me on both cheeks. I gave a slight bow at this courtesy.

"I note the gorgeous renovations and paintings that my brother commissioned for your Temple," I said, pointing my staff at the entrance walls. "It is my first look at the completed work. The stonemasons and artists did a remarkable job, did they not?"

Maya turned his considerable bulk to look at the walls and sighed. "It is beautiful workmanship. I only wish we had been consulted beforehand."

"It was a gift," I suggested. "Amunhotep wished to please you with this surprise."

"And with a mural of him praying to Re-Herakhti," he responded with disgust as he pointed to a colorful wall painting showing my brother, his arms outstretched toward Adon's yellow disk, its rays emanating and culminating in arrows. "A nice touch… which we will now have to live with and explain to our faithful."

"But you countenance other Gods," I said. "And Amun and Re can be thought of as one and the same."

"We are here not to argue the Gods' case," he replied, "for

there are weightier matters to discuss, away from prying eyes and ears." At that, he turned and walked away, with me following. I say walked away, but in reality, Maya did not exactly walk, he waddled like a duck, leaning heavily on his staff and even groaning every few steps. The largess of the High Amun Priests was as well known as their gluttony, and I often saw their families about town with more ostentatious jewelry than members of the Royal family.

After a short walk through a pillared courtyard where priests helped people with prayers and pried donations out of them, we entered the inner sanctum of the temple, where the altar for sacrifices to Amun stood. Maya turned a corner, and we ended up in a small private room. Unlike the rest of the ornate temple, this room was mostly bare. There were no paintings on the thick stone wall, nor any decorations or furniture, save for two chairs and a small table. Upon the table sat a pot of tea and some freshly cooked bars of sweetened fig.

"Please, help yourself," Maya said, pointing. "I am afraid it is too much for a small man like me." I always marveled how short people, no matter their physical bulk, often referred to themselves as small or tiny. But I said nothing and instead reached for a bar and took a bite.

"My dear Maya, this is delicious. I have heard that the bakers in your temple are the finest in the Two Lands. Now I know this to be true. You must try one."

"Well, since you insist, I will be sociable and partake… a small taste." He ambled to his chair, and I noted he helped himself to three of the bars.

"So, you have called this meeting, Maya, and deem it urgent."

"Yes, I will not beat around the bush any longer, Aharon. And, please allow me to say that although you are the Chief Priest of Adon or The Adon… I am not sure which is correct… I admit to not understanding who this God really is and what he represents. I have not seen even one statue of him, despite your brother's lofty building projects."

"Nor will you ever see a statue of Adon," I responded, which caused Maya to sit upright.

"None? But how can that be? How will your adherents pray to him? His essence will not be present in your temples without a physical representation of him where a part of his spirit will reside." Maya spoke these words with uncommon enthusiasm.

"Please let us leave that discussion for another time, Maya. I welcome that day, but now I suspect that you have called me here for other purposes." I was happy to deflect the conversation, for even as we sat in that room, Amunhotep was undoubtedly communicating with Adon and further refining our beliefs day by day.

"Alright, then, to the point. I understand that Amunhotep has engaged Ineni to build a temple to his Adon right here in Nesut-Towi. Is that true?" I knew that to deflect this would not be possible, for I was certain Maya already knew as much as did I, for his spy network, had its tentacles spread throughout Kem. This was merely a ploy to see how transparent I would be. Our game board was now set and in play.

"Yes, he and Ineni, with my help, of course, have completed the plans. Building should commence soon." I thought quickly that I better show goodwill. "It will be built on the eastern side of Nesut-Towi, far from here."

Maya's fingertips turned white as he clutched his staff. He thought for a moment, took a deep breath, and let it out slowly through pursed lips.

"Aharon, you know we cannot allow that." I feigned shock.

"Cannot allow? Surely I misheard you. The King has decreed its construction. You have no say in the matter."

"Co-regent King, may I remind you, and ill-gotten at that. It was thrust upon us by the true King, Amunhotep the Third, for we otherwise would have never approved his ascension."

"Well, then, you have proved my point, have you not? With the support of his father, my brother is in an enviable position."

"That is if you believe the true King will, in fact, support his son in this… this endeavor."

"I know you lead to a point, Maya. Please get to it then."

"I will, but please help me first to develop a fuller picture."

"Help you to undermine my brother's rule?" Maya ignored that comment.

"You know as well as I do, Aharon, that I already know or can find out whatever I like. I am trying to lay this out clearly for both of us in hopes that we can reach an agreement that will benefit us both. There is no reason this Adon of yours cannot exist as another God. The tent of Amun is large enough for all Gods."

I chose not to argue this for fear of distracting him from the more pressing current issue he saw. "Go ahead then," I offered.

"I understand that he plans to dedicate this Temple of Adon at a Sed festival. Is that true?"

"Before I respond, please lay out whatever else you feel needs to be aired."

"Alright, if it is to be a Sed festival, which we both know would be highly unusual for a co-regent, then it would be in, what, three to five years? I mean allowing for building of this Temple to Adon." I did not want to tip our hand in terms of the shorter timeline. I thought it best that he did not have adequate time to prepare.

"Maya, let me say that this temple will be quite small. It will not compete with the Temple of Amun in either size or grandeur."

"Ah, so this Sed festival maybe sooner." Nothing passed by him without notice. He reached out and finished the final fig bar.

"Possibly, although no firm plans have been made." I could see in his eyes that he doubted that last comment.

"We make progress then. Now on to the final issue, after which I think we may forge a notable agreement that preserves ma'at." He stood with difficulty and groaned, the crumbs from his bars tumbling from his robe.

"We, of course, know that he is planning a new city to

the north, although we are not fully certain of its true purpose, and I will not ask you to compromise yourself and shed light on it. Don't look so surprised that I know. He has commandeered every architect of note in Waset and beyond. I cannot even get Ineni to design a latrine for us." At that, we both smiled.

"We also know that he is single-minded in establishing temples to his God. You have been training acolytes to your priesthood. We have no objections to that." I marveled at the arrogance of the Amun priesthood.

"Here is what I suggest." He returned to his seat and leaned close to me. "You are as a brother to him. You have spent your entire life devoted to his, how shall I say this, his deficiencies." At this, I raised my eyebrows.

"Aharon, let not my poor choice of words distract us. Here is the opportunity. Encourage Amunhotep to build his city with the utmost dispatch, if I may be candid. Have him declare it the new capital of Kem if he likes. Let him build his temples. But make sure that he leaves us… and Waset, alone."

I could hardly believe that Maya made such an offer or thought himself powerful enough to do so. It was at that very moment that Adon's light shone down upon me and lay open the entire matter in my heart. It took all my training to restrain myself from laughing.

"Well done, Maya," I said slowly. "Very well, indeed. An unholy pact. I have much to learn from you." I reached for the pitcher and poured myself some tea. After I took a sip, I looked directly at him. "And why did the King himself not offer this solution?"

"What do you mean?"

"You said we should lay things out on the table. You would not have put this before me, no matter how powerful the Amun priesthood is, or believes itself to be, without the consent of the King himself." Maya averted my gaze and looked to the stone floor.

"He only seeks to protect his son," Maya finally offered. "He felt it would put a dagger in the heart of his relationship with his son were he to suggest such an arrangement. Yet I hope you will agree that this offers a way to avoid chaos as the King approaches his passing to the next world. He is ill, Aharon, as you well know, and my physicians fear his days are numbered."

My mind now spun with troubling thoughts. Did the King actually fear Maya and his powerful supporters? The wealthiest people in Kem were beholding to Maya for contracts with the temples. Was Aye involved in these plans? How could he not be?

Now it was my turn to stand. "I will give this serious thought, Maya. You know I do not approve of some of the practices of your priests or even of your leadership that tolerates and even promotes such practices. Yet I respect your accomplishments and your ability to see things clearly. I will be in touch very soon." I bowed slightly, and as I stood, I noted a sparkle in Maya's eyes. His tight lips held back a smile.

As I walked back through the beautiful stonework of the Temple of Amun, I stopped at the towering statue of Amun at the entrance. I looked up, and his countenance raised gooseflesh on my body. Did a spark of his spirit truly reside within? Did his gaze penetrate the secrets of my heart? I will not deny that I said a little prayer to him then, for I knew that in this decision we faced lay the very future of the Two Lands.

Scroll Four

Set-Maat

Ra rose to a clear sky, cresting the bare, rocky mountain that framed one side of Set-Maat. Kha opened his eyes, his head aching from his celebration with his work crew supervisors the night before. He tried getting back to sleep, but his full bladder would not allow it. He rolled over quietly, trying not to disturb Meryt's sleep.

"Are you alright, love?" Meryt whispered.

"Yes, I must relieve myself." Kha slipped his feet into his sandals, walked through the children's bedroom, both sleeping soundly, picked up a game piece in the family room and placed it in its acacia wood box, and stepped outside. He squinted at Ra's bright disk, stretched his arms above his head, and began to walk down the main path of the small village. After thirty cubits, he turned off the path and walked toward the mountain. At its base, he stopped to relieve himself in the latrine.

As he walked home, he saw two women walking his way along the narrow path that divided the town. The lane was so narrow he flattened himself along the wall of a neighbor's house to allow the women to pass. They smiled at him.

"You look well, Kha," one of the women said.

"Thank you, Henet-Towy," Kha responded. "I feel well. And how is your family? I saw one of your boys a few days ago.

He is a strong child, nearly a man now."

"He is. We pray that in a year or two, he will be fortunate enough to be on one of your work crews." Kha smiled.

"Amun's blessings on both of you," Kha said as he turned to walk home.

"Here, take this list of items for the market," Meryt was instructing two servants. "I told you what we need for today's meals, but make sure you get coriander and cumin for the bread and some honey. With the list, you can ask one of the shopkeepers if you have forgotten anything before you come back. One of them will know how to read." Meryt turned to pour tea from the kettle on the open fire. She handed it to Kha.

"What are your plans for today?" Meryt asked. "I will be busy all day with the children's lessons and a meeting with some of the other wives to form a helping group for the elders."

"Thank you for helping the village run smoothly. As far as my plans, it is the seventh day of the work week. I have to go to the Valley of the Kings to see the progress they are making on King Amunhotep the Third's tomb."

"Are you near to finishing? You have worked on it for years now."

"We approach the end of the fifth year," Kha answered, "But, yes, we are close to completing it. The King… actually, it is Aye who is getting impatient. I fear he will visit soon, so I must make sure the crews are hard at work."

"They will do whatever you feel is right," Meryt said, putting her hand on his arm. "Now, come and eat first meal while I wake the children."

Ra was now three hand widths above the mountain, its heat baking the sand and the stone houses within the walled village of Set-Maat. Kha was deep in conversation with two of the crew supervisors that reported to him. They began the climb to the Valley of the Kings, some three thousand cubits from the village. A line of servants followed them, leading donkeys laden with water and food provisions for the tomb workers. By now, the work crews had been at the tomb site for several hours.

The crushed stone and sand path they traversed hugged the wall of the mountain as it wound its way up and around, trending north. After an hour of hiking, the path curved to their right, and they came to a security hut. Two guards stood watch and waved at Kha and his cadre of supervisors. For a few minutes, they exchanged news of the village and the work being done on the tomb. Behind the guards, a cave had been carved out of the mountain, and shelves built inside to house the tools and sharpening stones needed for tomb construction. The guards protected the tools from robbers.

Halfway down the climb to the tomb of Amunhotep, as they saw the workers below ferrying supplies into the entrance, Kha stopped his men.

"We have been at this for many years now, and, I have to say, the work is the finest we have ever done," he said smiling. "But we are at the very edge of the King's patience lately. I have been told that Aye will be visiting soon to see the preparations."

"That is most unusual," one of the supervisors said, turning to the others, who nodded.

"Yes, I was surprised at this, but that merely shows that we must push our crews extra hard to make sure we can give Aye a definite date. The next step, I am told, is that Aye wishes to bring Amunhotep himself here to witness what we have prepared for his Afterlife.

"Is… is Amunhotep ill?" Another supervisor asked, his concern reflected in his furrowed brow.

"Oh, there are rumors, yes. But are there not always rumors? Truthfully, I have not heard anything definite. Let's all work in unison today to give encouragement to the crews and help them understand that they must work harder and perhaps longer hours so that we may finish our King's tomb quickly and to his satisfaction, for he will spend eternity in this house that we have built together." The men all nodded in agreement.

The area outside the tomb was a beehive of activity. Crews were divided into left and right units, each side with an experienced supervisor who instructed crew captains on the long-term plan and the daily tasks. There were separate right and left crews for chiseling the stone rooms and passages and those responsible for plastering and painting the intricate murals.

Each crew had a supply retinue that anticipated their needs for tools, tool sharpening, plaster mixing, and crushing of rocks to extract the pigments needed for the paints so that there was a constant flow of men in and out of the cave. Each man knew his job, and despite their joking, cursing, and teasing, they worked harmoniously. Periodically a captain would shout out an instruction.

Kha had timed his arrival to coincide with a mid-day break for a meal. The support crews had arranged water, cheap beer, bread, and cheese on tables set against the cliff wall opposite the cave entrance. When the captains saw Kha's party arriving, they called for the break to begin.

After a succession of brief conferences between the supervisors and captains, and Kha's entreaties to work hard, Kha entered the tomb with his party. The heat inside the cave was oppressive. Rock and plaster dust hung heavy in the air, making it difficult to breathe. Kha and some of the supervisors coughed upon entering.

Oil lamps were scattered on the floor during the work break, but when the men worked, assistants had to hold the lamps close to the wall so the artists could see what they painted. Tables were set up with sketches on papyrus detailing what the artists should paint, with dabs of color to indicate the color scheme. Small jars of paints in various colors were arranged in a semi-circle at each artist's station, with their brushes cleaned and neatly arranged atop each jar.

"Praise be to Amun!" Kha exclaimed, holding a lamp close to the walls as he walked. "These paintings are beautiful."

"Look, they are exactly like the sketches you had the artists make," a supervisor said, holding up a corner of one sketch.

"I especially like the blue and green we were able to use. I don't know how Aye is able to get these for us. There is no artist beyond Set Maat that can afford such luxury." Kha turned from his inspection to face his supervisors.

"By the looks of it," Kha continued, walking further into the tomb, "we should be finished and ready for the furniture and jar makers in three to six ten days." He turned to the supervisors, a slight smile on his lips. "Tell the crews that if they are ready in four ten-days, they will each get a bonus food ration for their families to honor their hard work."

The supervisors cheered before exiting the tomb with the good news.

Scroll Five

City of God

I had much to think about after my meeting with Maya. I did not want to present the idea to Amunhotep without thoroughly exploring all its ramifications. Fortunately, Amunhotep had made elaborate plans to visit the proposed site of his new city, taking with him a large entourage. I decided that it rested in my hands to convince my brother that Maya's proposal was the wisest course to take. However, I dreaded the meeting and delayed it far too long, in part because I felt it was to our advantage to keep Maya waiting. So the trip downriver turned out to be fortuitous.

The journey began with much fanfare. The elderly King allowed Amunhotep to use his Royal barge for the immediate family and for Ineni and me. All other travelers, plus a store of tents and provisions, were kept on accompanying boats. Four boats of soldiers from Captain Horemheb's guards flanked the Royal barge. An entire boat was devoted to Ineni's architects, draftsmen, and their supplies. Altogether, twenty-seven smaller boats made up our flotilla.

The journey was easy, as it typically is when traveling north downstream towards the fertile delta. The oarsmen had little work to do, and the helmsman gently guided the boat to accommodate the route plan. Amunhotep took the time to instruct his girls in the way of our people and of Adon. We passed many small villages, the mud-brick farmhouses and thatched roofs contrasting greatly with the lavish stone palace that the girls were raised in. They asked many questions, and I marveled at the loving patience Amunhotep and Nefertiti showed them. I noticed many times how the crewmen stole glances at her radiant beauty. Her motherly compassion reinforced their notion of her as a Goddess queen. Those moments reinforced my belief that her mere presence would help Amunhotep's rule.

Fishing boats made way and parted when they saw the colorful pendants flying from the Royal barge. They stared in wonder as we glided past, then bowed and shouted praises, and I often had to hold up my staff to bless them.

At one point, as we neared a bend in the river, the girls watched a herd of goats grazing slowly at the river's edge. They laughed as the youngest goats ran, jumped, and frolicked. At one point, a very young goat jumped on the back of its mother. Meritadon, the oldest, held Neferneferuadon on her lap and pointed, both of them laughing that sweet, contagious laugh of children.

As one of the young goats wandered near the shoreline, a huge crocodile suddenly burst from Mother Nile, sprays of water flying from its body in all directions, its green and black scales shimmering, reflecting Adon's disk. This happened so quickly it brought gasps from the children and even the adults. The goat turned toward the sound, and in one swift motion, the crocodile grabbed the young goat by its head and dragged it into the water. The children screamed but could not take their eyes off the bloody spectacle. The crocodile spun the goat around and around, then sank under the water to drown it. Other crocodiles left their perches on shore and paddled furiously to the kill. Blood turned the water crimson, and as quickly as it began, silence replaced the chaos.

I immediately went to the girls, who were distraught and crying. Amunhotep and Nefertiti were under the canopy at the stern and had not seen what had transpired. They arrived as I held Mekatadon in my lap, with Meritadon and Neferneferuadon each holding tight to my arms.

"Shhh," I whispered over and over, rocking back and forth until Mekatadon's crying softened to gentle sobs. Amunhotep and Nefertiti each took a child and sat next to me.

"But why do crocodiles have to kill such a baby?" Mekatadon finally asked, turning her tear-streaked head up to me. Amunhotep nodded, giving me permission to answer.

"It is the way that Adon has created the world," I said as calmly as I could. "All animals must eat, Meka. We raise cows so we may have milk and meat to sustain us. We must kill ducks and geese and fish to eat. Adon has also given us grains to eat and to make into beer. But crocodiles must wait and eat whatever comes carelessly near the shore."

"But, it was horrible!" Meritadon said.

"To look at, yes, it was, but it was not horrible to the crocodile, for he now has sustenance and will live a few days longer with a full stomach. Each day animals throughout the Two Lands awaken and think will I eat today, or will I be eaten?"

"I hate crocodiles!" Mekatadon said.

"They are surely mut spirits, like the hippopotamus," I said, looking at all three girls. "That is why we must always be on guard when we are near Mother Nile. She gives us marvelous gifts, but they are not free. We must work to earn them, and we must respect the power that Adon has gifted to the other animals that she nourishes.

"But… but why…."

"And that is enough discussion for now," Nefertiti interrupted. "Speaking of nourishment, it is time for the mid-day meal, so you will all come with me. I suspect your father and Aharon have matters to discuss."

Amunhotep sat next to me as we gazed at the banks and the people who busily farmed the land. "It is perfection, all that Adon has given us," he began. "I thank you for explaining that to the children."

"Speaking of children," I note that Nefertiti's breasts are enlarged. "When is she expecting?"

"Does anything pass your keen eyes unnoticed, brother?" We both laughed. "And I say that as a compliment, for I know, I am too often absorbed in deep thought and miss many things." It felt good to have Amunhotep recognize my contributions.

"I plan to have my Sed festival right after she births our next child, so I am thinking in month eight of my fifth year as co-regent. I need you to prepare for that. I will inform Aye, too."

"Of course. I know Aye will not be happy. Nor will Maya, but that hardly needs to be said."

"They both need to accept it, but I feel Adon's wishes are ever more pressing." Amunhotep hesitated. "There is something else I wish to share with you. At the Sed festivities, I will change my name. I have thought much on this and have decided on Akhenadon."

I nodded my approval. "Effective for Adon. That is a powerful name, and it serves as a warning for those who will attempt to oppose you."

"As they opposed my Temple to Adon in Waset?" Amunhotep laughed. "I had wanted to make it even grander, but Aye dissuaded me."

"As he should have, Amun… should I call you by your new name?"

"Much as I wish you to, I feel it is best to wait and not tempt fate. Maya's tentacles spread far and wide. In any event, I only agreed with Aye and you, I might add, that we move the capital to the new city because I knew that there we would have temples to Adon like Kem has never known. Let Maya think he prevailed for the moment. He will soon see what he is up against."

That last comment distressed me, for my brother was not adept at understanding the intricacies of power, history, and people's motivations. His naïveté, his devotion, and his purity of ka was both his strength and weakness.

"I have seen Ineni's latest plans for the city. Most impressive."

"But you have not yet seen the land I have picked out. Once you match the plans to the site, you will be further impressed." Amunhotep shifted to a seat directly opposite me. "I have also thought of a name for our new city. We shall call it Akhedadon, the Horizon of Adon," he said, stretching out his arms wide, "for it will appear to stretch here to there, waiting for Adon's light disk to arrive and depart each day." He smiled with contentment.

In two days, we came around a curve in the river and reached the barren land that Amunhotep had decided upon. Once we climbed the embankment to a plateau, I was surprised at how flat it was but quickly realized that was exactly what Amunhotep wanted. I had to credit him with understanding the power of a symbol, of showing his believers that Adon reigned uninterrupted from east to west across all lands.

The sand and rocks seemed to stretch forever until, in the far distance, they met a range of small mountains. Coming from the cooler waters of Mother Nile, the intense heat of this plateau was unforgiving. I wondered if Amunhotep had considered its impact on our future residents.

Ineni followed, hobbled as he was by age and weakness in his joints. His entourage stayed close to his side. "So, as you can see, we have already put out markers for the various buildings and roads," he said once he regained his breath. The children were already running around the site, their harried handmaids trying their best to keep up.

"Be careful of vipers!" Nefertiti cried out, and one of the servants waved her hand in understanding.

We spent the day walking what would be the main road that led to the palace, various administration buildings, storehouses, small temples to Adon, and my quarters. Then we walked a good distance, and Ineni stopped. He called over two of his draftsmen and unrolled a papyrus upon the sand wider than a man's two paces. On it was painted the most elegant structure, I had ever seen. Nefertiti's eyes lit up, Amunhotep drew a sharp breath, and I staggered backward a step in amazement before steadying myself with my staff.

"This… this is striking," I said in disbelief. "Upon what do my eyes gaze?"

"Even I have not seen this final painting," Amunhotep exclaimed to us. "It is gorgeous. Even grander than I have imagined." He turned to Ineni and actually bowed slightly. "Ineni, you have achieved beyond my highest expectation!" Ineni bowed his head in gratitude.

"Just what are we looking at?" Nefertiti asked.

"This," Amunhotep said, drawing his hand over the papyrus, "is the Great Temple of Adon."

"But, you have not finished the drawing," Nefertiti observed, then looked to Ineni. "What will the roof be like?"

Amunhotep took Nefertiti's hands in his. "There will be no roof, dearest one. This will be the first temple in the Two Lands to have no roof. Adon is there," he said, pointing to Adon's disk, "and we must all be open to his blessings each day as he travels through the sky. We will worship him in the open."

Nefertiti was unable to speak. She first looked at her husband, wondering if he teased her, but she saw the seriousness in his eyes. "Is it not glorious, my love? We shall ride each day from the palace to the Great Temple to pray with all who live in Akhedadon." He turned then and lifted his arms to the sky disk. "We shall pray to you, Adon, the One and Only God of all creation, who sends us his glowing disk. We thank you, oh great, wondrous Adon!" Tears flowed freely from his eyes, and Ineni and his assistants quickly looked away.

That afternoon, following our meal, Amunhotep asked Ineni and me to walk the perimeter of the Great Temple with him. I noticed that Ineni seemed nervous, his eyes flitting across Mother Nile frequently.

"Is something wrong, Ineni?" I asked.

"No… I mean, yes, possibly. I have noticed that there are two men who have watched us intently all day. I dare not point to them, but they are across the river, on that hill behind me," he said, pointing to his chest. Amunhotep and I saw them clearly for the first time.

"Do you know them?" I asked.

"I cannot be sure from such a distance, but it would not be unusual. In my work, I have many imitators, architects in name only. They try to bribe my draftsmen, or they hire some poor man to steal my papyruses. Then they quickly build something similar and claim they thought of my design first. May their hearts be heavy as a stone!"

"I have my doubts they are interested in stealing your plans," I suggested. "I think those men may be employed by others."

"Such as?" Amunhotep asked.

"Such as Maya, or perhaps your father."

Ineni looked from Amunhotep to me, then cleared his throat. "May I speak candidly, my King?"

"You should always do so, my friend."

"It is not my position to say what I am about to say, for I am an old architect, not a politician, Amunhotep. I may be doing myself a disservice in being so forthright. But I will preface it by saying that your passion excites me greatly, and I would be inclined to better understand your Adon so that my own ka could be so taken by him."

"Speak freely," I offered to him gently, for he was shaking with nervousness. "The King has the utmost respect for you."

"Then I shall. My fear, Amunhotep, is that in building this magnificent city of Akhedadon, you will be creating a rift so wide that no mortal will be able to cross it."

"Rift?" Amunhotep asked.

"Yes, master, a rift. One between you and the Amun priesthood. Between Adon and the God they represent. A rift that could tear the Two Lands apart."

Scroll Six

Amun's Anger

"Have you seen this, this… drivel that our esteemed King has written?" Maya said, throwing the parchment down on the table before him.

Gathered around the table were his three highest placed Amun priests and Ramose, Mayor of Thebes and Vizier of Upper Egypt under Amunhotep the Third. As Ramose picked up the parchment to read it, Maya snatched it from his hands.

"Allow me," he said, anger and mockery in his voice.

Beautifully you appear from the horizon of heaven, O living Adon who initiates life—
For you are risen from the eastern horizon and have filled every land with your beauty;
For you are fair, great, dazzling and high over every land,
And your rays enclose the lands to the limit of all you have made;
For you are Re, having reached their limit and subdued them for your beloved son;
For although you are far away, your rays are upon the earth and you are perceived.
When your movements vanish and you set in the western horizon,
The land is in darkness, in the manner of death.
(People), they lie in bedchambers, heads covered up, and one eye does not see its fellow.

All their property is robbed, although it is under their
heads, and they do not realize it.
Every lion is out of its den, all creeping things bite.
Darkness gathers, the land is silent.
The one who made them is set in his horizon.

"My, is he not grandiose with his words?" Maya
taunted, raising his eyes from the parchment. "Oooh, I am
frightened, what will his Adon do? Let us see."

But the land grows bright when you are risen from the
horizon,
Shining in the orb in the daytime, you push back the
darkness and give forth your rays.
The Two Lands are in a festival of light—
Awake and standing on legs, for you have lifted them
up:
Their limbs are cleansed and wearing clothes,
Their arms are in adoration at your appearing.
The whole land, they do their work:
All flocks are content with their pasturage,
Trees and grasses flourish,
Birds are flown from their nests, their wings adoring
your Ka;
All small cattle prance upon their legs.
All that fly up and alight, they live when you rise for
them.
Ships go downstream, and upstream as well, every
road being open at your appearance.
Fish upon the river leap up in front of you, and your
rays are within the Great Green.

The priests and Ramose were rapt, waiting for Maya to
continue. "That is it!" he said forcefully. "I mean, there is
more, but that is more than I can tolerate. Drivel, as I said.
What type of man writes such nonsense? Is he to be a King
or an Isis poet?"

Everyone looked down at their hands, no one saying a
word. "My point is he is no King. He is a weakling. A
grotesque figure. He cannot even talk without that

annoying lisp and stutter on his tongue. It is hard to even look upon him." Everyone at the table nodded in agreement.

"Yet what of it?" Ramose offered. "His Sed festival is upon us in two more months. People are gathering from all over Kem to pay him tribute."

"And to imbibe and gorge themselves," Maya said with disgust before sitting with effort in his rush chair.

"We await your orders," Pi-Hor said. "We will do as you wish, now and always."

"Of course, you will. As Chief Servitors, you have sworn an oath to me in order to gain your exalted positions," he noted angrily. Then he hung his head in his hands, rubbing his eyes and his bald head. He sat straight up.

"Alright, we will act as one. But we must play our moves as on a senet board. To do that, let's accomplish first things first. We must get Aharon to convince that idiot he calls brother to agree to develop Akhedadon to his heart's content and to move there with his entire Royal family. I have seen the site, and I cannot understand why he chose this land that has been forsaken by the Gods. In any event, I have already met with Aharon. Here is how we shall accomplish this first part of our plan."

The men leaned forward. "Ramose, you will arrange a meeting with Aye and suggest to him that you have heard the rumors and feel that it would be the best course of action. He has already approved of this idea, but your comments will reinforce the rightness of the plan."

Maya was at his best when implementing plans that advanced the cause of the Amun priesthood and mortared his power. His eyes were unfocused as he continued. "I will speak with the true King. We all know he is devoted to Amun. He has already blessed this plan, but it is always good to keep such plans in front of him lest he forgets."

"But I hear he is ill," Pi-Hor interrupted.

"Yes, he is, so it is critical that I get to him soon, which I will. This move must be settled before the Sed ceremonies." Maya turned his attention to the priests. "And you men will have to do your part, and quickly. You will put all other work aside and meet with each of our benefactors in your territories. These are the most powerful men in all the land. We reward them with contracts for their crops, grain storage, buildings, sculptures, military equipment, and more. See what they think of our strategy. Let them know how allowing this new Amunhotep to live in Waset would be a grave mistake and a threat to our survival… and their fortunes. I am certain they will get your meaning. You must suggest they relay their thoughts on the matter to Aye, and the King, if given a chance."

"May I suggest one other tactic?" Ramose said. Maya nodded.

"Nefertiti," he responded. "She will be important to our success. From what I have seen and heard, he depends on her for every major decision he makes."

"I agree, but how will we get to her?" Titia asked.

"Tiye has worked hard to develop a close relationship with Nefertiti since the Queen's mother lives in the next world," Ramose explained. "To their credit, I imagine they both know the challenges they face with Amunhotep the Fourth as King."

"But Tiye is from Goshen, is she not?" Pi-Hor asked.

"She is," Ramose said. "Does it matter?"

Maya smirked. "I think what our brother suggests is that her people are originally from Canaan. Some of those tribes worship a God they call Yahveh."

Ramose appeared confused. "Is that a problem? I do not understand." He looked at the other men.

Again Maya responded. "When I say they worship Yahveh, that is the only God they worship. They believe in a single God and reject all others." He turned then to Pi-Hor. "Are you suggesting that she harbors a preference for this Adon that Amunhotep worships?"

"I do not know that for sure. However, we have to consider that perhaps she has influenced Amunhotep as he grew up under her care."

"Interesting…" Maya said, his eyes closed in thought. "I had not considered that." He paused, thinking. "I have always felt that these foreigners influence us in bad ways."

"With respect, Maya," Ramose said, "I have known Tiye since before she was elevated to Great Royal Wife. It is true that her parents, Yuya and Tjuyu, were from that tribe you speak of, but they also allow that other Gods exist and people are free to worship them. Tiye was raised fully as a Kemian and is an adherent of Amun, as you well know. And a major supporter of your priests and temples."

"You are probably correct in this, Ramose, but I will keep an eye open for any tendency on her part to support this Adon. In any case, you and I will talk privately about the best way for you to recruit the Great Royal Wife into our service. As you say, she always appears to serve the best interests of the Two Lands."

After I received reports of this meeting, I felt the timing was right for me to discuss Maya's offer with Amunhotep. As it turned out, just days later, I learned that Aye not only supported Maya's plan for separating the power centers of Waset and Akhedadon, he had actually designed it himself. Once he convinced Amunhotep the Third of its merit, the two brought in Maya and sold the idea to him. I arranged a meeting with Aye, and he told me that Maya had agreed even before he was finished laying it all out.

One moon cycle after we returned from Akhedadon, and just two months prior to his Sed festival, I sat Amunhotep down to explain the arrangement to him.

"And what would you see as objections to agreeing to this?" Amunhotep asked me. Below us, we watched the King's Royal barge being provisioned for a trip. Supervisors called out to the servants with orders for where they needed to store the various items.

"There are positive and negative elements to it. However, I believe when they are weighed, the advantages outweigh the disadvantages." Amunhotep stood by the portico railing and simply stared at the workmen below.

"Realistically," I continued, "many members of the Royal family, those connected to it, and the wealthiest of Kem reside in Waset. Your father's palace, the administrative centers, the major temples...."

"And the Temple of Amun with its power-hungry priests."

"True, and if your plans for the new city materialize as planned, you will be located far from them. They have the power to undermine your rule... and the well-being of the Two Lands. Better to keep them at arm's length while we go about our business of building worship to Adon."

Amunhotep turned his back to Mother Nile and leaned against the railing. "No matter whether I choose to stay in Waset or move to Akhedadon, I will be forced to battle them, Aharon. Close or far, it matters not. But here is what does matter," he said, his eyes wide, his hands animated.

"I cannot bear to live surrounded and polluted by those men and their false Gods. Adon does not condone it. I will build our new city. It will become the center of all of Kem, dedicated to the One True God who has created the heavens and all that lives, that crawls or flies or swims. I will choke the very breath out of Waset and elevate Adon to his rightful place."

Amunhotep's focused devotion to Adon frightened me at times. Yet his unwavering passion also excited me. And while I always tried to stay grounded in the real world of trials and scheming that confronted us on all sides, when I let my guard down, his fierce beliefs flooded my ka and carried me away to unimagined heights. On that day, I was doubly convinced of the rightness of Amunhotep's vision and the might of Adon. But I also understood that right and might are but two edges of the same sword, owned by he who wields it.

Scroll Seven

The King's Tomb

The day was like any other in Set-Maat. Ra had risen to a clear, blue sky and the women and children were up, each doing their prescribed chores. Smoke rose above the houses as breads were baked and vegetable stews simmered for lunches. A few older men sat on stools in the shade of their doorways, watching people passing by and exchanging greetings of the day.

Suddenly a group of boys and girls ran past the guards and burst through the gates of the walled village, and ran away excitedly, pushing and laughing. Ahead of them was the daily line of donkeys from the nearest town, slowly making its way toward Set-Maat. Each donkey carried two large water jars strapped to its sides, with provisions on its back between them.

The children ran to the men leading the donkeys, who knew each of them by name. Some carried sweets in their kilts to hand out to the eager children. Each man was bare from the waist up, their skin dark and wrinkled from exposure.

The supply line continued along the eastern wall until they reached the guard gate, where they stopped. One by one, a man and his donkey were let in, where a team of servants met them. The water jugs were unstrapped and, with great effort, were carried to a deep stone-walled pit. The men upended jar after jar for the village residents. Soon a line of servants and older children lined up to take back water to their homes.

Outside the walls, the crew of donkey keepers unstrapped sacks of grain, sticks of firewood, cooking oil, ointments, and simple garments for the women, children, and workers. "In the name of the King, these blessings for your service," the leader of the donkey crew announced. He bowed to the women who had gathered for their household rations, turned, and motioned to his men to leave.

As they left Set-Maat and made their way back to their own village, from the southeast came a long line of servants carrying baskets heavily laden with fish from Mother Nile. The guards allowed the servants to pass through the gates, and each one made haste to deliver their bounty to their respective houses. They soon were busily gutting the fish to be dried.

In the midst of the commotion, Kha was in his reception room meeting with his three most senior supervisors. Suddenly one of the older village boys burst in, out of breath.

"He comes now, Kha! We have seen his boat leaving the east shore." Kha turned to his men.

"Remember, let me do all the talking. If you are asked a question directly, answer honestly but briefly. Very briefly. I will then take over the conversation." The men all shook their heads in agreement.

The walk to Mother Nile under Ra's disk took longer than they anticipated, as they shared the sand and dirt path with servants carrying heavy loads. They arrived just as Aye's royal boat was being tied to the dock. All the men bowed as Aye stepped from the craft, helped by his servants. They quickly unloaded the canopied carry chair and placed it next to Aye.

"Welcome, Vizier Aye," Kha announced as he stood. "We are honored and pleased by your presence."

"We shall see if you are still pleased by my presence when I depart," Aye responded with a forced smile. He stepped onto the carrying platform, sat in his chair, and waved to the servants to begin. Kha's supervisors walked behind the carry chair while a relief crew of carrying servants walked behind them. Kha walked beside the chair.

As the entourage passed through the village, Aye turned his head left and right and even craned to see behind him.

"Why do I only see women and children here?" Aye asked, a puzzled look on his face.

"All the workers are in the midst of their eight-day work week, Vizier. They sleep in little caves in the mountain, so they don't have to make the difficult hike back and forth every day, especially in the heat of the day. They come down for their two-day rest, then back to work."

"Of course they get celebrations off and for births and deaths, right?"

"Yes, they do. And for other necessities. Yet all the work gets done."

"I know it is a long walk to the tomb," Aye began. "That will give us ample time to talk about that work. Please fill me in on progress and when it shall all be completed." One of the supervisors hurried to the front to direct the carriers.

Kha betrayed no emotion. He held onto the bar that supported the platform. "The work goes well. In fact, very well. The entire tomb was excavated, which was a very difficult task because of the hardness of the rock. The chisels had to be sharpened…."

"Spare me the details, Kha. Give me the overview, and I will ask for details as needed."

"I am sorry, Vizier." For the next hour, Kha described the work on the tomb, frequently interrupted by precarious footing and some scrapes as the carriers maneuvered the platform around bends in the narrow trail. Every few minutes, a servant came forward, offering Aye water, beer, nuts or cheeses, and bread. As they climbed up the mountain, the carry servants traded places smoothly without ever setting the chair back down.

"So, as I said, the tomb is fully excavated, the walls smoothed and plastered, the paintings designed to please King Amunhotep are done, and the results, I must say, are strikingly beautiful. You will see for yourself how the work progresses."

"Progresses? After all, you described, I thought you were done! How much longer will the King have to wait? He is even more impatient than I am." Aye looked at Kha, who stared straight ahead. "Look at me when I speak!"

Kha bowed slightly. "We are only 2-3 months away from it being ready, Vizier." He paused and looked ahead to be sure of his footing on the rocky path. "We are waiting for the… well… to be truthful…."

"To be truthful? Is there something you are trying to tell me, Chief Architect?" The supervisors walking behind the carrying platform were obviously nervous at Aye's raised voice, trying to glance around it to see Kha.

As they approached the tomb guards' station before descending, Kha asked the carriers to stop for a moment. He put both hands on the bar.

"My Vizier, I have served you and the King faithfully since I have been a boy. I have never lied to you or withheld information, even if it does not reflect well on me. Yet in this instance, it is not upon me that the reflection is muddied."

"Then who? Tell me, who is holding up the King's tomb? Who?"

Kha took a deep breath and swallowed. "Vizier, it is you." Many years later, the two would joke over a beer about this moment, but now Kha's legs shook with fear.

Aye twisted in his chair. He leaned toward Kha and whispered. "Me? Do you say that I have held up completion? How is this possible?"

"It is the craftsmen shops that report directly to you. We have ordered all manner of furniture, food jars, mirrors, you name it. You instructed me in what the King preferred to have waiting for him in the Afterlife. I sent messengers to the shops many times and told them to create these items in haste. I sent messengers to you with word that they were lazy."

"And, what? Did I not respond?"

"You did the first time. But I heard from a man who used to be on my plastering crew. He is now employed at one of the furniture shops. He reports they get drunk in the morning and do little all day."

"Ah, I see," Aye said quietly. "I struggle every moment of the day to keep ma'at stable throughout the kingdom, yet in this instance, it is I who have upset it. An embarrassment, for sure."

"Only before me, dear Vizier, and I have made more embarrassing mistakes than you could ever do in your entire life. A nice beer from the brewers in Nekhen, and we shall leave it between us."

"It is a deal, my friend, but it comes with one condition. I shall issue an edict tonight that you have been appointed Chief of the tradesmen shops. I wish you to cross the river tomorrow and do whatever needs to be done to get these shops to follow orders. Dismiss whomever you must and hire ones you can trust with your orders. You shall have soldiers at your disposal. Leave one of your trusted men to supervise each shop if you feel it necessary. Extra rations… no, lavish rations to you and all who help with this endeavor." With that, Aye waved them on.

Kha could not believe what had just happened. He took a deep breath and signaled to his supervisors that all was well. Then he caught up with the Vizier.

The visit itself went well, and Aye repeatedly complemented Kha and the supervisors on their work. Kha kept deflecting the compliments to his supervisors and the workers. As they reached the inner chamber where the stone sarcophagus lay open, its lid propped against a wall, Aye motioned for Kha to come closer.

"Please ask your men to leave us for a time." Kha nodded and left. When he returned, Aye leaned against the sarcophagus.

"Kha, there are things I must confide in you. But I must secure your vow of silence in this matter, even in bed with your wife. No one else is to ever hear this from your lips." Kha was frightened, the candlelit tomb adding to his anxiety.

"Our King, son of Amun, is old, Kha, and not well. His hearing goes, and his eyes do not see clearly anymore. His doctors tell me that he shall journey to the next life soon."

Kha put his head down and murmured a prayer as Aye waited. "It pains my heart to hear this, Vizier. Amunhotep the Third has been our King since before I was born. What will we do without him? He has brought greatness to our land. Ma'at sits like a warm blanket upon us."

"True, he is a great man and a great leader. His son, Amunhotep, the Fourth, is being readied to assume the kingship. Amun will bless him and watch over him as he has his father."

"May it be so, Vizier. May it be so."

"I confide this in you, Kha, but I urge you... no, I command you not to make it seem like his death is imminent to your supervisors, captains or workers, or anyone in Set Maat or anywhere in Kem. But a little pressure on the workmen would be beneficial at this time. I know you understand me."

Kha looked at Aye. "I will do as you command. I will serve you faithfully, as always."

"That means much to me now, Kha, but it will mean even more in the time to come. When Amunhotep begins his journey, ma'at will be unsettled, and mut forces will seek entry to do evil. I see change coming, change that must be managed. And it will start here, my faithful friend. The change, I mean. It will start as soon as this tomb is sealed.

Scroll Eight

The Line Is Drawn

The time prior to the Sed celebration was one of intense action and little sleep for me, as Amunhotep placed me in charge of the event. Waset had grown to become a large city, and many changes had to be made to be ready for the official ceremonies, for hundreds were involved in the Sed festivities. The procession down the main street, for example, meant that shops had to be closed, people relocated, and buildings scrubbed clean of sand, grime, and vermin.

Officials who were arriving from every nome of Kem and emissaries from foreign countries had to be lodged and fed. For the common people, this provided an opportunity to fare better by boarding guests in exchange for food, beer, wine, and other staples, even foreign jewels, and clothing. For those visitors not able to secure lodging, large tents were set up outside the city, housing foreign delegations and their families. Fortunately, Amunhotep had decreed that I would have at my disposal whatever servants and soldiers I needed. Still, on restless nights I feared that all the servants and soldiers in the Two Lands might not suffice.

As if all this were not enough, two issues plagued me greatly. Amunhotep insisted that the Amun priesthood not be involved in the ceremonies. This was unthinkable. I could not have imagined his insistence on this, and we fought for many days over what I believed was a spiteful and unnecessary action. I spent sleepless nights trying to imagine what my conversation with Maya would be like in relaying this information to him. In fact, he sent messengers nearly every day asking what role the priesthood, and even more Amun himself, would play in the events.

If it were not for the nugget of gold that Amunhotep also gave me in dealing with Maya, I might have exiled myself to the deserts of Kush. That is, he finally agreed to the scheme plotted by Maya and Aye. We would relocate Amunhotep and the entire Royal family to Akhedadon, along with the administration of Kem. And while Maya was not at all happy with the arrangements for Sed, he derived great satisfaction from knowing that the larger plan for separating the two powers would be implemented. Little did he, or I for that matter, know what else Amunhotep had secretly planned for Sed.

I will not give a full account of the ten-day prior to the event except to say that it involved many parties, much imbibing, and accompanying debauchery among the visitors. Food was plentiful, with herds of penned goats and cattle ready for butchering, bakers turning out fresh bread throughout the day and night, and wagons of fresh fruits and vegetables continuously replenishing supplies. Rather than join in the festivities, Amunhotep chose to spend the time in quiet reflection and prayer to Adon, interrupted now and then by meetings with foreign dignitaries, a task he quite simply detested. If not for Nefertiti's presence and my keen eye and ear, the meetings would have been disastrous. For my part, the shocked looks and crude whispered comments of those dignitaries upon seeing my brother's bodily appearance for the first time troubled me greatly. While I regretted its truth, I have come to believe that we are all cursed by the false importance we give to first impressions.

On the day of the event, all preparations were in place. Waset was packed with people standing shoulder to shoulder, children on the shoulders of their fathers, noblemen, and envoys in special stands erected for them. A line of soldiers stretched from the beginning of the procession to the Temple of Adon, which was still in the final stages of construction.

Amunhotep was to exit the palace, followed by his father and Tiye, and walk the short distance to the Temple of Amun. In the end, Amunhotep agreed that the procession would at least start in the Temple of Amun, as it had done for hundreds of years, but the Amun priests would be given no opportunity for ritual blessings or sacrifices.

Amunhotep was carried by ten servants in a curtained palanquin, as none were allowed to see the King until the procession began. When the servants gently lowered the palanquin, he stepped out. It is hard to describe the reaction of the assembled priests of Amun, for they gasped and were entirely speechless and immobile. Jaws dropped, and eyes widened, both in shock and in fear. It took them several moments before they bowed, so transfixed were they on Amunhotep, for before them stood a man, a flawed mortal, unadorned.

He wore his white, pleated linen kilt and his gold-gilded sandals, and that is all. His deformed body was there for all to see, and upon his face, he wore no adornment. His head was shaved for the ceremony, making his long face appear even longer. Even I must say, looking back at the moment, that he presented a frightening appearance. That he was not adorned in the kingly regalia required by the solemnity of the occasion was a statement in itself. And in this way, I realized that Amunhotep would forever be a force of change. The Heb Sed was a display of the renewal of the King's rule, of rejuvenation, of rebirth. Amunhotep would proclaim to the Two Lands that Kem itself was about to be birthed anew.

Amunhotep waited as his eyes scanned the hundreds of priests brought here by Maya to attest to their power as they bent prostrate on the ground before him. "Rise!" he said in his high-pitched voice. He then turned to me, ignoring Maya, who now stood before him.

"You will accompany me on the procession on my left side," he said to me, then stared at Maya. Every other king in our long history had the Amun priest in such an exalted position. Maya stared back, unwavering.

"Nefertiti will be on my right." This last statement must have shocked Maya, for he would even be deprived of this public role. I suspected that Amunhotep would position his wife in a similarly exalted position as mine, for they were as one in body, prayer, and rule. "Let us begin."

And so, without a blessing from the Amun priests, indeed without even a word from them, Amunhotep stepped back into his palanquin. We walked out of the temple, where the rest of the processional awaited, but not before I witnessed the hateful look that Maya cast upon Amunhotep.

A smiling Nefertiti stepped toward the palanquin and gave a slight bow. Amunhotep returned her smile, for she looked radiant, dressed in a shimmering white gown, bedecked in gold, green emeralds, and orange sapphires, her eyes lined with black kohl and her eyelids with green malachite. Her black hair shone with exotic oils, and her bejeweled gold crown sparkled under Adon's disk.

Amunhotep called me over as the processional stood by waiting. Amunhotep the Third and Tiye waited impatiently, Aye at their side. The Royal Guard troops tried unsuccessfully to keep their eyes from Nefertiti.

"Raise your staff over us in blessing," Amunhotep said to me. As I did so, he continued. "Adon, my father, I beg you to shine down upon us your blessings this day. Bring me the strength to carry out your wishes. Bless Nefertiti, my beloved Queen, in our rule. Bless Aharon as an instrument of your message. I offer this as the last time I will pray to you with the name of a usurper God, for the next time I visit with you, I shall be reborn as a true servant of your glorious will." My heart skipped a beat, for I knew that contained in that prayer were every manner of difficulty.

Now the processional began, with me walking to the left

of the partitioned palanquin and Nefertiti to the right. Horemheb, a Captain who recently returned from a border skirmish, was given the honor of leading the guards protecting the palanquin, and I soon saw his strong leadership in action. As soon as we left the temple and moved onto the processional route, the people rushed to touch the Queen and receive her blessing. They threw flower petals at her feet. Dancers with sistras and musicians sang their praises to her and to the two Kings. They kept up their fervor for the second palanquin that carried Amunhotep the Third and Tiye. It was not long before it took the might of all of Horemheb's guards to protect Nefertiti from her adoring crowds. I witnessed several over-eager men being clubbed lightly over the head as a reminder to keep away from the Queen, who somehow managed to keep her emotions under control. Instead of panicking, she smiled and raised her right hand in blessing.

When we reached the Temple of Adon, the palanquin bearers moved to a tent that had been erected in the central, open courtyard. Amunhotep slowly stepped into the tent, where I crowned him with the Double Crown of the Two Lands, representing Upper and Lower Kem. Gooseflesh raised on my arms at the sanctity of this moment, for this was the first time in our long history that Heb Sed prayers were offered in the name of Adon.

Once the crowning was done, the crowds would finally have an opportunity to see their King. Although he refused additional adornment, he did allow us to place the gold breastplate upon his chest. I was glad of this, for it minimized his weak constitution. At this auspicious time, I felt it imperative for him to project a strong image. I need not have worried.

The temple stood on high ground. Below us, more than a hundred thousand people had gathered, stretching down the entire processional route, down every side street and alley, and into the foothills. They waved furiously, screaming and singing praises to their co-regent. I noticed that Amunhotep the Third looked drawn, pale, and quite frail, and it occurred to me that the people were, in fact, praising their soon-to-be future leader.

When the crowds started to calm down, Amunhotep raised his hands. Quiet began to spread throughout the assembled. Four scribes rushed to sit on the side of the temple to record his every word. More than one hundred Adon priests stood on platforms within the crowd to repeat Amunhotep's words for all to hear. Amunhotep began with a blessing and wasted no time charting the future of Kem. Despite the heat of the day beginning to rise, I felt a shiver pass through my body.

"My people, who I love dearly, I offer this blessing in the name of Adon, the One and Only True God, who speaks through me, his only son." He spoke slowly in his high voice, allowing the Adon priests in the crowd time to relay his words.

"May you all be blessed with his love. May you all have a happy and secure future filled with enough food and drink. May you have loving relationships with your families and friends. May you prosper in business and work. May you help build glorious temples to the great Adon, who will guide me in achieving all this." He paused to look over the crowds, gathering strength for his next words, as the priests yelled out his words for those far from the temple.

"As of this day, at this very moment, I say that I leave the name of Amunhotep to my father, the great Amunhotep the Third," he said, turning and pointing to his father. The crowd was not sure where this was going, and only a scattering of applause was heard. "From this moment on, Adon has instructed that I be known as Akhenadon!"

The crowd did not know what to make of this, but I had prepared the priests for such a declaration. They began to chant, "Long live Akhenadon," and soon, the crowds picked up the chant. For the longest time, the crowds cheered wildly. Akhenadon was pleased. As they began to quiet, he raised his hands again.

"As many of you know, I am building a city north of

Waset in honor of Adon. You will learn more about Adon as I build the priesthood and temples to him with the help of Chief Priest Aharon. Within a few months, I will move the Royal family to this new city, which is called Akhedadon. It will be the new capital of Kem and a tribute to the glory of Adon." Akhenadon looked at me and nodded. I bowed low to him as I thought him to be done. What happened next shook me to my core.

Akhenadon turned back to the crowd and raised his hands once again, waiting for quiet. "Look to the sky, my good people of Kem and all you foreign visitors. The disk of light and warmth you see is Adon's work. It represents him, but it is not him. His disk is but a small portion of his might. His light and warmth sustain all life on Earth."

"From this moment onward, and for all eternity, the people of Kem shall worship Adon and Adon alone!"

I felt my knees weaken, and I leaned on my staff for support. The crowd knew not what to make of Akhenadon's words, and pandemonium broke out. He had not told me he would make such a pronouncement, perhaps because he knew I would try to dissuade him. I looked at the spot where Maya and his high priests stood. Maya was stunned. He stumbled and had to be supported by his acolytes. He turned slowly in my direction, and I saw an expression that, to this day, I could not fully interpret, a mixture of sadness, desperation, anger and resolve and even fear.

But it was Aye's reaction that spoke to my heart. Aye just bowed his head, eyes closed, and shook it back and forth slowly in disbelief. Both of us clearly understood what Akhenadon's impulsive edict portended for the Two Lands.

Scroll Nine

What to Believe?

It had been a long and difficult climb. King Amunhotep the Third sat in his chair, a strap concealed around him to prevent him from falling off, so weak was he. In the second carry chair sat Tiye, resplendent as always. The rest of the royal retinue followed as they snaked their way over the mountain pass to the tomb below.

They were now all within the tomb itself, admiring the intricate paintings on the walls, colorful birds, and scenes of the King and Queen before Anubis, their hearts lighter than a feather on his judgement scale. Every cubit of space was a wonderful scene from the King's life and his future in the Afterlife.

The furniture was carefully arranged in the tomb, and the jars were open and ready for the food that would fill them upon the King's death. The only items missing were the canopic jars and the King's mummified body.

"This is just beautiful," Amunhotep said to Aye, his voice barely able to rise above a whisper. "I cannot thank you enough for what you have accomplished. It is far beyond what I ever imagined."

"I thank you, my King. But it is this man," he said, turning to Kha, "who did the actual planning and supervision. "Kha is the Chief Architect of Set Maat and the Valley of the Kings."

The King and Queen turned to Kha. Tiye looked at him with a penetrating gaze. "You have done well, Kha. I commend you highly." With that, she tipped her head toward Kha. Gooseflesh ran down his body, and he immediately bowed low to the King and Queen.

"Rise up, Kha," Tiye said. "There is much we must discuss with you," she added, looking at Aye, who nodded his understanding.

The King breathed in deeply as he surveyed the sarcophagus room. "I will soon be at rest in that box, yet my ka will again greet my mother and father, my departed son, and all the people of Kem who patiently await my arrival. I look forward to it… to my journey."

That evening, the King and Queen officiated at a celebration in Set Maat. All the villagers were present as the King's couriers brought beer, bread, cheeses, and meats as rewards for the completion of the tomb. In the midst of the celebration, Aye grabbed Kha by the elbow.

"Let us walk to your home. I must talk to you." Kha nodded, and they walked down the narrow lane and into Kha's reception room. They sat on cushions that covered the stone benches.

"You saw for yourself today how weak the King is," Aye began.

"Yes, I expected it, but it was still a surprise."

"His physicians believe it is a matter of ten days, not even months before his journey begins." Kha lowered his head in dismay. "And that is why I must ask for your help once again, my faithful servant." Kha sat up to look at Aye.

"You must now begin to design and plan to build the new King's tomb. Amunhotep the Fourth is co-regent now, and he will ascend shortly after the tomb is sealed."

"But why so soon? He is yet very young."

Aye looked toward the stone floor, swept clean of sand by the servants. He wiped his eyes with his hands and shook his head. "Yes, he is young. But there are matters of… of ruling a kingdom that you have not experienced. Yes, Amunhotep the

Fourth is young, but he is strong-willed and has ideas that are a challenge to the Amun priesthood and to others in Kem."

"I hear rumors," Kha responded, "amongst the villagers here in Set Maat and from visitors that there is something wrong with Amunhotep the Fourth. He is not in good standing with the Amun priests. Is there truth to these rumors? I tell the men that these are all just women's gossip. Yet he was not here today for the dedication nor the celebration. Few have ever seen him."

Aye looked at Kha in silence, trying to make a decision that would have far-reaching implications. He took a deep breath before continuing.

"You have surely earned my trust, Kha. You workmen, you each call yourselves brothers. I see you the same way. To me, you are like a brother who I have come to trust, so I will continue to confide in you and bind you to secrecy. Shall I go on?" Kha nodded, his eyes wide in anticipation.

"The young regent is different, in looks and heart. His body is twisted and difficult to look at. But he is also strong in heart. His religious beliefs differ from the Amun priesthood, in many ways."

"Such as?"

Aye looked around before resting his eyes back on Kha. "He believes in one God."

Kha scrunched his shoulders and held out his hands questioningly. "We all believe in at least one God, or a few or many. Why is this a problem?"

Aye gave a quick laugh. "Yes, we do, but not the ascending King. He believes that there is one God and only one God."

"I do not understand. Does he truly believe that there is only one God and none others or just that his God is the most powerful?"

"There is only one God and none others. None at all. He calls his God the Adon, and he says that Adon created all that we see on land, in water, and in the heavens."

Kha sat back against the wall. "Oh, I see. This may be a problem. I see that now."

"It is a problem, Kha, for the Amun priests will not tolerate this. That is why we must quickly establish the legitimacy of the new King, and one way to do that is to begin the construction of his tomb. The other ways I will try to handle, but they do not involve you. If I can depend upon you to not question the young King's beliefs but instead be a rock in service to Kem, then we will guide Kem through whatever comes."

Kha nodded his understanding. "You may always depend upon my unquestioning obedience, Vizier."

"Thank you, brother," Aye said as he stood and turned toward the doorway.

When the Royal party left, Kha told Meryt to put the children to bed and not wait for him, for he needed to walk to clear his heart. He reconstructed the talk with Aye and what it portended for him, his family, Set Maat, and his beloved Kem. He resented how little he understood about how the wealthy, the powerful, and the priesthood worked to chart the course of a nation. He was but a fly on the back of an elephant.

Yet even that was not what bothered him most, he realized. Something in what Aye told him lay like a burden upon his heart. He was not a religious man. He was always too busy. He worshipped planning, governing the village, inspiring his workers, and creating beauty from rocks. Yes, he believed that there was an order to life that surrounded him, but he never understood how the many Gods that his friends worshipped worked. His crews worked to accomplish something tangible.

He thought of Meryt, who worshipped many Gods, with carved stone and wood figurines placed carefully in every nook in their home. There were figures for Tawaret, Bastet, Hathor, Isis, and Amun-Ra. Within each, Meryt believed a piece of the God or Goddess' spirit resided, ready to aid believers.

He recalled that as a younger man, he had traded for a figure of Ptah, the God of construction and craftsmen, although he had never had the urge to pray for Ptah's intercession in his work life.

Why was he not a religious man, a believer in all these Gods and Goddesses, Kha wondered, suddenly realizing he was talking aloud as he climbed. He turned to be sure no one was near.

He often felt confused by these many deities, unsure of what they supposedly controlled. If the events of their lives together went well, Meryt was quick to attribute that to a God or Goddess. But if things did not go well, like the stillbirth of their first child, she blamed it on other causes and not on the hippopotamus Goddess "Tawaret, to whom she had constantly prayed for a safe pregnancy and a healthy baby.

Why was no God powerful enough to be King of all the others? And why would such a powerful God need lesser Gods to do his work? Perhaps Amun-Ra was that God. But was the young Amunhotep's God, this Adon, simply Amun-Ra by another name? If Amunhotep's God was so powerful, did he truly exclude all others? Could this possibly be?

Kha sat upon a flat boulder that protruded from the mountain. He held his head in his hands, his thoughts whirling in his heart. Too many questions and no answers. In frustration, he stood, took a deep breath, and turned toward home.

Scroll Ten

A Father's Lessons

We were in the final days of the season of Shomu, the point of Mother Nile's lowest flow. Crops were all in storage or had been sold or traded. Farmers slept late, families had time together, and walking through small villages or cities, one could even feel the air lighter.

Yet we awaited the dreaded five days of Heriu Renpet when ma'at hung by a thin thread, and we all spent those days in repentance, prayer, and helping the less fortunate.

"And that is the very core of the problem," I explained to Akhenadon. "Your edict concerning Adon is causing much confusion throughout the Two Lands. The people are used to praying and repenting for the past year's sins."

"Fine. Let them pray. The more they pray, the better." Akhenadon seemed distracted.

"But your edict prevents them from praying to the Gods they have always prayed to, and they…

"And by that, I assume you mean Amun. I recall you once telling me that Heriu Renpet is the time of year when the corrupt priests take in most of their treasure."

"Yes, then, and also at harvest." Akhenadon was silent.

"A travesty. My poor people must sacrifice their meager treasure to atone for their supposed sins? Deprive their families of food? With Adon, they need not do any such thing. They merely have to believe in him and worship him. That is it. His love fills the entire universe and all that is in it. That is our greatest failure, Aharon. We must educate the priests and spread understanding of Adon throughout Kem."

"I agree, but we are faced with what to do in the meantime. Heriu Renpet is upon us."

"Adon has made clear to me that he wishes for the worship of these false Gods to end. But I will not prosecute those who seek the old Gods this year. However, beginning the next year, I will issue further orders to stop these abuses. Be prepared, Aharon. Our work will not be easy."

"I am well aware of that, Akhenadon. Aye told me that Maya meets his supporters and has bound them in a tight cabal, ready to pounce at the first opportunity, at any of your failures. Their treasure is rapidly diminishing as they try to stay relevant. They secretly hold temples open in the dark of night."

"Thank you for this information, Aharon, but I am stressed from it all. I need time to reflect and ask Adon for guidance. I will tell you when he has made his wishes clear to me."

Heriu Renpet passed without incidents, in large part because Aye and I squashed attempts by overly zealous Adon priests to stop adherents of Amun and other Gods from praying to them during the most austere days of our calendar. We now looked forward to hearing from the priests in the temples to our south that Mother Nile would be sending us the blessing of her flood waters.

During the five days of Heriu Renpet, Akhenadon, at Nefertiti's urging, had the Royal barge outfitted, and we spent the time sailing from Waset to Akhedadon and back. I marveled at Akhenadon's patience with both Nefertiti and their now four girls as we sailed the river's waters. He spent much of the day instructing Nefertiti in the ways of Adon, and she listened attentively to his every word, asking questions when she did not comprehend his vague answers.

But it was the children, as I have learned children will do, that challenged Akhenadon's teachings, for children have a rigid sense of right and wrong and do not discern that truth often lies at their intersection.

I sat peacefully one afternoon with Meritadon on my lap, and the other three girls scattered next to Akhenadon and Nefertiti.

"Why are there no statues of Adon, father?" Meritadon suddenly asked. "Not in the Temple of Adon in Waset and not in the temple being built in Akhedadon, nor in any others I have visited with you or mama. The other children at the palace asked me that, and I could not answer them. We all want to know what he looks like."

Akhenadon smiled at her. "Then I shall give you an answer that you may give them." He scooped up tiny Ankhespaadon and placed her on his lap. "You see, our Adon is big... huge! Think of it. He has created all that we see every day, as far as we can see, and even beyond every foreign land. He has created the light we see arise in the heavens every night. He has created the life-giving disk that rises every morning and sets every evening. How can his might be contained in a statue?"

"I see," Meritadon said, "but the other temples have statues of their Gods in them, and the priests say that parts of their God live in them."

"Yes, they do say that. But let me ask you a question, my smart daughter, who is just like her mother. When you see, such statues, do you feel caring coming from them? Did you ever feel warmth in their presence?"

"Oh, no, they frighten me!" Meritadon replied.

"Me, too!" Mekatadon echoed. I laughed because I suspected that she was too young to have ever stepped into a temple dedicated to another God.

"Well, here is my point. Adon fills the universe with love, not fear. I know this because he is my father, and I feel his love... every day. No statue could ever radiate his warmth. That is what the sky disk does. It is a reminder of his love and his desire to always create life. That is why we do not have statues of Adon."

The conversation, of course, did not end there, for the

children began asking silly questions to which there were no answers. Instead of irritation, Akhenadon and Nefertiti laughed with them. Their loving natures made my heart swell with pride. Yet it also raised in me great anxiety. How would Akhenadon's peaceful nature deal with matters of aggression by our neighbors? How would they deal with the next famine that would certainly visit us?

At this point, the four nursemaids arrived to take the children and prepare them for their evening meal. I felt it was a good time for me to take my leave. I learned later from a deckhand what transpired between my King and Queen.

"You always call him your father," Nefertiti said. "It sounds strange to me."

Akhenadon contained his smile. He looked out at the river bank and the now barren fields waiting for Shomu. Soon they would not be able to sail upon Mother Nile for fear of her fierce currents sending them aground.

"When I stand under Adon's warmth, I feel infused with his love, a love I never felt with my blood father. When firstborn Thutmose was killed in that accident, my father never really recovered. He paid no attention to me. Because of my bodily problems, he hid me from contact with the Royal Court. I also had my speech problems, so I could not plead my case." Again, Akhenadon fiddled with his kingship successor ring.

"I felt that I could never live up to his expectations for me. I was neither strong nor fearless, my body not pleasing. My speech twisted. He ignored me mostly, but I felt his unspoken scorn."

"We have talked of this many times, and I agree it must have been awful. I know, I saw your pain when I was a child, and I see it continues to gnaw at you. Yet Tiye is so different."

"Yes, I could always go to my mother, who would at least listen. She is a strong woman and often would force me to overcome my weaknesses."

"Your weaknesses are only in your heart, my love. You

are far braver than any man in the Two Lands."

"I cannot understand you saying that. I can barely control a chariot, and I have never lifted a sword in war. And my body...."

"Stop!" Nefertiti said angrily. "You are beautiful to me. The expanse and depth of your ka no man can comprehend. It is free to wander the heavens, to communicate with Adon."

Akhenadon reached out and took Nefertiti's hand in his. "And your beauty transcends your body. Of all people, you are my most trusted."

"Aside from Tiye."

"Including my mother, for she sees things only through a mother's veil. I love and respect her, but even she has always advised me to consider the source when seeking advice."

The two sat quietly before Akhenadon leaned forward to touch the water, watching it slip effortlessly between his fingers. "It is not only that Adon listens to me and fills me with goodness, but he... he also speaks to me."

"I know, and it both excites and frightens me. What does he sound like?"

Akhenadon thought for several moments. "In truth, there is no sound, not specific words anyway. It is more like a low hum. It is like a thousand priests chanting in their lowest voices. But, his thoughts penetrate me, and I hear them clearly in my heart. He does not answer all my questions, but when he does, I hear them through my body, and the words form in my heart's eye."

Nefertiti sat, pondering what such conversations would be like. She closed her eyes and faced the sky, but she felt nothing. "What is happening with your blood, father? Is his health improving?"

"Ah, my blood father. He is weak but still has his wits about him. I spoke with him and Aye about our move to Akhedadon. It was something that the two of them had cooked up with Maya without discussing it with me. I was angry to learn this, and I confronted them. He insisted he was looking out for my best interests, that his knowledge of rule from more than thirty-five years brought him to the realization that I was far stronger than he had ever credited me but that my very strength was a sword with two edges. He felt that my youthful passion needed time to mature, or it would risk destroying ma'at."

"Hmmm. I see."

"And yet the most puzzling part of our talk happened toward the end after he asked Aye to leave." Akhenadon turned to face Nefertiti. "What he said still amazes me. It is a gift from Adon, for I would never have imagined this could happen."

"What is it? Quick, tell me."

"He said he had thought for a long time about my beliefs and was convinced that I was correct about Adon."

"Oh, my, that is amazing! You must be filled with joy. He has been listening to you all the while. And he acknowledged your strength."

"I was speechless. I wanted to tell you immediately, but I also had much to think about first. He wishes to build a temple to Adon here in Akhedadon as soon as it is dedicated next month. But he also cautioned me that he would continue to visit other temples and pray to those Gods for the good of Kem."

"It is what he has done his entire life," Nefertiti offered. "Yet, I wonder how much of his change is due to the work of your mother."

"How so?"

"After all, she was raised to worship Yahveh, the one God of her tribe, and she raised you to understand her family's beliefs. It certainly had an effect on you."

"True, but she and my father have been together for more than forty years. Why is he doing this now?"

"To support you? To show how you have brought Adon into his heart? To finally give your mother what is due?"

"I have been wrestling with similar thoughts for these past days." Akhenadon stood. "I feel a need to write, my dearest if you will excuse me."

I watched the two in earnest conversation and saw Akhenadon leave and walk to the bow, where my scribe joined him. For the next hour, the scribe wrote, scratched out, and rewrote as Akhenadon dictated. Finally, Akhenadon left, and the scribe continued to work on a final copy. In due course, he brought it to Akhenadon. He read it carefully and then brought it to Nefertiti for her to read.

> *The Hereditary Princess, Great of Favor,*
> *Mistress of happiness,*
> *Gay with the two feathers,*
> *At hearing whose voice one rejoices,*
> *Soothing the heart of the King at home,*
> *Pleased at all that is said,*
> *The great and beloved wife of the King,*
> *Lady of the two lands, Neferneferuadon Nefertiti,*
> *Living forever.*

I saw tears of joy in her eyes as she rose to hug her husband. It was while they were still in a comforting embrace that the captain waved to get my attention, pointing to the shore. There, Horemheb, Captain of the Royal Guards, stood, waving the King's pennant. It was apparent that he had been dragged away from maneuvers, for he was filthy with mud and sand. Aye stood beside him, dressed in his stately white linens and gold armband and necklace. The captain steered our boat closer to shore, and Horemheb bade him dock. I thought this most unusual.

As soon as we docked, Aye boarded the boat. "Come with me," he said as he passed me. He rushed to Akhenadon's side.

"What is the commotion?" Akhenadon asked, his brows knitted in worry. Before Aye answered, he first bowed low to the ground.

"I come with news, my King. Your father has begun his journey to the Afterlife."

Scroll Eleven

A Mother's Love

The dedication of Akhedadon had to wait at least three months for Amunhotep the Third to be mummified, and his funeral held. Tens of thousands of people from every Nome in Kem attended the funerary procession and burial in his tomb. Foreign countries sent delegations to show respect for a King they had known for nearly forty years. It was a time of worry when mut sprints roamed the Two Lands, and ma'at hung in the balance. Nor did it help that this solemn occasion brought out the worst in those opposed to Akhenadon's rule.

I could well understand the anxiety that was widespread throughout Kem. Amunhotep the Third had ruled for two generations, and the people had known no other ruler. There could be no doubt that he brought greatness to his beloved country. The shame of the Hittite invasion and rule a hundred years ago still burned in our hearts. The historical papyruses kept in the temples were taught to all children able to be schooled and heard in sermons in the Temples of Amun and Adon. But starting with Amunhotep's great-grandfather, we expelled the Hittites and reclaimed our right to once again call ourselves the most powerful nation.

Under Amunhotep, our trade routes expanded, temples and great monuments were built, riches were made, food storage increased, our army was made mighty, and peace treaties with our neighbors strengthened. It was indeed a golden age.

Now, his constancy was gone. The common people were already confused about Akhenadon's religion and what it would mean for them. The seventy days of his father's mummification and funeral ceremony were like an extended Heriu-Renpet. Courts were closed, people talked in whispers, and everyone stayed in their houses, windows covered at night for fear of mut spirits invading their homes.

It did not help matters that Mother Nile was sparing with her flood waters this year, as if mourning the great Amunhotep had dried all her tears. Of course, Maya and his priests spread false rumors that Amun's anger with Akhenadon had forced Mother Nile to withhold her precious life-giving water. The majority of the common people believed the rumors, as I learned from my priests.

Throughout that mourning period and for two months after, I traveled from south to the north, east bank to the west, stopping at villages and temples of Adon to tell our priests and the common people not to worry that good times were yet ahead. I was not well received in Upper Kem, for the Amun priesthood and those who supported them were still strong there. But in Lower Kem, in Goshen, and the delta communities, Tiye made sure that I was warmly welcomed. I found ample opportunity there to strengthen our alliances and form new ones.

Three months after Amunhotep's funeral, I finally felt it was propitious to hold the dedication for Akhedadon. To wait any longer would play into Maya's hands and weaken Akhenadon's rule. Crops were just emerging from the fields, turning the brown mud of the Inundation a soft, bright green carpet that pleased the eye and lifted everyone's mood. Colorful barley, flax, and vegetable crops sprouted wherever Mother Nile had decided to leave her fertile, life-sustaining mud, albeit not as generously as in recent years.

The celebration was to be held beginning in the third month

of Proyet when the crops would be well established, and people would have ample time to participate in the ten days of feasting and prayer. But a month prior to the event, we received a messenger from the Great Royal Wife, telling us that she would be arriving soon. I quickly met with Ineni to make sure that the Queen's house that Akhenadon had built for her would be ready for her visit.

All that was needed in Akhedadon for the celebration was ready. The King's palace was complete, as was the Great Temple to Adon, and the road linking them was paved with crushed stone from the quarries south of Waset. My house was nearly complete, and thousands of workers still labored on other projects throughout the city.

When Tiye arrived, I arranged a dinner in her honor at the palace. Despite her recent loss, she appeared in good spirits, and her small stature was eclipsed, as always, by the large presence of her ba. I knew that she liked to hear the sound of harps, so I hired a group of musicians to play softly throughout the evening. Just prior to dinner being served, Tiye pulled me away and whispered that she wanted a private meeting with Akhenadon and me after the meal. I advised Nefertiti of Tiye's request, and so after dinner, she excused herself to put the children to sleep.

"Mother, how are you feeling with father gone to the Afterlife?" Akhenadon began.

"It is difficult… in many ways. My body is well, but my ka is unsettled. It is of this that I wish to speak."

"But first, is your home here to your satisfaction?"

"Oh, Ineni has done a fine job with it. There is ample room, even for my servants. You should be proud of this… this entire city." Akhenadon beamed.

"Wait until you see the Great Temple," Akhenadon was quick to say. "I dare tell you that I do not believe in all your travels you have seen anything like it."

"So I am told, but it is not buildings that I wish to discuss with you and Aharon. I know that Aye will be here in a ten-day, and I will speak with him about other matters then, but for now...."

"Why must Aye be included?" Akhenadon asked, surprising both Tiye and me.

"Surely, you know," Tiye began slowly, trying to regain her wits. "Aye has faithfully served your father. He is wise beyond his years. His eyes and ears are spread wide throughout Kem. You will need his information and advice as surely as I sit before you." Now she turned to me. "Aharon, am I alone in valuing Aye's abilities so highly?"

I was unsure how to answer, for Akhenadon and I had never discussed Aye's presence in his rule. I had just assumed it so, as Adon's disk rises each morning.

"Never mind," she continued, addressing Akhenadon. "I will get straight to the point, dear son. You and I have always been close, and you have known me to never hold my tongue. So I say this without hesitation. You need men such as Aye and Aharon to temper your passions. Women, too. Nefertiti and I will be by your side. I cannot question your devotion to Adon. But to be King of the Two Lands requires far more than your religious devotion."

I could see that while Akhenadon looked at his mother out of respect, his heart was elsewhere. Often the look he had on his face right at that moment would be followed by him writing another poem or creating music for Adon. I thought it best to bring him back to the reality that his mother graciously served him.

"Akhenadon, I do think your mother is correct. We must listen to her and make plans that will help Kem continue to prosper." Akhenadon just nodded his head, whether in agreement or not, I had no idea.

"As you know, my son, there is much anger in Waset over what you have done to the Amun priesthood."

"What I have done?" Akhenadon responded, his voice raised. "Those thieves have been stealing from the people for hundreds of years. I have only helped our people."

"You have deprived them of treasure," Tiye answered, keeping her voice under control to calm Akhenadon. "You have cut off all their funding from your treasury and instead put it into Akhedadon."

"How else am I to build this city that Adon demands of me? We must have a place, a grand place, to pray and sing his praises."

"I understand that, but you must also provide funds for the priests of Amun to at least buy food and…."

"And I understand where you are coming from. I will take it under advisement."

"You may dismiss the words of all others in this world, but you may not dismiss mine!" Tiye said forcefully. "Follow my advice or not, I grant, is your decision. But to hear me out is not for debate."

Akhenadon sat back in his chair, collecting his thoughts and trying to calm his ba. "There are two other matters I wish to bring up, whether for discussion or not is up to you. The first is that you must consider a strong minister to conduct your foreign affairs. The second is that you must assemble a council to manage the internal affairs of Kem." Tiye could read from Akhenadon's face that his heart was drifting away. She shifted her gaze to Mother Nile.

"I am tired from my journey. Let us put these matters aside for now and return to them before I leave." With that, she embraced Akhenadon and left for her palace, which adjoined the King's.

The next morning, as I walked past Akhenadon's palace, I noted that the children's nursemaids were walking away toward Mother Nile. The children were excited and busy giggling and talking as they ran. This was unusual, for the Queen enjoyed her morning time with the children while they were eager and not tired and grouchy. As I passed Tiye's palace, I saw that she was in conversation with Nefertiti. The two were alone.

As I found out later, Tiye had asked for time with Nefertiti, and they spent the entire morning together, even having lunch prepared by Tiye's chef, who was from Lebanon and created tasty dishes with exotic spices that were often copied throughout Upper Kem. Nefertiti was expansive in her praise of the lunch. But of course, it was in the content of their discussion that I was interested.

As was her custom, Tiye began with praise for the beautiful children the Queen had birthed and for how well she managed the palace.

"How is your daily schedule?" she asked. "I mean from the time you awake to the time you retire."

"I spend the morning with the girls, helping them with their lessons that Aharon insists they do. At noon I accompany Akhenadon in his chariot to the Temple for…."

"Do you say my son actually drives it?" Tiye said, laughing.

"Yes, although he does insist on going slowly, even though the horses are well trained by Horemheb and his guards. They accompany us on either side to make sure the horses do not stray." Tiye found this amusing.

"We spend the entire afternoon praying to Adon, receiving his gift of light, warmth, and sustenance."

"Even in the intolerable heat of the mid-day?"

"Yes. Akhenadon insists we become used to it, for this is Adon's gift to us, and we should accept it with gratitude."

"And then?"

"Following that, we leave for rest and then dinner, and after that, we pray as Adon's disk retires for the night."

"And can I assume from your fertility that your sexual relations with my son are satisfactory?"

Nefertiti blushed. She hesitated before responding. "Yes, they are. Your son is very attentive to my needs. I am very satisfied."

"Good, then let's move on, for I did not come as a physician to counsel you on sexual relations," she said, laughing, as did Nefertiti.

"I am quite frankly concerned about Am… I mean Akhenadon's seeming lack of interest in matters of Kem."

"Such as?" Nefertiti felt it best to appear naive on the matter.

"My dear daughter, are you aware of the letters he has received from Tushratta, King of Mittani, begging for assistance?"

"No. I have heard of Tushratta, of course."

"Well, they are being threatened by the Hittites. Are you aware of the status of the granaries in Upper Kem?"

"I have no knowledge of them." Nefertiti felt anxious. "We have been focused on building Akhedadon and developing the Adon priesthood so they can spread the practice. There is so much to do so that the people can understand what is required of them to serve Adon."

Tiye clasped her hands together in her lap and looked to the sky. She took a deep breath and continued. "This is all well and good, Nefertiti. I support Akhenadon in his religious journey. After all, the people I come from are familiar with the worship of one God. I have exposed Akhenadon to those beliefs since he was a child.

"But there is also a kingdom to run, a mighty and diverse kingdom with people of many interests and persuasions. And right now, your husband is not paying attention to all the other aspects of kingship. If he continues on this path, and I have no doubt he will, there will be no Kem in which to worship Adon." By now, Nefertiti was frightened.

"I do not want to hear these words, mother. Akhenadon assures me that Adon will provide for us and for all of Kem."

"And perhaps Adon will, but only, and I do mean only if these other matters are taken care of. No matter what the God, I have learned that they only help those who help themselves. And that is where you come in, Nefertiti. Not just you, but also Aharon, his sworn brother, Aye, his wisest advisor, and me, who was my husband's foremost ally throughout his rule. You must rise up, Nefertiti. You must assume a sort of co-regency with your husband. You must take off his shoulders those matters which he does not take to naturally. You must help him govern, even dissuade him from disastrous actions he might take." Tiye stood to make her point.

"But, I am a mother and a dutiful wife. I have no time for

what you suggest."

"I promise to help you to do this, but you must take on this role willingly and forcefully, for, without it, I fear Akhenadon's rule will fail." Nefertiti nodded in agreement, for she knew in her heart that Tiye spoke the truth.

"He has strong internal enemies lined up against him. He has foreign powers standing outside our borders, ready to make mischief. He has matters of governance that must be addressed. We can help, but only you have his ear in those quiet times between husband and wife. You must firmly establish yourself as the future Great Royal Wife, Queen of the Two Lands, a force that no person in Kem dare cross."

Tears now ran from Nefertiti's eyes. She looked upon Tiye, who had accomplished all these things and more. "You speak truth to me, and for that, I will be forever grateful. What you suggest terrifies me, but I know you are right." At this, Nefertiti stood. "I will do my best to stand beside Akhenadon and help strengthen the Two Lands."

"Good. Then we shall form this little cabal of ours, all in support of Akhenadon's rule."

"And of Adon's," Nefertiti added.

"Yes, of course, and of Adon's," Tiye reluctantly echoed.

Scroll Twelve

Akhedadon

Today was the day that launched ten days in Akhedadon to officially commemorate its opening as the new capital of Kem. Dignitaries from every Nome were present. Ministers of every part of Akhenadon's rule were here in force. Foreign dignitaries from countries as far away as Kush to the south and Lebanon to the north sent emissaries. Only one group was not represented, and that was the Amun priests. Against my advice and that of Aye and Tiye, Akhenadon refused to have them violate his sacred space, to use his very words.

Akhenadon had already been crowned King in a quiet ceremony upon the death of his father. Although this was not truly required since he was already co-regent with Amunhotep, Aye felt it was worthwhile doing so to legitimize his ascension. However, in a stunning act of defiance, Akhenadon insisted that the ceremony not be held in Waset, the home of Amun, and instead, it was held in Inabu-Hedj. A search of our records showed that this had never been done before and would give cause to his enemies that he was an illegitimate ruler if he was not blessed by the Amun priests. Yet Akhenadon did not see it that way, for his righteousness and devotion to Adon blinded him to the reality of life in the Two Lands. What Aye did not suspect, nor did I, was that Akhenadon's decision in this matter was part of a larger plan that he later said was given to him by none other than Adon himself.

Now, however, was not the time to concern ourselves with the larger matters of Kem, for we faced thousands of people entering the city to witness the morning prayers to Adon, led by Akhenadon, which would set off the celebration. As the first sliver of Adon's disk peered over the horizon, Akhenadon stepped from the palace, Nefertiti by his side. Horemheb stood by Akhenadon's chariot, and two of his guards held the halters of the horses. As Akhenadon grabbed the reins, Horemheb held out his hand to assist Nefertiti. When they both were settled, Horemheb mounted his horse.

To say that Nefertiti was resplendent would be insulting her, for she radiated beauty and serenity, dressed in a plain sheer linen gown. Due to the solemnity of the occasion, she was not bejeweled as usual for public appearances but wore a simple gold chain around her neck and her gold armband. She wore a plain gold crown on her head, and her lustrous black hair flowed freely down her back.

Akhenadon wore naught but his coarse white linen kilt and a simple tunic, so intent was he to show the people his humility before Adon. With the snap of his wrists, the chariot took off at a slow pace and was joined on each side and a length behind by two chariots of soldiers. Horemheb, dressed in his usual splendid Captain's uniform, rode stately upright behind them, the muscles in his arms working the reins of his nervous horse.

Adon's disk rose big and bold in the clear blue sky, bathing the sand and buildings and the far brown hills in golden hues. Ibises took to flight from the marshes below Akhedadon, their loud cries in sharp contrast to their beautiful purple feathers lit from behind by Adon's light. I felt these were auspicious signs.

The road leading from the palace to the Great Temple of Adon was lined with many hundreds of people, in some places four or five deep. Soldiers, with spears linked to form a fence, kept the crowds from rushing in front of the chariots. As the King and Queen passed, people bowed low. Nefertiti smiled at the children while Akhenadon nervously focused on controlling his chariot. As the procession passed, people broke away to run toward the Great Temple.

The Great Temple of Adon. There are no words to describe it fairly. The common people who ran to it upon seeing it for the first time froze in their tracks, their breath coming in gasps. People pointed their fingers at parts of the pure white structure, but viewing it in its entirety made one feel small, as Ineni and Akhenadon intended. For this was to be a tribute to Adon, in whose presence we are all but specks of dust.

As the people moved closer to the temple, which was cordoned off by guards, they noticed that there was no roof at all, and they looked from one to another, not comprehending what they saw. But Akhenadon had always visioned that any temple devoted to worshipping Adon had to be open to the skies above. That was how he had Ineni design and build the Gempaadon in Waset, and the immense structure before us now echoed and magnified that plan.

The temple grounds had two large features, with the entire complex surrounded by a large wall and plenty of space for the faithful, both priests and lay people, to gather. The Sanctuary was located in the far east, and the Long Temple was on the western edge. I recalled the day that Ineni and Akhenadon giddily designed the east-west axis of the grounds to trace the path of Adon's disk across the sky.

Akhenadon's chariot stopped at the door to the Sanctuary. Two priests dressed in white robes swung the heavy wooden door open, and the King and Queen stepped through. They were greeted by Panehesy, Chief Servitor of Adon, who managed the entire Temple grounds under my supervision. Panehesy bowed low, and when he arose, he led the pair, with me behind them, through the outer court and to the alter where offerings of fruits, vegetables, and flowers were set upon a table as offerings for Adon. Akhenadon opened his arms, his palms up, and recited a blessing. Together, the four of us sang a simple hymn to the

Adon, composed by Akhenadon.

Next, we walked to the open-air Long Temple. There nine hundred alters were set up and scattered throughout the space. Only the people who lived in Akhedadon were allowed in, and they streamed to the alters, some as singles and others as married couples, even some with children in hand. Huge columns vaulted to the heavens, with no roof to act as a barrier to Adon. Prayers were free to ascend directly to Adon, to be embraced by his love and caring.

Since Akhedadon was so new, only a third of the alters were occupied, each one with a priest standing ready to light the brazier to send the adherent's prayers skyward on the now blessed smoke. But before that could happen, Akhenadon rose to lead the people in worship.

You are in my heart and none other knows thee
But your son Akhenadon.
You have given him understanding of your designs and
your power.
The people of the world are in your hand
Just as you have created them.
All men since you have made the earth you have raised for
your son
Who came forth from your body,
The King of Kem who lives in truth,
Lord of Crowns, Akhenadon, whose life is long.
And for his beloved wife
Mistress of Two Lands, Neferneferuadon Nefertiti
May she live and flourish in eternity.

I stepped forward, raised my staff, and asked all people to turn to Adon's disk and pray to him and feel the warmth that brings food and life to the Two Lands. I asked them to pray for the health of Akhenadon, who has come forth from Adon and who is the only mortal to receive Adon's word so that we may know it.

Thus we stood for the next hour, far longer than most of the people could bear. As Adon rose in the sky, the heat became unbearable, and I saw some of the older people holding on to the alters for support. The children were restless. The crowds outside the Temple were curious and began harassing the soldiers to get a closer look.

I turned to Akhenadon, who faced the heavens, smiling in contentment, oblivious to the people standing in the Long Temple. Nefertiti, bless her ka, saw me and nodded. I again stepped forward and ordered the priests to light the braziers.

"What... ?" Akhenadon muttered, opening his eyes. "I am not done with my prayers. Adon was about to instruct me...."

"It is alright, my love," Nefertiti whispered. "We must bring along the people slowly, for the worship of Adon is still new to them." Akhenadon appeared confused, but he nodded and took her hand as the smoke from hundreds of braziers rose to the heavens.

For ten more days, the celebrations went on. I did not stay for the duration, for Tiye had asked a curious favor of me to accompany her entourage to Goshen, the place of her birth, where her extended family still dwelled. I, too, was born there and still had childhood friends who kept me updated on the mood of the people. Tiye had brought me to the palace in Waset upon hearing that my parents were killed in a horrible drowning accident while on a trip to Bubastis. When she heard I was orphaned, she graciously took me in as a future servant in the palace. As providence would have it, I made fast friends with her son, Amunhotep. Once that happened, I was moved to the palace with a room adjoining Amunhotep's. And so began our loving brotherhood.

I left my duties in the capable hands of Panehesy and continued downstream with Tiye, past the white walls of Inabu-hedj, the capital of the Two lands founded under King Narmer, may his name be blessed for all eternity. Where Mother Nile splits into five smaller rivers and fans out further to form the fertile delta, we took the easternmost tributary and made a small stop in Bubastis to meet with the newly appointed Adon priest, who reported to us continuing tensions with the Amun temple.

We next sailed to our destination, Ha'at Wurat, not far from the Great Green, where I soon found out Tiye's reason for requesting my presence. Tiye had arranged meetings with those wealthy landowners and administrators with whom she felt a kinship and who were completely trustworthy, many of them enriched or appointed to their positions due to her efforts. I began to see how her soft power operated.

Certainly, there was no doubt as to the fierce loyalty the people we met with had for Tiye. She was not merely their benefactor but also an advisor. She knew each of them intimately, their families, their interests, and, I came to find out, their secrets. Her power was so strong she rarely needed to exercise it. She had always been the force behind the throne of Amunhotep the Third.

But it was something entirely different that both amazed me and buoyed my spirits. The people of Goshen, at least the ones related to Tiye or me, were from a stock of nomadic shepherds. For untold generations, they were reviled because shepherds were considered unclean by those in Upper Kem. In fact, it was forbidden in Kem to mix linen with wool, for then the linen would be polluted. Of course, a contributing factor was Kem, having once been conquered and ruled by the Hittites, also a shepherding people.

But as the generations passed, the people of the Delta began to make contributions to Kem. By the time of Thutmose and Amunhotep, many of them had risen in rank, including Tiye's family. But there was yet another aspect of their lives that merged perfectly with Akhenadon's belief in Adon. Some of the tribes in Goshen believed in a God they called Yahveh. They worshipped him alone. But unlike Akhenadon, they accepted that others worshipped different Gods. Thus they were more easily able to understand and accept Akhenadon's God. As a result of these meetings, they even agreed to support our priests in establishing temples and growing a following in the Delta.

I left these meetings empowered, knowing that there were those we could depend on as we made administrative and religious changes in Kem, ones that would be strongly resisted, especially in Upper Kem. I knew Tiye, and I would need to work hard to maintain these alliances, and I felt content that they would bear fruit. Bitter fruit, as I eventually found out.

Scroll Thirteen

War He Shall Have

The harvest was now in the storerooms and granaries throughout the Two Lands. Grains and vegetables had been sent upstream from the Delta to waiting merchants in Waset and further south to Kush and north and east as far as Babylon. The harvest was only modest yet sufficient for all our needs until Mother Nile gave forth her blessings once again.

Akhenadon sent for our Akhedadon Vizier, Nachpaadon, and the Vizier for the Delta, Aper-El. Both were also trusted Adon priests.

"I hear the harvest was good," Akhenadon said after we had finished our mid-day meal. Aper-El and Nachpaadon looked at each other.

"My lord, it was only sufficient, I would say… we would say," Aper-El responded, waving his hand to include himself and Nachpaadon.

"Mother Nile sent a flood of medium height," Nachpaadon added.

Akhenadon seemed troubled, although I had told him about the harvest many times over the past two ten days.

"You are certain of this?" Akhenadon asked.

"Yes, yes, of course," Aper-El said, sitting up straight in his chair. "I have seen it with my own eyes. I am among the farmers all the time."

Akhenadon sighed. "And the taxes, are they being

collected?"

"Of course, Akhenadon. The collectors are doing this as we meet. I do not know about Upper Kem, but from Akhedadon down to the Great Green, taxes are being collected."

"Scrupulously," Aper-El added. "We tolerate no cheating."

"Good, good," Akhenadon said, rising from his throne, his favorite cat spilling from his lap. "You must see to it that all pay their taxes. We have much to do to complete Akhedadon and build new temples for the people to worship Adon." The two Viziers nodded their ascent, bowed, and left the room.

"I fear we have a problem," Akhenadon began as soon as they left. He paced the stone floor, his two cats scattering in opposite directions. They each stopped at a pillar and lay down in the light of Adon's disk, rolling over and stretching in its warmth.

"If you are concerned about the treasury, I have it from Aye that it is sound," I said. "Sound, but not overly abundant. It will allow us to carry on all aspects of administering the Two Lands."

"I have spoken with Ineni, and the projects I wish to continue, and new ones I wish to begin, will cost far more than I anticipated. From what I am hearing, we will need all the treasure we can have."

"That could be a problem, you are right. There are all the ministers and their staff that have to be paid, food stores distributed as needed, temples to be supported, and…."

"Now you have come to the nub of the problem," Akhenadon said, returning to his throne. "I have been thinking much on this, Aharon, and have come to a decision. I will issue a decree, saying that from this day forward, no temples but those devoted to Adon will receive any funding from the King's treasury."

I felt as if someone was sitting on my chest, so heavy were Akhenadon's words. I had to force myself to breathe.

I looked up at him and could see in the set of his face that no amount of persuasion would deter him from this grievous act.

Within a ten-day of his edict, we received word from Aye that Maya and his priestly council urgently requested a meeting. To that, Akhenadon sent a letter thanking them for their service and offering them similar opportunities for service to the One and Only True God.

Within days of Maya's receipt of the letter, Aye came to my quarters and requested that I accompany him to the palace, where he had already secured an audience with Akhenadon. Surprisingly, when we entered, Nefertiti was seated next to the King, who was dressed in his rough linen robe.

"Oh, I am sorry to interrupt," Aye offered, bowing.

"You are not interrupting," Akhenadon replied. "I have invited Nefertiti to be part of this meeting which you feel is so urgent."

I know that Aye wanted to look at me, but his training kept him staring straight at the King. "I see," he said, then turned and bowed to his daughter.

"Father, you need only bow to me when we are in public," she said, smiling. Akhenadon took her hand in his.

"Go on, Aye, for it is approaching time for prayer, and I have much to discuss with Adon today." Aye once again strained to avoid looking at me. I noted that Akhenadon appeared tired. He had dark rings under his eyes, and he slouched in his chair.

"I understand that you refuse to grant Maya an audience."

"Yes, that is true."

"May I ask why?"

"I am tired of his constant pressure to continue sharing our treasury with his trained thieves and their false God. I felt it was better to cut them off cleanly rather than wound them and allow the cuts to fester. As far as I am concerned, I am done dealing with them. They can be free to pursue a nobler calling, like raiding caravans on the route to Kush."

Aye nodded his head but betrayed no other emotion. I could see that Akhenadon was bothered by that. The Queen sat rigid on her throne, her hands folded in her lap, alternately staring at Aye and me. She wore a simple white linen gown and no makeup, yet her gaze was penetrating. Every so often, when she glanced at me, she raised her eyebrows as if prodding me to speak. My heart went out to her, for she faced a terrible choice of siding with her father or husband.

Finally, she spoke. "If it pleases you, Akhenadon, I would like to at least hear why the Vizier has called for this meeting." I marveled at her reference to her father as the Vizier, thereby subtly signaling to her husband that she would not be swayed by emotion.

Akhenadon turned his head to look at her, then shifted to Aye. "Of course. Go on, Aye."

"First, I understand your frustration with the Amun priests and with Maya in particular. I also understand that our tax collections this year have not been good. Most of all, I understand your devotion to Adon and your desire to see him venerated as quickly as possible." Aye paused, looking at each of us in turn.

"You also have every right as King to do as you wish on this matter and all others. However, there is a line to be drawn between doing the right thing and disrespect." At this point, Akhenadon sat up straight.

"Disrespect? They have mastered disrespect in dealing with me from my very birth!"

"I see my words upset you. I have known you your entire life, Akhenadon. I served your father before you, and I have spoken my truth to him just as I do to you now. Dealing with people with different interests is not your strength, so I am here to tell you that your actions in regard to the Amun priesthood are deemed disrespectful by virtually everyone in Waset and even amongst most of the leaders of the Nomes. It is one thing to make a firm decision, even when others do not agree. It is yet another to at least listen to those whom your decision affects."

With that, Aye sat silently. After several moments of silence, Akhenadon turned to Nefertiti. "And your thoughts?"

"You know I will support you in whatever you decide, for you are King, son of Adon, and my husband." Nefertiti looked to Aye. "However, in this case, I do believe that your Vizier is correct. It would be wise to at least agree to a meeting with Maya and his council of priests to hear their position. If there is room for compromise, and I do not suggest that there is, but if they can leave with even a morsel from you, it is worth the effort. If you are not persuaded by their arguments, then at least you will be judged as having been fair and just."

I felt pride in Nefertiti's counsel, forever since Tiye's talks with her, she had asked for my advice on a variety of matters in order to broaden her understanding of the issues we faced as we increased the worship of Adon. I knew that she also sought counsel from Aye and Tiye whenever they were together.

It took a full month for the meeting with Maya to take place, in part because Akhenadon waited for Ineni to put the finishing touches on the Great temple and to the palace. Maya and five of his priests made the journey from Waset to Akhedadon in the Royal barge that we advised Akhenadon to send as a gesture of goodwill.

I arranged for the group to be shown all around Akhedadon, and I do not believe they were prepared for its impact on their senses. Despite their obvious initial reluctance, they lavishly praised the buildings and grounds, all but the Great Temple, of course.

For more than an hour, Maya presented his case to Akhenadon, with his priestly council members adding their thoughts as they felt were needed. I thought it interesting that Akhenadon did not offer to have them sit, despite their advanced ages. As a colleague priest, I felt I must also stand, but at Akhenadon's side.

For his part, Akhenadon sat there impassively, his hands folded in front of him and periodically leaning forward to hear them better or to ask a question. Maya's main argument was that the people needed to feel the support of whatever other Gods they wished during times of crisis or when they needed special favors.

"And cannot Adon provide them with all the support they need?" Akhenadon asked.

"It is not that he cannot," Maya responded, obviously anticipating the question. "It's that the people are comfortable with appealing to their own Gods and Goddesses, ones that their families have worshipped for uncounted generations. Women near childbirth wish to pray to Tawaret and Gods other than Amun, and we accept that."

"So you feel that the common people will never be able to adjust to worshipping only Adon?"

"I… we would never use the word never, but the people of Kem have worshipped many Gods for eternity. Why such a radical change right now and… and so quickly? We can be of invaluable assistance in your rule, Akhenadon. Please do not reject what we have to offer."

Akhenadon's face contorted into a crooked expression that I had not seen before. He looked quizzically at Maya and then the other priests.

"Please wait here." He rose and left abruptly. Maya and his council looked at each other, not knowing what to do other than bow at his passing before them. Maya turned to me, but I merely shrugged my shoulders.

We all watched as Akhenadon walked to the portico and leaned against the railing. He raised his arms to the heavens, and we saw his lips move as he began to pray.

"We were in the midst of the meeting…." Ameneman started to say before Maya held up his hand to quiet him. The priest lowered his head.

When nearly one hour passed, the priests were increasingly restless, and all were tired of standing. I, too, felt my back aching and wondered what Akhenadon was attempting. This surely was not his usual manner.

All eyes turned toward Akhenadon when we distinctly heard him in conversation, his head facing Adon's disk.

"What is he doing… he is mad!" Harmena whispered

loud enough for us all to hear.

We watched as Akhenadon nodded his head, said a few more words, nodded again, then turned and walked back to his chair and sat with a pleased expression on his face. We all sat at his gesture to do so.

"The Adon has spoken to me, and I to you," he began, looking from man to man. "You are to accept Adon as the One and Only God of our people. From this day on, you are forbidden, under penalty of death, to worship any other God."

It was as if Akhenadon had attacked these men with a mace, for they mumbled and gasped. The eldest priest fell to his knees and had to be helped up. They began to speak unintelligibly, to object, to wave their arms, begging Akhenadon to reconsider. Instead, he rose. The priests, even Maya, were still in shock. Akhenadon looked at me, and for some unexplainable reason, I knew what he wanted.

"Fellow priests, the King has stood." Maya looked at me, his face uncomprehending. It took a moment for him to understand my words, and he slowly rose and bowed, shaking low to the ground. The rest of his council followed. The elderly priest looked at Akhenadon with hatred and simply bowed his head ever so slightly. Akhenadon stared back at the priest, then walked from the room.

"What are we to do?" Harmena whispered pitifully. "We cannot allow this to stand! We…"

Maya held up his hand and began walking out of the room through the visitors' entrance. As the council passed me, I heard his whisper, and to this day, I believe he intentionally said it loud enough for me to hear.

"If it is war that he wants, then war he shall have!"

Scroll Fourteen

Trouble in the Kingdom

In the months following Akhenadon's proclamation closing all but Adon's temples, confusion reigned in the Two Lands. The proclamation hit hardest in Upper Kem, where Amun's presence was most passionately felt. The people in the Delta included a large following of Yahvehites and did not feel as strongly.

Akhenadon stationed troops in Waset, keeping people away from the Temple of Amun. People who mourned or wished protection from evil forces protested loudly, and injuries were reported as devotees of Amun tried to force themselves into the Temples.

I had to act quickly on two fronts. The first was that I needed to recruit embalmers to service the needs of Kem's wealthier, more powerful citizens, not an easy task when virtually all embalmers and funeral preparations were the exclusive provinces of the Amun priesthood. And, Akhenadon reminded me, one that brought them indecent amounts of revenue. But the reality of the situation dictated that I would have to travel to Waset, where I was most desperately needed and despised.

The second was more difficult. I decided that while in Waset, I would speak with Maya in secret, for I had heard reports that several of the people reported injured in skirmishes with our soldiers were, in fact, suspected of being family members of Amun priests.

"I assure you these are baseless rumors," Maya said, looking away, and I could tell by his dismissive manner that he lied.

"I am happy to hear this, Maya, for that would be a dangerous game, indeed, and one I would urge you not to play."

"I take your warning to heart but remind you that I have governed more than a thousand priests, more than a hundred temples, and more land than even your vaulted King and his entire royal family hold."

"Our King," I said as calmly as I could.

"My point is that you have no experience in these matters, and I urge you not to play in matters that are far above your station." I am sure my face paled upon hearing his words. I swallowed hard before speaking.

"I take that as a threat, Maya, and will give you a chance now to retract it."

"My dear fellow priest, I would not think of threatening you. I was just offering kindly advice, as it were." I felt like wiping the smirk from his devious face. "Besides, closing down our temples is perhaps the least of the challenges that your King… our King faces."

"Meaning?"

"Oh, haven't you heard of the intrusions at our northern border? I'm sure our southern border will be tested, too. To the people, it appears as if our King has not the will to protect our interests."

"I am always impressed at how your tentacles reach into the most delicate places. Yet I caution you here as the former Chief Priest of Adon. You seriously underestimate the power of our God and Akhenadon's devotion to him. I fear your many duties have hardened you away from the power of the God you started out to serve. You have become a slave to the trappings of your office, like a king hoarding his treasures.

"Akhenadon cares nothing of these trappings. He is a true devotee. He brings the power of Adon to all people of all lands.

In this, I will threaten you, Maya. Do not try to do battle with Adon, for you will lose."

It was not until I arrived back home that I realized just how far Maya's spies had infiltrated even Akhedadon. No sooner had I unpacked my meager belongings when a messenger came to my door bearing a request from Nefertiti for a meeting the next day, after prayers. When I saw her at prayers, she seemed agitated, not her usual self.

"What is the problem?" I asked as soon as we sat down. We were in her private quarters, and the children were in the nursery with their servants.

"I have asked my father to come down as soon as possible. I am concerned, Aharon. Tiye warned me of this, but I did not think it would come to it."

"What is it, Nefertiti? Please be out with it."

"We… I should say Akhenadon has received numerous communications from King Tushratta of Mittani. He requests assistance… oh, he requests gold as well, referring to promises that Akhenadon's father made to him years ago. But that is no matter the immediate problem. He claims that Hittite raiding parties are testing Mittani. He is afraid they will invade in force."

I pictured the bearded Tushratta, who I had met on occasion. "That is serious, indeed." My thoughts immediately went to Maya's words during our meeting. How did he know of these developments before I did?

"He refers to the alliance we have with them and asks us to send troops and supplies."

"And so what is the problem?"

"Akhenadon refuses to reply. He tells me that the problem is between Tushratta and Suppiluliuma, the Hittite King."

"I see."

"With all respect, Aharon, I do not think you do. Akhenadon says that Adon will resolve this, and we need not worry. But I have heard through Horemheb that the Hittites are also making moves towards Canaan. And the

Ta-Tjehenus threaten from the west."

"Did you discuss this with Horemheb?"

"No, I did not think that appropriate. I overheard him talking about this with one of his captains after prayers a few days ago."

"Have you heard from your father yet?"

"He is arriving in three days. Something to do with the granaries. He is to meet with the Vizier here and in the Delta. He said he would arrange to meet with me."

"Good. I wish to be part of those meetings." I saw Nefertiti wring her hands together in worry.

"Remember what Tiye told you," I offered. "We must stick together, you and I, your father and Tiye, to help Akhenadon achieve his dream for the Two Lands. Adon will prevail, but we must also help ourselves so that He can." Nefertiti shook her head in agreement, but I could see on her brow that my assurances did little to lessen her concerns.

"Look, Nefertiti, I have known you all your life. I know you did not plan for your life to be fraught with such heavy burdens." She looked at me with such sorrow, I immediately rose and went to her, and she stood so I could hug her to me.

"You are like another father to me, Aharon," she whispered before sitting down. She wiped her eyes. "I feel blessed in that. I am blessed with my children. And I feel blessed to have known Akhenadon."

"'To have known Akhenadon'. That is a strange choice of words." She stopped to think.

"I suppose it is, but it is true. I have known him since my first memories in the palace. When I was older, my palace friends sometimes asked me how I could tolerate his looks and mannerisms. But the truth is that from the very first, I never really noticed that he was different. I mean different in looks, yes.

"What I saw was that he was different in his heart. So very different. So beautiful. His ka was deep. To have known him taught me the important things in life. To have known him has shown me the way to live here and in the Afterworld. Life with him has not been easy, but I do love him, Aharon. Sometimes I feel that my love for him runs as deep as his devotion to Adon."

In my heart, I saw the similarities in our love for Akhenadon. We anchored him during his storms, but we also sailed with him in his dreams. Our lives were interwoven, but all threads emanated from Akhenadon.

Soon after we began our meeting with Aye, we agreed that the three of us should meet with Akhenadon, which we did the very next day. Aye very carefully laid out the issues with Mittani and suggested that we send troops and gold to Tushratta immediately.

"The Hittites are savages, Akhenadon, and will stop at nothing until they see us respond with strength."

"We must defend our borders, my love," Nefertiti added.

If there was anything to say in defense of Akhenadon's reaction, it was that he had learned to listen. He sat there, attentive and even questioning us, before he spoke.

"I hear your concern, I truly do. But I also hear the fear in your hearts, for you still do not comprehend Adon's power. Think now. He sends his disk into the sky every day. Think of the power in that alone! He gives us that despite our actions that often do not deserve this loving gift. Yet He also gifts the Hittites as He does us.

"Adon is at work. His plan unfolds every moment of every day. Is the world not perfect already? Are there not plants in abundance to nourish us? Are there not animals that Adon has created to serve our needs? Look around you," he said, sweeping his long arms from side to side, "what you see is perfection. Adon knows all that transpires."

It is an odd thing when Akhenadon speaks such. Since he was but a ten-year-old, his passion held me, hostage, to his odd beliefs. I sat there knowing with all my heart that he was wrong about the Hittites, that his beliefs clouded his vision. Yet I could not but believe with all my ka that I would follow him through the gates of the Underworld.

"So, you will do nothing for Tushratta?" Aye asked.

"I did not say that. I will do something, something more meaningful. I will pray to Adon. I will ask him to reveal to me his plan so I may ease your fears. When he speaks to me, I will inform you. Until then, I shall not respond to Tushratta's entreaties. Let him negotiate with Suppiluliuma himself."

Akhenadon rose and extended his hand to Nefertiti. "Come now, my love, it is time to retrieve our daughters so that we may share Adon's love with them." Nefertiti looked to her father, but Aye just shrugged his shoulders.

When they left, Aye went over to the table of refreshments and poured us a tall draft of barley beer. "Here," he said, handing one to me. "We need this."

After we drank, Aye turned his chair to face me directly. "Aharon, you are the closest friend that my son-in-law has. You are sworn brothers. I know you are his Chief Priest, but we must work together on administrative matters." I shook my head in agreement.

"It has come to my attention that Maya is corresponding with Tushratta."

"What? How can that be? He is not a foreign minister. That is traitorous!"

"Only if it can be proved. Maya is too sly to ever make such a mistake. No, I only have come to know this through a source that I cannot reveal. But, the source is reliable."

"A woman. Interesting."

"But I did not say it was a woman," Aye protested.

"No, but you referred twice to a source. You avoided saying a man. I suspect he is a she."

"Aharon, you are learning the craft of statesmanship all too quickly. Well, whether it is a man or woman is of no consequence. All I do know is that Maya is desperate, and there is nothing more dangerous than a cornered animal. I will keep my sources on alert, and you must cultivate sources of your own, starting with your most trusted priests. But even there, be careful, for I am certain that some of your priests that serve

Adon also serve Maya."

In a month, I heard a knock on my door, and my servant answered. He came to my room, followed by Aye. I jumped to my feet and shooed my servant away. I poured us two glasses of Lebanese wine.

"What brings you here unannounced?"

"Tushratta has taken a hostage."

"A hostage? What are you talking about? A Kemian?"

"Yes, not only, but a trusted negotiator in the King's service. Well, to be precise, in my service."

"Aye, I do not understand this. Be clear."

"The King approached me and requested, no demanded, that I send a negotiator to meet with Suppiluliuma to find out...."

"Suppiluliuma? What could possibly be gained...."

"Exactly, and that is what I said to Akhenadon. Yet he firmly believes that Suppiluliuma can be won over by Adon and be guided by his light. In any event, while crossing Mittani land to get to the Hittites, the negotiator was captured by Tushratta. He now demands that Akhenadon pay him the gold statue that Akhenadon's father promised him and that he send five hundred soldiers to defend his border with the Hittites."

"Oh, sweet Adon! What are we to do?"

"I have already counseled Akhenadon on what I feel are the best measures to take. Whether he follows my counsel is yet to be seen."

"Does he know of Maya's plotting in all this?"

"No, and I hold you to our pact and bind you to secrecy on this. If he were to know of Maya's involvement, in his zeal, he would come down too hard and send ma'at plummeting to the netherworld."

"When will Akhenadon tell you if he will follow your advice?"

"We will know in two or three days."

So it was that three days later, two of Tushratta's highest placed ministers were returning north from Waset on

Mother Nile, we assume with messages from Maya when their ship rounded a cliff that jutted into a narrowing in the river. There, to their surprise, was a cordon of the King's ships blocking the river.

With Akhenadon now holding two of his trusted advisors, Aye was able to negotiate a quick agreement with King Tushratta that brought all hostages home. But the events surrounding this affair caused the Mittanis to question their reliance on Kem's word. And while Maya had lost this skirmish, Kem itself was the bigger loser. In any event, one thing was certain. It was a signal that the war that Maya threatened had begun.

Scroll Fifteen

Need Your Help

"I fear the situation on our borders is deteriorating," Tiye said as Nefertiti refilled her cup with water. It was the height of the day, and the heat was oppressive, even in the shade of Nefertiti's quarters. A servant entered to replenish the alabaster pitcher, but Tiye waved her off.

"You cannot be too careful," Tiye whispered, "for the walls of a palace are thin, indeed. Maya has his eyes and ears where one least expects." Nefertiti nodded, realizing that she was too trusting and would need to be more vigilant.

"The stakes are high, my dear. I have received reports that you are managing the internal affairs of Kem very well. Roads are being maintained, courts are in session, the granaries are well supervised, and temples to Adon are opening throughout Kem." Nefertiti blushed at Tiye's words.

"However, now it is time for us to do more to help Akhenadon's rule."

"What are you thinking, Tiye?"

"There is much fear throughout the Two Lands. Too much remains unsettled. We need to have time for ma'at to again settle comfortably over the land, to give time for Akhenadon's reforms to take hold. The last thing we need is foreigners invading."

"The Hittites?"

"They and others that threaten us from all sides."

"And what do you propose?"

"We must step up and do more. We must begin to…."

"But, mother, I am doing all I can. I manage the palace as well as the country. Akhenadon depends on me to also help with rituals to Adon. His prayer sessions alone take hours from my day. And they are exhausting, standing in the heat for so long. The afternoon nap does little to restore me."

"Dear, dear Nefertiti. I recall you saying the very same thing to me when I first proposed that you assume a larger role in governance. Yet you managed to do so, and very well. Please suffer the words of an older woman who has experienced much in her lifetime." Nefertiti sat back in her chair, holding her cup of water.

"Men are by far the stronger sex… but only in physical strength. They make decisions that affect us all and seek pats on their backs for doing so. Yet they have all the time they need to think these matters through, and they have counselors and friendships to offer advice.

"A woman must do all her work while having a child tugging at her gown and another at her breast. Peasant women must plan meals, buy food, control vermin, and much, much more, all without anyone praising her efforts." Nefertiti found herself nodding at Tiye's words.

"But here is the thing, dearest Nefertiti. Somehow we manage. We do whatever it is we must. You may have to give up your nap, and, yes, you will be tired and exhausted, but you will sleep better at night. Soon it will develop into a routine. But, mark my words, you will manage. That is what we do."

Nefertiti sat silently for many moments. She took a drink from her cup and set it down on the short bullrush table before them. "I will do what I must to help my beloved Kem, to make Akhenadon's rule one for the ages. But you are my mentor. Tell me what I must do."

Tiye smiled at her protege. "Good. We are both strong

women. I have faced my share of hardships in my husband's long reign, and now you have yours. I suggest that you form a tighter bond with your father, for Aye sees things in ways that regular people do not. He makes connections between people, events, and ideas that create opportunities. Require him to be here on a regular basis. Side with him more when he advises my son.

"I plan to talk with Aharon about his need to support your efforts, but we must be realistic as to what role Aharon can play."

"What do you mean by that?"

"If ever two men were meant to be brothers, they are the shining example. If ever I did one thing right in my life, it was putting those two together. Akhenadon was always a very special child, but his bodily differences, his strange thinking, and his speech difficulties made it hard for him to have friends. Aharon is special, too. He never saw those differences in his heart. He loves his brother and will do all he can to protect him. He always has. But, that has limits, for he is also bitten by the same spirit that infects my son. He is a believer and suffers from the same blindness as our zealot King. You would be wise to always bear that in mind."

"I hear you, mother. Your words have helped me understand something that has bothered me for years. There are limitations to Aharon's role."

"But also strengths. Let's not forget that. The kas of my son and Aharon are bound together as one." This last comment caused Nefertiti to think quietly. She had to acknowledge that the thought of such an intimate connection caused her some jealousy.

"So, is there anything else I should do?"

"Yes. You will need to make strong connections to the army, for Akhenadon does not relate well to force or the need for war. He has always shied away from such things, and I have heard from one of his generals, a good friend, that the army is concerned. You must learn more about the art of foreign relations, about when it is best to negotiate when to threaten force, and when to actually use it." Now Tiye stood and steadied herself behind her chair.

"There is a captain in Akhenadon's guard here in Akhedadon that I have heard good reports about. His name is Horemheb."

"Yes, I know of him."

"Good. I understand he has already proven himself in battle and is well respected by his men. He is forceful with them but fair. I suggest that you seek his counsel on matters that relate to the army, its capabilities, its limitations, its strategy, and its tactics. My sources tell me he is also respected by his superiors, and as he rises in rank, you will be well placed to ask his guidance on matters that might involve the use of armed force, as opposed to the withdrawal of trade or treasure."

When Nefertiti and Tiye reported to me separately about their meeting, I was pleased to hear of their increasing bond. Of course, neither of them relayed to me their discussion of my own strengths and limitations. For that, I had to rely on one of Nefertiti's servants, which made me smile to think of Tiye's words on the subject of palace walls.

I agreed with the need to bring in Horemheb as a trusted advisor on military matters. As soon as I confirmed Aye's next arrival in Akhedadon, I arranged a meeting between the four of us. I held it in my quarters, which I could guarantee would be free of unwanted ears.

Aye, Nefertiti and I were already present when Horemheb arrived. The servant who brought him into the room was a full head shorter than Horemheb, accentuating his robust frame. He wore a white kilt with a leather waistband attached to a leather strap that went from his waist across his chest and down the back, separating the muscles in his chest so that they bulged with strength. His sword hung from his belt, as did a menacing dagger on the other side. His sandals were tied all the way to the top of his calves.

Upon entering, he bowed low to the Queen and Aye and held his position until Nefertiti bade him rise. She pointed to the empty chair, and he seated himself properly, moving his sword to the side in a smooth, practiced motion. He sat erect, his hands on his muscled thighs.

We began as we rehearsed, with Nefertiti setting out the purpose of the meeting and its implications.

"We invited you to this meeting today, Horemheb because it has come to our attention that you are a capable soldier and leader of your men." At this, Horemheb shuffled his feet back in embarrassment.

"I only do my sworn duty to Akhenadon, to you, and to the Two Lands," he said, avoiding the Queen's gaze. Nefertiti looked beautiful in her white gown and Queen's jewels. Her eyes were lined with black kohl, making her gaze irresistible. Horemheb wished to avoid embarrassing himself.

"We wish for you to give us advice on things military." I watched Horemheb's face, and he looked surprised.

"But why me, my Queen?" He looked desperately from Nefertiti to Aye and then me. "You can ask one of the King's generals or the Chief of the Army for such advice."

"It is quite simple," Aye said, turning his chair slightly to face Horemheb. "The Chief is in Waset, where he is stationed permanently, and the nearest general we trust is located near the Wat-Hor, as you well know. We need someone close to us that we can call upon at any time, for as you also know, matters involving the military are often pressing and immediate concerns."

Horemheb thought for a moment, then shook his head in agreement. "I do see your point," he acknowledged. I thought it interesting that he said no more. He was obviously trained not to volunteer information unasked.

"The three of us, being trusted servants of King Akhenadon," Nefertiti continued, "who alone is God's messenger, would like you to be available to us… to me, really, as Vizier Aye is often away and Aharon has his priestly duties." Again, Horemheb sat straight-backed, listening to the Queen but saying nothing. "Are you in agreement?"

Horemheb hesitated. "I will serve you and my King in whatever way I am asked."

"Good, then tell us what you have been hearing regarding the situation at our borders," Aye asked. Horemheb looked uncomfortable and again hesitated.

"You need not fear us," Nefertiti offered, kindness evident in her tone of voice. "You have our word that anything you say will be held in the strictest confidence, and none will know where the information originated."

"Similarly," I added, "we require that anything you hear in these meetings or those with the Queen also be held in confidence by you, Horemheb. Do we have such assurance?"

"But what about the King? Is he part of this group?" Horemheb asked. Nefertiti looked to Aye.

"He is not," Aye responded. "As you have seen with your own eyes, he is busy establishing Adon as the only God in the Two Lands. That has occupied all his time and will continue to do so for some time to come until all of Kem has accepted this. The Queen has assumed some of his non-religious concerns, and the military is one of them. As far as the King is concerned, you are the Captain of the Royal Guards and no more. We will protect you from any repercussions beyond that. Do I make myself clear?"

Horemheb was in a difficult position, as we knew he would be. He sat thinking for a long moment. "I am honored that you would have such trust in a humble soldier, Queen, Vizier, Chief Priest," he said, nodding to each of us in turn. "However, my allegiance is to the King first and for eternity and, of course, to the safety of the Two Lands. Therefore, I cannot accept this assignment." A broad smile crossed my face, for I had foretold Nefertiti and Aye that this would be his response. Fortunately, we were prepared.

"I admire your integrity," I said, putting my hand in my robe and withdrawing a small scroll. "Candidly, this is one of the main reasons we have chosen to approach you. Here is a scroll from the King, naming Nefertiti to the role we described."

Horemheb studied the scroll and ran his fingers over the King's seal. He handed it back to me.

"Shall we begin then?" he simply asked.

For the next hour, we questioned Horemheb about what he knew regarding the status of the borders. His appraisal was frightening, having heard stories of incursions from his fellow soldiers returning for rotations. As we were wrapping up our discussion, Horemheb leaned forward in his seat.

"May I speak freely of things you have not asked?" he said, so softly I had to lean forward to hear.

"Of course," the Queen said without hesitation. "Now and always."

"I hear rumors from Waset, and I must say they are only rumors, for I have not been there in more than a year. Apparently, there is much dissatisfaction from Upper Kem about the King's proclamations against the Amun priesthood and the closing of all the temples not devoted to Adon. Further, there is much concern being expressed about recent developments with the Mittanis, Hittites, Ta-Tjehenus, and others. I know not the details, just the general sense expressed to me by my fellow soldiers."

"And superiors?" Aye was quick to ask. Horemheb sat silently. "Do not feel you must respond. Your silence speaks loudly enough."

"I feel this is a good start," Nefertiti said as she stood up. The rest of us stood immediately. "I look forward to your counsel, Horemheb. We shall meet every ten-day or more as needed. I do hope we can avoid another war with our neighbors, but... well, we shall see." She turned to leave as Horemheb bowed deeply.

With the Queen and Horemheb gone, Aye and I discussed what the next steps should be. We agreed that we would discuss them with Nefertiti so that she could take command and charge Horemheb with his first actions.

The following ten-day, the two met again. I only had a small amount of time to devote to the meeting due to pressing concerns with the temple construction in Inabu-Hedj. This time Horemheb arrived sweaty from a maneuver he had just completed with his fellow guards, instructing them in close-up fighting. When he entered, Nefertiti's eyes roamed his glistening, dirty body as he apologized for his appearance. The Queen then dropped her gaze.

"You have no cause to apologize, Horemheb. You are a warrior first and foremost." Once they sat down, Nefertiti offered Horemheb and me a drink of barley beer, which Horemheb immediately quaffed. Then Nefertiti began.

"Based on your reports last week, I plan on the following course of action. Vizier Aye has arranged with your commander to increase the size of your Royal Guard troops fourfold." Horemheb was stunned.

"But, my Queen, how can I handle that? My role is to protect the Royal family and patrol Akhedadon."

"It will be up to you to organize them in any way you see fit, once you hear what it is, I ask of you. You may promote whomever you trust to positions of authority to help you as you deem appropriate.

"The first action you must take is to quell the raids by the Ta-Tjehenus, for word has come to the King they test our resolve not only for their own benefit but possibly to aid the Hittites. Take as many fighting men as you need to do this, but do it with dispatch. We need a convincing win to put to rest any thoughts of more incursions by the Hittite puppets."

"My Queen, I worry even more about Tushratta and his shifting allegiance."

"As do I," Nefertiti agreed. "What do you suggest?"

"Under normal circumstances, I would suggest sending a delegation to negotiate matters back to normal. But from what I have heard, I fear he is now set in his ways and feels he must prove himself to his people.

"I suggest you allow me to send a rumor his way that there are some in Kem who feel we should prepare for war. Then, allow me to send a battalion of chariot soldiers near our shared border to conduct training exercises. I believe the combination will serve its purpose."

"Brilliant! Good ideas," I said. "But now I must take my leave to deal with the Inabu-hedj problem. "Carry on. We are making good progress."

I left feeling good about the manner in which Nefertiti had accepted her new role. I knew that Tiye would be proud of her. Without a doubt Aye certainly was. The day had begun strongly, and I felt happy that my brother would have his most detested responsibilities removed from his shoulders by the work of our group and would be free to worship our God as he wished. It appeared that, finally, things were going according to Akhenadon's plans. What I did not consider is that Adon had his own plans.

Scroll Sixteen

Ma'at or Chaos

With Horemheb off to the northwestern border to deal with the Ta-Tjehenus, our group felt confident that we were advancing Akhenadon's vision, and he seemed happier than ever. Yet instead of celebrating the progress, he used the time to pray ever more frequently and for longer periods of time. His daily prayers at the Great Temple increased so that even his most devoted adherents had difficulty attending. Many fainted during the sessions, and the Adon priests had to care for those taken ill, causing confusion during the service. My response was to train a cadre of helpers who administered to those so stricken, but Akhenadon seemed not to notice the tribulations of his followers.

Since our meeting with Horemheb, Nefertiti had extracted a concession from her father to take a more active role in helping her with Akhenadon's administration, to which he agreed. One day following the morning service to Adon, I found him waiting for me in my home. As soon as I entered, he held up a mug of cold barley beer for me.

"Ah, you are a messenger from Adon!" I said as I grabbed the mug and drank a long swig.

"I figured you would need it after one of Akhenadon's services," he said. "Honestly, I don't know how you take it."

"If it were not for his passion and our love for Adon, I would not be able to," I replied. "But he is most persuasive when he reads his poetry or sings his songs to Adon. His voice…"

"It is like a woman singer."

"Yes. Yes, it is, but that gives it a heavenly stature. I close my eyes and feel myself floating, wandering amongst the clouds. But, it is when we are forced to stand there doing nothing, basking in Adon's glory, that the problems emerge. Akhenadon seems not to be bothered by it. We all try to emulate that."

"Yes, like all of us, the son of God is also used to ignoring the heat of his father." We both had a good laugh at Aye's observation.

"What brings you here, Aye?"

"We must talk, Aharon."

"So, talk, but not until I refill my mug," I said, rising. "Will you have more?"

"Perhaps half. Thank you." But he simply put the mug on the short table before us. "You must do more, Aharon, to temper Akhenadon's zeal. It is not healthy. And I fear that by removing all other responsibilities from his shoulders as we have done, he has nothing but time to indulge his obsession with Adon." I had to admit that Aye's words rang true in my heart.

"Am I right to interpret your silence as agreement?" he asked. I placed my mug next to his and rose to pace and sort out my thinking.

"Yes, I have had the same thoughts. The very same. Yet…, I do not know how to encourage moderation in my brother. The truth is I have never known how to do this since we were children. Now that he occupies the throne, he has thrown any semblance of moderation to the wind. He is possessed, Aye, truly possessed." I wiped my brow with my hand as I paced.

"When I see him praying alone in his quarters when I walk in and he does not see or hear me, I believe he is truly conversing with his godfather. He talks and listens, so he must hear Adon answering, for he talks again as if they are standing next to one another, as we do now. They profess their love and devotion. At times I understand that Adon has admonished him, for he apologizes. And promises to do better.

"So, what am I to assume, Aye? That he is unhealthy, ill, mad? Or is it that we, you and I, the Amun priests, who are ill, for we do not hear the words of the one true God? Can you answer that?"

From the heat of the prayer service and my emotional outburst, I felt exhausted, truly of spent all energy. I sank into my chair. Aye leaned so far back in his chair he gazed at the ceiling.

"I had a meeting with Maya before I came here," Aye said, still reclining. "I called him into my administrative offices in Waset and gave him all but a dagger into his heart. Perhaps I should have done that, too. But first, I had gathered information from my sources within his priesthood who were beholden to me. Did you know, Aharon, that the Amun priests wring what they can from the people because they have taken a vow of poverty? Of course, you do. It makes no sense.

"But did you know that these very vows often mean a life of poverty for their families? That is the opening that we seek in prying open the door to information. Many of the priests are grateful for our, shall I say, subsidies to their families. All done in secret, of course, so as not to shame them for their poverty or to raise the suspicion of Maya.

"In any event, I told Maya that he had better back off. 'You will gain nothing by courting foreign allegiances and warring with the King,' I told him so he knew from the start that I had a spy or two within his inner workings. 'You may vanquish the King yet lose the kingdom,' I warned him, 'for it is ma'at that we all seek to strengthen, not chaos'. I believe he understood my message perfectly well."

"Well done, Aye," I offered, realizing that I was but a novice in such weighty matters compared with Aye and, truth be told, even Maya.

"We shall see how effective the talk was. I suspect it will last a short while. He will be distracted and will spend much energy trying to find out who the spy is in his ranks before hatching new plans. In the interim, we must address how you will use your relationship with Akhenadon to, at the very least, temper his behavior."

I listened to Aye's advice that morning, putting aside other duties to try hard to understand how to apply his ideas and suggestions. Yet here is what I learned. Aye grew up as an only child, the son of two very powerful and wise people who lived well into their years. Could he ever understand growing up without parents, being cast from one poor relative to another? Could he understand the gratitude of being rescued and raised in abundance? More than all these, could he even imagine the bond between two sworn brothers, boys who shared their dreams, who trembled in fear, holding tight to one another under a blanket when thunder roused them from sleep?

To Aye, Akhenadon was a man with strengths and weaknesses that had to be managed for the good of ma'at. To me, Akhenadon was more than merely a man. He was my brother. We were two kas intertwined and inseparable.

Akhenadon was always different. I was three years his senior when we first met, and rather than being repelled by his strange looks, I was curious, fascinated even. I found that if I peered deeper, behind the physical, I was captured by his heart. He thought of matters that no one spoke about.

At night Tiye would tell us stories about her people, about marvelous places she had traveled to, and about the different religious beliefs of people in foreign lands. I would be satisfied with the stories and fall deep asleep, dreaming of tall, cold mountains covered with a white powder, only to be wakened by Akhenadon. Do the heavens have an end? he would question. Do all Gods that people worship report to a higher God, and is He the highest of all? Are all people, Kemians and foreigners alike, all loved the same by the highest of the Gods? These are the things that tortured his heart, and he wrestled with them throughout our youth.

I soon found that I could not keep up with Akhenadon's

deep thoughts. Yet I loved him dearly and did not want us to be parted by our differences. And so, I vowed to myself to become a better listener. I soon learned how to listen to his heart, not just his words. As we grew into youthful manhood, I became an adept scribe and wrote down his thoughts and eventual beliefs about Re-Herakhty, who eventually crystallized into Adon. His passion swept me up so that our beliefs merged, and he made me his Chief Priest, now supervising a vast system of hundreds of priests, helpers, contracts with farmers, and more. So, what could Aye tell me that I did not already know about my brother?

Still, I took Aye's advice into my heart. For many days I struggled with thoughts of how to better manage Akhenadon's passion, but all I saw for the effort was conflict, alienation, and perhaps even more zealotry. Yet I also knew that Aye was correct, and we faced enemies and pressures all around, even from within. That soon proved all too true when I received one of Aye's messengers some fifteen days after our meeting in my home. My knees buckled upon reading Aye's parchment, and the messenger had to help me to my chair.

I sat thinking for the longest time, settling my breathing and clearing my head. I composed myself and went straight to Akhenadon's palace. I could see he was deep in prayer, but when I coughed, he began to stir. I waited until he was fully present before I relayed to him Aye's news.

"Killed himself?" Akhenadon muttered to himself. "But why? Akhedadon is his masterpiece, the crowning achievement of his life. Why would he do such a thing?" The King paced back and forth, wringing his hands, his brow knotted in confusion. Finally, he turned back to me.

"You remain silent, Aharon. Have you nothing to say? You worked closely with him. He was as dear to you as he was to me."

I looked deeply into my brother's eyes. "I am quiet because I fear burdening you with…."

"Stop, Aharon! Just tell me what I must know."

"There is no doubt in my mind that Ineni was murdered." I

suspected Maya's foul hand in this, and I imagined that Aye felt the same, for Ineni's conversion to Adon was a slap to Maya's face.

I have learned to judge a person by their manner of speech and the words they choose. Even the rise and fall of their voices reveal to an adept priest much about that person's ba. Yet the truer way for a person to reveal their true nature is by their actions. When talk and action conflict, trouble brews. But when the two are aligned, it is as if Adon has sent one of his spears of light through a person's ba and fuses it with his ka, as in a metalworker's fire. Therein lies the true nature of a man.

And so it was that day, that moment, in Akhenadon's chamber. For when I revealed to him my truth in the death of Ineni, he took a deep, shaking breath and slowly turned from me. He slumped into his chair, placed his head in his hands, and cried, the wordless sorrow of his ka manifest to Adon's ceaseless light.

At that moment, I knew. All my hopes and fears became clear in that instant. Akhenadon did not react in anger at those who plotted against him through this evil deed. He did not raise the specter of the King's might coming down in force upon these murderers. No. Instead, he cried.

I knew then that my brother's naivety, his simple devotion to the higher purpose of our God, was all that mattered to him. He could not face the pure evil that resides in the hearts of some.

A shiver of fear ran through my body, raising gooseflesh, and my heart gave a furious beat, for I knew then, despite my love for my brother and for Adon, that Aye was correct. Kem was damned.

Scroll Seventeen

Returning Warrior

On the very next day, following the news of Ineni's murder, as I walked back to my house after morning prayers in the Great Temple, I heard a loud commotion coming from the other side of Akhedadon. Although exhausted from a sleepless night, I stood on the road to see what was happening, and steadily, the noise and crowds approached closer.

In a few moments, I could see what the fuss was all about. People cheered wildly as Horemheb and his soldiers rode triumphantly through Akhedadon towards the stables and their barracks. Horemheb was in the lead, but he looked weary, covered in sweat and caked with desert dust, and with a bloody bandage on his arm. His calf was also bandaged, and I saw a poultice of moldy bread surrounding the wound to prevent infection, obviously applied by the physician priest I had sent with the expedition. Even Horemheb's horse wore a dirty bandage on one of his forelegs. The chariots and horsemen behind him look equally bedraggled, many of them wounded.

Nefertiti and I felt it was proper to give Horemheb time to recover and attend to his men before asking him to a meeting. Yet in two days, we received a message from Horemheb requesting that meeting as soon as possible, and so the next day, following worship, we met again in my house. By then, all of Akhedadon buzzed with stories of the exploits of the soldiers on which I had been briefed.

"Please excuse my tardiness, but Meritadon is ill with fever," Nefertiti said upon arriving.

"Shall I send my priest physician?" I asked, concerned.

"He is already by her side," she answered. We waited for her to sit, and then we did the same. Horemheb still looked weary, but he had bathed and put on a fresh kilt. The military physician had also changed his bandages. I saw Nefertiti staring at them.

"Are the wounds severe?" she asked.

"I am fine."

"And your soldiers?"

"We lost three men, and nearly two dozen were wounded. I am sorry for their losses. I should have anticipated better."

"Anticipated what?" I asked.

"That is why I have asked for this meeting so quickly." He tried to lift his wounded arm onto the armrest and winced in pain.

"I have heard how you received that wound," I offered, looking from him to Nefertiti. "You acted heroically to save one of your men." Nefertiti turned her gaze to Horemheb.

"I only did what we are trained to do. On the battlefield, all men are brothers."

"Continue," Nefertiti said, staring intently at Horemheb.

"All skirmishes recorded with the Ta-Tjehenu as far back as we have scrolls documenting them follow a pattern. We learn this in training as officers. They are raiders, cowards, really. They intimidate women and the elderly. But as soon as they see our soldiers appear, they whoop and holler and run."

"Yes, I have read the same as I trained for the priesthood."

"Except this time, that did not happen."

"What do you mean?" Nefertiti asked, now at the edge of her seat.

"They did not run. Not at all. In fact, they had a carefully thought out plan for engaging us."

"What? How could…" I was stunned.

"After the skirmish, we captured some of the wounded. They were not Ta-Tjehenu at all. They were Hittites, shaved and disguised."

"Hittites? Not good news," I said.

"They had trained the Ta-Tjehenus in swordsmanship and spears. If they had also trained them in charioteering or if there were even a dozen more Hittite warriors present, I probably would not be here now reporting to you." At this, Horemheb looked to the floor.

"I am proud to tell you, my Queen, that my men fought valiantly. Kem owes them much."

"I have no doubt they fought bravely," Nefertiti said, "for they have you as their leader."

"I, too, have heard the stories of the battle, Horemheb, of how you rallied your men, reorganized them in the midst of the furor, and led them to victory with you at the front line. This victory was critical." Again, Horemheb merely looked at the floor.

"And after the battle?" I asked.

"First, I thank you for sending one of your priest physicians and a scribe along. The physician was sorely needed in the aftermath. I believe we only have a few infected wounds. After the battle, we executed the remaining Ta-Tjehenus and dispatched the headless bodies back to their homeland, as we have always done. We recovered the bounty they stole from our people, and I will send a delegation of soldiers to the Nome they raided to return our people's belongings."

"Thank you, Horemheb," Nefertiti said, obviously affected by his report.

"As for the Hittites, we executed all but three of them and have brought them here bound as slaves. I await your orders on how to handle them."

"We will speak with Aye on that matter," I suggested. I knew that Aye would have the means to wring information from them.

Nefertiti stood and began to pace slowly, her hands joined before her. We rose, but she bade us sit. "This is disturbing. The involvement of the Hittites and their training of the Ta-Tjehenus is most troubling." We both nodded our agreement.

"But we must face this new reality and adjust. I ask you, Horemheb, for suggestions. What must we do to protect our people?" Now she sat back down as we awaited Horemheb's response.

"I have had much time to think on this on my return to Akhedadon. If the Chief Priest would be kind enough to allow me the use of his scribe, I will have my suggestions put to parchment."

"That is well and good," I said, "but we would like a summary now."

"Of course." He paused to collect his thoughts. "First, we must retrain our troops for what new tactics to expect in border skirmishes and how to counter them." We both nodded. "Next, I urge the King to consider adding more soldiers to the army so that we may reinforce the troops in the border areas, for we are sure to be tested further. I have heard reports in the last few ten days that there is unrest and border raids in the Mafkat and along the Wat-Hor route to Canaan."

We sat quietly once Horemheb was done, thinking of the import of his words. Nefertiti was the first to speak.

"Horemheb, first I must thank you in my name and that of the King for your valor and strength and leadership. You are a true hero to us all." Horemheb, obviously embarrassed, bowed his head.

"Next, I have a report for you," she said, smiling. "Your ruse with King Tushratta appears to have worked. He recently sent a conciliatory letter to King Akhenadon. In it, he referenced the army drills you ordered on his border and how happy he was to see them, which he took as a sign of our promise to protect Mittani." Again, Horemheb bowed his head.

"And now I must leave to speak to the King and to convince him to increase our troops. You have the King's permission to retrain your troops at all the northern borders. Aharon, please have Aye send a proclamation to all the southern border posts to be on alert, using whatever guidelines Horemheb recommends. Horemheb, we will meet again in a ten-day, if not sooner. I pray for your quick healing," she said, pointing to his wounds.

Later that day, after evening worship and time playing board games with their girls, Nefertiti's servants bathed her. As she was being dried off, Akhenadon appeared, and she walked with him to their bedroom chambers. This followed several ten days that Akhenadon had devoted to intense prayer and communion with Adon. His mood was buoyed, no doubt in part because Nefertiti had assumed many of his administrative obligations.

"Have I told you recently how much I love you?" he suddenly said. "I have devoted so much time to Adon, yet a poem to you, my love, burns deeply inside me. I shall write it down and perhaps put it to song."

Nefertiti smiled broadly and went over to kiss him. She appreciated his full lips, and by his touch on her waist, she sensed it would be a night of intimacy. She thought of their beautiful girls but also wished to carry a son for Akhenadon. The thought of a night of sex pleased her. That it might help advance her request for troops entered her thinking.

"I must discuss a situation that I recently became aware of as I deal with the military."

"The military?"

"Yes, if you will recall, Aye and Aharon suggested that I take that responsibility off your shoulders, and you agreed."

"Oh, I had forgotten. I am so pleased that you do so."

"There have been numerous incursions recently at the northern borders, both east and west. Horemheb, the captain of your guards here in Akhedadon, has recently battled the Ta-Tjehenus in the western desert. They have been raiding us again.

"In any event, Horemheb suggests that we increase our troop strength along the northern borders and the south as well. Aye and Aharon both agree with his strategy. We would like to draft a proclamation for you to sign." Nefertiti was pleased with her presentation. When she looked at Akhenadon, she saw that he merely eyed her body from top to bottom.

"Come here, my gift, and let us make passionate love together." He reached for her hand.

"You have no idea how much I yearn for that, but I wish first to have an answer."

"You torture me, you mut spirit!" he said, laughing as he stood. She looked down and saw that he only had thoughts of sex.

"Seriously, love, I will pleasure you with my body in a moment, but first, tell me you will sign the proclamation in the morning. The Two Lands must have our protection."

A scowl appeared on Akhenadon's face. "You know I dislike dealing with such issues at night... or at all." Nefertiti turned and undid her hair dressings, letting her hair fall down her back, which she knew would tempt Akhenadon. She turned to the wash basin and brushed her teeth with a crushed acacia twig dipped in mint juice.

"I understand your request for more troops," Akhenadon began as he disrobed, "but I am distressed that you... you and Aye and even Aharon do not yet understand the workings of Adon."

"Meaning?" she asked as she moved toward the bed.

"Adon would never allow anything bad to happen to me, His only son."

"Of course not, nor did I ever think he would."

"And that is why I will not approve additional troops, especially at the border, where our neighbors might view it as an affront. Adon will provide. You must... we all must have faith in the one true God.

Scroll Eighteen

At War with Amun

We had been standing in the Great Temple for more than an hour as Adon's disk baked down upon us. A fine desert dust hung suspended in the air, making breathing difficult and causing the distant mountains to shimmer in the heat. People coughed loudly, and Panehesy, the Chief Servitor of the Great Temple, quietly supervised a cadre of helpers in passing out jugs of water for people to drink. Even I felt weak. Daughters obligingly poured water on the heads of their parents. Mothers soaked rags in the water and used them to cool their restless children.

Akhenadon signalled to me, and I walked to the center of the platform, looking out at the crowd of more than four hundred adherents. I raised my staff, and the people looked up to the sky. I said a brief prayer of blessing over them. As soon as I was done, Akhenadon stepped forward to speak. Nefertiti stood at his side, her hand intertwined with Meritadon's, whose unsteady feet betrayed her need for a nap.

"My beloved people, believers in Adon. Is it not a glorious day? Adon blesses us every day with His disk so that plants might grow, cattle might fatten, and we may benefit from both to sustain us. As we stand here at this moment, priests and celebrants across the Two Lands are also welcoming Him, worshipping Him, praising Him for all eternity, for a mighty

God He is.

"Soon Akhet will be upon us, another blessing from Adon, through Mother Nile, to us, another example of Adon's undying love, for He is eternal. His being is everywhere, throughout the entire universe. Everything is perfect, everything according to ma'at.

"Listen, believers! Adon is our God. Adon is the one and only God."

With that, Akhenadon held his arms high to the heavens, and the believers did the same and repeated the phrase that had become the rallying cry of devotees. Now the priests and helpers distributed bowls of fruits, nuts, bread, and sweets on the tables around which people stood. Akhenadon and Nefertiti smiled as the people partook in the bounty. Nefertiti pointed to one family where the baby had smeared dates all over its face, and Meritadon laughed. After watching for a few moments, Akhenadon led Nefertiti and Meritadon to his chariot and left for the palace.

That afternoon I left my home to meet with Akhenadon and Nefertiti. It was pitifully hot, the sand even burning through my reed sandals as I walked to the meeting. Thankfully, Nefertiti offered me a tall mug of beer when I arrived.

"What news do you bear?" Akhenadon asked.

"Good news, my King, for Sothis has been spotted in the night sky."

"Wonderful news," Nefertiti exclaimed. "Akhet will soon be upon us."

"And even better," I added, " the priests report that the flood looks to be promising."

"It is like I said, all is perfect, thanks to Adon. It is all ordered, all part of His plan. We never need to worry, so long as we worship Him as He instructs me to do." Akhenadon lifted his mug and drank.

"My love, will you supervise the various festivals for Akhet?" Nefertiti hesitated. "I do not mean to do all the work yourself. Just make sure that the governors of the

Nomes, the ones on your council, each does his part." Nefertiti nodded.

"And you, Aharon, please make sure that the priests throughout Kem honor Adon properly for Akhet. I feel this is very important as we continue to battle the Amun priesthood. I had hoped that by now, I had choked off enough of their treasure to…."

"They have their own way of raising treasure," I interrupted. "They have raised their rents on their lands and, well, to be blunt, they still manage to hold prayer sessions to Amun."

"And they expect people to lavish them with gifts for that," Nefertiti said.

"They even have created a series of smaller Amun statues, which they bless so they can worship him secretly in homes. Of course, the statues are only for those who can afford it, but since they, too, are violating your edict, they tell no one for fear of being found out and punished."

As I look back, I question whether I should have even mentioned this to Akhenadon, for the very next day, he summoned me to his quarters. He looked straight ahead, with dark circles under his eyes. He had difficulty walking erect, and in slumping as he did, his tortured body pained my heart.

"I was unable to sleep last night. I had not heard of the way that Maya had evaded my edicts. I have drafted a solution. Here, read this," he said, grabbing a parchment from the small table in front of his chair.

I had to read it twice to be certain of what I read. My heart pumped furiously, and my hands trembled. "Akhenadon, are you sure…."

"How did I know you would say that?"

I ignored his remark. "This is… how can I say it? Surely you must understand what this will mean?"

"Yes, of course, I do," he replied, but I felt sure that he did not, for he spent every day in contemplative prayer, creating songs and poems, and designing temples to Adon, rarely traveling the Two Lands to see with his own eyes the challenges common people face. My childhood friends in the Delta and my new acquaintances through Tiye all sent me reports on the tribulations they faced.

"I have given Maya plenty of time to join us. He refuses. He has already declared war on Adon. Now I will deliver a blow from which he cannot recover."

Although he wanted to implement these drastic measures immediately, I managed to persuade him to allow Aye to give us counsel on how to implement them in an efficient manner. I was surprised he agreed. I dispatched an urgent message for Aye to come to Akhedadon.

The night before our meeting with Akhenadon, Aye, Nefertiti, and I met to discuss how to handle him. Fortunately, we were in agreement that he must be dissuaded from issuing this proclamation. So, we entered the meeting confidently.

"I wish to first make sure we fully understand what you are proposing, Akhenadon," Aye said.

"Always a good way to proceed," he replied, smiling and looking at each of us in turn.

"You are proposing to have the Army disburse units throughout Kem, in every Nome, and literally destroy every temple of Amun. Do we understand that correctly?"

"As far as you went, but I also want every statue of Amun to be destroyed."

"Yes, I was going to state that next. And non-compliance would be punishable by imprisonment or even death, correct?"

"Very simple to understand, is it not? There is no room for Maya and his cronies to wiggle out of it." Akhenadon leaned forward, lifted his cup, and sipped his morning tea.

"My King, I am but your humble servant...."

"Servant, yes, humble I am not so sure of," Akhenadon joked. I looked at Aye, who seemed as surprised as I was, for Akhenadon rarely, if ever, joked.

With a faint smile on his face, Aye continued. "It has only been two years since your father passed. Can I at least convince you to slow this down, to start with something simpler as a first step toward eventually…"

"No."

I wish I could say that we succeeded in changing Akhenadon's heart that day, but we did not try, though we did. Even Nefertiti, usually able to at least draw some concession from her husband, was not successful. It was left to Aye to meet with Yanhamu, Chief of the Army stationed in Waset, and convince him that Akhenadon was bent on these actions. Thankfully, Aye knew Yanhamu well from meeting with him many times on King Amunhotep the Third's business. They had a friendship built on trust, respecting each other's expertise.

"You cannot be serious!" Yanhamu protested loudly. His booming voice matched his large body, outsized in the small chair he sat in. In his youth, Yanhamu was quite impressive, muscular, broad-shouldered, and a fierce fighter. Time had left his scarred body just as broad but without the muscles of his youth. He stormed out of his seat and walked straight at Aye, pointing his finger.

"This has gone far enough, Aye! We have worked together on military matters throughout Amunhotep's last twenty years on the throne. I cannot believe that the Two Lands that we have pledged our lives to defend and prosper, have come to this. We have an idiot on the throne! A weakling, who is penned up in Akhedadon afraid to show his grisly face."

Yanhamu paced away and then rushed back to Aye. "Here it is, then. I will not do it!"

Aye looked directly into Yanhamu's face, not wanting to show timidity to a man that most people feared greatly.

"You are a soldier, Yanhamu. A brave and loyal soldier. You have a sworn duty that you have never taken lightly. As friends, I will ignore your traitorous comments. You are angry, I understand that. But, you will do as your King commands, and that is all there is to it."

Yanhamu returned to his chair and sat with such force Aye thought the chair would break. He picked up his beer mug and drained its contents. Red-faced, he sat back and stared at Aye for a long time, neither of them speaking.

"Tell me, my old friend, a man I have always respected. How can you tolerate serving Akhenadon, who is more woman than a man?"

Aye leaned forward, crossing the fingers of his hands as if praying. "If we have ever been dishonest with each other, I know not of that time. I will not start now. I tell you that my work is not easy. Akhenadon is like no man I have ever known.

"You call him a weakling, and he is certainly weak in body, I grant you that. But do not make the mistake of thinking he is weak in heart or resolve. He can be as bull-headed as you, my dear friend. You call him an idiot, but doing so could only serve to reveal you to be one. But the truth is that neither of you is. It is anger that moves your mouth.

"What I will tell you is that he is a true believer, dedicated to his Adon, a God that I admit I still do not fully understand. But that is of no matter. He believes passionately, deeply, with all his heart. He speaks to his Adon, he receives messages from Him. And who are we, Yanhamu, to say this is all madness? What if you and I are simply deaf and blind to the calls from the heavens? What if our hearts are so hardened by the weaknesses we have seen in men that it has also hardened our kas so they cannot fly to the heights of this God? And what if, just what if, Akhenadon's heart is light enough to rise so?"

Over the next few days, Aye met with Yanhamu, and together, they drafted a plan to close some temples, destroy others, and create safe havens for the Amun priests. Maya would still retain his title as Chief Priest of Amun, but he would lose his administrative staff and continue to be deprived of any of the annual treasure from the King. Proclamations would be sent to every village, town, and city, telling the people they were forbidden to worship any God but Adon or to hold any statuary or amulet to another

God. It was a deal that would release every mut spirit in the Two Lands, Yanhamu warned in a last plea.

Yanhamu divided his troops into units that would enforce the decree in all forty-two Nomes. They were trained in what to do, yet it did not go easily. In town after town, people whose families had prayed to Amun or Tawaret or Isis or any of the many others we all worshipped for generations rebelled at the destruction. Devotees of Amun described the destruction as an assault on their bodies. Change always brings out fear, yet this was worse, far worse. Akhenadon was committed to converting people from the comfort of Gods they knew to a God they did not understand.

There were physical altercations with the troops. Farmers using shovels and sticks, desperately tried to block the soldiers' entrance to the temples. But Akhenadon was resolute in enforcing his decree, even resorting to watching the destruction of a temple near Inabu-hedj from a nearby hill.

It was hardly a secret that the Amun priests encouraged these demonstrations of discontent, and we all knew who was behind it. The war that Maya had promised was now fully engaged, and I could not anticipate where all this would lead.

Scroll Nineteen

A Believer

"When I was in Waset, I spoke with three of the priests from Nekhen, three Amun priests... well, former Amun priests, that is. Now they are priests in Akhenadon's service." Meryt sat on their bed, anxiously twisting her hands.

"Is that wise, Kha?"

"Wise? If I were wise, you would be calling me Vizier." Both laughed at the welcome break in the earnest conversation...

"But seriously, we spoke well into the night."

"And you supplied the beer."

"Yes, I supplied the beer. But these men, they are true believers, Meryt. They are not young, impressionable men. They are experienced. They have managed entire temples."

"And what has convinced them of Akhenadon's beliefs?"

"They believe in him, the man. And not because he is King of the Two Lands. They believe he speaks with this Adon and that Adon talks directly to his heart. They believe that he then speaks Truth. Truth such as none of the corrupt Amun priesthood knows anymore. They are so passionate, my love. True believers." Kha was animated as he paced before his wife, his eyes wide open, his face red from exertion.

"And you, my dear husband, what do you believe?"

Kha stopped pacing and stared at his wife, before looking away. Now it was his turn to wring his hands as he spoke. He continued to pace, now staring at the floor, trying to summon up the words that would answer Meryt's question, then realizing it was as much his question.

"You know me better than anyone else. You know I am a planner. I never decide quickly. I ask questions, I ask for opinions, for other ways to do something."

"Of course, I know that."

"So I did the same with this… situation. I also spoke with Amun priests and with my own workmen who also serve as Amun advisors to our community.

"Surely that is risky, Kha. Why would you do that? What did they say?"

"Risky, yes, but so are the decisions I make for building the tombs. The men looked like they would think about it and promised to attend meetings where this was to be discussed. The Amun advisors, however, saw things differently."

"In what way?"

"They fear their extra provisions for their families will be taken away. They fear extra days off hard labor to instead supervise religious festivals would also be taken away. They have also been told that such a move would endanger ma'at."

They sat silently for a time. "Yet I have learned a few things," Kha started again. "Each time I have these meetings, I come away with the same feeling. There is something missing in our traditional beliefs."

"Missing? We have many Gods and Goddesses," Meryt protested, throwing up her hands. "Many. This imposter King has only one. How can we be missing something in our beliefs? Our Gods cover everything, every part of our lives!"

"Yes, but that is the very point. Why are so many Gods needed? Why…"

"Do not insult me, husband! I pray to Tawaret for childbirth and to Isis for being a good wife to you and… and that is not always easy!"

"I am sorry, sweet wife," Kha said softly, now sitting beside Meryt and taking both her hands in his. "I know I have not been easy. My work is far too demanding." He breathed deeply. "But allow me time to explain what I feel. This is important to me."

Meryt squeezed his hands. "Go ahead. Forgive my impatience."

"I have always admired your devotion to the Gods and Goddesses you worship," he said, glancing at the alcoves in the room that were crowded with figurines of Goddesses. "But you know that I have never felt a kinship to them. I have spent many nights thinking of this since I was a child. Why has there not been a God strong enough to bind them together for the good of all? Is that not what happens here in the Two Lands with our King and his ministers and servants? Would it not be simpler to pray to one mighty God who has created and governs all that we see? That is what I believe and have always believed. And now the only difference is that Akhenadon has put the thoughts that have swirled through my heart into words that make sense to me." Kha stood again. "That, to me, is Truth."

Meryt rested her face in her hands for several minutes, lost in thought, troubled by Kha's words. Finally, she looked up. "And why do you tell me this, Kha? What would you have me do?"

"Men are simple creatures, Meryt. As far as the home goes, they go where their wives lead them," Kha said, looking at his wife. "I would like you to talk to the wives."

"What? How can I...."

"Wait. All I am asking is for you to persuade them to come to a meeting or two, meetings where they can hear the truth of what Adon is truly about. Not the lies that the Amun priests sling like crocodile dung, but the truth from the Adonite priests that understand Akhenadon's words.

"Set Maat is intentionally isolated. Our work has always been seen as holy. Amun priests never set foot here, only our workers who double as priestly assistants for extra rations or days off from work. They all report to me, and I report to Aye. I can sweeten the pot for all of them, of that I am certain. I plan to have prayers at Adon's appearance in the heavens. Eventually, they will come to see the wisdom in becoming adherents of Adon."

"What about our life here in Set Maat? We have houses with strong stone walls, not mud brick. We have three rooms, a yard, a kitchen, and even two underground storage pits. What happens if the Amun priests are offended and they convince someone to kick us out as troublemakers? What then?"

"Meryt, there is no someone they could convince. The King, the Queen, the Vizier, and even the Royal Mother are believers. Akhenadon would throw the Amun priests out on their ears."

Meryt looked away from Kha and began rocking in the bed, eyes closed. A single tear ran down her cheek.

"I do not doubt your plan, Kha," Meryt said, her voice weak. "You are a careful thinker and even better planner. But there may be more to this than you are considering. How do I know that I, or my friends, the wives, sisters, daughters, and mothers of Set Maat, will be treated equally under this Adon? Or the women of any village in Kem? Amongst all nations, our Kem by far gives women the most rights.

"Shall all women give up their inheritance rights, rights to own a business, to divorce, or ask for a fair judgment in court for those who harm us? Will we yet be able to teach our daughters to read and write as we do now? Will women be used for sex like the Hittites do, just to satisfy a man's needs, with no thought to a woman's pleasure?

"Men are free to think of lofty matters, of building for eternity, of the role of Kings and Gods. We women must attend to the practical, to birth, to nurturing, to home, and life.

"So, as always, husband, I will stand beside you. I will persuade women to at least listen. But of this, I will assure you. If this Adon does not give equal importance to the needs of our women, he will never become the supreme God of our people. Never!"

Scroll Twenty

Turmoil in My Heart

A month after the start of Akhenadon's decree, I was called to Waset to mediate a potential problem with the small Temple of Adon that was close to the immense Temple of Amun complex. It appeared that a difficult situation arose when the statues of Amun were being removed from the temple or, in the case of the larger ones, toppled and smashed. This action provoked impassioned riots. Waset, after all, was the home of Amun, with a strong following there.

I, myself, witnessed angry mobs besieging our Temple of Adon. I froze in fear. Stones were thrown at our laborers. "Do not take Amun from us!" they shouted. I even heard one woman... a woman shout, "Kill the heretic King!" People threw balls of hippopotamus dung at our priests. Adherents were afraid to attend our services for fear of retribution from their neighbors.

Then a curious thing happened. Akhenadon's decree required the Amun priesthood to be disbanded, leaving Maya with a title in name only. Where would his priests go? The Servitor of our temple had an idea. Since several of our most ardent priests were formerly Amun priests and had strong connections with their brethren there, our Servitor thought to shelter them within the Temple of Adon. I felt this was not a good idea. I knew it would infuriate Akhenadon should he find out, so I hurried to Waset to settle the conundrum, which I was able to quickly do. Gold, jewels, and offers of food stores helped settle many seemingly intractable problems. We found other lodgings for those priests who did not voluntarily convert to Adon priests.

Upon my return to Akhedadon, I was summoned to Akhenadon's palace. I was surprised to see Thutmose, the sculptor there, sketching the face of Akhenadon as Nefertiti watched and heaped praise upon him. Soon, we were joined by the chief artists of the Royal tombs, administrative buildings, and temples. By the time all had eaten and settled down, I was eager to hear the purpose of the meeting.

"Aharon, come here and sit beside me," he said, pointing to the seat to his left. Nefertiti sat to his right.

"My dear artists, you are undoubtedly the finest in all the lands. I have asked you here to give you some instructions, as given to me by Adon himself." Murmurings ensued as the men were either awed or skeptical of his claim.

"Many of you have asked me for direction as to how to depict Adon in your paintings. Thutmose here has asked to create a statue of Adon for the temples we build. I waited until now to explain this to you." He looked out upon the crowd, smiling.

"There will never be a statue or painting depicting the Adon." He let this sink in as the group whispered to each other. "There is no likeness that can be made of Adon," Akhenadon continued, "for He is everywhere at all times. His presence is throughout all lands and all-sky throughout the entire universe. He created all animals and plants, but He is not like them in appearance.

"I know this is strange to you, for you have spent your lives making representations of Amun and all the other false Gods that we used to worship. But Adon is greater than any of them and even all of them, if ever they existed, for before all else, and above all else, Adon rules, and I with Him.

"So, I have made here a drawing," and he unrolled a large

parchment, "which shows Adon's most familiar representation, which is the disk of light and the heat it sends forth that we see and feel every day. The rays that emanate end as life-giving helping hands for all our benefits. This, my dear artists will be how you will draw Adon, how you will sculpt Him on walls, for Adon is the one who built Himself by Himself, with His own hands. No craftsman knows Him or can ever know Him."

With that, Akhenadon handed me the scroll and told me to have my scribes copy it for distribution to all the artisans, craftsmen, and sculptors in attendance. Akhenadon and I had discussed Adon's physical existence many times growing up, as he devoted his life to Him. But this was the first I knew of how Akhenadon perceived our God. I found this most humbling, and I recall that it sent gooseflesh along my body, for somehow Akhenadon had captured the essence of our God in his representation.

Yet Akhenadon was not through. "There is one other matter for which you need guidance. I have noticed that in the tombs and buildings you are painting and sculpting in Akhedadon, you are depicting me in the same manner kings have always been depicted. I command you to change that." Again, the artists whispered to their neighbors. Akhenadon waited for the chatter to die down.

"From now on, you will represent Nefertiti and me as we are… exactly as we are. There shall be no embellishment. Both Nefertiti and I are Adon's creations. You all are Adon's creation. We are created in His image, but not His physical appearance, for as I explained, He has no physical appearance. We are each created in His image in our heart, in our ka. Our beauty shines within. Some of us, like the Queen, have outer beauty, too, but outer beauty only matters to those of us who are too shallow to see where true beauty lies in our inner reflection of Adon's beauty." Nefertiti smiled her love of Akhenadon on display for all who were present that day.

In the ensuing ten days, Aye sent me reports of unrest

throughout Kem, but most notably in Upper Kem. No matter the punishment, and many were indeed severely punished, the common people were angry. It did not help matters that Mother Nile was less generous during Akhet than was predicted, and the harvest was meager. The Amun priests would normally give out grains from their storage to those in need, but now the granaries were locked and guarded, and grains rotted or were eaten by vermin. People started to attack the granaries to feed their families.

Aye requested that I keep these reports from Akhenadon until he had an opportunity to meet with him. First, he met with Nefertiti and me so that we could present a united front in our meeting with Akhenadon, although we no longer harbored hopes for our success. I could not help but note Nefertiti's upset upon hearing of the discontent throughout the Two Lands. At one point, I noted that she cradled her abdomen, and I knew she was protecting her as-yet-unborn child. I had the distinct impression that the burdens of childbirth, motherhood, administrative duties, and, most of all, her marriage to Akhenadon had taken its toll.

"And you say you have witnessed these disturbances with your own eyes," Akhenadon asked Aye.

"I have many times. The people have always been taught that the essence of the God they pray to is contained in the statue. 'Who, then, are we to pray to?' they ask."

"I understand," Akhenadon responded, although I suspect that we all believed he did not. "We must do a better job of explaining the worship of Adon to them. Aharon, this will fall to you. I wish reports on how it proceeds."

"I will do so," I replied, "but there is more that must be done."

"Such as?"

"The people must see you more. There must be new festivals where they can celebrate rather than spread evil gossip. Without them seeing you celebrating the glory of Adon, they feel unguided, leaderless. They neither fully understand Adon nor do they understand their King, His son."

"And in your absence, Maya or his supporters are able to say what they wish," Aye added.

"Really? Please tell me what my dear friend Maya says to the people."

Aye took in a labored breath. "Maya is saying that you are at war with Amun. This has proved to be a battle cry for Amun adherents and their supporters."

"The peasants know nothing!" Akhenadon said, leaning forward in his seat.

"Not only peasants, Akhenadon. Amun's followers include some of the wealthiest, smartest, most powerful people in all of Kem."

Akhenadon sat back and smiled. "Well, despite what Maya says, there cannot be any war with Amun," he responded in his quiet voice, "for there is no Amun. There is only Adon, the one and only God."

By the end of the meeting, we were only able to extract minor concessions from Akhenadon. He would distribute grain and other stores from the royal granaries to people in need. He would also provide work to any Amun priests who willingly give up the priesthood. He allowed us to open refuges for priests who were willing to be retrained in return for food and shelter.

Still, Akhenadon sheltered himself in Akhedadon and rarely ventured out, choosing to spend his time with Adon, Nefertiti, and his girls, who grew in beauty like their mother. One of the few times Akhenadon left was to see the completion of the new Temple of Adon in Inabu-hedj, on the site where the Temple of Amun once stood. It was larger than the ones in Upper Kem, for the people in the Delta were more accepting of Akhenadon's one God. While I accompanied him there, I witnessed something so strange, so unexpected, it caused me to tremble.

As we entered the open prayer courtyard, a miniature of the Great Temple in Akhedadon, Adon turned to one of the wall artists who had attended his meeting in the palace. He pointed to a spot on the wall where his cartouche stood in bold relief.

"Do you see my cartouche there on the wall?" he asked the man, whose hands were still white from working the mortar and plaster. The man nodded nervously, fearful of reprimand. "It is excellent work, but I am afraid you must remove it and replace it."

The man did not comprehend, for it would be an offense to remove the King's cartouche. I stepped forward and bowed before Akhenadon. "May I speak with you privately?" I asked.

"Of course." We walked a few paces away, leaving the poor artisan shaking.

"What you ask cannot be done, my brother. It is forbidden. We cannot strike your name."

"Oh, but they must. It is only temporary. They will replace it with a new cartouche." Now I was puzzled. I leaned against my staff, anticipating yet another chance for Akhenadon to disturb ma'at. He did not disappoint.

"A new cartouche? Do you intend to abandon the Two Lands to a different King?" He laughed.

"Not at all, Aharon. It will be replaced with two names in the cartouche, Adon's and mine. Adon is co-regent with me on Earth."

For a moment, I could neither speak nor even breathe. What Akhenadon was suggesting was pure heresy. Never, in all our history, had any King placed another name within his cartouche. This would have enormous implications, for even though Akhenadon often referred to himself as the son of Adon, this would announce it physically to the entire land. Our people would not be able to comprehend its meaning and might even attribute the change to evil spirits. I knew in an instant that Maya would use this to accuse Akhenadon of believing himself equal to Adon. But, as usual, Akhenadon could not be deterred.

As soon as we returned to Akhedadon, with Akhenadon in high spirits, I dashed off a message to Aye so he could be prepared when word of this spread. In three days, he returned a message expressing his consternation and asking me to find out if Nefertiti agreed to this.

As I walked toward Nefertiti's administrative quarters, I saw Horemheb walking with purpose to his scheduled ten-day meeting with Nefertiti. His face was contorted in what seemed to me to be anger. I thought it best to wait until after their meeting and then speak with Nefertiti privately.

I learned later that day from Nefertiti what transpired, but not all of what happened. The rest I learned much later.

Horemheb stormed into the meeting out of breath. "My Queen, may I speak with you privately, I mean with none of your servants present?"

"Of course," Nefertiti replied, ushering her staff and servants out of the room. "Now, what has you so upset?"

"I… it is… Aaah, my anger has tied my tongue." He wiped his hands on his kilt several times to collect himself. "It is the decree the King issued. It has taken time for my guard troops to be trained in what we must do. There are no temples to Amun close to Akhedadon, so we were not called upon to act until seven days ago."

"I see," Nefertiti said softly.

"With all the respect that I hold you in, I do not think you see… at all. May I speak from my heart?"

"It would seem to me you already are, my friend." Rarely had Nefertiti seen such emotion in a man, let alone a battle-hardened soldier. A servant started to enter the room, and she waved her away.

"I think you and the King do not understand how difficult it is for those who must administer the destruction of temples that are holy to…."

"I must interrupt, Horemheb, my valiant warrior. I have been enclosed in this room since this morning dealing with the King's business. And you are excited. It might be best for us to walk in our garden along Mother Nile. It would be restful to our bas and would allow us to speak from our hearts without distraction."

Horemheb seemed uncomfortable. "If that would please you, then… then I would be happy to walk with you, Queen

Nefertiti."

As they walked, gardeners stopped their work to bow. Potted plants from Nubia, Kush, Lebanon, Canaan, and lands far east grew along the path, creating shade and a profusion of reds, purples, greens, and oranges. Servants drew water from the river to fill ponds and water the many trees. At the end of the path that Nefertiti chose, a grove of trees sheltered an acacia wood bench from Adon's blazing disk. Nefertiti's open hand pointed to the bench, and they both sat, half turned toward one another.

"I can only imagine how difficult it must be for your men to tear down temples, Horemheb."

"Many of my men grew up nearby. Their families have worshipped Amun for a thousand years. When my men appear in a town to destroy their temple, the people weep. They plead for us to stop. They throw themselves at us, men and women, risking blows. My men are soldiers, not used to such service to the King. But they carry out their orders, for they are soldiers with sworn allegiance to Akhenadon."

Nefertiti looked down, full of sorrow for what Horemheb described. She felt his pain as leader of his men, ensuring that they followed his orders.

"I am sorry for you to be put in this position...."

"I do not ask for pity," he said, turning to correct her and placing his hand atop hers without thinking. "I only ask for you to try to dissuade the King in his pursuit of...." He realized his transgression and quickly withdrew his hand, blushing.

"I cannot, dear Horemheb. I cannot."

It was as if time stood still, the two of them staring into each other's eyes, not a word spoken, but much said and even more understood. Suddenly Nefertiti drew a sharp breath and stood. "We must return to the palace," she said, starting to walk, at first stumbling before she regained her balance. Horemheb reached out to steady her, but she quickened her pace. Horemheb followed in silence.

When they reached the palace, Horemheb turned to Nefertiti. "I am sorry, my Queen," he began, bowing low to her.

"I should not...."

"You did nothing that requires an apology," Nefertiti replied in a whisper. "It is the turmoil in my heart that I must examine." She then turned and walked up the steps into the palace.

For the next few days, I heard little from Nefertiti. Her maidservant reported to me that she was ill, but I knew better than to believe that since she always asked for my advice concerning her health as I trained in the medical arts as I advanced in my priesthood. I decided to let it go. That day, Akhenadon invited me to share the mid-day meal with him. He was jubilant.

"Dear brother, look at what I received last night from my beloved. I am at a loss for words. Here, read this," he said, thrusting a papyrus scroll toward me.

I unrolled it and looked quickly to see that it was written by Nefertiti. It was a poem and one that explained Akhenadon's mood.

> *My beloved one, King of my soul, the only master of my body.*
>
> *You are the most majestic tree, I come to lie down at your feet, covered by your warm arms...*
>
> *Your gaze all over me is an albatross song, I'm your inner tide, I get back to you from dawn to nightfall...*
>
> *Our hearts beat together, my skin is perfumed with red hibiscus scent,*
>
> *I befuddle you with my divine nectar that you drink from my golden cup...*
>
> *After love, we'll bathe in the waves of the Nile, watching over the pyramids, and whispering one to the other: 'I love you!'*
>
> *We'll draw our love line with our blood, throughout poems written by the immortal Gods, deeply engraved on the gate of our eternity.*

Scroll Twenty-One

Tombs For None

"A Royal runner comes from a boat," one of the boys in the village shouted toward Kha, who was talking with a group of workers in the early morning light. The runner stopped at the entrance to the village, and one of the guards pointed toward Kha's group. In another moment, the runner stopped in front of Kha and handed him a short scroll with the wax seal of Vizier Aye. The workers looked from the scroll to Kha and back.

"It is official business. I must attend to it," he said. But as he unrolled the scroll and quickly reviewed its contents, a column of soldiers began to enter the gates, obviously headed for Kha. The workers cautiously stepped back.

"We have been instructed to accompany you back to the palace to meet with the Vizier," the captain announced, his gaze falling on the workers. "Only Chief Kha. The rest of you may go about your business," he added, pointing his spear for emphasis. Two Supervisors nearby quickly took charge of the workers and led them toward the mountain and the Valley of the Kings.

The wind upon Mother Nile was gentle, and the rowers shipped their oars in favor of tacking back and forth to the other side of the river. They disembarked, and the soldiers led Kha up the stone stairs of the meticulously planted embankment to the palace. Flowers in many colors lined the sides of the steps.

At the top stood Aye. Before Kha could bow to the Vizier, Aye bowed his head lightly to Kha, who was shocked by the gesture. He hurriedly and awkwardly returned the bow, his face a deep crimson.

Aye smiled, then opened his hand and directed Kha toward his side of the palace. They walked side-by-side until they entered a modest meeting room with ten chairs set around a circular table. Aye passed through this room to a smaller one, with but three chairs and a small table already set with a pitcher of beer, mugs, cheese and bread, and dried fruits.

A servant followed closely behind. "Will the Vizier need anything else?" He asked.

"Nothing else, but make sure we are not disturbed." Kha felt anxious.

"Sit," Aye said, motioning to the woven rush chairs with the wave of his hand. As Kha hesitated, he added, "Anywhere." Kha quickly chose the nearest seat.

Aye poured beer into each mug and raised his. "To whatever God you believe in or is the current favorite of our King," he said, smiling. This surprised Kha, but he took a gulp of the beer.

"Not bad, eh?" Aye asked. "It's from Nekhen's finest brewery. It is said to have been King Narmer's favorite, may his name be blessed forever."

"Yes, may his name be blessed," Kha repeated.

Aye put down his mug and turned to Kha. "You are probably wondering what this is all about, my dear Chief of Set Maat." He stared at Kha for uncomfortable few moments.

Kha wiped his hands on his kilt. "Yes, my lord, I do. I… perhaps I have done something that has displeased you or, perish the thought, the King himself."

At this, Aye tilted his head back and laughed heartily. "Oh, Kha, forgive me. I mean, no insult by laughing. I just find it funny. I deal with scoundrels, thieves, and incompetents every day, it seems. But you… you, my friend, are the shining exception. You manage the entire village of Set Maat. You manage the workers, and they actually like you and find you tough but fair. Your designs are nothing short of perfect, and your construction is always as you say it will be. So, no, you have not displeased anyone, least of all the King or me." He sat quietly and smiled at Kha, who hung his head in embarrassment.

"I have heard rumors, Kha, that you have formed a small group of believers in Adon in Set Maat." Kha nodded.

"That is no small accomplishment, considering how firm a hold the Amun priesthood has indirectly held on your important village for so many generations." Kha sat silently, looking at the stone floor before him, noticing the poor workmanship in the gaps between several of the stones.

"Do you wonder how I know of this?" Aye asked. Kha nodded.

"It is through the complaints from the few remaining Amun priests here."

"Oh, I am sorry to have caused trouble."

"Trouble? Since you have no idea of courtly troubles, allow me to explain to you what the trouble is that you have caused." Aye raised his mug and took a long swallow, then wiped his lips with the back of his hand.

"You would think that Akhenadon would be the major cause of trouble, and he is, certainly. The Amun priesthood detests him and the changes he brings. It is a daily struggle I face with them. A battle, really.

"But what frightens them even more, is what you have managed to accomplish. People in villages throughout Kem are convinced of Akhenadon's God. Certainly not all, perhaps not even a majority, but enough. That frightens the Amun hierarchy. But Set Maat is an intentionally walled city dedicated to the secrets of the Afterlife for the Royal family. It never changes. It must not change. Yet you have brought the Adon to them and convinced a good number of the families, you and your good wife, to embrace him. Your effort has been noticed, Kha." Kha was speechless. He did not know how to respond.

"You are a man of few words, my friend. On the other hand, I am a man of too many words." Kha looked at Aye, and when he saw Aye burst into laughter, he joined him.

"I am a … a true believer," Kha ventured, now sitting up straight. "In my whole life, it is as if I have waited for someone to offer a truth that would sit solidly in my heart. This Adon is a powerful God, full of love for people, whether man or woman, whatever color of their skin, whatever country they call home, for we are all His creations. I believe that, and I will offer that truth to whoever wishes to hear it."

"Well, then, Chief Kha, you will be happy to know that I have shared your work and the story of your beliefs with both Queen Nefertiti and King Akhenadon. And I have arranged for you to meet the Man-God, the only one to whom Adon speaks directly."

Kha paled. "They are here in… in Waset? I do not… I am not worthy of being in his presence, my lord Vizier. Please. Please do not make me do so." The stone walls of the room suddenly began to look like Mother Nile's waves. His breath came in quick gasps so that Aye called for his servant, who placed wet rags on Kha's face and neck. In a few moments, the panic attack passed.

"Kha, I understand your fearing meeting the King and Queen, but meet them you must. We have many things planned for you, wonderful things that will elevate Adon in the eyes of all Kem and all nations. The Two await your presence, so we must leave at once. They very much dislike being in Waset and wish to leave as soon as possible."

"So we meet right now?"

"Yes, this very moment. Come, you are ready."

The two walked through the palace to the other side, a grander and more expansive building. Huge columns supported a grand room with high ceilings. They walked through this room where guards stood watch. At the far end of the room, they entered a wide passageway into a smaller but no less grand meeting room. At the far end sat

Akhenadon, and behind him Nefertiti stood, resplendent in a white gossamer robe, a simple gold necklace, her hair tied back with two gold and bejeweled clasps that accented its lustrous quality. Kha felt his knees weaken, and he was grateful for the excuse to bow low to his human Gods.

"Arise, Chief Kha of highest achievement," Akhenadon called out. Kha was taken aback by his high-pitched voice. He stood, his legs still shaking.

"The Queen and my Vizier have shared with me your work at Set Maat. They have shown me drawings of my father's tomb and your design for my tomb, which I understand you have already begun to construct."

"Yes, my King. We have cut the opening and the reception room. All has been done with the guidance of the Vizier."

"Yes, and they have shown me the drawings of my relationship with Adon, and I have cried at their beauty. You have exalted Adon as no artist in the kingdom has been able to do."

"I am a believer, my King."

Akhenadon and Nefertiti both looked at Aye and smiled. Akhenadon raised his hand, and two servants immediately entered the room.

"Bring two chairs for my guests," he ordered. As soon as they arrived, the Queen sat on her throne next to the King, and the Vizier and Kha sat.

"Well, my dear Chief Kha, I am certain that you heard that I am building a new city in lower Kem called Akhedadon. It will be the most beautiful city ever imagined, open to the glory of Adon. There will be no separation between him and the people He so loves. Do you understand?"

"I can only imagine, my King. It will be without equal."

"Yes, yes, it will, thanks be to Adon. However, there is one problem that remains to be settled, and it plagues me greatly."

"What would that be, my King?" Kha asked, turning from Akhenadon to Nefertiti to Aye.

"I am in need of a burial tomb."

"A burial tomb? I do not understand. We are building you

a burial tomb."

"Not mine." Kha sat back in his chair, rubbing his sweat-soaked hands on his kilt. He took a deep breath.

"Please explain, my King. I am but a poor manager, and this does not make sense to me."

"May I?" Aye asked.

"Yes," Akhenadon replied. "Please do."

Aye turned to face Kha directly. "Kha, the King wishes to journey to be with Adon from Akhedadon, not from the Valley of the Kings. This is very important. The Valley represents all the beliefs that went before, the many false Gods and Goddesses that contradict the truth of Adon, the one and only God."

"I see," Kha said.

"And so," Nefertiti suddenly said, smiling, "we wish for you to be the one who designs and builds Akhenadon's tomb in Akhedadon."

Kha stared at Nefertiti for so long and so intently that he realized this might be taken as improper. He shook his head and looked down.

"What do you say to that?" Akhenadon asked.

"My King… my King who speaks to our God, I don't know what to say. I have lived in Set Maat all my life. My wife and children live there. My entire work crew lives there. They are all busy building you… well, they were… we thought we were building your tomb. How can this happen as you desire?"

"If I order it to happen, it will happen. I am King of the Two lands and the son of Adon. All I require is your willingness. If you agree and do so with all the love in your heart, then I will close down Set Maat and move you and all the workers and all the families to Akhedadon. You will live there in plenty and build the tombs for Nefertiti and for me. Your children will build the tombs for our children and your grandchildren for our grandchildren down to all eternity."

Tears were now falling freely from Kha's eyes. His body

shook as he sat. Finally, he slid from his chair and bowed to the King and Queen. When he lifted his head, he looked at them.

"My heart is full to overflowing, my King and Queen. Full as never before. I will do this for the love of you and for the love of Adon. I will faithfully serve you now and unto death and beyond."

Scroll Twenty-Two

Neferuneferuadon

Following her meeting with Horemheb, Nefertiti threw herself into her work to help stabilize the Two Lands. It was as if that meeting had crystalized in her mind how tenuous was the Royal family's hold on power without the consent of the people they ruled. And how could the comforting blanket of ma'at fall over the land once again with enemies like Maya standing in opposition?

I learned later that Nefertiti used the time to examine her own heart. Horemheb was a strong, irresistible force, but she now knew deep inside her heart so was Akhenadon. Her commitment to her husband was sealed with her latest pregnancy.

Nefertiti came to our meeting exhausted. She was a tiny woman, and her bulge was huge, as her due date was close at hand. Yet she still worked long hours so that Akhenadon could commune with Adon. In her own way, she was as passionate a believer as he.

"You look exhausted, Nefertiti," I said. "You must get more rest if not for you, then for the baby."

"Would that could be," she replied, sitting carefully in her chair while holding her hand on her abdomen. "Tiye was so right."

"About what?"

"She advised that I take on more responsibility but that it would come at a cost. I am living proof of that." She patted her stomach as she leaned back.

"I see that the governors are arriving. Are you ready for your meeting?"

"I am never sure with any of these meetings. I always feel as if new things arise that I am unprepared for. However, I feel that we have a good plan, and so long as we stick to it the meeting should be good. I do worry, though, with all the discontent in the Two Lands. I worry that these twenty men will challenge me, and I will not know how to respond."

"Yes, that is disconcerting," I said, my hands gripping my staff. Nefertiti took a deep breath and exhaled slowly. She turned to me, her sad eyes penetrating mine.

"You know, Aharon, I love Akhenadon as you do. We both believe in Adon and in Akhenadon's righteousness. But... I know I can confide in you, Aharon. Has it ever... have you ever felt that Akhenadon is not suited for rule, that perhaps he should be Chief Priest or one of those prophets of Gods that we hear of from Canaan?"

I placed my staff across my thighs. "You are not alone in these thoughts," I said, "whether it be our love for Akhenadon or our doubts. I believe your father feels the same, and his job is far more difficult than ours. Adon places burdens on all people, Nefertiti. Some must worry about where their next meal comes from or how to survive with a crippled arm. Survival is not our worry, but we have our own burdens.

"Tiye undoubtedly saw your inner strength. She believed in you and has been proven right. You must continue to be strong. You are Neferuneferuadon, beautiful is the beauty of Adon. You have the strength and wisdom of Adon behind you and inside you. Your outer beauty is only a shell. It is your inner beauty that truly shines."

She smiled at me and reached out and took my hand in both of hers. "Thank you, Aharon. You are a brother to me, too." She bent over and kissed my hand before letting go.

With advice from Aye and Tiye, Nefertiti had formed a

council of governors from ten of the largest nomes in Kem and ten of the smallest. This would be their first annual planning meeting since the Council was formed. The purpose was to determine what their most pressing needs were for the coming year and for Nefertiti to gather information about the feelings of the people.

Before the day of the meeting, the governors were taken on a tour of Akhedadon, and those who had not been here before were much impressed. Those good feelings did not last long, as they were required to attend the following morning's prayers in the Great Temple of Adon. At the dinner meeting that evening, there were many whispered conversations that ended whenever Nefertiti or I neared. Aye chose not to be in Akhedadon during this time for fear of diluting Nefertiti's power.

If there is one thing that people tend to underestimate, it is the power of gathering information from servants. All of the servers at the evening dinner were in my employ, so I was able to meet with them singly to learn what they overheard. It was not good.

There were the usual comments, of course, about his long neck, his paunch, his elongated arms, his strange face, and the like. What plagued our guests the most was the way Akhenadon carried himself as if he truly believed he was the co-regent of Adon. He was haughty, removed, distant. He had no desire to meet with them, to hear of the needs of his people. His arrogant self-righteousness was apparent to all.

This carried over into the meetings the next day with Nefertiti. The first day's sessions were business-like. The governors discussed their Nomes' needs in terms of roads, food distribution, housing, services for the poor, health issues, construction, and, of course, taxes. At one of the sessions, governors of border Nomes complained of security fears. All these issues were duly noted by scribes assigned to each group, along with proposed solutions. Nefertiti did an admirable job of keeping the meeting progressing.

It was after the mid-day meal on the second and final day that trouble began. The day was hot, and the men had worked hard all morning. Many had too much fine barley beer, and all were tired.

"Governors, thank you for the hard work you have done," Nefertiti began. "The King and I will take all these matters under advisement, and I will be in contact with you with our decisions and proposed actions. Are there any other items you wish to bring up that have not been dealt with in these meetings?

The men looked at the table before them, at their hands, at the mud-brick walls of the meeting room, all avoiding meeting the Queen's eyes.

"Well then, I would say that the meeting is…."

"Where has the King been the past two days?" one of the Governors called out. Others in the room nodded or echoed his words. Nefertiti and I had anticipated that question.

"As you men know, the King has appointed me to this task. At the moment, he is busy with the many other issues that occupy your King's time. He has meetings with the treasury, with the foreign ministers… well, you know how busy he is."

"Busy? Yes, I suppose he is, but by busy, if you mean creating edicts that forbid the worship of other Gods, then I question whether he occupies his time in the right affairs." At this, the room erupted, with most of the Governors agreeing but some shouting at the others for their disrespect. Men yelled that their constituents complained vociferously about the destruction of temples. They did not understand Adon. They questioned the sanity of Akhenadon. Throughout, Nefertiti sat at the head of the table and listened, turning from one shouting man to another. When the room finally quieted a little, she rose, putting her hands on the table and allowing her baby bulge to overhang it.

"Governors, I have heard you, and as your King's representative, I will do all in my power to…."

"Crocodile dung!" one of the men muttered, loud enough

for everyone to hear. Some tittered, but others sat wide-eyed.

"And which of you will be brave enough to stand and defend that slur?" She looked around the silent table and waited for a moment, and no one stirred. "Coward, as I thought. So let me be clear. I am Neferuneferuadon, Queen of Kem. Do not be fooled by my appearance or my fertility, for my strength does not derive from that.

"Adon is my strength, and His son is my guide. You will obey the edicts of King Akhenadon, no matter what they are. If you feel they are ill-advised, then you will discuss that with me." She again gazed around the table at each of the twenty men.

"And, Governors, hear this," she said, leaning forward on the table. "If any one of you dare… dare!… to interrupt me again while I speak, I will have you flogged… in public!" With that, she turned and left the room.

Days later, Aye arrived and called a meeting with Nefertiti and me. As usual, we met in the safety of my quarters.

"First, I must congratulate you, dear daughter. From what I heard about your meeting with the Governors, you made quite an impression."

"It nearly caused the death of my baby. I find it hard to understand how some men can be so gracious, and others so badly behaved."

"Well, from what I have heard, they left feeling you did a good job but also fear you. That is always a good thing in a ruler."

"Except I am not the ruler," Nefertiti answered. I looked at Aye and saw that we both thought otherwise.

"In any event, I am here for another purpose. Are you familiar with King Ribaddi?"

Nefertiti hesitated. "He is the King of Byblos, is that right?"

"He is, and always a reliable ally to Kem. We have had good trade relations with them, and in the past,

Akhenadon's father sent troops to deter aggression from their border."

"With the Aziru," I added. Nefertiti nodded.

"Well, the Azirus are back at it. They have sent troops to the border and appear to be threatening Byblos. King Ribaddi requests help. Aye pulled a parchment from his robe and uncurled it. Nefertiti read it.

"It is addressed to my husband," she said, looking up at her father.

"It is. In truth, we intercepted it before Akhenadon had a chance to read it and respond."

"But, this is… treason!"

"Calm down, Nefertiti. It is simply the craft of rule, not traitorous. We three know full well that if Akhenadon reads it, his reaction will be to deny such aid, and that will be it. We would not have any recourse to do otherwise. Yet Aharon and I certainly know that Byblos is very valuable to us. We must keep them as allies, and we must keep the Azirus far away from our borders.

"Besides, Akhenadon has no interest in these matters. I felt it would be better for us to respond, in his name of course, and be done with it."

"I agree," I offered. Nefertiti looked at me.

"It does not seem proper, but then I suppose that few things seem proper from outside."

"I wanted to get your approval, but if we are brought to task for doing so, I want it known here that I will take full responsibility. I believe I can justify to Akhenadon that it was too minor a matter to bother him with."

"How do you suggest we handle this?" Nefertiti asked.

"I suggest you charge Horemheb with this task. He has proved himself adept at such dealings. I have heard that he is about to be promoted due to his work here and against the Ta-Tjehenus. He is well-liked and respected by his soldiers." Nefertiti was surprised.

"He did not mention this promotion to me. Is he to be moved from Akhedadon?"

"I do not think he knows about it yet. But I will do all possible to dissuade Yanhamu from moving him. I feel better knowing that you are well protected under his leadership."

"Well protected? Is there an underlying meaning to that?"

Aye looked at me and gave a half smile. "She has picked up much wisdom, has she not?" He turned back to his daughter.

"Yes, there is an undercurrent to my words, for I fear that if we do not get things right, we will have riots even here or at least nearby. In that case, we want a good military leader here whose soldiers would follow him to death."

And so, the very next day, Nefertiti summoned Horemheb and assigned him to take soldiers to Byblos and to try to calm the situation. He took two hundred men along the difficult march. In two months, Horemheb returned and met with the three of us.

"It is Suppiluliumas," he said. "He is agitating the Aziru and offering them a share of the spoils when he invades us. We had a small skirmish with the Aziru, and they backed off for now. But I tell you this. Suppiluliumas is agitating to invade. He must be stopped."

Nefertiti felt a sharp pain and rose. A gush of water issued from between her legs. Her labor had begun.

Scroll Twenty-Three

Tortures of the Body

It was a perfect day. Adon's disk shone brightly, and a few scattered clouds graced the heavens. The air was cool, a true treat for those who had attended the lengthy sunrise prayer session in the Great Temple, where Akhenadon spoke eloquently, but as usual too lengthily, of Adon's blessings. The children were eager to play and run, and so after the mid-day meal, Akhenadon arranged for the family to walk along Mother Nile.

The children were excited, already running before their parents, their nursemaids yelling for them to slow and trying to keep up with them. Nefertiti walked with her arm through Akhenadon's, and as I trailed behind, I couldn't help but smile at their loving relationship.

"Momma, may I hold Ta for a little while?" Meritadon said as she ran up to Nefertiti, out of breath. I marveled at how quickly she had grown.

"First, catch your breath," Nefertiti said as she turned to the nursemaid by her side, who held an infant swaddled in a thick linen blanket. "Satiah, let Meritaten carry Neferuneferuadon Tasherit a while."

The nursemaid knelt and gently placed the baby in Meritadon's arms. A broad smile graced her face. She looked at Nefertiti. "She is so cute, Momma! I adore her." With that, she walked slightly ahead of the couple, cooing at the baby.

"She will make a wonderful Queen someday," Akhenadon said proudly. "In another year or two, we must begin thinking of suitable pairings." Nefertiti squeezed her arm tighter against Akhenadon's.

In a few moments, Meritadon returned with the baby. "I must return her to your keeping," she said to Satiah. "My sisters need me to keep an eye on them." With that, she dashed off to join them.

"I will also run to them," Akhenadon said, turning to Nefertiti. "You can stay with Ta or join me."

"I'll stay. She may need to be nursed."

"Meritadon, wait for me!" he yelled as he took off, his long strides gaining on his young daughter. He looked awkward doing so, his long neck protruding forward and his paunch jiggling up and down. But his infectious enthusiasm caused me to smile. I soon caught up to Nefertiti, who now held a fussy Ta.

"It is wonderful how much he loves the girls."

"It is," Nefertiti replied as she moved off the path to sit on a rock and placed her nipple in Ta's mouth. "He is a very devoted father."

Once the baby fell asleep and was back in Satiah's arms, we continued ahead. When we got to the bend in the path, we saw a commotion down by the river and hurried down the embankment. There lay Akhenadon on his back, with the girls jumping on and over him, all of them laughing hysterically. In Akhenadon's hand was a gigantic bullfrog.

"Look, they are all frogs!" Akhenadon laughed. He turned over, put the frog on the ground, and began hopping after it. "Gribbit, ribbit, ribbit!" he kept repeating as the girls did the same.

"Momma, come join us," Mekatadon yelled, but Nefertiti waved her off. Instead, she put her arm through mine and leaned her head against my shoulder.

"He is nothing more than a child in an adult body," Nefertiti said, laughing herself. How true, I thought, remembering our times as children when we were away from adults, and he would invent silly games that I could not bring myself to join.

Soon Akhenadon caught the frog again, and the girls circled around him as he explained its features and behavior. That led to him telling them a story about why Adon made frogs. When he was done, they demanded more stories. We sat behind them and listened for more than an hour.

I thought to myself how idyllic this moment in time was, a perfect day, two loving parents, and the future of Kem in the laughter of children. But a priest learns through experience how fleeting such moments are and this day, this time, was no exception, for, in Upper Kem, another gathering was taking place, far different from this.

Across the banks of Mother Nile from Waset, in the dusty brown hills, four men met in an unfinished tomb carved into a crevice. Six guards stood outside, armed with swords and daggers, and high above, on a rocky plateau, four archers knelt, scanning for intruders.

"I have spoken with each of you privately," Maya began, standing before the seated priests, "to determine if you are willing to sacrifice your lives for the good of Kem. I believe you all have a suspicion of what I am about to propose, and when you leave here, there will be no doubt in any of our hearts.

"There are two issues that we must all agree upon before we create the details around this plan. First, everything we discuss here and from this point forward must be held in absolute confidence. No one, not family or friends, must know what we plan. Second, our pledge of confidence is secured by the promise of death to anyone who violates it." Maya looked into the eyes of each priest in turn.

"Upon our sacred vows to Amun, do you all agree to these conditions? If not, now would be the time to leave our… our holy group." All three priests nodded their agreement.

"It is settled then. We are bound in this alliance by our oaths to Amun and to each other. Let us begin." Maya sat down.

"There is no need to recount what Akhenadon, may his

name be stricken, has done to the worship of Amun and to his people. You have been informed of his every move and have even seen them with your own eyes. He is destroying our temples, smashing our God statues, barring the priesthood, depriving us of our rightful treasure, forbidding the people to worship Amun... is there any need to go on?" The three priests sat with their heads down.

"So it is a most difficult decision we must make together. Shall we allow Akhenadon to live, or shall we help him die of... natural causes?" Maya leaned back in his chair. For many moments no one spoke, each man lost in his own thoughts.

"This is a momentous decision," Pi-Or whispered. "To even know of a plot to kill the King and not do anything to prevent it is against our laws, a grave sin, let alone to actually be part of such an act."

Titia nodded his agreement. "It is as if we were to throw ma'at to the Underworld and allow chaos and Nun to return as before creation."

"And do you men truly believe that this has not been done before?" Maya retorted. "You have all studied the holy parchments. You know Kings have met with sudden death due to so-called natural causes even as far back as the First Dynasty."

"But we also know that the King is an agent of Amun, he is...."

"Surely you joke, Harmena. Akhenadon has rejected Amun. He has said Amun is not even a God. For him, there is only his Adon. Even the lesser Gods are forbidden."

The group was silent yet again before Pi-Or spoke up. "My fellow priests, I believe this is a moral issue for each of us, but I will tell you how I come down on it, apart from what Maya believes. It is an issue of the King or the nation. I accept the fact that Akhenadon feels a direct connection with his God, and who are we to argue whether that is real or not? But, at the same time, he has endangered the Two Lands beyond anyone's worst fears. It is not only an issue of religion but of foreign affairs. Our very existence is being threatened by outside forces. Plagues afflict us. Hunger is everywhere. And what does Akhenadon do? Nothing."

After another silent break, Harmena spoke. "This is a very complex issue," he began. "Even if we were to dispose of Akhenadon, there is Nefertiti to deal with. He relies on her as one would a co-regent. She manages all except for religion."

"And poetry," Maya added, half joking. The priests laughed.

"Are you suggesting we dispose of them both?" Titia asked.

"No, I am not, but we must consider all options for this to succeed," Harmena responded. "And Nefertiti may be an unfortunate casualty of her marriage."

"Which brings up another point," Titia said. "What would success look like? Just the removal of Akhenadon? The restoration of Amun? Allowing other Gods to be worshipped? Going to war again to defend our borders, as did Amunhotep the Great? And if any or all of these, can this be done without chaos ensuing?"

"You make good points, Titia," Maya said. "Even if we removed both Akhenadon and Nefertiti, their children have justification for ascension. Meritadon would need a co-regent, of course."

"And that would give Aye legitimate access to the throne if he were to marry his granddaughter," Pi-Or pointed out.

"Many complexities, obviously," Maya said, "so here is what I propose. We each should take on one of these issues and do whatever probing you feel necessary to make a good decision. You will not communicate at all with each other, only with me directly and only in personal meetings. No written communications whatsoever. We must be very careful, just in case one of you is caught, for the heart of no man can long withstand the tortures of the body.

"Pi-Or, you are closest to Akhedadon, and you have reason to be there more than the rest of us because of your close connection to Tiye. I want you to observe the comings and goings of Akhenadon and Nefertiti. Oh, and that so-called

Chief Priest Aharon. Is their schedule predictable? What are their favorite foods? Are any of their servant's faithful believers in Amun?

"Titia, you were the former Servitor of Manuscripts in Nekhen, You will go through the ancient manuscripts and look at various methods of… of aiding natural deaths. The method must be untraceable back to us. I've always been partial to undetectable additions to food, eh? Understood?" Titia nodded.

"Harmena, since you are located here in Waset, you will help me develop a list of prominent Kemites who we would count on to help us stabilize the Two Lands after Akhenadon is gone. We will need to also come up with a way to approach these people.

"We must all also consider ways to remove Akhenadon that do not depend on his death. I know it would be difficult for any of us to imagine such a turn of events, but we are obliged to try. In fact, if there were such a way, I am certain that even Aye might agree to join us. "I can only imagine how difficult he finds Akhenadon, even if he is his son-in-law." Maya stood, the weight of their decisions heavy upon his shoulders.

"We are done for now. I wish you all a safe journey home. Be safe and safeguard your every move. We will leave one at a time, hours apart, again for security reasons."

"If I may, Chief Priest," Titia said. "Do you not think it wise for us to offer a prayer to Amun to safeguard us?"

"Oh, oh yes, of course," Maya said, stumbling over this oversight. "Titia, why don't you lead us?"

Titia rose, as did the others. They raised their arms to rest them on their fellow priest's shoulders. "I have no words to say, so monumental is the task we undertake. Let us each pray silently to Amun for guidance so that we may avoid chaos and restore ma'at throughout our beloved Kem."

Scroll Twenty-Four

Destroyer of Ma'at

Over the next few years, it is hard, even painful, to describe what went on in the Two Lands.

The first I must report on is an attempt on Akhenadon's and Nefertiti's lives. Even now, it is difficult for me to write this, so vile is even the thought of such an act. To plot against the King is against all that Kem stands for. I reconstructed the events after speaking with all who were involved. In this case, it is best to let them speak in their own words.

"Are you sure of what you tell me?" Horemheb demanded. He shook with fear.

"I can only tell you what was told to me, Captain. One of Nefertiti's servants has poisoned their food."

"When? Just now?"

"I think so. We have her in captivity. Her husband told a friend that she was up to something evil, that he could not believe what she was going to do. He tried to stop her, but she left their house through a window. The friend came to tell a guard, and he told me."

"Damn it!" Horemheb yelled. "They sail right now on a boat. They wanted to have their evening meal alone. They will have no chance to get to a physician in time." He spun around, thinking quickly.

"Get my guards to mount up immediately. We must get to

them before they eat. Hurry!" Horemheb checked that his dagger was by his side. His heart raced, knowing he had not a moment to spare. He ran out the door and to the stables. Five of his men were already there.

"There is no time to prepare the horses. Mount them bareback!" he shouted. With one jump, he mounted, kicked his horse, and rode off. His men followed.

"I know their route," he yelled back to them. "This way!" They galloped along the river's edge and onto a peninsula that jutted out into Mother Nile.

Horemheb slid from his horse before it fully stopped and spilled face down on the ground. He got up quickly, blood running from his nose. Adon's disk was setting, yet the King's boat was visible halfway across the river.

"You men keep shouting to them. Use your swords… your buckles… anything to signal the captain."

"What will you do?" one of the soldiers asked. Without answering, Horemheb tore off his tunic and ran straight for the water. Four large crocodiles blocked his way.

"We saw what we saw," the soldiers told me later. Whether true or not, this did not hurt Horemheb's stature as a heroic leader. He ran straight for the largest crocodile, jumped on its back, and propelled himself into the water before the creature could even react. Then he swam furiously toward the boat.

The aftereffects of this event were complicated. The woman turned out to be a former acolyte and priestess in the Temple of Amun in Inabu-hedj, far from the Amun power structure in Waset. Horemheb took her questioning upon himself rather than wait for Aye's participation. It was not a pretty affair.

After being tortured for days, she would not reveal who had put her up to this heinous act, sticking to her story that she acted alone. She was bound to a chair, and her husband was brought in. She was given a chance to reveal who put her up to this. She refused. Her husband was decapitated, and his severed head was placed on her lap.

"I understand this evil bitch has a grandson," Horemheb said. "Bring him here."

When her only grandchild was placed before her, dagger held against his neck, she refused to come forward with the truth. The child was mercifully spared for one day to give her time to tell us what we all suspected. She died that night after bashing her own head against the stone wall of her cell.

What we learned was that the poison was of such a rare type, few in Kem would have even known of it. Yet one of my priests, formerly in charge of the library in Nekhen, found that what was likely the same poison was suspected in the death of a Fourth Dynasty King. Only priests had access to those scrolls. No matter who we questioned, we could not establish a connection between the servant and Maya, nor any priest in his employ. Rather than create a huge confrontation over this crime, we decided to act as if nothing had happened.

Following this event, which threw us off balance for many months, I received reports from Aye, Horemheb, and my priests throughout Kem, descriptions of horrible events I thought I would never hear of that could never occur in the Kem that I loved. Due to the limited number of soldiers that could be spared to enact the King's orders, the destruction of temples was still happening, but now more slowly and located in remote areas. At one point, I sat with Aye lamenting these matters.

"I would have thought that the more remote areas would have fewer protests than the larger cities, but this is not proving true," I said.

"These farm families are not used to seeing soldiers at all," Aye replied. "They are also not used to feeling the heavy hand of the King's administration upon their heads… except at tax time, of course."

"Whatever the reasons, the protests are escalating. I am getting reports of soldiers being seriously wounded and, in some cases, killed!"

"I receive the same reports," Aye responded.

"Have you spoken to General Yanhamu? What does he

say?"

Aye sat back, taking a breath. "You bring up an important matter, Aharon. He is sympathetic to the cause of the common people, but he cannot allow disrespect for the military. He has relaxed the requirement that citizens not be harmed."

"Is that what happened in that incident at..."

"Yes, in the heat of the moment, crowd control broke down. Impassioned people pushed upon the soldiers. Sadly, they responded with clubs and even swords. Many people were wounded or killed. I fear there will be more such incidents."

So it was not surprising that I received word from Horemheb that he wanted an audience with Akhenadon. It took a great deal of convincing, but Akhenadon eventually agreed, although he felt that nothing would come of it.

On the day of the meeting, Horemheb arrived, freshly bathed and in a clean kilt. Only his dagger hung from his belt, and he chose not to wear his shoulder strap. He bowed deeply to Akhenadon.

"Arise, loyal servant," Akhenadon said from his throne. I pointed Horemheb to a seat, and I took the remaining chair.

"Welcome, Horemheb," Akhenadon said. "I know I have been remiss in doing so, but I must compliment how faithfully and carefully you execute your duties. And you undoubtedly saved my life and the Queen's. I know I need not worry about my family with you in charge of Akhedadon. I extend my gratitude."

Horemheb was taken aback by these words, which I had suggested to Akhenadon. He thanked the King profusely.

"What do you feel requires an audience and cannot be solved through Aharon or Nefertiti?"

"My King, I have come to beg you to reconsider and stop the closures and destruction of the temples. I fear for my soldiers and for the Army in general. You have no idea how difficult it has become. We face violent reactions wherever we go. People have begun to disrespect our authority."

"But your authority emanates from Adon through me. How can they possibly disrespect that?"

I could see the frustration building in Horemheb, for he was a man used to receiving orders and carrying them out or giving orders and expecting them to be obeyed. Arguing fine points behind the orders was new to him. "But, Akhenadon, that is my point. In disrespecting us, in questioning our authority, they point the finger at you."

I took a deep breath, for although what Horemheb said was certainly true, Akhenadon was never challenged so directly.

"Dear Horemheb," Akhenadon said, "are you married?"

"No, my King, I am not."

"So you do not have children?"

"No, my King."

"Even so, would you counsel a couple to allow their children to be undisciplined, to run amok doing whatever they pleased?" I could see where this was going, and all I could do was shake my head in disbelief.

"I do not see your point, my King."

"My point is the people out there are like children, Horemheb. They are ignorant of the ways of Adon, but as our temples and priests increase, they will understand more. But now, they must be disciplined. And like children, they will be angry and rebel. Such is the way of life. But children, so disciplined, do not stay angry forever. I know this from my own daughters. They adjust, they calm down, and eventually, they understand that it was for their own good. And so it is here and now in Kem.

"Look, Horemheb, Adon has spoken to me and told me all this. He has given me a vision of the whole. Do not be afraid, my loyal subject. Your bravery is legendary. Continue with the eradication of these bad influences and help bring people to Adon. You will soon see things change, and peace and fulfillment will spread throughout Kem." The King sat back and smiled at Horemheb.

"I do see your point, my King. But what do we do now? We

are outnumbered. My soldiers cannot continue to maim or kill innocent Kemians. Even my soldiers will rebel at some point. Rumors are rampant in the barracks."

"And I see your point, Captain. I have an idea. I will bring soldiers back from the borders to help with this business. That will add to your strength, and people will not even consider endangering your work."

Both Horemheb and I were shocked into silence. How could Akhenadon suggest such a dangerous move? It took a moment for me to respond, and I jumped in for fear of Horemheb saying something insulting.

"Akhenadon, I would suggest we discuss this further before actually implementing this order. Troops are sorely needed on the borders, so...."

"Now you are the one governed by fear, Aharon. You are the Chief Priest of Adon. You know how powerful He is and that He surely would never allow Kem to be attacked now that we recognize Him as the one and only God. He has spoken thus to me."

"I only mean we should explore other options before making a quick decision."

"Do you not realize that Adon watches everything He has created? He sits beside me every moment. We share the same serekh. He has told me that as soon as the job of eradicating these false Gods is done, people will forget them, and ma'at will rest comfortably upon the Two Lands.

"Is there anything else you wish to discuss, Horemheb?" Horemheb sat with his shoulders slumped. "No, my King. I am, as always, your loyal servant. I will do my best."

"You will do what is necessary," Akhenadon casually replied. "And by the way, Horemheb. I plan to send a message to General Yanhamu requesting promotion for you. Aharon, would you kindly stay for a few more moments?"

Horemheb stayed in his chair, looking down, I believe, wondering what had just happened. "You are dismissed," I whispered to him. He slowly stood and bowed to the King and left.

Instead of reporting back to his men, Horemheb went straight to Nefertiti's quarters. "She is not here," one of her assistants told him. "She is supervising the gardeners." Immediately, Horemheb turned and stalked to the garden.

"I must talk with you!" he said when he found Nefertiti speaking with her head gardener. She sensed his urgency.

"Come," she said, pointing to the now familiar walk to the secluded bench. As soon as they reached it, Horemheb grabbed her wrist. She spun around, and they fell into each other's arms, both of them hugging the other with a passion born of fear, frustration, and need. When she felt Horemheb move his head as if to kiss her, she put her hands on his chest and pushed away, her heart beating furiously.

"Sit, my dear Horemheb, and tell me what lays heavy on your heart." Horemheb had to regain his breath before continuing.

"I have just met with the King. He is impossible to deal with. He does not listen to reason, even as it sits before him plain as Adon's light. I do not know what to do. Danger surrounds us."

Nefertiti took a few deep breaths. She waited until his breath matched hers. "Before we discuss this further, Horemheb, there are things we must resolve, private matters between you and me. I do not deny that my feelings for you are… delicate. You are a strong and brave man, a natural… no, a great leader. But no good is to come from our being disloyal to Akhenadon. He is my husband and the father of our children. We must… I feel we must only see each other on official business."

"Yet he fathered the boy Smenkhkare with his sister, Kiya. How special could you be to him?" Nefertiti had never seen Horemheb argue so passionately.

"It was his right to do so, Horemheb, we both know that. I have given him six daughters and no heir. I approved of this arrangement, and with the birth of Smenkhkare, he no longer shares his bed with her."

"But he is also ill, Nefertiti. He is mad, whether, from his illness or his love of Adon, I know not. I fear for you. I expect that if this persists, you will be killed along with him. He will be the ruin of Kem. People say that he is the destroyer of ma'at." Horemheb picked up a stone and flung it into the river. "Damn!" he shouted.

Tears ran from Nefertiti's eyes, knowing full well how frustrating this all must be to a loyal soldier. "Even if what you say is true, if he is indeed ill and mad, then it is so ordained, for he is the King of the Two Lands until death. That is our law. You know that I, too, believe in Adon and that in the end, He will prevail over all on Earth who harbor ill intent. I do not pretend to understand my husband's absolute devotion to Adon, but there is no doubt in my heart that there is a connection between the two, for I have witnessed it. I am sorry, dear Horemheb, but that is the way it must be."

"Then hear me out one last time, dearest Nefertiti. I care for you deeply, beyond a soldier's ability to say the right words. I envy Akhenadon's poetry and the songs that he writes to you. It pains my heart to hear them, for I harbor the same feelings toward you. But I also respect you and will honor your wishes.

"But, should the time ever come when you must forego this madness, or if ever there comes a time when you feel yourself in danger, you need only send me a message, and I will come immediately. That is my promise to you."

"Please, go now, Horemheb, for my heart cannot bear this pain any longer." Horemheb stood, never taking his eyes from Nefertiti.

"Goodbye, my Queen." He bowed, turned, and walked away.

Nefertiti waited until her tears dried and then got up slowly from the bench. She stumbled as she began to walk when she felt the first quickening of the life that grew within.

Scroll Twenty-Five

The Meeting

We were now in the midst of the four months of Shomu. Mother Nile ran low, the harvest of Proyet was safely in storage, and the intense heat of Shomu was upon us. I was again in Waset at the invitation of Aye and Tiye, for we had much to discuss.

I walked through the old city in the early morning, a time when most people were asleep. Adon's disk was just rising above the surrounding hills, carving deep shadows in front of the rocks and hills of sand created by night winds. I needed to clear my head for the meetings we were to have, and an early morning walk had always been my way of doing so.

Now I was on the outskirts of the city, and a wholly different mood enveloped me, for here were the everyday farmers who supplied Waset with fresh food. Many now spread manure on their land. Dotted here and there were the artisan shops that produced the plates, cups, and other objects of need and desire. They were up early, getting in as much work as possible before the heat became oppressive. Women carried buckets of water from the desert springs in the nearby hills. Young boys gathered wood for the kilns and set off for foraging in the foothills.

The dry desert air began to stir as Adon's disk rose in the heavens, creating the morning winds. Desert dust clouded the air, and I had to cover my nose and mouth with my robe so I could breathe. Still, it was comforting to see my people at work, not rebelling and causing chaos.

Returning to the city, a few people came to me asking for a blessing. But most people either avoided me or else cast me angry glances. I proudly wore the King's gold armband on my upper arm, and so women peering from their second-story windows called their children to witness my passing.

As I walked to the Great Wife's palace, children began to pour forth from their homes. Some headed to the schools that we established in our temples. Others went about doing chores for their households, emptying slop jars, sweeping, or setting off to the local market for eggs, fish, or whatever else the mother of the house needed.

Cats roamed the streets freely, for, in our land, no animal is more revered. Some were well groomed, others neglected and flea-ridden. Yet each served its function, whether pleasing their masters or ridding the streets of rats, mice, and vermin.

When I finally reached the palace, I was filled with gratitude for all the blessings that Adon provided. They were there for all to see. But, people are often blinded to those blessings and remain discontent. A pity. I sighed as I walked up the steps to the entrance.

After our morning meal, Tiye brought us into an enclosed room with no windows. It was made of large stone blocks. I smiled inwardly, for I suspected it was created for just such a purpose as we were now engaged.

"Tomorrow, I have a meeting with Maya," Aye started. "I am concerned and wished to get advice from each of you," he continued, nodding his head to Tiye and me.

Tiye reached for her cup, and her servant suddenly appeared to pour it for her. Tiye shot a knowing look at Aye, who also realized that we were being watched from the doorless entrance. "Please call in Bakennifi," Tiye said to the maid, who bowed to her before leaving. We waited quietly until he appeared, a tall man, well muscled and armed with a sword and dagger.

"Bakennifi, stand on the outside of the entrance and do

not let anyone within earshot or sight." The soldier bowed and took his position.

"He is the Captain of the palace guards and has been here for many years. Amenhotep trusted him, as do I. Proceed, Aye."

"I am not completely certain of Maya's reason for the meeting. We have not communicated for many months now."

"I can guess," Tiye said. "I am sure our concerns overlap."

"Perhaps, but I felt it would be good to compare our perceptions so that I may be prepared for whatever he proposes. What have you heard, Tiye?"

"He is speaking with many of the supporters of the priests and temples of Amun, the wealthy nobles in Waset, Nekhen… throughout Upper Kem. I have never trusted Maya, but somehow Amunhotep was able to work with him. I always felt he was not a problem so long as we provided from the treasury." I listened, fascinated. Although I was brought up in the palace with Akhenadon, we were sheltered, always in the shadows of Akhenadon's older brother, Thutmose, so we were not privileged to such conversations.

"Yes, I agree. We did not pay enough attention to his use of those funds to build alliances, buy property, to make people dependent upon him. He gained power, and I regret that now."

"Well, regrets or not, it would appear that we need to help you be ready for whatever poisonous stew Maya has cooked," I offered. "But I fail to see what I can offer."

"We will get to that in a moment, Aharon. First, let us be clear on what he may be up to and how I can respond. Are you good with that?" I nodded.

"I suspect that with matters in the Two Lands being so perilous at the moment, Maya will try to negotiate a deal with us to undermine the King's power in some way…."

"That cannot happen," I said angrily. "We all know how evil Maya is. He must be stopped."

Aye, avoided my outburst. Instead, he turned to Tiye. "We have worked together for many, many years. I think you will agree that we face the biggest crisis Kem in all our lives. And, I suspect we both know where this is all heading." Tiye nodded forcefully. Now Aye turned to me.

"Aharon, you asked me what your role is in this. I will tell you. The Queen and I asked you here because we know… we feel we know how things will go. We will do our best to save Akhenadon's rule, but the survival of Kem is our paramount goal." My stomach tightened with these words.

"You are a friend, confident, sworn brother to Akhenadon. He trusts you more than even his own wife or his mother. Whatever is decided, it will be you who will have to convince Akhenadon of its necessity. I will help, but you must prepare him for it."

I sat back, shocked. I panicked but resorted to my priestly training and brought calm back to my ba. Then it occurred to me that Aye was, indeed, correct. We each had a role to play in this drama. Even though Aye and Tiye had vastly more experience in these matters, for Akhenadon, this would surely be more of an emotional issue than one based on reason. With a nod, I accepted my role.

The next day, Aye arrived at Maya's modest quarters, a small, single-story mud-brick house in a fashionable neighborhood at the edge of Waset. Maya greeted him at the door. "Welcome, Aye. I have dismissed my servants so we may speak in private." Aye was wary.

They sat in the front room, an unlit cooking brazier in the center. Overhead the room was open to the sky, other than a series of dried rushes laid across timbers that provided shade.

"I hope your walk here…."

"Skip the pleasantries, Maya, for my suspicion is this will not be pleasant at all."

"We are old hands at this, are we not, Aye? I know you are aware of what goes on in Kem, but I wish to give you my perspective. It is not just the Amun priesthood that is upset, yes, and even angry. There are more nobles and businessmen than you can imagine who are also unhappy.

These powerful people are incensed. And why wouldn't they be?

"There are no more festivals to the Gods of our history. Sickness is everywhere. Plagues of vermin assault us. Our enemies attack us from all sides. And what does Akhenadon do? Nothing!" Maya could not contain himself. He rose and leaned over the back of his chair.

"He does nothing but destroys everything that might bring comfort to his people. I fear he is ill, Aye. Seriously mad." At this, Aye leaned forward.

"Maya, would a fine barley beer, the ones that you Amun priests hide from us peasants, be available that we could share? I feel that we must lower the temperature here for our talk. Wouldn't you agree?" They both smiled.

"Well said, Aye, well said. You are a master, and I still learn from you. I will return in a moment." But he returned so quickly, Aye was sure that there were others within earshot.

"Here, my worthy adversary." He handed the mug to Aye. "To Kem, may the Two Lands prosper." They both drank.

"So, you have laid the groundwork, Maya, and now to the finish."

A few days later, Aye and I met with Tiye.

"And what was the finish?" I asked as we sat again in Tiye's palace meeting room.

"He says that many influential people have reached the end of their patience," Aye explained. "They see Kem disintegrating before their helpless eyes, our enemies waiting at the borders. He said they are ready and willing to do something drastic."

"Drastic?" the Queen Mother asked.

"Naturally, it is Maya alone, he would have us believe, that has kept them from such drastic action… at great cost to him, of course."

"Of course," the Queen agreed.

"But what drastic action?" I asked.

Aye closed his eyes and brought his hands together before his chest. He took several breaths before he spoke. "He feels that we must formulate a way in which Akhenadon leaves." The Queen's face paled, and she slowly leaned back in her chair.

"What? He cannot be serious!" I shouted. "His attempt at murder failed, so now he proposes this!

At that, Bakennifi peered around the entranceway to be sure we were safe.

"Neither of you will be of help if you react this strongly," Aye said softly, grabbing another sweet from the table and taking a small bite of it. I admired his restraint.

"What would you have us do?" the Queen asked.

"I feel that Maya would not have risked this meeting if there were no truth to his telling. We have heard similar reports of dissatisfaction, have we not… Tiye… Aharon?" We nodded.

"I also believe he would not have met with me unless their… his plans are far enough advanced. There might be too many ways for us to undermine his plot if they were only at a beginning stage. I feel we must take his proposal seriously."

"Taking him seriously is one thing, but acting upon it cannot be!" I shouted. "It is wrong, it is against ma'at, and… and Akhenadon will never agree to it." In that instant, Adon shone a light in the dark places of my ka, and I had this overwhelming feeling of Akhenadon's frailties and insecurities. He would destroy his country, his loves, and his very children to achieve his vision.

Aye stood and bent over as if to stretch his back. "I sometimes think I am too old for this intrigue," he said wearily, and I realized then what a toll this was taking on him. He had lost a lot of weight and was beginning to walk bent over.

"Whatever the case, I have secured his agreement that we will come back to him in one year, and no later, for it will take that long to investigate our options. He was not pleased with the delay, but he is smart enough to know that reasonable minds will ensure a more stable result. As for your objections, Aharon, allow me to respond.

"Whether what Maya suggests is wrong or not lays in the eye of the observer, something I learned early in my career. To be successful in any negotiation, you must always see things through the eyes of the other.

"In terms of Akhenadon agreeing to this, or anything else that he would perceive to be a threat to Adon, I agree with you. He will not. But when you say such a proposal is against ma'at, with the utmost respect, I believe you are wrong. From our eyes, we seek to preserve ma'at by keeping Akhenadon on the throne, but from their eyes, ma'at is already threatened and chaos but a stone's throw away."

Scroll Twenty-Six

My Father Adon

It is both a pitiful and awe-inspiring thing to witness, and I vacillate between the two every day and on some days more than once. It is as if Akhenadon has withdrawn from the world of living beings to be with our God.

Horemheb now must spend his time forcibly keeping people from Akhedadon, such is the unrest amongst the people outside. It is a good thing that Akhedadon is so removed from the rest of Kem, which was one of the main reasons for him choosing this desolate spot. We had such high dreams for Akhedadon. Never did I imagine that it would become a prison of our own making.

Sometimes the anger of the common people can be heard even from within the palace. People are hungry, the disease spreads through entire villages, and even thieves and tomb robbers have become emboldened. As we try to develop new policies to help our people or try new tactics to lessen the burdens of the King's edicts, Akhenadon sequesters himself, praying ever more fervently to Adon.

"It is because I am not praying hard enough," he said one day as we met for an evening prayer session. "I am not truly dedicated enough. My father Adon is not pleased with me as His co-regent."

"Why do you think this? You are dedicated. Your devotion is real and deep. You do enough… more than enough. Please, you cannot do anymore."

"I must, Aharon, for when I fulfill Adon's expectations, He will guide us, all of Kem, to glory once again. I must especially do this for my son, Smenkhkare."

"What about the people? Do they not have a role in all this?"

"Of course they do. I see that they fail to be as deeply devoted as they should. They are bringing on their own calamities. We must do more to make them true believers."

"We are all doing the best we can, Akhenadon, as are you. If you do not rest, you will be of no use to Adon."

Such words, repeated over and over in slightly different ways, had no effect on Akhenadon. We were approaching the end of the one-year grace period that Aye had negotiated with Maya, and so, out of options, we agreed to meet over several days to make sense of the situation and to plan.

"So where do you stand on our situation?" Aye asked me. The day was overcast, a rarity in Kem but one that suited our moods.

"To be perfectly candid, Aye, I am torn between my love of Akhenadon and Adon and the realization that Kem is truly falling apart."

"I understand," Aye replied. "I have the same conflict within me. But as you know, I do not have as close a relationship with the King as do you. So for me, the scales tip toward easing the burdens placed upon the Two Lands." I sat with my forehead leaning against my staff that I held between my knees.

"I must ask you a difficult question, Aharon." He hesitated for a moment, then blurted it out. "Do you think that your brother is mad?"

For some reason, I expected that question, for I asked it of myself often enough. I looked up at Aye. "I do not know, Aye. I truly do not know. What is madness? Is it something we label because the other person experiences something we do not? It is said in the scrolls that King Narmer, may his name be blessed for all eternity, had visions from Horus of a united Kem, the Land of the Papyrus and the Land of the Lotus living together in harmony as one, an impossibility in his day anyone would have thought. Many lives were lost in achieving his vision. Was he mad?"

"I see your point, but it does not help us to make a decision. If we both firmly believe he is mad, it would ease my conscience, for one." He gave a big sigh and looked toward Mother Nile, flowing behind me.

"Aharon, I have given council to two Kings now, as well as Queen Tiye. I have lived 50 years studying, learning, and practicing my diplomacy. Yet I will admit to you that I am frightened. Not frightened because of an impending war, or a tax revolt, or… whatever. I am truly frightened that we may not survive as a nation if this continues any longer.

"To be honest, I feel that Maya is right, hard as that is to admit. I will say it here, now. We must seek safe exile for Akhenadon, or he will either be killed by them or will destroy Kem. I see no other option." I could not but agree.

"Our history is long, Aye, with some defeats, but mostly a glorious past. As far as I know, this has never happened before… to exile a sitting King."

"Perhaps we have not had an official exile, but we both have read the scrolls and understood what lay unseen between the lines of holy words, enough at least to know that more than a few Kings have been murdered. And I would rather negotiate Akhenadon's exile than have to help my daughter through grieving her beloved."

I thought for several moments. "We must involve Nefertiti in the plan. She is effectively ruling the Royal court."

"I agree, but I do feel we would be better served if we first finalize what we feel is a workable plan, and one that Maya might accept, before approaching her. She is the mother of six and pregnant again, I understand. It would be better if she just approves rather than helps develop the plan." I nodded in agreement.

Over the next three days, we worked from after morning prayers until past dark, discussing, arguing, and finally completing a plan that we felt would work. None of it could be certain, for there were too many people who would need to approve, modify or possibly reject it. We arranged a meeting with Nefertiti for the next day.

As we entered her quarters, Nefertiti was handing over Setepenre, the sixth daughter of the King and Queen, to her nursemaid. I had to admire the fortitude of Nefertiti, or any woman for that matter, to keep trying to conceive a boy despite the difficulties of pregnancy, childbirth, and motherhood. What I found even more amazing was how Nefertiti managed to retain her figure and her beauty. Yet the trying times had taken their toll. She had dark circles under her eyes, and she always appeared tired and fatigued.

"Welcome, father… Aharon. Refreshments are in the other room," she said, and we followed her to the adjoining room. It was elaborately furnished with a few settees, a couch, and several chairs. A table that could accommodate six people sat in the center of the room, and alongside one wall was a long, narrow table filled with plates of fruits, nuts, and sweets. Pitchers of barley beer stood on either end, along with mugs.

"Please help yourselves," she said, holding her palms out to the table. "Setepenre was up most of the night with a stomach ache. I am thoroughly exhausted." She sat down in the softest chair, sighing.

"I worry about you, daughter. You work too hard with all your other responsibilities."

"Worried?" she said with a laugh. "I work hard because of you and Tiye. You have recruited me to be co-Regent and to be part of this… this cabal." I sat silently, trying to determine how much of what she said was offered in jest or as painful truth.

"You know, I used to think amidst one crisis or the next that things would calm down, and I would recuperate, perhaps have some time alone to reflect. After fifteen years as Great Wife, I realize those times never come. They cannot, for we rule a vast empire, and pressing matters arise every day." She looked out at Mother Nile and a clear blue sky.

"I know you did not come to hear me complain. What is today's crisis?"

I looked to Aye as he looked to me. I knew that neither of us wanted to be the one to explain the plan to Nefertiti.

"Well, then, it would appear that this is a serious one, my councilors. Allow me, then." She got up to pour herself some beer. Her baby bulge was already apparent.

"You do not have to waste time telling me that things in the Two Lands are unsettled. My own servants tell me how desperate it is outside Akhedadon. Our best efforts to turn the tide have failed. So, what have you two planned to finally put an end to this?" She eased herself into the chair, holding her back in obvious discomfort."

"Perhaps we should come back another time... when you feel better," I suggested. Aye nodded in agreement.

"Well, that will be in six months, when I am done with this pregnancy, would that be okay? I thought not. Let's get on with it, then. It is only the backaches I have had with every pregnancy."

"I know not how to tell you this, Nefertiti, so I will be blunt. Akhenadon must be exiled." I expected her to gasp, to protest, to raise her voice against our foolishness. But she did not. Instead, she stared at Aye, then me, as if peering into our very kas.

"I believe it can be temporary," Aye continued, "and if handled correctly, we may eventually prevail and restore Akhenadon to the throne."

"Unless Adon himself takes my husband by the hand, I cannot think of any way to achieve this," she said.

"We will explain it all to you," Aye said, "but you must understand that whatever we do will have to be negotiated with Maya and others. I believe Tiye will agree to it in general terms but may have additional ideas. But here is the main point. Assuming you agree with what we describe, you will have to help us convince Akhenadon that this is something he must do."

Nefertiti began to giggle, then laughed aloud. She had to use the hem of her gown to wipe her eyes. "Convince Akhenadon... hmmm. You are joking. How successful have you men been in that endeavor?" I admired her wit but also her maturity. She was far from the retiring young girl she was when she married.

"Apparently, I am only listened to when he needs his sexual desires filled. But aside from that, he no longer listens to what I have to say. Even when I am in his presence, he does not cast his eyes upon me. He no longer sees his children, for he is too busy praying and talking to Adon." She again arose, her hands now clasped in anguish.

"We have not slept in the same bed for… well, since this," she said, pointing to her abdomen. "And it was months and months before that. All he cares about is Adon." She paced before us. "I am frightened. Every day I awake to wonder what the day will bring. Will my husband grow wings to fly back to his father? Will we all be killed by Supililiuma? Will Kem fall into total chaos?

"I must tell you what happened when we last shared a bed together. 'We have not had a son together to ensure our rule', he said to me. 'Yes, I do have Smenkhkare now, but I wish to have a son with you. My father, Adon, told me he wishes for us to try once again.'

"Yes, that is what he said. He had sex not for us but for Adon. His father, Adon."

Scroll Twenty-Seven

The Queen is King

It took almost a year for all arrangements to be made. While Maya was irritable about the delays, I helped him to understand that the problem was fifteen years in the making, in part due to his refusal to compromise with Akhenadon at the start of his reign. Had he simply committed to eradicating corruption, things might have gone differently.

In truth, the entire plan was made without the knowledge of Akhenadon, and even at this late date, he knew nothing about it. His only care was to be left alone with his God. So Aye, Tiye, and I laid the groundwork for the wheels to turn, and when it was all set, we advised Maya in order to get his approval.

Since the very survival of Kem was at stake, we felt the best way to afford the meeting the severity it called for was to meet in Tiye's palace in Waset. I learned from my able mentors that this immediately accomplished two things. First, it was a gift to Maya that he would not need to travel to Akhedadon but that we would require him to come to Tiye's quarters. The meeting place itself was a decided advantage for us.

We met, once again, in Tiye's secure quarters, with Bakennifi standing guard outside. All was prepared in anticipation of a long and grueling meeting. Yet we felt confident that we had explored and resolved all aspects, with face-saving measures for both sides.

"Right at the outset, we will say that we grant your wish to have Akhenadon removed from Kem," Aye began.

"Exiled?" Maya asked.

"Yes," Tiye responded so that Maya was assured of the Queen's concurrence.

"This must be done respectfully and without any harm coming to the King or to anyone who travels with him into exile."

Maya did not hesitate. "Granted, of course."

"None of this will happen unless all of it is agreed upon, so I will continue." Maya sat still in his chair as I watched his reactions to what was to come.

"We will arrange for Smenkhkare to marry Meritadon and…."

"What?"Maya interrupted, his face showing his surprise. "That will only serve to perpetuate Akhenadon's line."

"Excuse me," Tiye responded. "We agree to exile the man, not the dynasty. Even you would have to agree that Akhenadon is the problem, not my late husband Amunhotep or his forebears all the way to Thutmose the First. It is their lineage, too." At that, Maya bowed his head, not wanting to insult the Queen.

Aye continued. "We will agree that before her marriage, Meritadon will change her name to Meritamun." Maya nodded, obviously pleased at this.

"Further, Nefertiti will be allowed to stay. Since Smenkhkare is still far too young, Nefertiti will be left in place to administer Kem. Her popularity with the people and her knowledge of daily operations would add stability as the changes occur." At this, Maya twisted in his seat, obviously uncomfortable.

"Are you done?" Maya asked.

"No, there is more. Be reasonable, Maya, this is complex. Never before in our history has a king been forced into exile."

Maya suppressed a smile that I saw begin. We all knew quite well the alternatives to exile that had previously been employed.

"Smenkhkare will serve in a temporary capacity until Tutankhadon comes of age. Then Smenkhkare will step down in his favor."

"Tutankhadon? I have not yet seen the child, but I understand he was born with a club foot. What if he is not fit for the throne? What if he is a misfit like his father?" Tiye sat upright at that, obviously upset by Maya's callous remark.

"He is normal in every other way," Tiye said angrily. "He is healthy and vigorous."

"So you say, Queen Tiye, but I don't believe the people I represent would agree to that without proof of his fitness."

"We are prepared to grant that to you, but it must be a fair test of fitness, and it must be judged impartially by a majority vote of three physicians." Aye leaned forward to take a sip of his beer. "And now we are done, is that right?" he asked, looking at Tiye and me. We both nodded.

"I will have to speak with others to make sure that they are in agreement with your proposal. I will also now have to insist on a few things."

"Such as?" Tiye asked.

"First, we do not care to what God Nefertiti prays, but she is never to do so in public, even if it is Amun to whom she eventually prays." Aye looked at Tiye and me, and we agreed.

"Next, we may have serious reservations about Smenkhkare. I understand from reliable sources that he is, well… a spoiled brat, wanting to please his now absent father, not listening…."

"That is why we are insisting that Nefertiti acts as secret co-regent for him."

"But she is not even his mother!" Maya protested.

"She was in favor of Akhenadon trying for a son, however he could," I replied. "However, as often happens, as soon as Smenkhkare was born, she became pregnant with Tutankhadon. The Gods play cruel tricks on us sometimes, do they not, my fellow priest?"

In a ten-day, it was all decided in a larger meeting with Maya, Pi-Or, and Harmena witnessing the telling of the agreement and Tiye, Aye, and me representing our side. Ramose, the Mayor, agreed to be the impartial witness, as his allegiance to both Tiye and Maya was well known to all. Nothing was put in writing for fear that the contents of the agreement would be seen by the wrong eyes.

When the meeting ended, I was prepared to walk out when I realized that Aye was not behind me. As I turned to wait for him, Tiye took me by the arm and escorted me out. "Leave them be", she said. "They are probably just saying their goodbyes." By the tone of her voice, I suspected that Tiye was not telling me the truth, yet I could not make sense of that. But as I learned later, there was one matter, one aspect of the plan, a horrible one, from which I was mercifully excluded.

By agreement, Maya gave us time to arrange all matters and to reveal the agreement to Akhenadon, a prospect none of us wanted to face. Between meeting with my priest network throughout Kem and being part of these plans and negotiations, I had not seen Akhenadon for months. Even I was shocked by his appearance.

We had agreed that the best approach was for Aye and me to meet with Akhenadon, as including Tiye or Nefertiti would put them in an untenable position as mother and wife. When we arrived at the palace, even the King's main servant just shook his head when we asked how things went.

Not surprisingly, Akhenadon had forgotten about the meeting, and so when we arrived, we were forced to wait an hour while he finished his prayers. When he walked in, we were both taken aback. He was thin as a rope, haggard looking, black rings surrounding his eyes, and stooped. He sat on his throne rather than on the chairs that we had arranged during his absence.

"What brings you both here? I haven't seen you for quite a

while… I think." He appeared confused.

We had agreed that I would be the one to speak first. "Akhenadon, my dearest brother…."

"You are my only brother," Akhenadon interrupted. I was not sure from his facial expression whether he was joking or just reminiscing. I smiled at him, but he did not respond.

"Yes, we are the only brothers to each other, and my love for you is wide and deep." I let that sit in his bag for a while. "Unfortunately, we come to you today with difficult news." Aye nodded.

"Go ahead, for there is nothing too difficult for Adon." This brought a lump to my throat.

"Do you want me to continue?" Aye whispered. I shook my head.

"Akhenadon," I continued, "the Two Lands that you love so dearly are in chaos. Ma'at no longer sits comfortably upon our land. I know not what Adon has in store, but I do know this. He is testing you for a reason. You must leave Kem for a while, perhaps a short while, so that things might be set straight again. We have developed…."

"What do you say, Aharon? This is against ma'at! I am King, and nothing can change that except death. We both know that. The three of us surely know that."

I turned to Aye, who continued. "My King, I fear you do not understand what is happening in Kem. People are hungry. They rebel violently against your edicts. They have drawn a line in the sand about worshipping the Gods they wish. There are plagues that come and go, and not enough physicians to treat the ill. Supililiuma is at our border, ready to invade, and he has created alliances with our former friends.

"If you do not follow our advice and allow yourself to be exiled, it will come to terrible violence, and in that case, no one can guarantee the safety of you, Nefertiti, and your children."

"As has always been, I will be at your side for however

long or short this exile will be," I added.

"I think it is the two of you who do not understand. This is a test for Kem, not me. A test for all its people, not just those who pray to Adon. When things look to be at their lowest point, He will appear and save us all, proving He is the one and only God, all-powerful and just." He took a deep breath and held his head to the heavens, and smiled.

"You now have a male heir with Nefertiti, brother. If you insist on staying, you may be condemning Tutankhadon to death, too. Then who will rule Kem, Maya? Ramose?" This had the effect of causing Akhenadon to think. He lowered his head to his hands and rocked back and forth.

"I have never done anything to harm my people," he said, looking at us with tears in his eyes.

"Not intentionally, for you did what you did out of your love for Adon, and perhaps this is all part of His will," Aye responded, his brow wrinkled in sadness. "But, it is not as if you did no damage, Akhenadon. You destroyed the very foundation that the Two Lands were built on. You would not be patient and wait. You threw ma'at to the beasts of the underworld with your sudden edicts, and now people believe that Kem is plagued by mut spirits that wander through the lands every night. It is as if you have killed the people's spirit, and in so doing, you have injured more than one Kemian. You have harmed many of our countrymen, our very brothers, and sisters."

Scroll Twenty-Eight

The King Must Go

Changes happened quickly. After our meeting, Horemheb was put in charge of the daily administration of Akhedadon, which he initially objected to but ultimately handled with military precision. The King refused to even grant an audience to Nefertiti, retreating ever more into his communion with Adon, and so her desire to support him through this terrible time came to naught. To keep the peace, and under our direction, we converted my home into Nefertiti's palace, and I moved into a lesser home just a stone's throw away. Whether he knew of Nefertiti's leaving, I was not sure and feared asking.

Akhenadon continued to hold his prayer sessions each morning to greet Adon's rising, but now it was I who accompanied him in his chariot to the Great Temple, the short journey taken in silence except for the snorting of the horses and the grinding of sand under the wheels. These sessions were a terrible thing to witness, for none but a scattering of the most devout came. Akhenadon stopped giving his sermons about Adon, simply praying to him in silence, then singing his songs to him as if none of us were there. And sadly, there was no more poetry written to Nefertiti.

Aye took on all other tasks that were needed. He and Nefertiti prepared Meritadon for her wedding, explaining how she would simply be a wife in name only. Smenkhkare was told little, for he was just a boy. He vacillated between excitement over being King and boredom over the details. Yet, even so, he sometimes accompanied us to prayer, wanting to impress his father with his devotion.

The wedding was the least of Aye's worries, for he now had to deal with Maya regularly to prepare for the opening of the temples to Amun, reconstruction of others, and the building of entirely new ones to replace those that were completely destroyed. I had heard that every artisan in Kem was commissioned to create new statues of Amun and other lesser Gods.

Akhenadon took no interest in anything other than his prayers, fervently insisting that Adon would soon set things straight and he would rule triumphantly with Adon. I became so concerned about my brother's health that I dispatched a messenger to Tiye, asking her to visit and spend time with her son, for he always took solace in her presence. Within eight days, her boat docked at Akhedadon. No one but Horemheb and I were present to greet her, such as the state to which Akhedadon had descended.

Akhenadon's face lit up when he saw her, and he rushed to embrace her in his arms. I had arranged for a dinner to be brought to his quarters, and as soon as they were done, they retired to his outer room where they sat and talked, the first conversation of many they had over the next ten-day.

"I am fine, mother, really. You need not worry," Akhenadon said as they sipped Babylonian wine, the first time I had seen Akhenadon indulge in a very long time.

"Nonsense," Tiye replied, putting her mug down on the small rush and wood table between them. "I birthed you, swaddled you, and brought you up to be King. Do not tell me that you are fine. You are not, and I wish for you to tell me honestly what troubles you." Tiye was never one to parse her words.

Akhenadon moaned and leaned back in his seat, holding his mug on his paunch. "I don't know where to even start. My head is in turmoil. My stomach plagues me. Even my very bones hurt."

"I can see you are in pain, son. My heart goes out to you. Please, speak from your heart and allow me to help."

Akhenadon sighed loudly. "I… it's as if… I feel… abandoned. Despite my prayers, I feel as if Adon no longer listens to my entreaties." He turned to face his mother. "I do not pray for me… not at all. I pray for those I love. I pray for the people of Kem. I pray for peace among all people."

"I know. You have a loving heart. It is light as a feather."

"I do not believe in Anubis' judgment, mother."

"I realize that. I only meant that Adon must recognize that, too." Akhenadon nodded.

"They want to exile me. Did you know that?"

Tiye took a moment to collect her thoughts. "Yes, my dear, I did. I have been informed of these plans throughout and have come to feel it best. Does that surprise you?" Akhenadon looked at his mother.

"I suppose it should not, for you are still the greatest Queen Kem has known."

"I am not sure of that, but let me say that it was never my intent to hurt you in my being part of this small group that loves you so dearly. We are looking out for your interests while protecting the Two Lands that we all love so much… and to which we have a sworn loyalty."

"I understand your position, but I do not understand why exile is the only solution. I do not agree with it."

"My dear, dear son, how do I explain this any more than Aye and Aharon already have? The options are exile or your death at the hands of very powerful people in…."

"Maya is not powerful in the eyes of Adon. He is a speck in the universe, an abuser of my people, a parasite."

"He is not the only powerful man or woman who rallies against you, Akhenadon. But, let me be very clear, for I believe that you must hear this from me. Whether you are exiled is no longer for you to determine. It will happen, and all that is needed to accomplish that is already in motion. I am here not to debate its merits but to help you create a vision of what comes next."

"A vision? Of what? Of my failures? Of Adon's disappointment in me? Of our people lost to the glories of Adon? Or are you speaking of visions of my death from despair? What vision, tell me!" He slumped forward in his seat, his head in his hands. Tiye could not help but see Akhenadon as he was as a child. She waited for him to regain his composure.

"None of these, Akhenadon. You were young and impatient when you ascended to the throne. I speak of the vision of maturity, contemplation, and wisdom. I see a vision of you returning to the Two Lands stronger, wiser, and a true leader. You have this in you.

"Where you see failure, I see future greatness. Each year, my son, Mother Nile, ravages our farmland, destroying all she touches. But from that devastation comes new growth, sustaining life for all our people. Ever has this been so since we arose from the mound of Nun? So it was with you. That is my vision. This effort has been ravaged, but in that, it contained seeds of change, growth, and endurance. You must grasp that and move forward, proudly, standing tall, no matter what barriers others put in your way."

Akhenadon sat there, mesmerized by his mother's words. His eyes were wide open, his heart full of energy and ideas. "Oh, mother," he said, "never have I heard such words of wisdom. You are right. Perhaps I did move too quickly, but I did that out of love and conviction. Perhaps some time for reflection and planning will help. Yes, that is it. I feel it in my heart!" He rose to hug Tiye.

"I will take Nefertiti with me and do my best to show her how sorry I am for ignoring her these past few months... or years, and...."

"Sit, Akhenadon, for there is more to talk about... much more."

Tiye was exhausted when she related to me her talk with Akhenadon. I could see how difficult it was for her. But I could also tell that her words helped shine Adon's light into the dark places of Akhenadon's ba. In the end, it gave him the comfort and perspective he needed. In the end, I could not decide if what plagued him the most was what he saw as his failure before Adon or his abandonment of his beloved Nefertiti.

What Tiye suggested, and we all agreed to, was that Akhenadon would first go to Goshen, where Tiye traced her heritage. There he would spend a year becoming adjusted to the changes in his life as Kem adjusted to the new order, which still bordered on chaos. Maya had agreed to this transition period as he would need the time to reconstitute the Amun power structure.

It did not surprise me when Tiye called for a meeting with me after she had spent a few days with Akhenadon. We met in Nefertiti's quarters, in the secure room I had set up while I lived there.

"I have insisted upon Goshen for a reason, Aharon. You already know my people are from there. From Goshen, you will be able to monitor what is happening in the rest of Kem, at least until the end of one year when you will have to leave Kem entirely.

"Due to my ties there, if your party ever feels threatened, you can depend on my people to protect you or hide you in the mountains.

"But I chose Goshen for an entirely different reason, and that is where you come in, for the truth is, and has always been with my son, that you will have the hardest job of all." My brows raised at this, for I had no idea where Tiye was taking this conversation.

"Goshen is a settling point for all the misfits that Kem has not wanted to be part of the power structure, as far as possible from Waset. It harbors the descendants of Hittites, shepherds, mariners, and even those who believe in one God… and not necessarily Adon."

"I met these people on our last visit together. They were the people of Yuya and Tjuya, were they not?"

"Yes, my parents. They believe in a God they call Yahveh."

"I had heard you and Akhenadon speak of this when we were but boys. I have always wanted to learn more of this Yahveh, but I have been too busy with… other things."

"The difference is that the people who believe in Yahveh as their God also allow for the existence of Gods that others pray to. That is why my parents adapted easily to Kem. They accepted Amun, but I will tell you this in secret, Aharon. Until the day they passed to the next world, they worshipped Yahveh."

I was taken by Tiye's words. "You tell me this for a reason, Tiye."

"It is this. When you are in Goshen, learn as much as you can about Yahveh. When you have done so, introduce Akhenadon again to it… slowly… in more detail. Let him come to understand Yahveh's relation to Adon, for I suspect they are bound together in deep and mysterious ways.

"We both know that Akhenadon is impetuous, stubborn, devoted. But I feel he is yet destined for greatness. But he must learn that his beliefs are not the only ones that reside in righteousness. He must learn to temper his enthusiasm. He will need to experience some degree of deprivation to further shape his ba. He has had it too easy, despite his… well… deformities."

"But why do you feel I must do this? Why not you?" At this, Tiye smiled.

"Now we come to an even deeper secret, Aharon, at least for you. Your own parents were Yahvehites." My eyes revealed my shock.

"Is… is this true?" Tiye nodded.

"I have always believed that this is why you and Akhenadon came so naturally to Adon, for the idea of one supreme God is baked into your bones."

And so it was that we left Akhedadon the next month, marking the start of our one-year transition period. Horemheb planned the processions, from the packing of furniture and supplies to the organization of carts, horses, and accompanying soldiers. All had to be carefully loaded into boats for the short river and land journey to Goshen.

However, there was one item for which Horemheb did not plan. He refused Akhenadon's request to spend a few days with his beloved, Nefertiti. All that was left to the King and Queen was a meeting in the palace on the day before we left. Since Nefertiti brought their children with her, there was no time for them to be alone to say their goodbyes. I had my suspicions about why Horemheb acted so, but I still felt this was a cruel act.

It was indeed a sad day when we left. I had implored Horemheb to send all boats other than the ones carrying Akhenadon, the soldiers, Tiye, and me well in advance so as to respect the regency of the King. Surprisingly, Horemheb argued against doing so, but he finally relented, and by the time we left, only five boats remained at the dock, four for the soldiers and one for Akhenadon, Tiye, and me. Aye was off arranging Meritaten's wedding, which was to be held in Waset.

It was my job to get Akhenadon and take him to the boat. Walking in the palace now gave me gooseflesh. It was empty, devoid of servants, priests, and children so the sound of my sandals echoed against the unswept floors and made a scraping sound that was painful to my ears. I entered the King's bedroom and found him standing next to one of the columns, a shaft of light from Adon's disk highlighting his body. He looked upward, his arms raised, his hands extended to his God. He smiled, bathed in the loving embrace of his Father. He murmured to himself, and I could tell from the cadence that it was one of his prayers that he sang in gratitude, and the thought occurred to me that perhaps Akhenadon was not of this world and never was.

A lone servant entered the chamber from the side door, saw Akhenadon, and quickly turned around and left. I waited silently until Akhenadon was done. As he turned, he saw me and gasped.

"You seem surprised," I said softly.

"Yes, I thought you had left with the others." His stare penetrated me as if I were a mut spirit.

"Oh, my brother, never think that I would abandon you. Never, for you have shown us the truth and the way to eternal life. Indeed, you are the son of Adon, the son of the One and Only God. I am your servant to the end." Akhenadon's brow was deeply furrowed.

"They seem to leave in small groups, I notice," Akhenadon continued as if speaking to himself.

"Have you heard from Aye on whether they will allow our people to leave as a group from Goshen? I asked. "Together, I mean. All of us."

"Yes, yes. I have asked again when they visited me here, I think it was yesterday or perhaps a few days ago. It is never Aye alone anymore, always a number of them, asking unimportant questions, as if there is anything that is more important than faithfulness to Adon. My Father speaks to me and tells me that all will end well." Akhenadon spoke as if to himself.

"But did they give you an answer? I must prepare our people." Either he did not hear me, or he refused to answer. Instead, he stood smiling and staring outside, as he often did when thinking of our God.

"I shall speak with Aye today, with your permission, Great One. We must leave soon. I fear…"

Akhenadon turned to face me, his expression reflecting his confusion. "Why such a rush, Aharon?"

I turned to my brother and saw his confusion. "The crowds, Akhenadon, have you not heard them beyond the walls?"

"Yes, they seem angry, even as Adon blesses them every day with His light and warmth. He brings them life and sustenance. I have shown them His gifts. They are as clear as Mother Nile. Why do they not just bask in His light and rejoice?"

The journey north was uneventful, except for two items. The first was that Akhenadon appeared cheerful insofar as he had Tiye to converse with and to help him mold his vision. The second came about when, on the second day, Horemheb invited me to join him on his boat.

"Do you plan on leaving as soon as you deliver us to Goshen?" I asked.

Horemheb watched the far bank where a large crocodile basked. "I thought you knew. My detachment will stay in Goshen until the transition year is up."

"Is Maya that distrusting?" I laughed at the thought.

"Actually, it will surprise you to know that it was Aye who insisted on it, and Maya agreed. They fear threats to Akhenadon's life, and Maya, above all, does not want to be held responsible for that." I was surprised.

"So, you are assigned to protect the King for the next year, no matter…

"The soon-to-be deposed King," Horemheb interrupted. "My troops will guard him from a suitable distance."

"You do not like him at all," I said. "You two are so different, yet… and I say this gently, so alike." Horemheb erupted.

"Alike you say? How could you say that, Aharon? He is despicable, a poor excuse for a man. He is mad!"

I waited until Horemheb took several breaths before continuing. A fishing boat crew waved as they saw the King's pennant pass by. "You are both headstrong, set in your ways, unrelenting in your self-righteousness. And, most of all… and I say this wondering if you will take that dagger at your side and carve me up for the crocodiles… you are both brave men."

"And I say now that you, too, are mad, Aharon! He is weak, his body grotesque, his breasts and hips like a woman's. He would rather write poems and sing in that pitiful high voice of his than protect his country from foreign invaders."

"Yes, I expect you would think that. You are a soldier, and your bravery can take only one form. His bravery is not physical but spiritual. I will leave it at that for now. But I do thank you for your loyalty and service to the King. I also appreciate your honesty in your feelings toward Akhenadon. It is always useful to know another's position." I then left to re-board my master's craft.

It was only sixteen days after we arrived in Goshen that we received word that Kem had a new King. Yet we little expected what was to come next.

Book Two

Exile

Scroll Twenty-Nine

Exile

The transition year passed all too quickly. We were so busy in Goshen that the seasons flew by in rapid order. There were new alliances to be made, favors to ask and to give, and meetings with the many different kinds of people to be found in and around Goshen. This seemed to fascinate Akhenadon, and I watched his energy increase as he spent hours engaged in conversation with these men and women. And, of course, there was prayer, always prayer.

Yet even Akhenadon's prayers, at least those in public, were more subdued, and I attributed that to the joy he felt from his newfound friendships with the common people. He listened attentively and asked so many questions people were amused by his curiosity. I sat in on most of those sessions and I, too, burrowed deeper into the beliefs of the people. That openness soon proved its value.

It was after an intense discussion with three of the elders of the Yahvehites, who we had met a few times before, that one of them, a respected leader named Yosef, who I liked approached me. His long beard was yellowed with age, yet he stood erect, though still short in height.

"I have come with a strange request," he started. His missing teeth required me to listen carefully, yet he carefully gauged my reaction.

"Go ahead," I said, feeling the camaraderie between us.

"Would you be open to meeting with a family that lives a day's journey from here?" I was intrigued.

"I am not against such a meeting, but why?"

"It is something that Tiye and I feel might be of benefit to you. I prefer to say nothing else." My heart raced, thinking of what might lie behind this.

"How soon?" I asked.

"At sunrise."

"I am not sure I can have Akhenadon ready...."

"Not Akhenadon. Only you."

We journeyed in a small boat and arrived at a landing outside Bubastis in the early evening. The slight breeze hinted at a cool night, yet it also wafted a peculiar scent into the air, one that I could not place. Yet the smell felt familiar, a combination of marsh grasses, fertile mud, and sweet flowers. I breathed it in deeply, and it settled comfortably on my ba.

Yosef led me, along with the two other elders, up a dirt path until we crested the banks of Mother Nile's tributary. In the distance was a farmhouse surrounded by verdant fields. I gasped. I was dizzy and disoriented. I looked to Yosef, who was already staring at me. He smiled.

"Shall we go on?" he said softly. I could only nod, my heart thumping, willing myself to breathe.

It would be foolish to attempt to describe all that I felt as I approached the house, for memories, more like dreams, arose in my heart one after another. The smells, the sounds of the geese circling above, and the hazily familiar house with smiling people standing outside all bathed me in confused yet comforting feelings. As we arrived, all the pieces fit together, for I stared into welcoming faces that could have been mine.

Yosef turned to me. "Aharon, meet your Uncle and Aunt and your many cousins."

It was an emotional three days that I spent with my relatives, finding out where my roots spread, how my parents perished, and about my unborn sister who perished with them. But there was one thing that I learned that surprised me most.

Tiye was related to me.

Bringing me to the palace was not a random act of mercy, as I learned, but a carefully executed plan, for she had known me since my birth. For days after learning this, my heart was torn between appreciation of her action and the difficult questions that plagued me. Was hers a selfless act or a selfish one designed only to save her own son? Why had she not told me the full story? Why did she deprive me of the warmth, love, and acceptance that I felt in that farmhouse? Did Amunhotep know that Akhenadon and I were already related by blood before he pricked our fingers as sworn brothers? And why did Tiye feel the need to reveal this to me now?

I was sad to leave those hard-working people whose blood I shared, but on the way downriver, I realized that Tiye had given me a gift, many gifts, actually. I was raised in privilege, I was loved by Tiye and Amunhotep, and above all, I gained a brother. Tiye was still closely connected to my family, to her roots, to the fertile soil of the Delta. My respect for her rose to even greater heights.

My meeting with my relatives had another positive effect. Word spread of my connections to the Delta so that people felt more comfortable approaching our group. As a result, we gained new acolytes and priests since the people of Goshen were already more receptive to Adon. It seemed to fit comfortably into their own beliefs. Yet there was one acolyte who far surpassed the others in enthusiasm, intelligence, and, as it turned out, valor. His name was Joshua.

Joshua was born and raised in Goshen by shepherd parents but entered the Kemian army at an early age. By the time we knew him, at the age of 24, he had already served for ten years and was an accomplished swordsman, having seen his share of enemy skirmishes. Yet what he truly yearned for was a connection to something greater than himself, greater than the army, even greater than Kem. He was ready for Akhenadon and Adon's message when

Horemheb dropped us off in Goshen. Within months he was inseparable, and we welcomed this new firebrand to our midst.

And so, on the third month of Proyet, as farmers busied themselves planting in Mother Nile's fertile mud, we left the safety of Goshen and entered the barren desert of the Mafkat, as forbidding a place as ever a man could set foot upon. With Horemheb and his troops watching closely, we crossed over, our small group led by Adjo, a heavy-set, bearded man who was also a relative of Tiye. Adjo regularly plied the trade routes from Goshen to Midian, Edom, and Moab. Few men knew the mysteries of the Mafkat better.

Accompanying us was Joshua, who Horemheb knew and had allowed to be armed, knowing that our survival depended on being able to secure the wild game, although, in truth, I do not believe Horemheb cared whether Akhenadon lived or died, and the rest of us with him. Twenty others were from Adjo's tribe, all of them believers in Yahveh. While Akhenadon had already learned about their religious beliefs from these men, we both hoped to learn more during our exile, which we anticipated would be short.

As far as Horemheb knew, we were headed straight for Canaan, where the Midianites might provide Akhenadon with refuge. Only Adjo, Akhenadon, Joshua, and I knew the truth of where we were headed. We traveled for days, the days stretching into ten days, then into a month. Each day was the same. We woke at dawn and had a morning meal of unleavened bread with cheese. While the others packed, Akhenadon, Joshua, and I prayed. The Yahvehites also prayed, but their prayers had been set for centuries, they told us, and so all who worshipped Yahveh knew the prayers by heart and recited them quickly.

Once we started again, we had to cover our mouths and noses with a cloth to keep out the ever-present sand dust. By the mid-day meal, we were parched, and our mouths were filled with sand dust that ground against our teeth and coated our eyelids.

Water was more precious than gold, and we often thanked

Adon for bringing Adjo to us, for he seemed to know of every watering hole in the desert. We would stop, usually, at some cave entrance that hid a fresh spring, drink our fill of water and refill for the next leg of our journey.

It is odd that Akhenadon and I had many times been to the eastern and western deserts, but had never set foot in the Mafkat, that stretch of desert between the Two Lands and those of the Midianites, the Moabites, and the Edomites. Despite its oppressive heat and dryness, it was, without a doubt, a beautiful landscape. It was not endless expanses of sand dunes and little else. It was a land of mountains, caverns, and canyons with valleys between. There were acacia groves in some of those passes, and we gladly rested in their shade when possible.

It was on the second day of the third month that we awoke and noticed Adjo in animated conversation with Baki, Djal, and Labi, three of his trusted tribal companions. They gazed and pointed at the sky around us. They held up their noses and sniffed the air. Joshua and I looked but saw nothing unusual.

"What are they looking for?" I asked Joshua.

"I know not, but you can be assured that if they look to the sky, they suspect bad weather." Scanning the clear blue sky, I found that curious.

And bad weather we had. In just moments, Adjo began screaming to his men to pack the donkeys quickly. He ran to Akhenadon and yelled for us to move fast. A sandstorm was approaching and would be upon us sooner than we imagined. Yet the skies were still clear, and I wondered if he might be wrong. As we hurried, beating the donkeys to get them to move faster, we heard a sound far off, a sound of a thousand horses thundering toward us. I feared that Horemheb was about to attack us.

"Faster, faster, a sandstorm is upon us! We must make it to those mountains!" Adjo shouted over the din.

We struggled against the rising wind and the sand blowing into our eyes and mouths, stinging us like nettles.

In an instant, I lost sight of Akhenadon and Joshua, who had been right at my side, such as the thickness of the dust. Walking was now a struggle as the wind turned ferocious. I saw the shadow of Adjo before me, wrapping his robe around Akhenadon. Every step we took was an effort. I could hardly breathe.

For the briefest moment, the dust calmed slightly, enough for me to look up. And what I saw was the most horrific thing in my life. Towering above us, taller than the tallest mountain in the Two Lands, was a brown cloud, menacing, ready to curl and plunge down upon us. My legs shook in terror. I saw Joshua just ahead, Akhenadon draped over his shoulders, running with all his strength toward the base of a canyon just cubits before us. Then Djal grabbed me from the front, threw me over his shoulders, and began to run. As we reached a crevice in the canyon's wall, that black wave crashed down upon us in a swirling, blinding, terrifying wind.

All breath was sucked out of me. Over the furor, I heard Adjo scream for us to crouch, bury our faces near the ground, and breathe in shallow breaths. Someone threw a robe over me, creating a tent, and I prayed that Akhenadon was granted the same favor.

"It went on as if forever," I said to Akhenadon later that day when we had recovered and had gathered all the missing donkeys and supplies that had blown off their backs. "I thought we would be buried alive."

Akhenadon laughed. "It was most fearsome," he replied, "yet all the while it persisted, I marveled at the power of Adon to master such storms. Is He not truly a fearsome God?"

"We say of Yahveh that He can be an angry God," Adjo offered, "punishing us for sins. When I witness a sandstorm, I often wonder if some animal may have offended him, and He seeks to wipe it and its offspring from existence."

"An interesting thought," Akhenadon said. "We cannot know what goes on in the heart of our Adon or of your Yahveh. That is why we must be dedicated in our prayer and live a life that is good and does no harm to others." I marveled at

Akhenadon's seeming acceptance of worship to another God.

"In any case, we must make a sacrifice to Him today," Adjo said, getting up. He looked around him. "The blessing from the storm is that the next ten-day should be good weather. It seems like sandstorms scour the land of evil."

Yet some in our caravan did not make it through the storm. Some had suffocated, others had been battered against rocks. We buried four of our party before we moved on.

For five more days, we wound our way through narrow canyons of every hue of brown and high, rocky mountain passes. We were now in the midst of an enormous, far-ranging mountainous area. Our journey was so seemingly haphazard I knew I could never retrace it. At midday, Adjo stopped.

"We will stop here in the shade of this canyon and have a meal. We have reached our destination," he said. I looked about and could not imagine how such a forbidding place could be where we would be exiled. It felt as if Adjo might be in league with Maya, and we would be sentenced to a slow death by heat and starvation in this remote wilderness. I said nothing, for I did not want to insult Adjo nor worry Akhenadon.

During lunch, Adjo explained the plan. "My cousin, Tiye, wanted us to take you to a place where no one but us would ever find you." Akhenadon laughed.

"Well, I would say you have done well. Yet how are we to survive here? Have you a plan?"

"We do. Where we eat now is not the precise place." He pointed to the top of the mountain that loomed above us. "You see that peak? Upon it, hidden from anyone below, is a building. I sent men of my tribe before us to provision it. There are also ibex and dik-diks all over these mountains and valleys, so Joshua will be able to hunt them.

"We will journey here every three months with more provisions. Without so many men and donkeys, it will only take us one ten-day to get here. We always make sure we are not followed. Tiye believes that there always remains a chance that one of your enemies will try to kill you."

For the rest of that day, we climbed the mountain along switchbacks too numerous to count. Pieces of rocks made walking difficult, and I was glad that my staff helped me keep my balance. Some of the drop-offs gave me gooseflesh as they plummeted straight down to the valley below. Finally, we came to a sunken plateau between two peaks, and there, perfectly hidden, was a mud-brick building. Next to it was a large cave with storerooms within.

A warm but welcome breeze drew across the plateau, devoid of sand dust. I breathed so deeply I thought my lungs might burst, but the feeling was exquisite after the torments we had experienced on the desert floor. Joshua quickly climbed the smallest peak and bade us to join him. Indeed, the view from there was commanding, for we could see endlessly on such a clear day. Joshua certainly recognized the strategic importance of such a view.

"It always amazes me when I come upon places such as this," Joshua commented. "I have been in this region before, several times, in fact. I may have even passed right by this mountain on the way to our border to the east. I would never have imagined there would be such a place as this," he said, moving his arm around to encompass our new home.

The building itself was more spacious than it first appeared, for it was recessed into a fold in the mountain. As one went deeper into the house, the rooms became smaller and shorter, but there were enough rooms for each of us to have his own place to sleep. A fire pit and table were in the outer room, along with pots and utensils. The roof only covered a part of the house, allowing for coolness and some protection from Adon's disk.

The cave was stocked with all manner of foodstuffs. We had enough flour to feed a small army, as well as dried fruits and nuts. Cheeses hung from the walls. There was even a cache of dried fish, which added a pungent odor to the cave. There were two stalls for our donkeys in the back and a huge stack of hay on the opposite wall.

After two days' rest, Adjo and his men left to return to Goshen. We bid our goodbyes and prayers for a safe journey, confident that we had their unwavering support. It is funny how when twenty or more men get together, we hardly notice how much noise we make. It was not until after they left, and evening began to settle on the mountain, that we sat together, the fire not yet lit, and absorbed the complete silence of the desert. There was no wind, no water rushing, no trees rustling, nothing. Absolute silence. Akhenadon looked to the sky, his arms spread wide, and smiled. He had wordlessly spoken for us all.

Over the next two ten-days, Akhenadon and I worked to develop a routine, sort our goods, and pray. Yet Joshua could not stay still. He searched throughout our hiding place, hiked up and down our paths, sometimes going all the way from the valley to the tip of the higher of the two peaks that enveloped us. I was about to say something to him, but Akhenadon stayed me from speaking.

Finally, Joshua spoke to us at the evening fire pit. "I must leave tomorrow for Goshen," he said.

"What?" Akhenadon said in shock. "That is foolish, Joshua. It is too far a journey. You may get lost or killed in a storm."

"Why do you feel this need?" I asked

"Simple. We are poorly defended in case of attack by determined adversaries. The only weapon Horemheb allowed me to take was one sword and one short spear. I may be able to make a bow and a few arrows from the acacia trees I found in the neighboring valley, but it would lack power, and the arrows would be inaccurate.

"Adjo left me with a sketch of the route in case of emergency. I consider this an emergency. I must go. You are well provisioned, and I will return in two ten days."

Akhenadon and I tried to dissuade him, but the young soldier was insistent. "It is my sworn duty to protect you, my King. And I must have the tools to do so."

The two ten days without Joshua were difficult in some ways, glorious in others. We missed his company and joyous, youthful energy and exuberance. But the time alone gave Akhenadon and me the time we needed away from the distractions of Akhedadon and the rigors of rule to reacquaint ourselves. Of course, we ate and prayed together, but above all else, we talked. We reviewed all that had happened in the past twenty years, and I could see Akhenadon gaining new perspectives on his past behavior.

We also spoke about Adon and Yahveh and how each was similar and different. That, too, brought new perspectives to Akhenadon. One evening he asked me to ready some scrolls, for he wanted to formalize what the religion of Adon would mean to his followers in actual practice. And so, during Joshua's absence, we began that process.

Finally, twenty-four days after Joshua first left, I climbed to the smaller peak and looked out on a bright day. A tiny movement a few valleys over caught my attention, and I knew it was Joshua, pulling two donkeys behind his own.

Akhenadon and I hurried down the path to greet and help him with his supplies. At the bottom, we hugged him to us, happy that he was safe.

"How was your journey?" Akhenadon asked.

"Uneventful. I am late because I had to avoid a troop of soldiers patrolling the Wat-Hor."

"But that is on the other end of the Mafkat," I suggested.

"Yes, they were well out of their way. It is because of all the turmoil in Kem." Joshua looked away from us.

"What turmoil now?" Akhendadon asked.

"Perhaps we should wait until the dinner fire," Joshua offered.

"No, now," Akhenadon demanded.

Joshua shuffled his feet, still holding the reign of his lead donkey. "I am sorry to be the bearer of bad tidings, my King. I met with Tiye, who was in Goshen. She wanted you to know. Smenkhkare has been murdered. It was Maya's doing. Your son Tutankhadon is now King of the Two Lands. They have changed his name to Tutankhamun.

Scroll Thirty

She Ruled As Smenkhkare

It was the fifth time that Sothis rose in the heavens since our arrival here in the desert of Mafkat. Five long and lonely years with none but the three of us as a company, other than the periodic restocking of our provisions by Adjo and his men. They proved true to their word and to their family ties and appeared every three months as told by the alignment of the stars.

I cannot say that the exile was without its rewards, for it gave us all time to think, learn, and reorder our priorities. Joshua was an eager student, and both Akhenadon and I taught him nearly every day. I was surprised that he did not know our picture word language, so I taught it to him, and he soaked it up quickly.

For me, it was an opportunity to finally have lengthy periods of time with Akhenadon, during which we discussed what we had learned from his kingship and what we might have done differently. In the beginning, Akhenadon held onto his anger, but by the end of the first year, I noticed that the sharp edges had dulled a bit. We also had time to begin to formalize the Adonite religion. There was much to be done, and I often went to sleep worrying that we would never be able to accomplish what was needed. For, unlike my Amun brethren, we did not have two thousand years of tradition to rely on.

For Akhenadon, it proved to be an equally valuable time. Tiye was correct when she felt that Akhenadon needed to experience hardships to grow into the man he was capable of being. After the first month of exile, he insisted on gathering firewood and drying the dung from the donkeys for the fire. He enjoyed feeding and riding the donkeys to give them exercise, although it was a funny sight to see him astride one, the toes of his long, spindly legs touching the ground when he relaxed them. Sometimes they would catch on a rock, spilling him to the ground.

Life passed slowly. We developed a rhythm that differed for each of us yet also brought us together as a unit. Joshua was a disciplined soldier and kept up his exercises, even building a straw man against which he practiced his swordsmanship. He hiked down the mountain every other day to practice his archery. My days were spent with Akhenadon and then transcribing what he told me to write down.

But the evening meal was always spent together, from preparing the meal to the prayers, eating, and talking into the night. When darkness fell completely, I instructed Joshua on the constellations and what they meant.

Of course, we eagerly anticipated Adjo's visits, and he learned to come prepared for questioning by each of us. He made it a point to relay information from Tiye and Aye so that we knew what was happening in Kem. And, as we learned, much was happening.

Adjo explained that Smenkhkare had drowned while fishing in what Maya said was an unfortunate accident. Tiye sent along a sealed scroll for me, which warned me that Aye may have had a role in the murder. This came as a great shock to me, but I dared not tell Akhenadon until I understood Aye's motivation. But what surprised me even more, was that Aye had Nefertiti take on the male vestments of Smenkhkare, and for three years until Tutankhamun was old enough, she ruled as Smenkhkare, with Aye as her advisor. I needed time to untwist this disturbing information.

"No one saw Smenkhkare except at a great distance at public festivals. So the crown of the Two Lands and makeup hid Nefertiti's face," Adjo explained.

"Why did Aye insist on this?" Akhenadon wondered aloud. We sat quietly, each of us trying to make sense of these events.

"We will leave at sunrise," Adjo said to us at dinner.

"Why the rush?" Akhenadon asked, obviously wanting their company longer.

"We were stopped twice by Kemian troops. They have increased their patrols, and we are not sure why. It is better that they do not follow even in the same direction as ours. We were careful, but it is best if we leave quickly."

After dinner, Akhenadon and I sat separately with Adjo. "Tell me," Akhenadon began, "is there any word from Nefertiti?"

"There is. Tiye asked me to tell you, but I wanted to wait until we were alone… with Aharon, of course. Nefertiti sends her love and devotion. She says she still prays to Adon every day to have you return to her." Akhenadon hung his head, and I thought he would cry. Instead, he looked at Adjo.

"Please return this message for Tiye. Tell her to speak with Nefertiti and tell her that my love for her is undying. We will be together again, whether in this world or the next." My heart felt my brother's pain.

"What have you heard about Tutankhamun?" I asked.

Adjo hesitated. "Tiye says that Tutankhamun is growing quickly and that he is only slightly hindered by his clubfoot. He walks with a cane, so he must be in pain, but he handles it well.

"He is thirteen years old now. He feels ready for rule, but Aye and Nefertiti feel differently. Nefertiti is the one who instructs him, but Aye is the power behind the throne. He makes all the difficult decisions and is able to manipulate Tutankhamun to his will. Tiye feels that he also influences his daughter too much."

"I know that Aye will do what is right," Akhenadon said. This made a lump form in my throat, for I could not get Tiye's scroll out of my thoughts.

Before sunrise Adjo and his men rose, hiked down the mountain, and took off. I noted that they continued riding southeast so as to throw off any army unit that might have been tracking them. They would think that this was a trading route or, better yet, a smuggling route. Rewards were given for capturing smugglers.

Three days later, as Adon's disk was starting to set behind the mountains, Joshua sat upon our lookout and came scrambling down to our camp.

"Be quiet. There's an army troop approaching. I will go back up to watch them, but no fires and no noise. Find the goats and pen them." He then climbed back to the lookout. When night came on, he climbed back down.

"They are camped at the base of our mountain," he whispered, concern written all over his face.

"Do you think they look for us… for me?" Akhenadon asked.

"Hard to say. They are a good-sized unit. They may have followed Adjo's tracks, but he is smart enough to have taken a very twisting route before turning back to Goshen. If he suspects he is being followed, he may even go all the way to Edom to trade and then return."

"What do we do?" I asked.

"We wait. In the morning, we will see what they are up to. They are on the other side of the mountain in the neighboring valley, so they have not seen the path leading up here. Each night we scrub our tracks to be sure. Tonight, I will check our defenses, just in case."

I do not think any of us slept much that night, surely not Joshua, who ran up and down the path checking on the rock slides he primed, as well as armaments he staged at different points.

When Adon's disk rose above the mountains, Joshua climbed to the lookout. He was gone for an hour as we waited nervously. I heard one donkey bray, and I ran to the cave to feed all the animals to silence them. Finally, Joshua came down to us.

"They are leaving in the same direction as Adjo's caravan. That is the good news. The bad is that they have left a single sentry with what looks to me like supplies for a ten-day or a bit longer until their return. It should not be a problem, though."

"You say one thing, but your face reveals another," I said. Joshua smiled.

"I worry for you two. Remember, as long as he is down there, we cannot have a fire. We must eat what we can. Sound travels far in the desert, so we must remain very quiet."

For the next few days, Joshua kept a careful watch on the soldier below. Nothing appeared out of the ordinary. The man ate, slept, and occasionally wandered off to answer the needs of his body. But on the fifth day, Joshua came down quickly.

"He is bored and has started to explore, looking up and around. I do not think he suspects anything, and he cannot see us from below, but let's be sure not to move around too much. Certainly do not go near the path."

This went on for two more days. We were all tense, but that worsened when Joshua reported that the soldier had indeed found the trail.

"He probably thinks it is an ibex run. No need to worry, though. I will be vigilant."

That morning I went in to feed the animals. As soon as I left, pandemonium broke out in the cave as one of the goats jumped into the donkeys' pen and tried to eat their food. For what seemed like an eternity, they brayed and bleated at one another.

Joshua came barreling down from the lookout. "That did it!" he said. "He heard that and is on his way to the trail. Both of you go into the cave, behind the pens. Aharon, you take one of the swords that are in there. I have trained you enough. Use it if that becomes necessary."

"What are you going to do?" Akhenadon asked, his voice shaking.

"If he comes up to a certain point on the trail, I will have no choice but to kill him. I will have the advantage, as I will be higher. We will deal with the consequences later." He turned and left, patting his side to make sure his dagger was there. As he ran, he smoothly picked up his sword and disappeared down the rocky trail.

When he was halfway down, he stopped to think. He could easily kill the man as he passed him on the trail, for he now stood against an indentation in the rock wall that would afford him the element of surprise.

One thrust of his blade would end it without struggle. As he thought the move through, he realized that he had to dispose of the body before the troop of soldiers returned, and if they found sword wounds on the soldier's body, they would scour the mountains and not leave until they had Akhenadon. Not a good idea. He somehow had to make the kill without sword play. How?

He peered around the rock that hid him and some one hundred cubits below he saw the soldier sometimes climbing with difficulty, staying close to the mountain wall for fear of slipping off. Joshua squinted to make sure his eyes were not playing tricks on him. He knew the soldier! He served with him for more than a year. In fact, they had always been good friends since they came from adjoining villages in the Delta. Then the thought hit him.

He stepped out onto the trail and kicked a small rock down the trail. The soldier looked up, drawing his sword in one smooth motion.

"Who goes there?" Joshua yelled, his sword already before him. The two men stared at each other in amazement.

"Is that you, Joshua?" the soldier asked, incredulous.

"Praise the Gods! I cannot believe it is you, Buneb." Joshua put his sword back in its scabbard and walked down to embrace his friend.

"What are you doing here?" Joshua asked.

"It is I who should be asking that," Buneb said, still surprised at finding his friend here. "This is the most good forsaken desert I have ever seen!"

"I know, come, I will tell you all about it." He walked up to the indentation in the mountain and sat down.

"You have hiked up quite a way. You must be tired and thirsty. Here, have some water." He picked up a water bladder and gave it to Buneb, who drank thirstily.

"So, what in the name of Amun are you doing here?" Buneb asked.

"It is better I show you than try to explain." He stood up at the edge of the trail. "Look here, do you see that gold shimmering on the next cliff?" he said, pointing.

"Ah, I knew there must be a good reason." Buneb stood and carefully shuffled towards Joshua. When he was next to him, he peered at the cliff. "I do not see…" With a smooth motion, Joshua spun and leaned against the rock wall and kicked with all his might. Buneb fell to his death without a sound. Joshua looked down to see his friend lying on the valley floor, his limbs bent at unnatural angles. There was no movement at all.

Now Joshua raced up the trail to the cave. "Come out, both of you!" he shouted. When the three of them were together, he explained.

"I had to kill the soldier. In order for it to appear he had an accident, I have to recover his body and take it several valleys away, so it looks like he went exploring and fell."

"What if his troop returns?

"That is why I must do this right now. I do not like leaving you alone, but we will be in greater danger if I do not get rid of his body in a convincing way." Akhenadon and I looked at each other.

"Keep the animals separated from now on, and keep your dagger at the ready, Aharon. No fires, no noise until I return. I will use the soldier's donkey. I should be back in two days' time."

It took all that time for Joshua to retrieve Buneb's body, put it on the donkey, and then march it in the same direction as the troop and caravan, expecting all the time to be found. He found another valley with tall cliffs and an ibex trail, and he struggled up the path with Buneb's body on his shoulder until he was able to throw it off the mountain. He knew that by the time the troop found the broken body, half eaten by jackals and snakes, they would assume he had fallen. Joshua left his friend's wine bladder, nearly empty, close to the body. He thought it would go far to satisfy the captain of what had happened.

One day after Joshua returned, the troop came back to pick up their soldier. After a few hours of searching, his body was found and loaded onto his donkey. They left immediately for the comfort of their base.

Both Joshua and I were relieved, but the event proved more difficult for Akhenadon. He took off for the lookout, saying he needed time to pray. Later that night, I hiked quietly up to see if he was alright. I heard him speaking to Adon.

"Adon, King of the universe, why have you forsaken me? Why do you continue to test us so?"

I found myself nodding in agreement. I looked to the heavens wondering the same thing, wondering if it would ever end.

Scroll Thirty-One

In the Beginning

It had been three months since I saw Akhenadon, and when I finally viewed our mountain retreat in the distance, I was overjoyed. Still, I worried about his health and how my news would affect him.

"I can see you are happy to be back," Adjo said, riding beside me.

"I would not say happy, Adjo, for this is hardly home. We have been exiled far too long. But it will be good to be back with my brother, completing our plans for Adon. There is still much to do."

"And Yahveh, do not forget."

"Yes, and Yahveh. I spent many, many days with my priests and the Habiru leaders. Now I believe I understand Yahveh far better."

"And not much different from your Adon, is he?"

"No, not very different at all. It will now be my challenge to help Akhenadon also understand this."

"I have no doubt you will do so. You took a great chance going back to Goshen, but from all I have heard, it was successful."

"That is according to how you view success as far as our respective Gods go, yes. And I learned much about what is going on in our country, but the news was not all good."

"We do live in troubled times, Aharon. No doubt about that."

As we got close to the mountain, Joshua came running down to greet us and help ferry supplies to our hideout. It took the entire day to do so, for Adon's disk was scorching. When all was ferried up and stored, we sat for an evening meal. Akhenadon said the blessing. I watched him with new eyes due to my absence, and I saw that he had aged, not in my missing three months, but since our exile. He was bent over, and he now had a great white beard that blew in the wind. I had left my staff with him when I traveled to Goshen, for I did not want to be easily spotted. But I noted that he now used it just to get from one spot to another. My heart sank, thinking of what would happen if Akhenadon passed to the next world before our work was done.

I asked Akhenadon to wait for us to talk until Adjo's group left. After we finished eating, I introduced Akhenadon to the young scribe, Menna, whom I had brought back with me from Goshen. We had long recognized that we needed a true scribe to write down all the customs that we were developing since I was slow at this task. He brought with him a donkey laden with parchments, inks, and writing tablets. Menna was a trained and trusted Adon priest and had risen in the ranks, so he was now a scribe instructor to many.

That evening, Akhenadon and I sat by the fire while Joshua climbed to the lookout and Menna curled up to sleep, weary from his travels.

"Tutankhamun is sick, Akhenadon. Very sick. He has turned eighteen, but he has the mosquito illness, and his very bones are painful, I was told. It is Aye who runs Kem. Tutankhamun is hardly able to go out."

"What about Nefertiti?"

"She, like the rest of us, is aging and also in ill health. She is not involved in Tutankhamun's rule any longer, although I heard from my priests that her ministers... Tutankhamun's ministers... love her and visit her often to seek her advice."

"I sometimes think it to be a dream, Aharon, that once I loved such a wonderful woman. She was as beautiful on the inside as her outer beauty."

"Well, do I know that, brother. In my own way, I loved her, too. We all grew to adulthood together."

"Perhaps it is best to be left with the dream. None of her beauty will ever fade." He sighed. "Now tell me the rest."

"Our priests report that Waset is full of anxiety, worrying about succession. Apparently, Horemheb is the choice of the Amun priests and…"

"You mean Maya's choice."

"Not only Maya, for he, too, is aging and not in good health. But there are sources that say that Aye is trying to hold on to power, in one way or another."

"Well, of course, he is the most experienced. He would be a good advisor."

"Apparently not to Horemheb. The two are now enemies, rivaling for power… perhaps… perhaps even the throne."

"Nonsense, Aye is too old to be crowned King of the Two Lands. He has always been best behind the throne."

"Perhaps you are right. I felt it was critical that we get detailed reports from Adjo every visit. I have instructed my most trusted priest to gather all the information he can and meet with Adjo before he leaves. I have told no one where we are camped. My priest only knows that Adjo can get us messages."

"Well done, as usual, Aharon." Akhenadon poked the fire with a branch and threw on another stick of firewood. "While you were away, I had some excellent conversations with Joshua. He is a true believer in Adon and was raised to worship Yahveh. Of course, he continually tries to convince me to have more fighters here, but I tell him we are nearing the end of our exile."

"Do you believe that?"

"I do. Tomorrow I will hike to the taller peak. Joshua has made a place up there for me. I wish to be closer to Adon. I wish to open my heart, ask questions, to feel His presence. In a ten-day, when I return, I expect there will be much to discuss."

As promised, Akhenadon descended on the tenth day and joined us for the morning meal. He seemed… lighter as if a great burden was lifted from him. He often smiled during the meal. When we were done, and our plates and utensils cleaned, he bade us join him as we sat around the fire.

"Adon has spoken to me," he said, swaying from one side to another as if in prayer. "He has instructed me to prepare to once again lead my people. Not the Kemian people… the believers in Adon, for I now understand they are my true people. I am to mold them into a nation… a great nation such as has not been seen before." He paused to collect his thoughts. I saw that Joshua and Menna were transfixed by Akhenadon's words.

"We will make our way from Kem to Canaan and dwell there, for Adon said the land is the right one for us, far away from the temptations of Kem." He stopped, and we sat in silence, awe and fear, for many moments. The fire itself seemed to crackle with new intensity.

"Are you quite sure of this, Akhenadon?" I asked. "There is so much to be done."

"Yes, are you sure?" Joshua asked. "I have heard the Canaanites are a fierce people, full of giants, fierce warriors." Akhenadon smiled.

"First to you, Joshua. Of course, you think as a warrior, and I love that in you. You are strong and brave, and Adon has told me that we will need an army once we leave Kem. And you, my son, will be the General of that army." In seconds I witnessed the transformation in Joshua's face. He quickly beamed with pride. He stood up, then bowed low to the ground.

"No, no, please rise, Joshua. From here on, there will be no bowing to a King. From now on, I am the leader of Adon's worshipers, and that is all." I must say that those words surprised me.

"And for you, my dear, dear brother, I will say this. I have never been surer of anything. You and Joshua, and even young Menna, will continue to help me to draft the laws and customs that will bind the Adonites together. Adon himself has shown me the way, and it is as clear as the view from up above," he said, pointing to the peak where he stayed.

"Fear not, for when Kem was created from the mound of Nun, it was Adon who did that. But he made not only Kem, he created the entire world," he said, spreading his arms. "It was Adon then, and it is Adon now, for He will create a nation anew!"

The next months were a desert storm of activity. From morning to night, we sat, paced, argued, and put to parchment some of the laws that Akhenadon said Adon had wanted. I was able to amend some of them because, of all present, I knew best how ordinary people might react and turn away from Adon. Akhenadon believed in his heart that we must avoid angering Adon, for He could be a vengeful God, as well as a loving one. It all depended on how closely a believer hewed to His laws and customs.

So hard did we work that poor Menna actually ran out of parchment before Adjo's next resupply? I did have a few blank sheets to give him, and at the evening meal the night that the last sheet was used, Akhenadon asked Joshua if he felt comfortable going back to Goshen before Adjo left there to secure a large supply of parchment. When Joshua agreed, Akhenadon asked for one more thing. He was to bring back a few more soldiers, highly trustworthy and ones who were raised to lead and knew the desert like none others. With Joshua in charge, they would train together, looking to the day that Joshua would raise an army.

When Adjo and Joshua returned a month later with the caravan of goods, four armed men flanked the caravans, so we knew at once that Joshua was successful. Few things were discussed at dinner other than pleasantries and gossip, after we were done, Joshua asked Akhenadon and me to join him at the lookout.

"The news," Akhenadon said.

"Tutankhamun has died and was buried in an elaborate ceremony and royal tomb. It is said that the artisans surpassed all who came before them in provisioning his tomb for his journey. He was so young, and according to Nefertiti herself, his heart was light."

"I am sorry to hear of this, even though I hardly knew my son. I will pray for his ka tonight."

"There is more, master. Just fifteen days after his death, Aye married your daughter Ankhesenamun."

"He what?" Akhenadon exclaimed, struggling to get to his feet. "That would mean…"

"He now has a legitimate claim to the throne," I added. "This is most unexpected."

"He has been planning this all along," Akhenadon said. "I was so naive, thinking him of a light heart."

"Horemheb is away at war right now fighting in the east. When I left Goshen, they expected Aye to any day name himself King."

"Horemheb will be furious, I am sure," I said. "But there will be nothing he can do except wait."

"And I've heard that Aye is ill," Joshua continued. "He will not last long, your priests say. They urge you to yet wait longer."

"As if I have not waited long enough. It has been nine years!"

I signaled to Joshua to stay quiet, to allow Akhenadon to absorb all he heard. Then I spoke.

"Akhenadon, there is much to think about and discuss. Let us sleep on it tonight before deciding on anything. Would you agree?" He nodded and walked slowly down the slope, and entered his sleeping room. I started to follow him, when Joshua grabbed my arm.

"There is yet another matter, Aharon, but I had not the heart to tell him. You must be the one." He took a deep breath.

"What is it?"
"Tiye has passed to the next world."

Scroll Thirty-Two

Our Love is An Eternal Dream

As I write this, I find it hard to believe that we waited another three years before receiving word that Aye had journeyed to meet Adon, or perhaps Anubis in the Underworld, such was his duplicitous nature. I, for one, wondered whether his heart would be lighter than a feather. I felt like a hypocrite feeling this since Adonites do not believe in such an event taking place, but to some extent, we are all captives of our upbringing, are we not?

Yet the three years were not wasted. Akhenadon and I decided that we needed to enlarge our community in order to have a hope of completing our work. The first thing he did was charge Joshua with assembling a small army.

Surprisingly, rather than immediately recruiting former Kemian soldiers, Joshua journeyed to Shechem near Canaan and spoke with the general of their army. The Shechemites were enemies of Kem and would welcome the opportunity to help a Kemian rebellion. Joshua was acquainted with the reputation of Shechemite fighters from his time serving in the army. He left Shechem with the promise that one hundred of their soldiers would soon arrive at a mountain just a half-day's journey from our camp.

In Goshen, Joshua then discreetly recruited a contingent of fifty men, including brigade captains that he knew well, to join Akhenadon. All the men were from the Delta and sympathetic to our cause. They arranged to travel separately to a meeting place, where Joshua would guide them the rest of the way to our camp.

I accompanied Joshua to Goshen with an entirely different purpose. I was to recruit a dozen priests and their scribes to join us. Some of these young priests were like sons to me, having known them since they joined the Adonite movement. The priests would be formed into groups, with each group tasked to put together different aspects of worship for Adon. There were more laws needed, observances, rituals, and customs, for these are all essential to binding a people together. Our plans seemed to be coming together.

"When we were about to leave Goshen, one of my priests came to me with news," I said to Akhenadon.

"Why have I learned not to like it when you start with that? No news is good news, but news from Kem never seems to be good."

"Aye is dead. Horemheb has married Nefertiti's sister, Mutnodjmet. So he will undoubtedly be the next King." Akhenadon looked away, disgust registering on his face.

"Is that it?"

"It would be if I were any good keeping secrets from you. I am afraid the news gets worse." Akhenadon recoiled.

"One of your loyal servants remained faithful to Nefertiti, and when I was in Goshen, the servant was secretly brought by the local Adon priest to speak with me."

"Go on."

"She said that just before marrying Mutnodjmet, Horemheb appeared at Nefertiti's home in Akhedadon. She listened to their conversation. Horemheb said that he had always loved Nefertiti and that she had wasted her life and talents staying faithful to you. He berated her. According to the servant, Nefertiti never replied to any of his words. She just stared at him once and looked away. When he was done speaking, he turned and angrily walked away towards where the servant was hiding. As he passed her and left the room, he nodded to the Captain of his guards and said, 'In Amun's name, I beg you, be quick about it.'

"She is dead, Akhenadon... murdered." I could not contain myself from sobbing. When I had no more tears, I looked up. Tears ran from Akhenadon's eyes, but otherwise, he sat up straight, his hands on his thighs, staring straight ahead. It was not until many years later that I understood how Nefertiti's murder soured Akhenadon and allowed his unspoken anger to simmer in his ba. It changed him and affected everything he would do.

If there were not so many things for us to accomplish, setting up the priestly groups, developing the rituals, and training the soldiers, I believe Akhenadon would have lived as if his ka had gone on to the Afterworld. As is, his ba changed, and he was sedate, quieter, often seeking solitude and going to his mountain peak retreat for days at a time. I once asked if writing a poem to Nefertiti would help, but he just stared at me as if I spoke a foreign tongue and did not respond.

As it turned out, Horemheb did ascend to the throne and began changes such as Kem had never before seen. First, he restored the military to its former glory, sending troops far and wide and moving Kem's enemies far back from its borders. Several of these campaigns he led bolstered his reputation as a mighty King.

Once that was accomplished, a process that took two years to complete, he began fierce destruction of all things related to the four Kings that preceded him. This was not a casual task but a determined effort to wipe all traces of Akhenadon, Smenkhkare, Aye, and Tutankhamun from Kem's history. Soldiers, artisans, and masons literally chiseled their names from stone monuments and public spaces. Even tombs were entered to obliterate paintings and mentions of these kings. All of this, of course, was supported by the Amun priests. The Royal Court and the Amun priests worked together to tax the people to support these drastic measures.

To his credit, and more probably to reduce the

possibility of dissatisfaction, Horemheb allowed the worship of Adon to continue, but only in private. No temples devoted to Adon were allowed. None.

Horemheb also changed the judicial system. He appointed judges and allowed Amun priests to rule on legal issues. One change he instituted was opposed by many, yet he persisted. Horemheb divided legal power between Upper and Lower Kem, establishing clear lines of authority between the Viziers of Waset and Inabu-hedj. It was as if he was reversing the progress we had made since King Narmer united Upper and Lower Kem some two thousand years ago. But I knew that Horemheb was smart and well versed in palace intrigue, for a divided nation was easier for him to hold onto power. He had become a master at playing one side against the other.

I relate these events here with no emotion, for I need to simply put these down for future generations. Yet the truth is that Horemheb's actions did not come easy. They fell hard on Kem.

The destruction of temples to Adon was handled completely differently than Akhenadon's destruction of Amun's temples. In Akhenadon's case, it was gradual, for the military was weak, and resistance was strong. Horemheb's plan was based on the people's desire for stability, and the sooner, the better. He unleashed army units and civil servants to destroy temples quickly, using battering rams and employing thousands of workers. Some buildings were saved and repurposed as temples to other Gods, for he now allowed full worship of any Gods to resume.

At the same time, his troops were even entering private homes to strike out the names of the four kings. This was an arduous task, and at one point, when his army units were overworked, and the destruction slowed, he called in his top general. "If I see one remaining sign of their existence in the Two Lands, heads will roll!" he was heard yelling.

I must admit that soon Kem was as stable as it was when Akhenadon's father reigned. Yet this only served to anger believers in Adon. The Amun priests were again ascendent, reviving their contacts with the wealthy and powerful whom they had put into power in the first place. From one of my high priests, I also discovered that they had managed to keep their fortunes in gold and land by legal trickery. They had simply transferred their property to wealthy patrons, with a provision that if the new owner died, all lands would revert to the priesthood. Thus, if the new owner did not give back the land at their request, he or she soon confronted Anubis.

Akhenadon was so angry at these revelations I decided it best to withhold some of the more disturbing information from him. That concerned the treatment of our Adonite priests and followers. By decree of Horemheb, they were allowed to worship Adon, but the reality was far different. They were persecuted throughout Kem and often forced to work in the quarries due to default on debt or some other minor infraction.

Life as a quarry worker was unbearable, and none but the lowliest of Kem's impoverished would choose to work there. In fact, slaves captured in battle would serve out their terms working in the quarries until they were freed. Life there was harsh. Food consisted of a piece of bread for the mid-day meal, sometimes with moldy cheese or rotten meat, and similar rations to be taken home for their families. The work was grueling, prying rocks from the cliff face, hammering them, carrying them uphill to be loaded on wagons, all under the scorching heat of Adon's disk. If a worker slowed from fatigue, he faced the searing end of a leather strap, and many bore the scars of such encounters.

The days at our camp continued each day much the same, punctuated by certain recurring events like our resupply caravans. Due to our swelling numbers, we had to divide our supply routes. One came every three months from Goshen as always, and now one came from the Shechemites each month. The soldiers also hunted the nearby valleys and mountains for dik-diks and ibex to supplement our diets.

Each morning began with prayers to Adon upon the rising of his disk, led by Akhenadon and me. Fortunately, one of the lessons Akhenadon gained from his reign was that services had to be shortened. We were able to do this by having the priest group that concerned itself with formal prayers develop a regular service schedule based on Akhenadon's guidance. Soon, every one of the Adonites knew the prayers and participated eagerly. Some even led certain portions of the service.

Evening prayers were less formal and, in most cases, were led by one of the priests. While Akhenadon was reluctant to give up this task, he soon became comfortable with it and took pride in the involvement of so many others. It gave us both hope for the future.

Yet my brother was still plagued by the death of Nefertiti, which he bore on his shoulders like a heavy weight. He slept more than he ever had. People commented on how weak he appeared. Many were the times that I tried to talk with him about her, but he always sat silently until I was done. I began to worry greatly about him.

Until one evening, when I saw him approach Menna. They talked for a moment, and Menna handed him a scroll of parchment and a pen and ink. He took them and climbed to his retreat site. I did not see him again until morning services.

During services, he seemed more animated than usual. At one point, I noted him smiling when Joshua led a prayer. When services were over, Akhenadon came to me, took my hand, and led me to the lookout. There he gave me the scroll.

"I know not how to thank you," is all he said. He left me with the scroll and walked away.

Neferneferuadon Nefertiti, you were the most beautiful one of my palace.
Your face charming, your lapis lazuli smile is still the source of my joy…
My dearest one, my mistress, my queen, your sweet voice makes me happy.

*My heart is overwhelmed by your love, you're on my
temples.
Love gives me wings that will help me fly to you…
You are my only love, the brightest star, your shining
eyes bewitch me, your arms wrap me like wattle vines…
Your hair a trap where I let myself fall, your breasts like
delicious red apples…
I breathe each word that comes out of your lotus petal
mouth.
You offer me life to love you with my whole being,
even your name is vital to me like air and blood…
Stay close to me, with me, live in me – now and until
the end of time, as our love is an eternal dream.*

Scroll Thirty-Three

Sacrifices on the Mount

Our community of Adonists and Shechemites was now sprawled across three separate mountains, all surrounding the same narrow valley. The entrance to the valley was well protected by a narrow passage with high cliffs. Joshua's men had found a deep cave toward the back of the valley where they stored weapons, donkeys, and a few horses. The priests and scribes stayed in the original encampment, although we were now crowded together, and it took much patience and mediation to keep everyone doing what was needed.

Several more years had passed during Horemheb's reign, and from all indications, things went well in Kem. Prosperity had returned, but only for those who already had it. The one difficulty that evaded Horemheb's solutions was disease and illness, which swept through villages killing and sickening many.

The Amun priests were the ones responsible for training priest physicians, and Maya had always devoted much attention to see that the training and the supply of physicians was adequate for Kem's needs. But since Akhenadon's reign disbanded the Amun priesthood, training had lapsed. And since Maya's passing due to the illness that ate from within, no one had picked up that responsibility. Kem was faced with too few physicians.

We maintained our pace and progress. We had already

developed a series of religious practices that would stand our adherents in good stead with Adon. We debated fiercely over how to merge the beliefs of Yahvehites into our beliefs. It was not easily done, for while there were significant similarities there were also differences, most especially in the names of our respective God. As we argued the points, Akhenadon left for another of his retreats, and when he returned, he met with me.

"I fasted for an entire day, and when it was over, I made a grain sacrifice to Adon as an offering," Akhenadon explained. "Afterward, I ate, yet the food would not go down. I felt instead an urge to meditate, and as soon as I did, I felt something far more pleasant than food filling my body.

"Adon spoke to me then, Aharon, so clearly I savored every word. He told me that Yahveh was the same as Adon, only Yahveh was to be Adon's unspoken name from this time forward, for Adon Himself had grown from the seed of Yahveh. The four letters that comprise it in the Habiru language of the Yahvehites are never to be spoken aloud by our adherents. They will be written in our texts but not spoken until some future time when we have earned that right through our orthodoxy. The roots of Adon in Yahveh are too deep for any person to now understand."

"Then this would allow us to appeal to the Yahvehites," I said, excited by the thought of enlarging our fledgling religion. Akhenadon looked to the heavens and laughed.

"There is more, Aharon. Adon said for me his name, Yahveh. No, no, he did not exactly say it, it was… melodic. I could not describe it, for I have never heard such sounds before. He breathed it, Aharon. It was so soft, yet it vibrated through the earth, shaking me. I felt the wind blow through my ka as He said it." Akhenadon sat, swaying back and forth, his eyes closed, yet looking toward Adon.

Suddenly he opened his eyes. "And you shall hear it, too, Aharon. For Adon told me that the High Priest must also hear it, but none others. Not until the day that Adon reveals himself to us on Earth."

I was pleased but also frightened, for I had never heard Adon's voice. The thought made me shake. "If we cannot speak his name aloud, what shall we do when we see it written?"

We will simply call Him 'The Name... or Adon.'"

"The nameless Name," I murmured.

This was added to the scrolls of laws and customs that we had compiled. On future trips back to Goshen, the priests spread the word of how our two religious beliefs were now joined. The measure of our success was that Adjo and my priests in Goshen reported many more began to attend worship to Adon.

These reports did much to bolster our moods and gave us sustenance for our work. Life in our encampment went well for several years, with no change in our routine. That all came to a quick change one afternoon.

"A military patrol approaches!" one of Joshua's soldiers suddenly yelled from the lookout. Immediately, Joshua's emergency plan went into effect. Everyone stopped what they were doing and instead put into effect the plans we had rehearsed and modified over the years.

The scribes hurriedly packed their scrolls and materials and stored them in a secret crevice on the other side of our encampment. The priests and scribes then ran down the trail to our protected area and made their way to the military cave, where a contingent of well-trained soldiers would protect them and had enough weapons to hold off a good-sized troop. The cave was on a ridge that afforded an excellent view of the valley below and an advantage against anyone coming up from below. A second, smaller cave was located a short distance away but would allow our soldiers hidden there to attack from behind anyone approaching the larger cave.

Akhenadon and I were brought to the peak where he meditated. To get to that retreat, an enemy would have to hike up an exposed rock face, subject to the arrows and spears of Joshua's defenders.

The lookout signaled to the lookouts on the other two mountains using a polished gold mirror. The Shechemites would be ready to descend from their perches in moments once given the signal. Everyone knew their places and what they should do. In moments, complete silence descended on our encampment. All was ready.

Our lookout stayed well hidden but reported back down to Joshua, who commanded the soldiers that guarded Akhenadon and me. It took an eternity for the Kemian military troop to reach us, for they were not looking for anything special but just transiting from their base to wherever was their destination. It was rare for any traveler to come so deep into the desert mountains, but it happened occasionally. In those instances, the travelers just kept on passing and never were wiser to our presence.

However, when the troops reached our mountain, it was starting to get dark, so they made camp at the base of our mountain. We counted thirty well-armed soldiers, plus their servants. It was obvious that they were en route to a border skirmish.

The night passed with no incident, but Joshua was edgy and slept little. In the morning, we expected the troop to leave, but it was clear they planned an extra day's rest. Joshua's men watched as the soldiers below sharpened their weapons, fed their animals, and lay around in the shade of the mountain. The day also passed without incident.

That evening Adon's silver disk was full and shone beautifully on the desert. We could clearly see the troops below us. Whether it was Adon's plan or just a matter of chance, one of our watchmen stood up at the lookout to get a better view of the Kemian soldiers. Just at that moment, a Kemian soldier happened to look up and distinctly saw our soldier silhouetted before the night disk's glow. And with that, pandemonium erupted.

"There is a man up there!" the soldier yelled loud enough for us to hear him in the desert mountain air. The Captain looked up quickly just as our man tried to duck, but the movement was unmistakable. The Kemians went on high alert and posted guards around their campsite. We knew that the morning would bring trouble.

Joshua sent one of his men with his plan to the cave harboring our priests and another man to the Shechemites on the neighboring mountain, both dangerous missions. Both arrived back safely near dawn.

As soon as Adon's disk began to light up the sky, the Kemians awoke and mustered at the center of their camp. They sent out scouts around the mountain to survey for a route to the top. It did not take long for them to find our trail. By then, Joshua had his traps set. Before he took his position, he checked on our safety in the cave. Six of his best men crouched near the entrance, heavily armed with bows and arrows, spears and swords. They had rehearsed this countless times over the years.

Sooner than I thought possible, the Captain of the Kemians emerged from the trail and stood in the camp, followed by a dozen of his men, all of them with swords drawn, looking about nervously. They quickly saw the building we slept in and the campfire. The Captain walked to it as his men nervously stood next to him, ready to act.

"The fire is still warm," he said, looking up at a soldier with an armband indicating valor. "This was an established camp. Be wary. We may have lucked upon the encampment of the heretic King that we have heard so much about. There is a steep price on his head to be shared among us." He stood and looked around.

"You men, enter that building… carefully… and see what you can find. My guess is that they scurried away during the night like rats, and we will have to track them." Eight of the men carefully entered the building. As soon as they disappeared from sight, one of our men guarding the cave stood quietly and sent an arrow straight through the heart of the Captain. The other soldier had no time to react when another arrow pierced his neck in a burst of blood. Both fell silently where they stood.

Joshua appeared with ten of his men, and they took up positions on either side of the building. When the soldiers started to exit the building, each one was dispatched with an arrow from our cave defenders. Although the spectacle of such carnage made me ill, I admired the accuracy of our men, no doubt the result of Joshua's insistence on constant practice and refinement of their skills.

Finally, three Kemian soldiers burst out of the doorway together, swords ready. Joshua waved off the archers and instead had his men engage the enemy with their swords, for he later told me that his men needed the experience of actual combat. The skirmish was over quickly, with only one of our soldiers injured, albeit with a serious slashing wound.

"Well, we have entered new territory," Joshua said as he surveyed the scene. "We must finish the job so we can hide all traces of this, or else we will be attacked by forces we cannot even imagine."

The remaining Kemian soldiers had entered the valley, a force of some twenty men, some armed with spears and swords, others with bows and arrows ready to shoot. They moved slowly among the sand and rocks, staying together, examining the mountain walls for signs of their enemies. Not a sound could be heard.

We knew that Joshua would avoid a battle on open ground, for it would put his soldiers on an equal footing with the well-trained Kemian warriors. Using a hand signal, he had the men in the caves stand down.

When the Kemians finally found the path leading to our trail, they posted two guards and continued walking around the edges of the valley until they found the trail that led to the large cave on the second mountain. With that discovery, they split into two groups, each one ascending one of the trails they had discovered.

The going was difficult for them, for they had to avoid large rocks, all the while straining their necks to keep a vigil above them. When they were halfway up the trails, Joshua gave the signal to attack.

Joshua would like to have said that it was a glorious battle, fought hand to hand and showing our soldiers' valor.

But it was not like that at all. The Kemians were in a terrible position on the trail and vulnerable to the arrows and spears of our soldiers.

By Joshua's plan, the Shechemites had come down from their mountain base and stood by the narrow entrance to the valley to prevent any Kemians from escaping, but they need not have bothered. In but half an hour, every Kemian was dead or wounded, and Joshua gave the order to kill any that survived.

It was only as our soldiers, and the Shechemites dragged down the bodies and buried them deeply to erase any trace of what had happened that Joshua suddenly stood up, looking around in confusion. He turned and raced back up the mountain to our camp as the soldiers in the valley wondered what was happening, and many followed him. We had already come out of the cave by the time Joshua appeared in the camp.

"Where is my watchman?" he shouted. "My watchman, where is he?" No-one answered.

Joshua ran to the lookout and peered out. Far in the distance were a few dots of men on horseback. His shoulders slumped, and he stood for a moment, trying to gather his thoughts. Now he ran back down.

"Quick, get back down and send a contingent of ten good men on horses to chase those servants who escaped," he said to one of his captains.

"We do not have ten horses, sir," the soldier said. "We have but two, and the Shechemites may have two or three more."

"Alright, then send how many you can. We must kill those servants before they spread word of this to Horemheb. Go!"

I went to Joshua to see what was happening. "In the heat of battle, I forgot to post a watchman on the lookout. It is my stupidity. From what I could see, all the servants escaped."

The next days were fraught with worry as we waited for word from our pursuing soldiers. Finally, they began to come back in separate groups. They joined us as soon as they arrived.

"Some of them tried to escape on donkeys, and we caught up with them quickly. The ones on horses split up. We managed to capture only two of them. The rest got away."

Joshua hung his head, thinking of his next move. Akhenadon and I stood next to him.

"These deaths are troubling to me," Akhenadon quietly said. "The battle and the killing of innocent servants, they all plague my heart. Yet I know that this had to be done." Joshua turned to face him.

"We tried not to engage, but...."

"I know, my faithful servant, and I do not blame you at all. I saw that you did what was needed. But word will get back to Horemheb. We have no choice. We must move... now."

"Move? But where?" Joshua asked.

Akhenadon looked to the heavens but did not answer.

Scroll Thirty-Four

And So, It Is Written

Our journey was grueling. There were times when I thought we would not make it. For three long months, we journeyed across the length of the Mafkat before crossing over to Canaan and then to Shechem.

We now had more than two hundred and fifty people in our caravan, one hundred Shechemites, and the rest an assortment of our soldiers, priests, scribes, and adherents. It was a sad lot, for most of us had no experience with desert travel. We had to take very difficult routes in order to avoid Kemian troops, who were now on high alert after the report of the massacre. We traveled mostly at night, with Adjo guiding us.

Word reached us that Horemheb had dispatched more than a thousand troops to capture me. Fortunately, they spent months preparing for their campaign, assembling the troops, training them, and finally embarking. When they reached the approximate site of our exile, it took them two ten-days to locate the correct mountain, surround it, and try to negotiate with our ghosts. By then, we were almost in Canaan.

The Shechemites were welcoming to us, but many in their Royal Court did not want to risk harboring us for fear of Kem's might. Eventually, they settled us on Mount Ebal, as Joshua persuaded them of our need for a strong defense.

The Shechemite warriors who had come to our assistance in the Mafkat were happy to be home, but they were soon dispatched to the border, along with the rest of their army, in case the Kemian army found us through their network of spies and decided to come after us. In Waset, we were tried in our absence for killing Kemian soldiers, and the Shechemites felt there would be good cause for Kem to pursue us across the border.

While we waited to see what would happen, I immediately set up our working groups again, transcribing the laws and re-copying them over and over as they were revised. One day, in our discussion, the issue was raised that most of our adherents could not read. They would, of course, learn most of what they would need to know orally. But even then, we determined that Akhenadon needed to come up with some definitive laws or guiding principles that were easy to understand.

Akhenadon and I spent many nights discussing what we could do. One night I suggested that he consult the Forty Two Negative Confessions for guidance. He looked at me for the longest time, thinking.

"You are right again, Aharon. Why did I not think of this? Excellent idea. I will do so and also ask Adon for guidance."

As he sat in deep thought, I suddenly laughed.

"What is so funny?" Akhenadon asked.

"I must admit", I said, smiling, "that it is an odd sight seeing you with hair on your head and a flowing beard blowing in the desert night breeze".

"And white hair at that", Akhenadon replied, turning to look at me.

"Times have changed and we with it", I sighed, stroking my own beard. "If anyone doubts that we have severed our ties with our homeland, let them gaze upon us as proof". We sat silently, staring at the fire, lost in thought.

The Forty-Two Negative Confessions was the list of behaviors that a person facing Anubis had to state they did not engage in before their heart was weighed. It was a cornerstone of Kemian religious thought for a thousand years or more. I retrieved a scroll of the Confessions that I had brought with us from Kem. Akhenadon unrolled it before me one night, and we reviewed it carefully.

Forty-Two Negative Confessions
I have not committed sin.
I have not committed robbery with violence.
I have not stolen.
I have not slain men and women.
I have not stolen grain.
I have not purloined offerings.
I have not stolen the property of the Gods.
I have not uttered lies.
I have not carried away food.
I have not uttered curses.
I have not committed adultery.
I have made none to weep.
I have not eaten the heart [i.e., I have not grieved uselessly,
or felt remorse].
I have not attacked any man.
I am not a man of deceit.
I have not stolen cultivated land.
I have not been an eavesdropper.
I have slandered no man.
I have not been angry without just cause.
I have not debauched the wife of any man.
I have not debauched the wife of any man (to a different
God).
I have not polluted myself.
I have terrorized none.
I have not transgressed the Law.
I have not been cruel.
I have not shut my ears to the words of truth.
I have not blasphemed.
I am not a man of violence.
I am not a stirrer up of strife.
I have not acted or judged with undue haste.

I have not pried into matters.
I have not multiplied my words in speaking.
I have wronged none, I have done no evil.
I have not blasphemed the King.
I have never stopped the flow of water.
I have never raised my voice in anger.
I have not cursed or blasphemed God.
I have not acted with evil rage.
I have not stolen the bread of the Gods.
I have not carried away the khenfu cakes from the
spirits of the dead.
I have not snatched away the bread of the child, nor
treated with contempt the God of my city.
I have not slain the cattle belonging to the God.

"It is a start," Akhenadon said, "but I fear it is too long… far too long."

"I agree, we must simplify it."

Akhenadon left a few days later and went to a nearby cave protected, of course, by a contingent of guards. After five days, he returned.

"I have asked Adon which of the Confessions is most important for our people to abide… or if there are ones that should be added." Akhenadon looked troubled.

"He told me that he would not give me an answer but that we should wrestle with this and then bring to Him those that we feel are needed. Only then will He respond."

"This is a show of the faith that Adon has in you, brother."

Yet faith was perhaps the furthest from our minds when we were summoned to a meeting with Labaya, King of Shechem.

"My scouts tell me that the Kemian army, perhaps one thousand or more strong, are but two days from us," he said nervously. "They have sent a messenger to us demanding that we surrender the both of you to them, along with the warrior, Joshua."

"And what will you do?" I asked.

The King looked carefully at Akhenadon. "You are indeed a strange man, Akhenadon, in looks and heart. Some say a prophet, others an evil spirit. But your passionate beliefs go back in our history when we sheltered one of Tiye's relatives. Although I do not believe in your Adon, as you call him, I feel we have a duty from our Gods to protect you. So say our priests.

"So we will do our best, but hear me, so you are prepared. If Kem persists, there is nothing we can do to stop them. I will not sacrifice our small army to slaughter. If they invade, I will send a message to you so you may escape.

"In the meantime, I have called upon our alliances with the Moabites, Midianites, and even the Azirus to aid us. We shall see if they have the stomach for a fight."

All I could do was bow before Labaya and thank him. Akhenadon gave the King a blessing before we left.

The fateful day came, and we watched from our Mount as the Kemian troops began to appear far on the horizon. It was a fearsome sight. One thousand charioteers, infantry swordsmen, spear vanguards, and archers all marched in formation to the border.

"He is no longer in our territory," the General of the Shechemite army lied to his Kemian counterpart. "If you insist on wasting your time invading, we will not oppose you in the open wheat fields we now stand in."

"A wise decision," the Kemian General said, smiling, as his charioteer controlled the spirited horses.

"We wish no fight with the Two Lands. However, we will fight you in the hill country, which we know like the backs of our hands. Our allies are already here, and they will join us. Just as you would do, we must protect our land and people."

The Kemian General stared at his adversary, trying to gain a measure of the man. Was he bluffing? Would they dare risk a battle with Kem, a war they would surely lose badly? But a series of sneak attacks and smaller skirmishes would demoralize his troops. How badly did Horemheb want the heretic, a King whose reign had already been wiped from Kemian memory?

"I will give you two days to reconsider. At that time, we will make a decision. We have other border situations to deal with," he said as he ordered his charioteer to turn back. But they both knew that the decision had already been made.

With the withdrawal of the Kemian army, we jumped back into our work, and the first topic that we needed to debate was that of circumcision. Would we insist that adherents be circumcised? Was that truly necessary? This was a difficult issue because the majority of our believers were not circumcised.

"But the fact is that you, Aharon, Akhenadon, and the rest of the priests, even some of the scribes, are circumcised," one of the priests argued. "The people will want to be like you, like Akhenadon, like us."

"We all know how painful the process can be if not done properly," another priest offered. "If this becomes a requirement, I fear that many, many men will refuse to commit to Adon and will take their families with them."

"As priests, we shave ourselves to keep ourselves clean and free of vermin. With circumcision, there is not a bad smell from down there, either. It would be in the best interests to promote cleanliness wherever we can."

So the debate went on for many days before we put it aside, only to pick it up again and again. Finally, we came to an agreement. Circumcision would be required, and while there were several reasons for this decision, Akhenadon said it best.

"To be an Adonite will require a big commitment. It should not be an easy decision. If there is sacrifice involved, it will make that commitment even more significant. I will say that Adon requires it as a bond between Him and His people.

"However, unlike how it is done in Kem, and well, I remember my circumcision when I ascended to the throne as an adult, we will do the circumcisions soon after the male child is born. That way, he will have no memory of it, and he will be considered an Adonite from birth. We will also train priests to do this correctly, with sharp instruments bathed in juniper juice."

We debated the status of women, for Kem was the land that gave the most freedom to women in the entire world that we knew. Women in Kem had the right to divorce, the right to own businesses, the right to sue in court, and the right to pass on inheritances to whomever they wished. And our very King was legitimized only by his mother's or wife's royal birth. We decided then that the status of any person's right as an Adonite would pass down through the mother.

Slowly, painfully slowly, the laws, rituals, customs, and beliefs began to be expanded. Scroll after scroll was filled with our writings so that the stack they made was nearly as tall as Joshua's sword. The hopes of all of us were buoyed by our achievements.

"This has been an extraordinary time for us," Akhenadon said one night as we sat around a small fire next to his tent. "With you at my side, we have accomplished more than I ever imagined." He held out his hand, and I grabbed it, and we shook them together as we nodded. I thought I saw a tear in his eye.

"You know better than anyone, my brother, how I felt being King. I wanted it so badly when I was co-regent. I thought it would solve everything. It is only now, in my advanced years, that I realize that greatness, at least for me, did not depend on being King. No, not at all. Tiye was correct.

"Instead, I see my role clearly. To birth a new people, one devoted to Adon, the One and Only God… a just people, with firm laws, moral guidance, and rituals and customs to keep us all bound together in community. That is greatness. That shall be my legacy."

Scroll Thirty-Five

Reclaim Your Birthright

It was no more than three months after the Kemian army left us in peace that we received word from Goshen. Horemheb had been wounded in battle. His wound had festered on his trip back from Kush, and by the time he reached the physicians of the Royal palace in Waset, he was near death.

"But who is there to replace him should he pass from this world?" Akhenadon asked. Often recently, I look upon my brother as he speaks and think I am hearing a different man. He has aged greatly, and no one from his past life would recognize him with his white hair and beard. But his tortured body was still unmistakable, although greatly stooped. He now always walked haltingly with a staff.

"I am told his Upper Kem Vizier, Paramesse, was his choice," I explained. "He has great trust in him and has groomed him for the throne. Horemheb never fathered a child, so Paramesse will need to marry into your bloodline."

By now, we had all but completed the entire basic structure of Adon's worship. It was no small feat, for when we separated them into discreet sections, they were many scrolls worth. We had already begun training priests in the details of the laws, customs, and rituals so that they could serve as judges in disputes.

But the news of Horemheb's serious illness and the possibility he may already be dead caused a fierce debate within our community. Was now the time for Akhenadon to return to Kem to reclaim his birthright? Was it time to attempt to resurrect the worship of Adon? And if we did do so, was it to be exclusive or with an allowance for Kemians to worship other Gods if they chose to do so?

Abihu, one of my High Priests, who I had known since he was an initiate, and who was to me like a son, spoke up at one of our meetings. "I know, Akhenadon, that you feel you do not wish to return to Kem, but I urge you to reconsider. Please listen to why so many of us feel you must return."

"Must return. Those are words filled with strong judgment, Abihu." Akhenadon sighed. "I am old and frail," he continued, this time looking around the table at the other priests, many of whom had pieces of parchment spread before them.

"In my younger life, I thought that being King of Kem would make me all-powerful, that whatever I decided would be embraced by all. But I was a foolish youth. A King is nothing more than a figurehead, manipulated by those who have something to gain. Now, in my old age, I see what true power is. To start a new devotion, to bring people closer to God. To have people embrace the truth that there is only one God, Adon. That is what I wish to do until Adon calls me to his side."

Not a word was spoken in response. Akhenadon leaned back in his chair, obviously tired. "My brother, if you will but stay as you are and perhaps just listen, with open ears, to what Abihu has to say," I said softly. "There is no need to even respond. But I agree that you should at least hear him out, for there are things happening in Kem of which you are not aware."

"And you are in agreement that I should seek to regain my throne?"

"I did not say that, for I have strong doubts it would be a wise action. But I do feel that you should have the facts so you can speak with Adon and together make a wise decision." Akhenadon thought for a moment and nodded. I indicated to

Abihu he should continue. He took a deep breath.

"Master, when you left Kem, you left behind thousands of believers in Adon. They are passionate in their devotion and want to understand better how to worship our One and Only God. What I must tell you is that these adherents are suffering mightily. Not merely by not being able to worship in temples or together at all. No. Horemheb's spies have found them out, and he has banished every one of them from government service.

"They have been placed into forced labor for the most minor infractions. They are like slaves in the quarries, working for a slice of stale, sandy bread and perhaps a piece of moldy cheese, with no chance to pay off their debts. Even mothers are torn away from their children."

"I did not know this," Akhenadon said, turning to me. "Why was I not told?"

"There were simply too many other things to deal with and no possibility of doing anything about these affairs while Horemheb ruled with his sword." Akhenadon hung his head.

So it was that Akhenadon retreated for a ten-day to ask for guidance from Adon. While he was gone, anxiety, expectation, and even hope simmered within the camp, a thick brew that permeated everything we did. At the end of the time, Akhenadon called me to the cave where he rested.

"It was difficult," he began, "but Adon helped me to see things in a new light." He looked at me and smiled.

"Why the smile?" I asked.

"Because of my love for you, my brother. Because when I am most obstinate, when I am locked into a position and cannot see any way out, you come along and force open my heart, not with anger or harsh words, but with a gentle prod, with wise words often spoken as a question. For this, I am most grateful." I hung my head down in embarrassment.

"And I do it for my love for you, my brother." I looked up, and we connected as deeply as ever.

"My heart hurts with the hardships my adherents

experience. I birthed them into this, and I will not allow their devotion to die through my neglect. I will go back to Kem. I dread it, but I will return, but not to claim the throne. I have no interest in it. The love of my life was ripped from me. My mother is gone. The entire Royal Court and the Amun priests are like desert vipers.

"No, I will return to gather my people, and only them, and take them from Kem to a new land."

"But how?" I asked.

"I have thought about this. I will start with the simplest of ways. I will just ask the new King to allow our people to leave. There are probably only a few thousand of them. Kem does have laws. Our people are free to move about as they like. If anything, doing this will free the King and the Amun priests from having the Adonites to deal with."

"And if they do not allow you to just take our people?" Akhenadon waited to answer.

"We will deal with that at the time, for Adon assures me that He will be there at our sides. But, right now, there will be many things to do to prepare for the journey."

I did not pursue this any further, for I knew that Akhenadon was exhausted. My heart raced with the possibilities and the challenges that faced us.

Once the decision had been made, Joshua asked to speak with Akhenadon and me privately.

"Akhenadon, I must prepare the army for the march and for protecting you while you are in Kem. I need to plan with both of you."

Akhenadon looked at me before speaking. "Joshua, you have become like a son to me. You have saved us from certain death on more than one occasion. But hear me out on this matter." Akhenadon sipped from his beer.

"We will not be taking an army with us into Kem…"

"What? What do you mean? There are forces there aligned against you."

"I am aware of that. There is no point antagonizing the Kemian army, for they would squash us like dung beetles. We would be defenseless no matter how well-trained we are. I have another idea that I think will work, and I was planning to speak with you about it in the next day or two. Trust me, for Adon, has lit the path."

"Of course, I trust you and Adon. Will you allow me to provide at least a personal corps of guards as you travel around Kem?"

"We will discuss all of that when I present my ideas to you. Give me a few days, and then we shall meet."

The plan was simple enough but too simple for Joshua's liking. In order not to stir up trouble, Joshua would lead a small group of soldiers disguised as traders in a caravan to Goshen. There he would wait as more and more of his soldiers made their way to Goshen in small groups, either by caravan or boat. Once in Goshen, they would muster secretly under the protection of Adonite priests and Yahvehite believers.

The Shechemites would be ready to provide additional assistance once we were back in the Mafkat. Joshua had set up a horse and rider relay system to get a message to them quickly if they were needed. Akhenadon and I would have a small contingent of guards dressed as traders to accompany us to Goshen.

Several ten days before we were to leave, I received a message by boat from Adjo. Horemheb had died, and the Vizier Paramesse had indeed been named King and had chosen the name Ramses for the throne. Kem was as strong as it ever was, and indications were that Ramses would continue Kem's strong path. Our success was far from assured.

But our priests still in Kem, at my urging and those of the four High Priests I had named, had gathered a wide range of information that could help us achieve our goal. Not all things were good in Kem. The common people were upset with the taxes and corruption. They were plagued by illnesses and diseases. And it appeared that the government was not meeting the needs of the people.

And so, on the first month of Proyet, we were prepared to leave Shechem and began our journey home after so many hard years. Our plan was to sail down the Great Green to get to Goshen.

As we all sat waiting for word from Joshua that all was ready for us in Goshen, I marveled at the changes in Akhenadon. He was truly a changed man. He no longer claimed birthright to the throne. He only wanted Ramses to let his people be free to worship Adon.

Scroll Thirty-Six

Preparation

"May I remind you, dear wife, that despite your complaints, Aye has provided for us lavishly," Kha said, swatting a mosquito on his arm as he sat in a comfortable rush chair.

"Lavish? How can anyone call living in Goshen lavish?" Meryt answered back, hands on her hips as she turned from the pot she was stirring. "It is a place of idiots, of the basest people I have ever met. There is not one in a hundred who can even read!"

"We await Akhenadon's return, my love, and then all will be set right. You must continue to be patient."

"Patient, you say. For ten or more years, we have waited patiently. Is that not patient enough? We left all our friends and relatives back in Set Maat, first to bake in Adon's oven, and now...."

"Now what? Have you lost all faith?"

"Faith? Oh, no, I have faith," she said, holding up her stirring spoon as it dripped onto the earthen floor. "I have faith that these damned mosquitos will devour us! I have faith that Akhenadon will fly down on one of Adon's rays to save us all, and the Amun priests will all become believers in Adon." Meryt turned back to the pot.

Kha struggled to his feet, his back aching more from

sitting too much than from the hard work that he was used to. He put his hands softly on Meryt's shoulders. "You have been the best wife a man could ever wish for," he said. "And the best mother to our children, who have grown into strong and worthy adults. You have sacrificed much, my love.

"You are smart enough to realize that it is not Akhenadon who should command our anger. It is the King and his corrupt Amun priesthood. They have driven Adon's son, his messenger, from Kem because they could not tolerate the truth. They will pay for their sins."

Kha turned Meryt around and hugged her tight to him. "We must remain steadfast, Meryt. We must not surrender to doubt. I hear from Joshua from time to time, and all is well with Akhenadon. We are all in his heart. He will return. He will be victorious. I promise you."

"I do not know why I have such doubts," Meryt whispered. "I wish my faith ran as deep as yours. I will try harder, I promise." She turned to stir the pot of stew.

Two days later, a messenger arrived at their door to summon Kha to a meeting but would not reveal its purpose. They walked for a long time, using narrow alleys, at times doubling back, at other times stopping to await a nod from lookouts that were positioned at strategic points. Finally, they reached a cave near the base of a small mountain. Two guards allowed them to enter. Joshua rose to greet them, dressed as a poor peasant. The messenger then left the two men for their meeting.

"It is good to see you, Joshua," Kha began, moving with open arms to hug Joshua tightly.

"And good to see you again, Kha. It has been far too long. These journeys back to Goshen have become more difficult with Royal Guards and regular army soldiers working harder to find Akhenadon."

"How is Akhenadon's health?"

"That is difficult to answer, my friend. Outwardly he appears healthy. He climbs the cliffs up and down so that his body is in good shape. But he eats too little and sleeps even less.

His heart is plagued with worries. He misses Nefertiti. He misses you and his most loyal believers. He prays to Adon for guidance and has written down Adon's wishes for how we must behave.

"But what bothers him most is that he feels he must return to Kem to finish what he started. He hears of the difficulties his believers face under the thumb of the King and his corrupt priesthood. He has given up hope of ruling Kem. He simply wants to take his people out of Egypt and settle them in a new land where we can worship Adon in peace."

"Somehow, I do not think that simple. Do you think the King will just let the Adonites leave Kem... just like that?" Kha said, waving his hand toward the ceiling.

"And that is why I have set up this meeting, to discuss with you the preparations that will be needed."

"Preparations? For what?"

"I tell you this in complete confidence, Kha. You must keep this secret from everyone, even from Meryt. We are close to Akhenadon's return. Very close." Kha stood. He paced away from Joshua, his hands clasped in front of him, his heart beating quickly in his chest. After all this time, he could hardly believe what Joshua had just revealed.

"Is this true, Joshua? Is this truly to be soon?"

"I would not make a joke about something this serious," Joshua said, smiling. "The time has come. We must be ready. You will play an important role."

"Me? Now you are joking, right? Am I to build a new tomb here in Goshen? How am I to play an important role in his arrival in Kem?"

"Please sit, Kha, for there is much to discuss. And, no, I am not joking. Please take a breath and open your ears, for I relay a message directly from Akhenadon's lips. He has discussed this with Aharon and me, and we are all in agreement. You are the best man for the job that I am about to place upon your shoulders."

Kha just stared at Joshua for several moments. "Please

excuse me. I should have also asked about Aharon's well-being."

Joshua looked down. "Honestly, Kha, he is heavily burdened. He has always been the rock upon which Akhenadon stands. Without his brother, and I confide in you in this, I believe Akhenadon would have been deaf to Adon's voice and blind to his presence. I sometimes wonder which is the holier of the two. But it really is of no matter. I have come to understand they are truly as much one person as any two people can be. I believe that Adon planned it this way from their births, for no one person could carry the unimaginable burdens placed upon their shoulders."

Kha leaned forward, his fingertips touching. He nodded at Joshua's words, for this young man had expressed his own thoughts better than anyone had ever done. Finally, he took a deep breath and leaned back.

"So, what will you have me do?"

Scroll Thirty-Seven

Let My People Go

It took far longer for us to actually leave Shechem than we originally thought it would. We had to wait for Joshua to get his men settled and lodging arranged for the rest of his soldiers. Desert storms and wretched ones on the shores of the Great Green, where several of our soldiers and two priests drowned, caused interminable delays so that it was months before we actually were able to board our vessels, a ragtag collection at best. Yet such ancient, leaky boats would arouse no suspicion when we landed.

As soon as we arrived, Adjo met us and took us to a side alley. "This is unbelievable, but Ramses has died."

"Died? What is happening? He reigned for but…What? A year?" I was shocked by the news.

"Sixteen months," Adjo replied.

"Murdered?"

"No, not that we know. He had a bone illness and was in much pain. He died in his sleep."

"So, now what happens?" Akhenadon asked.

"He has one son who is off at war. He has fought the Hittites for years and is an accomplished warrior. He is supposedly very tough on the inside as well as the outside and commands the respect of his army."

"So he is away during the seventy days of

mummification. Isn't that unusual?" I asked.

"It is, but what can one do? It was not his choice to be away. He inherits a strong Kem due to Horemheb's rule, so he need not worry about not being here, so long as he returns to Waset before his father's funerary procession."

Once again, we were delayed in putting our plans into action, exposing us to discovery by the Royal family or the Amun priesthood. Because of that, we decided to seclude ourselves, and we asked Adjo and my four High Priests to be silent about our arrival. Still, Joshua was concerned and arranged for us to be safely hidden.

After the funeral of Ramses and the ascension of the new King, we gave time for King Seti Merenptah to become settled in his new duties. The new King's name meant 'Man of Set, beloved of Ptah', so there was no doubt as to what his religious beliefs would be. I sent a messenger to the Royal palace in Waset requesting a meeting. And with that simple request, Kem erupted into an uproar never before known.

To be sure that Akhenadon was still alive came as a shock to the Royal Court. Although Horemheb was the last of that Court to ever know Akhenadon, his legacy was known to many, despite the destruction of all he had created. Others considered him a mut spirit come back to do evil.

The Amun priesthood was particularly up in arms over Akhenadon's return, for in him, they once again saw a threat to their authority. Our priests reported meetings going on amongst them constantly as they tried to determine the effects of his sudden appearance.

Yet the biggest uproar, one that could not be anticipated or contained, was when our adherents heard that Akhenadon had returned. The streets of every village and town were filled with rumors that Adon had brought him back from the dead in order to lead his people to worship. They danced in the streets and sang Akhenadon's praises.

Dwellers in Goshen were especially taken by the news. It soon came out that Akhenadon was hidden in Goshen, and people rallied in the streets celebrating him and Adon.

Hundreds of farmers, artisans, and businessmen travelled from Upper Kem to Goshen, hoping to see him.

"We cannot contain this any longer," Nadab, one of the High Priests, said at a meeting. "There will be riots in the streets if you do not allow the people to see you and begin addressing them. It should also help your standing with Seti when you two meet."

"You know I am not a public speaker," Akhenadon replied gently. "I am old, bent, and my stutter is worse than ever. I cannot do this."

"We can do this together," I volunteered. "I have always been your spokesperson. I can do most of the talking, and my voice is loud enough for a crowd to hear." I could see Akhenadon wavering. "Will you let us give it a try? Our people need us. They are devoted to Adon. That has always been your desire."

He shook his head in agreement, and for the next several days, we made our plans while waiting for an answer from King Seti. None arrived. We truly did not expect an answer quickly. The request surprised the Royal Court, and Seti's advisors were seeking a way to deal with this new situation. That would entail meetings with governors, wealthy businessmen, government ministers, and above all, the Amun priesthood.

By the end of our planning, the priests had put word on the streets that Akhenadon would appear before them the next day, soon after Adon's disk rose. We had secretly been moved to the home of an Adonite devotee, a businessman trading exotic gifts from Babylon, Lebanon, and Canaan. His home was situated on a hillside.

Joshua's troops stood by, anticipating a small crowd, but that was not to be the case. More than a thousand people gathered, pushing their way to the front to catch a glimpse of their spiritual leader, all of them screaming, women ululating, all there to see the man who was steeped in myth, the Son of Adon.

Joshua called for reinforcements to cordon off the

hillside. "Move back!" the soldiers shouted. "Give everyone a chance to witness Akhenadon's return!" Only after they joined spears to create a human fence and pushed back forcefully, did the crowd obey.

And then Akhenadon walked out the door, holding his staff, his white hair shimmering in Adon's golden light, his white robe illuminated as if aglow, his long beard bent by the warm morning desert breeze. I had expected the crowd to cheer him raucously, but rather than bedlam, the crowd, suddenly grew silent. They stared open-mouthed, heads moving side to side to have a better view. It was probable that not one of them had ever laid eyes on Akhenadon as a King. To see his distorted face came as a shock to many.

Many held up their hands to him, and others dropped to their knees in the sand. Some bowed low to the ground, and most shook and wept uncontrollably. Then, slowly at first, some of the people began to cheer. In a growing crescendo, others cheered, and soon all did so wildly. They jumped up and down. Finally, there was no way the enthusiasm of the crowds could be contained, and they pushed through the soldiers' fence and rushed upward toward where we stood.

Akhenadon stayed his ground, pointed his staff at the advancing crowd, and held up his free hand. The crowd stopped, holding back in awe. While Akhenadon was not good at speaking, his singing was godly. And so, as the crowd quieted before him, he began to sing a few verses from his hymn to Adon, his sweet, melodious, high-pitched voice floating over the crowd dreamily, as if carried on a cloud. People stared at Akhenadon, breathing in his heavenly melodies, their hands clasped before their chests, tears streaming from their eyes. Others kneeled in tribute, overcome by Adon's son and messenger here before them, dressed in a simple white linen garment with no adornment.

When he was finished, Akhenadon looked out over his people, many crying uncontrollably. The people stood and again began cheering. In the midst of the crowd, one man yelled, "Glory be to Akhenadon! Glory be to Adon Mose!"

Others took up the chant. Some yelled "Adon Mose," and others just "Mose". Soon the crowd alternated between the two, some shouting "Adon" and others "Mose" so that they formed a rhythm that was deafening.

Suddenly I saw Joshua's men run from the scene, and I knew that Kemian soldiers must be upon us. We had planned beforehand that we would not engage in a fight with Kemian soldiers on Kemian land. I brought Akhenadon inside the home, and the owner barred the door. We walked out the back and were quickly whisked away to safety.

"You heard them," I said to Akhenadon that night. "They called you Adon Mose, 'You come from Adon'. Like Ramose, Thutmose, or Rameses, but here, for the first time, you have been acknowledged as being from Adon, not Ra or Thut. This is a miracle!"

"Perhaps a miracle," Joshua added. "And perhaps it will be a thorn in the side of Seti and the Amun priesthood. I think it is not a coincidence that Kemian soldiers appeared so soon. I suspect there was also a spy or two in the crowd that ran to them to curry favor."

Now that a thousand people had seen Akhenadon in the flesh, they spread the word to others, notably Adonites, but also curious others. Suddenly crowds gathered throughout Goshen, in towns large and small, delirious with joy and begging for Akhenadon to show himself again. And so twice more Akhenadon made an appearance, and the crowds doubled in size each time. Adon priests and even friendly government officials requested meetings with us, and we accommodated as many as we could. The chant now spread throughout the Delta. At every stop, people screamed, "Mose! Mose!"

Yet the most significant meetings for Akhenadon were those he held with just a few adherents at a time, in private and in secret locations. Sons of those forced into servitude pleaded with Akhenadon to free their fathers so they could provide for their families. Women cried over husbands and sons forced to work for nothing but scraps of food. Farmers complained of their land being forced from them for being late with a payment of grain that had not yet even sprouted, land that then mysteriously appeared in the records of an Amun temple. These entreaties weighed heavily on Akhenadon's heart.

It was not long before we received the summons from Seti that he would allow an audience and promised us safe passage to and from the meeting. We sailed up to Waset in a small boat. With us were High Priests Nadab and Eleazar. We all agreed that it would be best to leave Joshua and the two other High Priests in a safe area should any treachery happen.

As we entered the main hall where King Seti sat on the throne in full regalia, we saw behind and to the side of him an assortment of others. Two generals in battle dress stood on either side of Seti and behind him stood a cadre of Amun priests, as well as the Vizier of Upper Kem. I felt my legs shaking from the intimidating scene.

"Well, well, if it isn't the traitorous Amunhotep of heretic fame!" Seti called out. The men surrounding him snickered. "Welcome to the Royal palace… no, not the one in Akhedadon, which no longer exists, in case you did not know. I think your beautiful wife may be buried there. What was her name? Oh, yes, Nefer-something." None of us bowed.

"Oh, so you do not bow to the King? I could declare our grant of safe passage violated by you and have you all slain right here in front of me."

"We bow only to Adon," Akhenadon managed to say softly. "If you must kill us for pledging our allegiance to the highest being, then please do so quickly and spare us your childish insults."

Seti smiled. "Did the cat scratch your tongue, Amunhotep? It must have the way you stutter so. I will take pity on you, Amunhotep, for you are tired, old, decrepit. Your gown does little to hide that monstrous figure I have heard about. Yet your believers now call you Mose, I understand. Then it must be a pitiful God who has sent you!" Seti looked to each side of him to see that all were smiling.

I stepped forward. "As you point out, Akhenadon is advanced in years and is not well. I will speak for him. We are here to ask that you let our adherents leave peacefully."

Seti laughed.

"What? You mean leave Kem? Just like that?"

"Yes. They do you no harm. They merely wish to fill their lives with devotion to Adon, the One and Only God."

"How dare you vomit that rubbish to me!" Seti said as he moved sideways in his chair. His hands grabbed the armrests tightly. "Besides, if I let your people leave, who will mine our stone in the quarries? Who will clean the temples of the mighty God Amun and empty the latrines?" Again he looked to his sides.

"No, with all due respect to you, Chief Priest, and to you, Amunhotep, I think not. You may stay for a short while to get your affairs in order. Then you will be exiled once again until your God soon claims you for his own."

Seti turned to his personal guard standing by the entranceway. "Get them out of here. They sicken me," he said and waved them away.

As we walked out, Akhenadon suddenly turned and pointed his staff directly at Seti. I was shocked at this affront. "Hear my words, Seti, though they may be spoken with my affliction. Adon will no longer look with favor upon Kem. The land and its people will suffer greatly if you do not do the right thing. You... have... been... warned!" he shouted, then turned and left.

Scroll Thirty-Eight

From Darkness, Light

"I prefer to be alone," Akhenadon said as he hobbled toward the tomb of his beloved Nefertiti. It was a small tomb, put together in haste, as the Royal tomb that Kha had constructed for them both had been usurped instead for a nobleman in Horemheb's court. This act was Horemheb's final cruel affront to Akhenadon.

The workmen had cleared the site and unsealed the tomb so that he might enter. The entrance was low, so Akhenadon had difficulty bending to enter. I came to his side to help.

"I will wait for you here," I said. My heart was filled with sadness, remembering her buoyant spirit, her joyous motherhood, and the tragedies she endured.

After a few moments, I heard Akhenadon begin to softly sing a poem to Nefertiti, his voice cracking a few times in sorrow. Tears ran down my cheeks.

"My heart has been hardened," Akhenadon told me later that night. "I had no tears to cry for my beloved, no tears left for anything."

"You have seen many trials in your life, brother. It is hard to think of what might prompt more tears than you have already shed."

"What Adon requires of me has never been so clear. When I was young, my ba was formed by the misfortunes of my body and the way others treated me. Later I was blinded by my arrogant heart. I suppose the saying is true. One cannot make a horse from a donkey." He looked away for a moment. "And I was even at the wrong end of that donkey." I laughed, and so did he.

"Adon set me upon a path to create a new nation of people who believe in Him. I understand now, Kem could never have accepted that, no matter my power, my edicts, or anything else I might have done. It has too much history. Its customs, religions, Gods, government... everything is carved in stone.

"What is needed, what was always needed, but I was too foolish to see, is a fresh start. I am satisfied that we have developed the new laws and practices that will govern us."

"And that we have brought some of the Yahveh practices into our worship," I added.

It was now a year since we had arrived in Kem and held our audience with Seti, and still he refused to allow Akhenadon to lead his adherents to their destiny. Up to now, we felt safe in Kem and had even become friendly with some of the Kemian troops whose responsibility it was to keep a close eye on our comings and goings and to restrict the number of people who came to hear Akhenadon pray.

But now matters in Kem were worsening, and we had heard from our spies in the palace that Seti was considering going back on his pledge of safe passage within Kem. Despite Seti's military victories under Horemheb, Kem's borders were once again under attack, and his Generals were only partly successful in eradicating the threats.

While we instructed our priests to stop open rebellions by our adherents, they were helpless in the face of the anger and bravado that arose due to Akhenadon's presence. In villages and towns, there were demonstrations against Seti. This might not have been worthy of Seti's ire, except for the fact that these protests began occurring in the quarries that Kem needed for building.

On one terrible occasion, a brutal overseer in one of the

most horrendous quarries beat one of our adherents to death. When the brother of the victim witnessed this, he killed the overseer with a stone. When word of this reached Seti, reports said that he blamed Akhenadon directly for the overseer's murder. We feared he would either imprison us all or else have Akhenadon and me killed. Thankfully, Adon intervened to save us.

Internal events happened that had no explanation in the historical scrolls of the Amun priests. A red tide suddenly appeared in the Great Green, a tide so red and so widespread that none like it had ever been recorded. Fish began to appear floating on the surface, dead. At first, it was just a few here and there in various locations in the Delta. But within a ten-day, hundreds died, then thousands, then untold numbers.

The stench throughout the region became unbearable. Water running through the delta polluted with dead fish sickened thousands of people. With not enough physicians, people began to die and could not be buried properly, adding to the stench and disease.

The Amun priests blamed Akhenadon and convinced Seti to have him killed. I thought to use this to our advantage.

"He received the message I sent," I reported to Akhenadon, Joshua, and our High Priests. "He will consider it."

"Consider what?" Eleazar asked.

"To allow Akhenadon to lead our adherents from Kem."

"But you two already asked, and he said no," Nadab said, turning to the group.

I looked at Akhenadon, and he nodded for me to explain. "What I did was basically acknowledge that these events happening in Kem are due to Akhenadon asking Adon to send clear messages to Seti, demonstrating His anger and power. I told him that if he did not allow us to depart peacefully, worse things would happen. If they killed Akhenadon, I warned him that Kem would be consumed.

"And I also sent a similar message to the High Priest of Amun." I noticed that Nadab had blanched.

"Was this wise?" he asked. "I mean, Seti could kill us all in a moment."

"Have faith," Akhenadon said. "I am certain that Adon is working miracles on our behalf."

Word came to me that the Amun High Priests convinced Seti that this was a bluff. They suggested he wait and see what happened, and if nothing bad followed, he should arrange to have us all killed, a suggestion Seti appeared inclined to follow. In any event, the message from Seti said that he would never relent and that he advised Akhenadon to leave Kem quickly or he would not be responsible for what might happen.

Once again, I have come to believe that Adon sent more miracles. Kem is not used to rain, at least not in great amounts. Yet within the month, the skies opened, and torrential rainstorms deluged large portions of Kem. Roads were blocked, fields were drenched, and crops ruined. Cattle drowned in mud, and flooding was everywhere. Soldiers, already scarce due to the border skirmishes, were sent to help people, but little could be done. As soon as they repaired a road, it would be flooded again two days later.

One of the most miraculous things that happened, and that convinced me of Adon's intervention, was what the rains did in the oases. Frog eggs that lay dormant for years began to hatch. Mud frogs that can live deep in the mud for years emerged in great quantities. In the course of a month, there was a literal plague of frogs.

As they died, they created their own stench, but there was more, for, in the oases, there were also large biting flies. From consuming the flesh of the dead frogs, they reproduced and reproduced until there were clouds of flies that descended upon the poor people. Without enough physicians, the bites festered into sores and then horrible boils so that the people walked around with painful, inflamed boils covering their bodies. They could not even sleep, for the boils would rub on their straw mattresses and cause them excruciating pain. Many died.

The biting flies had another effect, one so horrible even I

doubted that even the One and Only God had a right to do this. I found out from a physician priest that since young children's bodies are so small, the flies are able to bite more of their bodies, infecting them greatly. They suffered terribly from the festering and boils, not knowing what was happening to them. As a result, they died in numbers far greater than adults. My heart hurt from this news as the deaths swept throughout Kem. Each morning villages were awakened by the hysterical cries of mothers and fathers mourning their dead children.

The effect of all these events and diseases was that the people of Kem rose as one, whether worshippers of Amun, Isis, Horus or Adon, whether dwellers of the Delta or Upper Kem, dark or pale skinned, man or woman, it made no difference. They blamed King Seti for one. But the heaviest weight they placed on the shoulders of the Amun priesthood.

I deemed it time for one last message.

King Seti, Ruler of the Two Lands,

By now you understand the power of Adon and the anger he holds toward you. Adon revealed to me that what is happening in Kem is just the beginning. He will strike down the members of the Royal family, men, women and children. He will render your army impotent. He will bring starvation to your people. Now is the time for you to do what is right. Now is the time to let my people go.

Moses

Scroll Thirty-Nine

Leave!

Five days after receiving our message, we received a summons from Seti to come to the palace. We were deep in the Delta, so the journey would be long and arduous. Joshua helped plan the journey and secured the boats, food, and medicines. Two boats were laden with Joshua's best soldiers, their weapons hidden from view. One boat held three physicians and their assistants, as well as Akhenadon and me.

As we sailed upon Mother Nile, the devastation that Adon had wrought was visible everywhere. Mutilated bodies floated along the banks, snagged by reeds as they passed. Crocodiles basked on the banks, bloated from gorging on the bodies. At one point, as we passed a large temple to Amun, we saw a crocodile slither into the water and pick up the body of a small child and bite it in half, swallowing the upper body in one gulp. I vomited at the spectacle.

We were not sure how it happened, but word had passed of Akhenadon's journey upstream to Waset. Every village we passed had people waiting on the shore, begging for help, supporting sick husbands, wives, or children.

"Please, great Mose, please help us!" they shouted. On the banks of one small town, dozens of men and women lined up and chanted, "Mose! Mose! Mose!" At other places, people pleaded for Akhenadon's intervention with Adon.

When we were halfway along, I moved to the bow to speak with Akhenadon. "Brother, we will soon come to Akhedadon. Do you wish to stop and visit it, perhaps for the final time?"

Akhenadon breathed in deeply and sighed. "I have heard that Horemheb destroyed it and used the materials to build temples to Amun elsewhere. I understand the ruins are now reclaimed by the desert sands. So, no, Aharon, I wish to remember it as it was, in all its glory, to Adon." With that, he turned his back to the city.

Even when we were far away from Waset, we could see that something was amiss. The closer we sailed, the more chaotic the city appeared. People were running here and there. Governors from the nomes ran toward the palace, their guards holding their identifying pennants. Emissaries from foreign countries, dressed in all manner of odd clothing and jewelry, prodded their guards to push through the masses of citizens.

As we brought our boats to the shore, we could see crowds milling around burlap blankets lining the waterfront. Upon each lay, a grotesque shape, hardly recognizable as human, so covered were they in open ulcers and boils. The biting flies still attacked their bodies as their family members, covered head to toe to prevent being bitten, tried in vain to help. Maggots wriggled in the ulcers as the afflicted moaned and begged for relief.

When the people saw the bearded Akhenadon, a strange silence spread over the crowd. I could instantly see in their eyes whether they saw him as a savior or a mut spirit. I quickly summoned the physicians we brought with us and bade them minister to the sick. When Akhenadon raised his staff in blessing, people near him shied away in fear.

"Do not be afraid, for I have come only to free my people." Akhenadon called out.

"Then why do you curse us with plagues like this?" one elderly man shouted.

"Akhenadon does not do this," I shouted back. "Our God is

angry with King Seti, for he refuses to allow us to leave peacefully. It has been more than a year since our request."

As the crowd continued to stare at Akhenadon, Seti's guards arrived and cleared a path to the palace. As we passed through them, one woman grabbed Akhenadon's arm and knelt on the ground. She looked into his eyes. "You are our Moses, he who has arrived. I pray to Adon every day. Please, my husband is near death in the quarry. Please free us, Mose."

Akhenadon placed his hand on the woman's head and whispered a prayer. Then the guards pushed us forward.

As we entered the palace, Seti was in a meeting with his ministers, yet the guards escorted us into the room. They all looked up when we approached, silent. As I scanned the group, I noted there was an unmistakable sign of respect, and fear, on the faces of several of the ministers, who nodded to us.

"You are dismissed," Seti said. "All except for you, Papper." The ministers rose, and surprisingly, a few of them bowed their heads slightly to Akhenadon as they exited. Vizier Papper stood by Seti's side as he leaned forward on his throne.

"So, Amunhotep, you change names like a desert lizard changes color. How shall I address you? Is it Amunhotep today, or is it Akhenadon? No, wait, how about your newest name? I believe the crowds call you Mose or Moses, the one who has arrived. Hmmm. Well, he certainly has, has he not, Papper?" Akhenadon remained silent, staring impassively at the King.

"I will not grant you that term of endearment if that be acceptable with you. According to the Amun priests, you are still Amunhotep the Fourth, the heretic King, and so you shall be with me." He rose from his seat.

"I debate with myself whether to have you killed right here, right now. You are no prophet, you are an abomination, a charlatan." He held out his arm and pointed at Akhenadon. "I know not what magic you wield, sorcerer, but I will grant that it is powerful. So, for the sake of the Two Lands and no other, I will allow you and your followers to leave. To be rid of you and that rabble stench will be a welcome relief, for you pollute the very essence of Kemian blood. Tell them what we have decided, Papper." Seti sat back down, his face reddened in anger.

Papper stepped forward but was still a half-step behind Seti. "You will pass word throughout Kem that your people will gather in one place… and only one place. Once gathered, you will leave. We grant you one month to gather and another month to supply and leave. Our army will ensure that you abide by King Seti's orders." Akhenadon simply nodded.

"That is all. Leave!" Seti said with a casual wave of the back of his hand.

I held my hand out to Akhenadon to stay his leave. "There is one other matter," I suggested.

"I fear you are wrong. There are no other matters," Papper responded in anger. I ignored his comment.

"We wish a guarantee, from Seti's mouth, with you bearing witness as Vizier and a High Amun priest, that we will not be slaughtered, gathered together as we conveniently will be."

"What? Surely you jest!" Seti said, bursting out of his seat and looking from me to Akhenadon. "I have told you what I will generously allow. No more is needed."

I looked to Papper. "It must be in the form of a decree, with the King's seal upon it."

"Get out!" Seti screamed, his face red, the veins in his neck bulging. "Leave, or I will order you killed on the spot!"

"I would advise against that, King Seti, for you have no idea what vengeance Adon will unleash against you, your family, and the people of Kem." I looked to Papper. "The edict?"

Papper turned toward Seti and whispered in his ear. Seti's anger did not ease. Papper whispered again and again. Finally, Seti looked at Akhenadon, turned, and stormed from the room.

Papper looked to the entryway and called to the guards. Six marched in, led by their Captain. They all wore their swords and daggers. Every muscle in my body was tense, for I knew what Seti was capable of.

"Summon my scribe," Papper said to the Captain.

Soon the man arrived, carrying a parchment and his pen and ink kit, wrapped in a leather binding, along with a small table. He sat cross-legged before the table, took out his pen and ink, and smoothed the papyrus paper on the table. "I am ready, Master."

Papper dictated the decree to his scribe, all the while looking straight at me. I felt then that as High priests, he of Amun and me of Adon, we somehow understood each other. When the decree was written, Papper had the scribe melt bee's wax on the surface. He removed a ring that hung around his neck and impressed it with the King's seal. He rolled the parchment and tied it with a linen ribbon that the scribe handed to him, and he walked it over to us.

As he handed it to me, he stepped in front of Akhenadon. He bowed, something neither of us expected. "You are indeed the Moses that your people have prayed for. May your Adon protect you, and may your people flourish." With that, he turned, dipped his head quickly to me, and left. Seti had let our people go.

Scroll Forty

The Gathering

Joshua knocked loudly on Kha's door. When Meryt answered, he bowed respectfully, and Meryt stepped aside. Joshua walked swiftly into the room, and Kha stood, surprise evident on his face.

"He has done it, Kha! Adon has worked his miracle through Moses. We are free! Seti has set us free!" Kha embraced Joshua, and they twirled around, tears running down their faces. Kha went over to Meryt and hugged her, too.

"Is this true, Joshua?" She asked. "Are we truly free?"

"Yes. A messenger just arrived from the palace. Moses and Aharon are sailing back here as we speak."

He turned to Kha. "You may not know this, Meryt, but your husband will be the most important man in all Kem, at least to our people, from now until we leave. Except, of course, for Moses," Meryt looked to her husband, confused but with obvious pride.

"Kha, the lists you have drawn up and the people you have recruited in utmost secrecy, today is the day to put all into action. Seti has given us only thirty days to gather all our adherents from across the two lands here in Goshen and a mere thirty days additional to organize them for the trip across to the Mafdet."

"The Mafdet?" Meryt cried out. "We will all surely die!"

Joshua took a step toward Meryt. "Fear not, dear woman, for Adon protects us, and Moses and Aharon lead us. My army, although small, will protect us. We have a plan. You have been patient long enough. Our time has come. Now you must place your trust in us." Meryt looked deeply into Joshua's eyes and saw a man who spoke the truth. She nodded.

That day, Kha kissed Meryt, telling her that he would be gone for many days. He explained that his job was to gather crews of men and women to gather foodstuffs enough for thousands of people and animals, to gather or construct wagons, to train Captains, and to stock the many things needed for such a journey.

"Not without me, husband! I have organized the women in Set Maat since we have been married. I have watched you supervise in ways that got the job done yet gained your men's respect. I will help the women do the same. As soon as you get settled in your tasks, you will call for me, and I will be ready."

Kha smiled. "As I have always said, my love, you are the best wife any man could have. And now you shall be the best Captain I have ever worked with." With that, he embraced Meryt and left.

Joshua quickly arranged for priests and messengers to travel throughout Kem, where there were known Adonite communities, even ones that met in secret. But it was immediately apparent to Kha that Joshua had not planned for the sudden influx of immigrants to Goshen. Families arrived by the dozens and then by the hundreds with no place to stay.

"Joshua, you need to give me command of fifty of your soldiers. I must train them to build an orderly tent village for our people and a way to feed them and dig places for latrines. The situation now is creating chaos."

Each soldier recruited ten men to help build modest tents. Within seven days, straight rows of tents were established. Now the crews devised ways to build faster. By the end of the thirty days, six thousand Adonites were housed on the site.

Every able-bodied man and woman was put to work. Meryt organized cooking units supplied by teams of men that Kha had secretly set up to purchase produce, meat, and cheeses from throughout Goshen, the most productive farming region in Kem. The money mysteriously appeared from treasure supplied by Tiye's relatives and from caches of gold that Tiye had asked her many relatives to hold for just such emergencies.

At the end of the thirty-day gathering period, Kha turned from his work when he felt a tap on his shoulder. He stared incomprehensibly at the faces of six men. They looked familiar, yet he could not believe they could be who he thought they were.

"Well, are you not even going to say hello?" the nearest one asked.

"Praise to Adon or Amun or whatever God you pray to… if it is not Amun-Nakhte and you, Djehuty. Hor-Min, Ipuy, Ka-Sa. What are you all doing here? Have you become believers in Adon, you scoundrels?"

The men looked around at each other. Ipuy spoke first. "We are not really believers in Adon, Kha. We are believers in you." Kha dropped his hammer. He did not know what to say.

"We heard what Seti decreed, and we figured you might need carpenters and tradesmen and captains such as we are. We figured the only way to finally get rid of you would be to come here and help you!" With that, they all laughed heartily. Kha hugged each of them.

"More men are on the way, some of them with their wives, to help Meryt," Djehuty added.

"My brothers, you have no idea how much this means to me and… and how much I truly need you. When can you start after your long journey?"

"Our tools are in our sacks," Ka-Sa said, holding his up. "Why are you wasting time?"

Scroll Forty-One

The Exodus Is Upon Us

Frantic. That was the word our leadership used over and over again, for it was just this side short of chaos, and only then due to the heroic efforts of Kha and Meryt and the volunteers they recruited. Even men and women from Set Maat, non-believers all, arrived to help.

My attention turned to the issue of governance. I urged Akhenadon to form a council of elders to help us organize, not for religious observance, that would be left to the High Priests, but for the immense challenge of governance. He agreed, and ten men, former ministers, government officials, and community leaders were chosen. Their first task was to lend help to Kha and Meryt in whatever way they needed. Frantic.

The Council used some of Tiye's fortune to buy every donkey available in the Delta and even as far as Inabu-hedj to carry the supplies for our journey. Joshua decided that horses would be useless, except for the soldiers, due to their greater need for food and water.

There were not enough wagons to accommodate our needs, so Kha's carpenters made as many wagons as they could in such a short time. Everywhere one walked, there were wheels scattered about, wood planks piled, and shouts to assistants to fetch this item or that one. Children ran about ferrying supplies to men and women.

The women banded together and sewed more than a hundred tents, all the while caring for husbands and children, another frantic undertaking.

By now, there was no use calling Akhenadon by his rightful name anymore, for the people had taken to enthusiastically calling him Mose or Moses.

"I find this somewhat disconcerting," Akhenadon confided in me one morning after prayers. "I know that many Kemians have used Mose in their names for generations. I remember Ramose of Waset well. And so did our Kings. Even my bloodline included Thutmose, and there was Ahmose and even Seti's father, Rameses. I do not wish to dampen the enthusiasm of our adherents, but…"

"But nothing," I said. "You will get used to it, Mose only means 'he has arrived', so what is wrong with that? You have arrived, as the emissary of Adon, to free His people, to create a nation devoted to Him."

"Perhaps you are right, brother. But I am in conflict about it. I do think that this might be a good thing to put my past life as a Kemian behind me. It is a clean break, for I know I will never return."

Each day began with prayers, even before the morning meal. This served to focus the men's attention, and by time they arrived back in their tents, food was ready, after which work began in earnest.

Evening prayers were done at sunset, after which the men had time with their families to share the day's events and to wonder about what Moses' plans were for the future.

At one of our planning sessions during the month of gathering, one of the Councilors talked about how the prayer services helped create order and discipline among those gathered. This Councilor was from generations of people from the Delta and had worshipped Yahveh his whole life.

"The people find it comforting to pray to Yahveh…," he began before being interrupted by Moses.

"Please, never use that term for Adon again," Moses said

somewhat sharply. "It is one of the holiest names for Adon."

"Yes, yes, of course, Moses. I forgot. Adon is mightier than any of the others, mightier than all the others." He smiled apologetically.

"No, Adon is the *only* God. There are no others. None!" Moses demanded. "You must remember that, you all must remember that. Adon is the One and Only God." Moses took a breath to compose himself.

"If you see His name written, say Adonai, my Adon, or The Name. When you say any of the secret names of Adon, it opens up hidden gates to the infinite that we can neither understand nor imagine. It can bring unpredictable consequences. When all people accept Adon as the One and Only God, then we will be able to say all his names. Only then." No one said a word back to Moses for fear of upsetting him.

Much of our time was spent with the High Priests, giving them more instructions as it became clear to us how to transmit the knowledge of Adon to a far larger group. The High Priests then taught the ordinary priests the laws and rituals of the faith. They, in turn, held small gatherings of people to help them learn the prayers and laws.

Fortunately, this was helped by something that happened by itself, with no prompting from Moses or me. The people of the Delta tended to live in tribes from their original homelands. Mostly these people originally worshipped the Yahveh of their ancestors, so it was easy for them to learn the full extent of Adon worship. They also were amongst the first to embrace it when Akhenadon still ruled Kem. But, most of all, the tribes competed with each other for Moses' favor, so they tried to quickly adapt their members to the laws and practices. They also tried to help newcomers.

As the month of gathering ended and the month of readiness to leave began, we sent the priests out to conduct a census. We now had some six thousand people, and although some still wandered in from the most remote regions of Kem, there was little change in numbers by the time we left.

One matter that we had not given enough thought to was the fact that a large number of our people also suffered from the plague of boils. Our physicians worked day and night to alleviate their pain, but as soon as the month of readiness began, complaints began to arrive from the people.

"When are we to move out?" a man shouted at a gathering that we had called for one of the tribes. "Our children suffer from these bites!" This same complaint was repeated for each session we held for the tribes.

While this was going on, the Captain of the Kemian army, that watched us from nearby hills, reminded us regularly of the time we had left.

Joshua was our constant companion as we worked through all these details, for he, like Kha, had a talent for organization. With but a ten-day to go before we were required by Seti's edict to leave, Joshua called me, Moses, and the High Priests into a meeting. Before us lay hand-drawn maps.

"This is the route my map makers have drawn out for our journey," he began, hunched over the map.

"I did not know we had map makers," High Priest Ithamar said.

"All armies have map makers," Joshua replied, smiling at the man's obvious ignorance, an ignorance that I, too, shared.

"Anyway, once we are in the Mafkat, we will journey almost due south and try to stay as close to the Dashret Sea coast as possible, to allow our people to fish for food. I have arranged for boats of fishermen to follow us along that part of the route, promising to buy from them all they can catch." All nodded our heads in approval.

"Once we get near the tip of the Mafkat, where the Dashret Sea splits into two, we will move due east across the most mountainous part of the Mafkat. This will be the most difficult part of the journey. You know well what that land is like," he said, looking at Moses and me. I shuddered at the thought of bringing six thousand people through those mountains and dry valleys.

"Once we are across the Mafkat, we will continue on due north on the other side of the Dashret Sea. We will be out of the mountains but in difficult desert until we pass Edom and Moab across the water from us," he said, tracing the route with his finger. "Then it will be easier as we approach Canaan."

"Perhaps this looks easy when traced on a map. However, you must all understand that this will be a very difficult journey. Our history does not tell of any people who have ever attempted to cross the Mafkat six thousand strong. It will be a huge challenge. But with good planning, strong discipline, and Adon's watchful presence, we will make it to Canaan." All heads nodded.

"And how long do you think it will take us, from start to finish?" one of the priests asked. Joshua took time to consider.

"I cannot be certain. My officers and I have discussed this, but with so many children and elderly, we cannot predict. I would say a year at least, probably double that."

"Oh, God!" High Priest Abihu said, falling back in his seat. "How can we sustain that? Six thousand men, women, and children…"

"It will not be easy, Abihu. We will face the intense heat of the desert, cold nights, rationing water and food, illnesses, viper bites… the list is long."

"And what choice do we have, my sons?" I added, for the four High Priests sitting next to me were, indeed, like sons to me. "We are enemies in our own land, not allowed to worship our God, forced to serve in quarries and the King's fields, beaten, taxed, denied land. We have gained our freedom but at a high price. Yet I ask again, what choice do we have?"

"The exodus from Kem is upon us," Moses said as he looked into the eyes of every person. "We will leave and not look back. We will forge a new nation of people faithful to the One and Only God."

And so it was that on the 20th day of the third month of Shomu, we began our exodus. Six thousand, two hundred hopeful believers, eleven thousand four hundred donkeys, three thousand wagons in various stages of disrepair, two hundred and twenty soldiers, ninety priests, a hundred horses for the army, and Moses.

Book Three

Exodus

Map of the Exodus

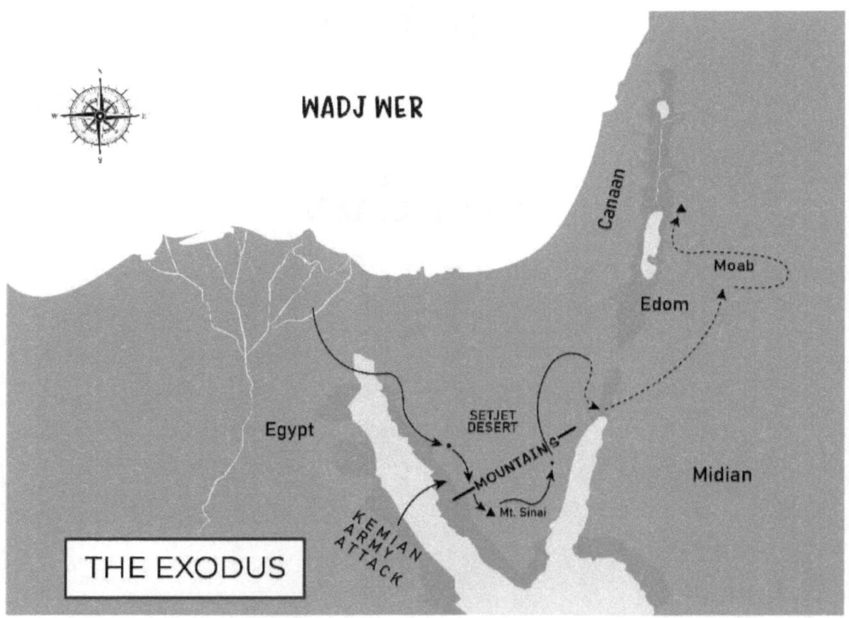

Scroll Forty-Two

Exodus

When I look back over the past eight months, it is hard to believe what we have all been through. The desert is a cruel mistress, but we are intimately bound to her all the same.

Through Joshua's careful planning, we left Kem by going around Lake Timsah in the far northeast of Kem, thereby avoiding having to cross the Dashret Sea. This alone was a trial, for the wagons bogged down in the marshy mud, and the entire army was forced to push and pull to pry the wheels loose. It took four whole days to make the short passage. One would think that our people were jubilant to now be free when we finished crossing, but that joy was short-lived when we faced the immensity of the barren, scorching desert.

Fortunately for us, we were led by Adjo and his men, who walked at the front of the column and were able to warn us of the many dangers that might confront us. They also led us to water when our supplies ran low. Above all, Adjo's high spirits kept our moods buoyed.

It is hard to contemplate how difficult it is to move six thousand men, women, and children, young and old, healthy and ill. By the time we broke camp each morning, Adon's disk was already in the sky, and in too few hours, it was time to camp again. Progress was painfully slow, and I now understood better why Joshua said it could take as much as two years to arrive in Canaan, the land that Moses felt would be best for our people to settle.

As we went, we modified our routine. We now started to break camp two hours before Adon's disk rose. There was no morning meal allowed. Instead, people ate as they walked or rode, from what they had prepared the night before. Usually, that was a few pieces of unleavened bread made in haste, a bite of cheese, and some dried fruits. We were also blessed with the fresh fish that Joshua had arranged, which we dried on the sides of the wagons as we walked.

The morning prayer was done in haste, just as we left camp. Moses led those that could make it to his side, offering prayers to Adon and asking for His blessing for that day. Then we trudged off, heading south, the Dashret Sea some distance to our right.

Joshua's soldiers were used to a far faster pace and were frustrated by our painfully slow progress and by the demands placed on them by the ill and infirm. Yet Joshua, as their commander, did a good job in training and disciplining them. He instilled in them a sense of community, helping them understand that they were not a military force subjugating us but rather part of us, dedicated to our protection. Still, constant breakdowns of wagons, burials, births and having to quell arguments often made them irritable.

As part of his planning, Joshua arranged for fifty of his soldiers to have horses, not only to be able to ride along the column quickly but also to offer help. As we went, he established small outposts and left a man and horse at each. That way, we had a messenger system that ran all the way back to Kem, apprising us of news. The truth is that Joshua did not trust King Seti and wanted to keep a close watch on what was happening in the Royal Court. Our spies and his military contacts supplied that information, and the messengers relayed that to us.

Fortunately, Siamun, one of Joshua's ablest soldiers,

who as a young man worked in one of the Royal stables and was an excellent horseman, was in charge of the messenger relay and frequently volunteered to make the first run himself. Due to their long friendship and service in the Army together, Joshua thankfully did not have to worry about this critical function of our journey.

As day followed day, and month followed month, nothing of note came out of Kem. But starting in our eighth month, Joshua began to receive unsettling information. Even after we left, Kem was riven by strife. Workers complained of poor working conditions and poor pay. The people were still plagued by disease. In addition to the biting flies, the wet weather brought mosquito illnesses. Food crops spoiled, and people went hungry.

To quell these disturbances, Kem's powerful advisors, members of the Royal family, business owners, and Amun priests pressured Seti to exercise his power as King to eradicate the instigators of the protests. This went on for months, as wave after wave of rebellion was met by military suppression. People were beaten and executed. Yet the protests still continued.

In a meeting that was witnessed by one of our spies who masqueraded as an Amun priest, those gathered around Seti convinced him of one thing, the root of the problem lay with Akhenadon and his success in freeing his people. Seti's advisors said that he had acted too quickly in granting Akhenadon's request, that his capitulation made him look weak, and that the protestors gained confidence from Moses' example. The Amun priests, who at the time of our exodus were frightened and cowed by Adon's miracles, suddenly reversed course and said they were natural events that would have abetted in due time. The only way to convince the rebels that their cause was hopeless would be to massacre the Adonites and their so-called Moses. As a successful military leader, it did not take long for Seti to embrace their view.

It took several ten days for word of Seti's decision to finally reach us. We learned that he had already begun to mobilize the army and plan the attack. Yet we knew not how or where it would occur. Moses instructed Joshua to keep this information secret so as not to create fear within our people, who were already stressed by our perilous journey.

"If they follow our route," Joshua said, "which is most likely, it will take them months to catch up, depending on how many soldiers they bring. Anything more than a thousand will slow them down considerably, and they will surely need at least that many. In any case, we should have enough time to get to the furthest southern point of our journey and then be in the mountains for protection."

"Protection from a thousand or more Kemian soldiers with only two hundred of your fighting men?" Moses asked, knowing well the answer.

"You say that mockingly, but I will tell you that Kemian soldiers are well-trained to fight in open battle. We wouldn't stand a chance. But, they are terrible in mountainous areas, where small numbers of our forces can ambush them and escape. Ten killed here, thirty there, and soon the numbers have an effect. After a while, they become demoralized. I say this from experience."

So we trudged on, nearing the southernmost tip of our journey. Joshua continuously sent Siamun back to begin the messenger chain to see if there were any signs of chase, but none was seen. Yet we heard from our spies in the Royal court that Seti had indeed set off after us and with many more than a thousand soldiers. Where were they? Could they have sailed along the Great Green, planning to wait for us when, exhausted, we reached Canaan, ripe for slaughter? Trying to figure this out was unnerving, and Joshua became short-tempered and disagreeable.

Making matters worse, our people began to complain mightily. They were exhausted from battling the heat and sand of the Mafkat. We had already lost a third of our wagons to breakage, with no excess wood for repairs. The majority of our people had constant pain from toothaches due to sand infiltrating all our foods and wearing down our teeth. Even our donkeys were down to skin and bone.

People began to question why they left Kem. They asked why Adon was forcing us through such hardships.

As we approached the point where the Dashret Sea splits on either side of the Mafkat, one of our advance scouts came across a reed sailboat beached on the sand. Waiting by the boat were two terrified priests, one of Amun and the other of Adon. They demanded to see Moses immediately.

"We have been waiting for you for five days without food," the Adon priest said between bites of bread and honey. "Seti is coming for you in great force. We barely escaped before being found out."

"And why are you warning us?" I asked the Amun priest.

"The two of us have been friends since childhood. I could no longer tolerate what my brothers in Amun were condoning against our own people, no matter who they worshipped."

"You say they are coming," Joshua asked anxiously. "Where? We have not seen anyone in chase."

"Because they are not in a chase. They will appear before you!"

"Nonsense," Joshua responded. "We cross into the mountains within a ten-day."

"Do you not wonder how we knew to wait for you here?" the Amun priest asked.

"Of course," both Moses and Joshua answered. The Amun priest pulled out a parchment from his robe and unrolled it. A map was drawn upon it. Joshua grabbed it and studied it.

"Moses! It is a map of our route, a close copy of the one I drew for you back in Goshen." Joshua turned to the priests. "How did you get this? Tell me!" The eyes of the priests opened in fear.

"I stole it from one of the Army Captains," the Amun priest said. "He talked of how… please excuse me for saying this, Joshua… he said how stupid you were thinking that Seti would not find out about it."

"You have a spy in your midst," the Adon priest said. "It is one of your messengers."

"Do you have a name?" Joshua asked, his face red with rage.

"No. Only the King knows who."

Joshua paced before the two priests. "How many soldiers?"

"The Captain said some two thousand. They felt they would need that many to complete the slaughter and make sure none escaped."

"I… I just can't figure out how two thousand soldiers and supplies were able to get ahead of us. It makes no sense. It's… impossible!" He stood thinking, his brows contorted in concentration. All of a sudden, he turned to the Amun priest.

"Unbelievable! They are crossing the Dashret!"

"As we speak," the Amun priest said.

Scroll Forty-Three

Adon Spoke

Joshua began preparations for battle within hours. The first thing he did was call a meeting of his Captains, telling them of Seti's pursuit.

"But, sir, that is impossible!" Rekhmire said. "My father is a fisherman. He would never attempt such a crossing at this time of year… certainly not with two thousand damned soldiers, horses, chariots, and weapons."

"I thought so, too," Joshua answered, "but there you have it."

"The Dashret is unpredictable. Storms can come up in minutes," Rekhmire continued. "Every fishing village along the Dashret has stone cenotaphs for lost fishermen. Seti is a madman."

"They are obviously eager to slaughter us, that is all I can figure," Joshua said. "All the more reason to be prepared. If we can make it to the mountains, we gain an advantage." Joshua paused to take in the mood of his Captains. "I look for strong leadership, men. All information is to be kept secret until Moses speaks to the people."

Joshua asked Siamun to stay in his tent. "Send a rider to gather all the soldiers stationed in the outposts going all the way back along our route. There is no longer a need for them to protect our flank. We will need every man here with us."

"I leave immediately," Siamun said, turning to go.

"Wait! Send someone else. I need you here, Siamun. You are my trusted friend and one of the best warriors I have ever fought with. Send another and instead gather your men, telling them to await orders. Then come back here, for we must make plans for what to do next."

I entered Joshua's tent shortly after. "Moses has told me that I am to assist you in whatever ways you need." Joshua smiled.

"I thank you, dear Aharon, but what must be done now is to prepare for war, and I fear that neither you nor Moses is equipped for that. What I need is for Moses to tell the people what is happening and to calm their fears."

I hesitated. "Before I go, I need to know. How bad is it?"

Joshua looked at me for the longest time. "If I lie, you will see through me, so I will tell you straight. It is very bad, Aharon. What we must do is make a mad run for the mountains tomorrow before morning if we have any hope of even a few surviving. The Kemian soldiers will not spare a person, whether man, woman, or child. We will have to leave whatever will not move quickly. We must stage a defense, not even knowing where that will be. It may be between where we are now and the mountains. We all have to pray that we have a ten-day to get to safety." He looked at the map that was spread on his table, tracing our route with his finger.

"This was well calculated… very well. One of my men… perhaps more… has betrayed us, and for that, I am sorrier than you will ever know."

That night, Moses called for a meeting of all men who could attend, and almost fifteen hundred assembled. The night was still, giving us good conditions to be heard. While Moses spoke in his melodic, high-pitched voice, I spoke those same words in my booming voice so most could hear. As well the High Priests relayed Moses' words to those standing in the back.

"My people, people of Adon, hear me. Adon has performed miracles that you have seen for yourselves. He has forced the King of Kem, the most powerful nation on earth, to free you from the most horrible conditions imaginable. He has inflicted suffering on all of Kem to punish them. You doubted our God once, but now you are believers. Despite the hardships we face now, they are nothing compared to what you suffered in Kem. Adon looks down and sees you persevere.

"You have taken an oath to serve Adon, to be faithful to Him, to pray to Him with all your heart. In return, Adon has pledged to be faithful to you, to protect you, and to make you prosper." For many moments the assembled cheered at this.

"We will now face another test of our faith, of your faith as well as mine. Apparently, King Seti has not learned his lesson well enough. He has revoked his safe passage for us, the pledge he gave upon his honor to allow us free passage to Canaan." Now the crowd was anxious. They began murmuring and talking to one another, fear on their faces.

"Is the King's army coming after us?" one man shouted.

"They will slaughter us like sheep!"

"Who will protect us?" another shouted. Moses held up his staff for quiet.

"This cannot and will not happen. Ever. There is no army, nor all armies put together, as powerful as Adon's might. Adon has promised me that He will lead us to Canaan, and that is what will happen. With Adon's help, Joshua and his soldiers will defeat the King of Kem and all his minions. I ask only one thing from you... no two things.

"One is to have faith in Adon, no matter what fears or doubts you may harbor in your heart. Go back to your families and be their rock, calm them, and hold up your faith as a model.

"The second thing is to pray, to lift your hearts and prayers up to Adon. Pray with your families. Place yourself in Adon's hands. If you will do but that, Adon will protect us and allow us to move on victorious."

Some cheered, but most left with their heads hung low, their muscles taut, their countenances full of fear and doubt. Yet that night, there was calm in the camp, and the murmur of desperate prayers could be heard throughout.

The next morning, well before Adon's disk rose, Joshua met with his captains and instructed them to send out their soldiers, telling everyone that they must leave behind everything not essential. That included all our wagons. Everyone needed to move quickly. The mountains were clearly in sight but so distant as to appear as mere hills.

For the next four days, we traveled from well before Adon's disk rising to well after it set. We slept in the open, not taking time to assemble and disassemble tents. Anxiety pervaded every aspect of our journey. The people now bemoaned leaving Kem and some of the most outspoken cast doubt on our faith. I sent out all priests to calm our people, helping them to pray, and trying to restore their confidence.

"They scream for Moses," one of my priests said. "They blame him. Some now call him a false prophet. They say they were better off in Kem, being beaten, for they fear being hacked to death by Seti's soldiers."

"Women are hysterical," another priest reported. "They want their husbands to turn back and have their families risk the desert alone, rather than the blades of soldiers."

The night of the fifth day, as we settled into a nervous night in camp, the mountains were so close I felt we could touch them. The Dashret was before us and to our right side. Joshua came to my tent, and together we went to Moses'.

"We are but a day or two from entering the pass we must use," Joshua said.

"But the mountains are so close," I objected.

"They are, but according to Adjo, if we enter anywhere but the path we must take, we will be lost."

"Better lost than dead," I said.

"True, but Adjo knows these mountain passes better than anyone, and he assures us we would not have defensive positions for another day or two. We would be open game for the Kemian troops."

"Have your scouts spotted them?" Moses asked.

"Not yet, but if Seti's generals have calculated well, and

I have to assume they have, then we should be seeing them any day. They may have already landed before us."

"Are you prepared?" Moses asked.

"As well as we can be. My men are well-trained, and we have developed some tactics for mountain skirmishes. Everything we will do is designed to delay their army, so you must keep the people moving, no matter what else happens. Day and night if necessary.

"Our hope is to thwart them long enough to allow you to get through these mountains to Midian, Edom, and Shechem. I have sent scouts to Shechem to tell them to expect us. They will be waiting on the other side."

"You are doing your best, my son," Moses said. "That alone will be enough to convince Adon to protect us. You will see."

The weather that night did not help our spirits. The wind picked up, blowing sand into our blankets and our meager rations. We could not have a fire for fear of the Kemian army spotting our position.

In the wee hours, we were startled awake by thunder in the distance. Soon rain began to fall, soaking our blankets and making sleep impossible. By morning we were already awake and packed to make haste toward the mountains. No sooner was I ready when Joshua burst into my tent.

"They are here!" he shouted. We ran to Moses' tent, but he was already awake and had finished his prayers.

"I know," he said calmly. "Adon has warned me. We shall see miracles today."

"We cannot outrun them. My men are getting the people to circle up so they can be defended as long as possible. Just before Adon's rise, my scouts killed all the advanced scouts in three boats that were camped on the beach up ahead. Two of my men were killed. Your physicians are tending to the wounded. I must leave now."

Moses grabbed his arm. "May Adon be with you… and with us all."

As our soldiers kept the people back so as not to frighten them with what was coming, Moses and I followed Joshua to a bluff overlooking the Dashret. The rain beat in our faces, and we were soaked. Nothing could have prepared me for the frightening scene that unfolded before me. As far as the eye could see, there were reed and wooden boats, hundreds filled with Kemian soldiers, shields at the ready, swords in their hands.

"Down to the beach!" Joshua yelled to two of his Captains above the roar of the wind. "We must attack them as they land." Two other Captains he instructed to stay on the upper sand to reinforce the ones below as needed. The rest he commanded to guard our people.

The downpour pelted us, and the wind nearly drove us off the bluff. As the boats got close enough for us to hear the shouts of their officers, the skies thundered again. Lightening pierced the sky. The officers tried to guide the oarsmen to avoid the jagged rocks as the wind and waves blew them off course. Their shouts were now frenzied.

Hundreds of boats were now on the scene, colliding with each other as the waves grew in height. Suddenly, the thunder and lightning rose in sound and frequency, and one could not help but believe that Adon was hurling the bolts of lightning at the soldiers. Some of the bolts hit the storm-tossed boats, spilling the crew out into the water and drowning them.

Joshua's soldiers stood holding their swords at the ready, looking at the scene, their jaws hung in amazement. None could believe what was happening. As the boats overturned, the soldiers, weighted down with their armament, quickly drowned. Our soldiers behind us could no longer contain our people, and they surged ahead and crowded onto the bluff behind us, witnessing the miracle.

We stood there, soaked from the driving rain, peering at what Adon had wrought, unprepared for what happened next. Abruptly, the thunder took on a higher pitch, such as we had never before heard. The winds increased, and the waves built-in height, tossing the boats upon the rocks and upon each other. Suddenly, the soldiers in several boats paddled furiously toward another, larger boat, making little headway. I could not make sense of their actions.

To my right, Moses lifted his staff and his free hand. He pointed toward the boat that the others were trying to save. Then I saw. In it stood King Seti, shouting to his decimated army. Moses closed his eyes, and in an instant, Seti's boat was swamped by an enormous wave.

The people cheered. Moses put down his arms, and I could read sorrow, not victory, in his eyes. Only later did he tell me that his sorrow was for the vanity of our people and not for the soldiers' death from Adon's wrath.

Moses and I walked away from the scene and had the soldiers push back our people. "We must stay humbled before Adon's anger and not revel in it," he said. Later in the day, the rains stopped, but the wind kept up, giving us a chance to rest and dry our belongings.

But Joshua's soldiers had no such rest, for they were charged with the terrible task of killing whatever Kemian soldiers were washed ashore yet lived. It was a horrible sight. As far as we could see, the beach was littered with hundreds of bodies, and the sand was soaked in deep red blood. Bodies washed up onto the shore by the tens.

While I understood the necessity of doing what our soldiers had to do, one aspect of it plagued me. I wondered whether had he lived, Horemheb would have agreed to partake in the crossing. Yet I knew in my heart that his anger towards Akhenadon was so great that he surely would have. But would he have done so if he had come to know the man as Moses?

Our soldiers also gathered every bit of armament they could from the dead Kemians. Entire chariots washed up on shore. Those horses that did not drown roamed the beach, and we gathered them up. Food and supply wagons were also salvaged, although some foodstuffs like flour, beans, and other perishables were ruined. Search though we did, Seti's body was never found, and he and his bejeweled, golden breastplate, gold arm and wristbands, and his sword undoubtedly dragged him swiftly to the bottom of the Dashret.

The next morning, Adon's disk rose to a bright blue, cloudless sky. A sleepless Joshua entered Moses' tent, where I sat with his scribe reviewing our account of what had happened.

"We have enough arms now to train as many men as will volunteer," Joshua said. "Some of the young ones are now old enough to start their training, for who knows how many soldiers we will need when we enter Canaan."

"And the Kemian supplies?" I asked.

"Enough to make up for all we left behind several days ago." He remained silent for several moments.

"To you, Moses, I say that in my heart of hearts, I confess my faith was not strong enough. I was prepared to die yesterday, and, worse yet, I… could only envision all of us slaughtered."

Moses half-smiled. "You are a soldier, Joshua, so you reacted so. Yet you are also a natural leader. I urge you to strengthen your faith, for there will be times when you must forego war for peace, and there is nothing that requires more faith than that." Joshua hung his head.

"My men will finish cleaning up today with the help of many volunteers among the people. They organize in tribes, and their leaders have great sway over them, which helps us. But this evening, I have yet one more item of war left to deal with."

Moses and I looked toward each other but said not a word, for we both understood what still plagued Joshua.

Joshua was busy throughout the day supervising his men and speaking with individual soldiers. When night fell, he met with all his Captains.

"It is time to assess what happened. Of course, Adon saw to it that we did not need to fight, yet I still wish to hear your assessments."

"It was a mighty show of Adon's power," one man spoke out. "I do not deny that my knees were shaking from fear and not from the enemy." The others murmured their agreement.

"To see our enemies fall so before our God… it was humbling." Similar comments continued.

"So then we are left with one matter that is quite curious," Joshua continued. "And that is, how did Seti know our route, how fast we progressed, and where we would be most vulnerable? How was he able to get those boats carried across the desert from Waset to the Dashret Sea in time to sail across and await our arrival here? Does that not seem strange to you all?" Heads shook in agreement, yet one head remained still.

"Does anyone have any ideas how this could have happened, for it will inform our strategy as we journey on? The lives of our people depend on us getting this right."

"Somehow, word must have gotten back to Seti," one of the Captains offered. "I can see how perhaps knowledge of our route was discovered since several people had to know about it, and they told others. But I cannot see how he figured out our progress, so he knew where to strike at exactly the right time."

"Yes," Joshua said."Your thoughts echo mine. So as I thought on this further, the only way Seti could get regular reports would have been through our messenger system, right? I hate to say that, Siamun, for you, were entrusted with that. Do you have any idea who in your relay team would have been a traitor to our cause? I mean, who would dare betray Adon and Moses? Who would betray an entire people who simply wished for their freedom?"

Siamun was quiet, staring straight at Joshua. "Are you thinking of who it might be?" Joshua asked.

"You know damned well I need not think on who it might be!" Siamun spat out angrily. All eyes immediately turned to their colleague in arms, a man they each had come to trust. One of the Captains put his hand to his dagger.

"It is you who the traitor is! You and that false prophet and his impotent Chief Priest. To think that he could ever have been King of the Two Lands. He is a torture to the eyes of normal men. He is…"

"Enough!" Joshua shouted. "Remove his sword and dagger. Bind him and secure him. Then round up each of the men in the messenger system and bind them, too, but far away from each other, so they can no longer plot against us."

The next morning, Moses presided at their executions. Siamun was stoned to death by his fellow Captains while his co-conspirators were forced to watch. Then each of them, Siamun included, was beheaded. All had their body parts scattered. In that way, given their obvious faith in Amun and the Afterlife, they could not achieve the next world, for their bodies would not be whole.

As for the rest of us, we packed and continued on, full of conflicting emotions. In two days, we camped before the mountain pass to which Adjo had guided us. We entered between two large cliffs, giving us daytime shade for the first time in months. We were now free to complete our journey in peace.

Or so we thought.

Scroll Forty-Four

The Tablets

For six terrible months we traversed that rocky, mountainous part of the Mafkat. When I say traversed, I mean back and forth, east, west, north, and south, again and again. We would take one route, always heading east to Adon's rising, and within a ten-day, find ourselves retracing our route back from a dead end. Adjo was both frustrated and embarrassed, although by his own admission, even before the journey, he had told us that this was the only area with which he was only slightly familiar.

The going was not easy, for the valleys were filled either with deep sand or large rocks and boulders, such that the chariots could not advance and, at times, had to be carried. Day after day, our people had to trudge through the sand and side-step rocks that turned their ankles. The going was painfully slow.

Our first true emergency came after two months in the mountains. Adjo was unfamiliar with the area we were in, and we could not find water sources. Water had to be rationed, which lasted only about a ten-day, and we still did not find water.

The people, as we surmised would happen, began to complain again. Only this time, Moses was angry with them. "Why do they lose faith so quickly? Do they not know by now that Adon will always provide?"

After morning prayers, Joshua and I helped Moses climb a hill next to our campsite to ask Adon for guidance, for Moses' ability to walk was hindered by the pain in his joints. He was so bent over he could not look forward and struggled to keep his balance. Later that day, we helped him back as he explained that Adon had given him a vision of a nearby mountain that would have water. Yet the next day, when we reached the place where Moses said he was sure Adon had indicated, we could not find a spring. We decided to camp for a few days to give our people rest and for our Council to meet and plan.

After two days, with water supplies almost gone, Adjo came to Moses. "I have been watching on that side of the mountain," he said, pointing, "and I notice that a healthy family of desert mice keep going in through a crack between a large boulder and the wall. I believe they are getting water there. We should try to get in."

Adjo and a few of Joshua's soldiers tried to crawl through the narrow crack, but even the smallest and thinnest man could not enter. They recruited several children, but even they could not pass through the crack. But the one who made it the farthest said he could smell dampness.

The soldiers disassembled a chariot and used the hard axle wood as a fulcrum to move the boulder, but after many tries, the wood cracked. Moses and I walked to the site to see how the men were faring. The group argued and cursed but could not come up with any alternatives. Moses looked to the sky and held up his arms to Adon, his staff in his right hand. I watched as his arm began to shake, and I immediately went to his side, thinking he was ill. His body gave off such heat I knew at once he was possessed.

When the shaking stopped, Adjo and I helped him climb over the rocks that led to the cave entrance. He placed his hands on the boulder and closed his eyes, his lips moving in silent prayer. He then retreated and told the soldiers to try again. This time the strongest eight soldiers wedged themselves between the boulder and the wall and pushed with all their muscled strength, groaning loudly with their efforts. As we stood in amazement, the rock gave way painfully slowly, advancing the width of a man's finger with each push, loudly grinding the sand beneath it. We held our breath until the space was wide enough for a man to fit through. Moses raised his arms, and the soldiers stopped and bent over, panting. Adjo immediately crawled in and, for several moments, did not emerge.

"Are you alright?" one of the soldiers called to him. No answer. He called again. In another moment, Adjo crawled out, held up his goatskin, and poured fresh water out of it. The crowd that had gathered went wild with joy.

"Adon has provided for you once again," I shouted to the crowd. "Let this be a lesson to all who would doubt Adon's miracles. He will never abandon us! Never!" Again there were cheers.

Thus fortified, we continued on. Adjo had taken it upon himself to continually ride ahead of us in order to find water. But now food began to run out, despite what we had salvaged from the Kemian army. In a month, rationing began, as did the complaining.

"I am tired of it!" Moses shouted at our small group of High Priests. "How can a people who have seen His miracles with their own eyes, who have been saved by the acts of Adon every time they were in need… how can they be so unfaithful?" He leaned on his staff, his head bent down from his exertion.

"You tell me that they wonder if they should go back to Kem. Do you know what I fear? After all this… this whining, they will anger Adon, and He will rain his wrath down upon them as He did upon the Kemians. Our attempt to bring up new people to serve and worship Him will be for naught." Now he pulled back his chair and sat.

After a few moments of silence, Eleazar spoke. "What would you have us do, Moses?"

"We will do anything you say," Ithamar added. "We are as concerned over their faithlessness as you are."

Moses closed his eyes, and we all remained silent. "I will again seek Adon's counsel. On the morrow, you will all help me climb atop this mount to talk to our God. I will be a few days at least, perhaps a ten-day. Let us pray I come down with an answer.

"And I will take with me the commandments that I have decided would be acceptable to Adon from the Forty-Two Negative Confessions. If he agrees with my choices, I will carve them in stone and bring them to the people. Then they will have a simpler way to govern their behavior."

"Yes, this is the right thing to do," Nadab said. "The people need this." Abihu, Eleazar, and Ithamar all nodded their agreement, as did I.

"We will prepare food for you," I added, "as well as tools."

The first evening that Moses was gone, a huge fight broke out in the camp between those who complained most fiercely about our conditions and those who defended Moses, the High Priests and me.

"It has been more than a year since we left our homeland," one man shouted. "And what do we have? We are weary and sick. The stale bread the overseers in the quarries gave us was more than we have now at Moses' hands. We have lost most of our possessions, meager as they were. For what? For a God that we cannot even see!" Most of the crowd shouted their agreement. No matter what our defenders said, others shouted them down.

"I say, let us at least have something real to worship, something whose spirit is contained within, something that can carry our messages to this Adon."

"Yes, good idea!"

"What should we make?"

"The Apis Bull!" a young man yelled. More shouting and cheering.

"That would be an affront to Adon," a woman carrying a young child called out.

"Let us make a calf, then. We carry much gold with us to

trade, and it melts easily."

I stood there in disbelief, not knowing what to do, and I fear that to this day, I have been damned by Adon for not forcefully interceding. Joshua raced to me, wanting to know what to do. I could have asked him to stop this madness, but something in my heart overpowered my reasoning, and I felt it best to let the people get this out of their system before Moses returned.

By late the next night, the fires that had been lit were ready for the gold to be melted and poured into molds dug into the sand. On the third day, when the two halves hardened and cooled and were fused together, the people brought it out with great joy and celebration.

I refused to be part of this sacrilegious behavior and hid in my tent, trembling, while the revelry went on all night. Little did I know that up above us, Moses had already been greeted with happiness by Adon over his choice of the commandments that would provide a simple frame, like a weaver's loom, for our people. Yet after carving the commandments, he would now share with all the people, Moses felt uneasy and knew he should return to camp. He slowly descended the mountain, carrying the heavy tablets cradled in one arm and his staff in the other. I shudder to think of how much pain he must have been in.

In the midst of the revelry, with people dancing, drinking, and exhibiting lewd behavior, a soldier looked up to the mountain and called out.

"Look, Moses is right above us!" he said, pointing. Immediately, as if a blanket fell upon the people, a crushing silence overcame them. Seeing their white-bearded father standing above them, stooped as he was, the crowd was overcome by guilt. Their shame caused them to look away. Hearing the sudden silence, I sprang from my tent, and in the blink of an eye, I took in what was happening. I, too, felt such shame and failure I wished Adon would strike me down with one of his bolts.

Moses continued to hobble down, grasping the tablets tight to his chest, until he was just the height of a man above them.

It was not until then that his failing eyes saw the golden calf, and they widened in shock, and tears flowed freely from them. His jaw fell open, and in one shudder of his body, the holy tablets fell from his grasp and shattered.

The effect this had could not have been imagined. The people fell to the ground, men, women, even children, and soldiers, begging for forgiveness. Men cried, women moaned, and people groveled before Moses.

"You have sinned!" Moses roared in a voice I had never heard before. "You have brought idol worship into our midst. You have polluted the sanctity of Adon with false Gods. This cannot be forgiven, for it is not me who must forgive. You have mocked the One and Only God, and for that, there will be grave punishment." He turned his gaze to me then, a gaze filled with such utter contempt and disgust that I felt my shame on public display. I fell to my knees in prayer and repentance. But in my heart, I selfishly wished for death.

The next day, Moses called in Joshua and ordered him to gather the leaders of the rebellion and all who had made or touched the golden calf. With Moses watching, they were executed, men and women both. I, too, was there to witness the punishment, yet I stood apart from Moses, for he wanted nothing to do with me. I did not blame him. My cowardice was a mark upon my soul.

Scroll Forty-Five

A Demanding God

Moses insisted that we stay in this place of memories - terrible memories - for another three months in order to purify it and ourselves and to recommit to Adon. I suspected another reason, too. Moses needed to help us mend our relationships. This work proved difficult.

I have come to believe that the difficulty lay within me, for I did not forgive my own inaction. I looked at our four High Priests as my sons and knew that they often took their charge from me. They looked to me for leadership during the golden calf incident. Instead, I hid.

Moses' way of dealing with this was for us to pray together each day before going out to lead services for our people. We also met every evening before prayers to discuss the day's events and to plan for the next day. Joshua joined us for those meetings. We also met with our Council to charge them with spending time with the people to hear their concerns and to encourage obedience to Adon's law.

After only two ten days of this regimen, Moses started as soon as we arrived in his tent. "I will go back up the mountain and will return with another set of tablets. I feel the people must have this soon to mortar their faith. They need guidance in proper behavior to be faithful to our God." I was pleased to hear Moses say this, for I, too, felt this was critical for our adherents.

"This terrible incident with the golden calf has also taught me something. Our people need to have real objects, symbols of our faith. That has always been a strength of worship in Kem. I was a fool for not recognizing this. Only then can our people's hearts be grounded in something comforting. Adon is too vague in their hearts. They crave real things, as they say."

"What kinds of real objects are you thinking of?" I asked. The other priests shook their heads in agreement.

"I am not certain of all the items needed," Moses said. "I will spend time meditating and communing with Adon over this.

"But I do know that what has always set the Amun devotees apart, aside from the statues of Amun, is that every temple has a sanctum inside, in which Amun supposedly lives. As you know, they believe that a part of Amun lives in these statues and praying to it sends the message directly to Amun.

"We obviously cannot build temples everywhere we travel, so for now, until we reach the land where we will settle, we will set up a special tent, a tabernacle, which we will consider the dwelling place of Adon. The Holy of Holies."

I could see that the High Priests were excited. "This is a wonderful idea, Moses," Nadab said. "The people truly need this."

"They are like sheep that need to be led," Ithamar added.

"It may be more like sheep to slaughter," Moses responded. "We shall see."

Moses was gone for forty days this time, the longest period I had experienced. Every few days, I sent priests up the mountain to bring food and to make sure he was not ill. They reported that he ate little and looked poorly.

Being a few years older than Moses, I, too, suffered from decrepit bones and stomach problems. Still, I decided to visit Moses on the mountain. Four priests helped me make the climb.

"I am sorry to intrude, my brother, but I wanted to be sure that you are eating and…"

"Please do not worry about me, Aharon, for I feast on the presence of Adon. Come sit with me in this place made holy by our God."

We talked for a time and ate a meal together before Moses spoke again. "I wish for you to meditate with me, for Adon will be placing many responsibilities on your shoulders as Chief Priest. Once the tabernacle is built, you will be the only one allowed to enter the sacred space." He took my hand and squeezed it, and for the first time since the golden calf, I felt a sense of peace. I breathed in deeply several times, and then we closed our eyes and meditated.

As Chief Priest and a trained scribe, as I aged, I came to realize how inadequate words can sometimes be, especially when only a very few have ever experienced what you try to describe. So it was that morning, for as we meditated, I experienced something that was indescribable in words. Yet I feel I must try for those in future generations who read this account.

In a few moments, I felt my breathing calming and grounding me, no separation between me and the ground I sat upon, and no pains in my body. And in the very next moment, I was no longer me. I was but a tiny part of myself, for another entity, something far greater than myself, had entered my body and heart. I was suddenly lifted up, high up, weightless, looking out at the miracle of abundance below me. Mother Nile flowed effortlessly beneath me to the beautiful Great Green. Everywhere I looked, I saw abundance. The fish in the sea, the animals and trees in the forests, the grasses of the Delta, the birds in the air. People of all looks and colors populating their countries.

My head spun. Then I heard Him. No, not a voice, certainly not a human voice. It was… there is no word I can use. The sound infused me, and it vibrated throughout my body. It saturated me with understanding. Light shone within me. For an eternity, I was light, only light, holy light. Never before was I certain of anything like I felt now that we are all part of the heavenly order and all part of Adon's plan. I felt happy, fulfilled, complete.

When I opened my eyes, Moses was watching me, a broad smile on his face. "He came to you," he said.

"He came into me... it was... like nothing I have ever experienced." I still was in disbelief, dizzy.

"We will not talk more about it for fear of lessening its impact," Moses said. I nodded, for I understood perfectly what he meant. Instead, we sat in silence. My heart yearned to hold on to the fleeting moments I had just experienced.

I descended the mountain a few days later with my brother, helping to support him as he insisted on carrying the tablets. Priests met us soon after we departed. This time Moses was not greeted by sin, but by a cheering crowd, for a few hundred of the most devoted had waited at the base of the mountain all this time for him to return.

As we neared the desert floor, Eleazar, Ithamar, Nadab, and Abihu came running up to meet us. I thought that they carried bad news, but their smiling faces told me otherwise.

"We heard him," Ithamar, out of breath, said excitedly.

"We all did, the priests... and the people," Eleazar added.

"We heard the voice of Adon!" Abihu explained.

"Yes, a few days ago, and only for a few moments, there was a sound... I cannot describe it... perhaps a rumbling," Ithamar went on. "But we felt the very ground shake, and when we looked up to the mountain, we saw a cloud completely surrounding the peak."

"It was God announcing the coming of what I hold in my arms," Moses said, and he hobbled past us all toward the crowds below.

"My people, people of the One and Only God, hear me. For our, God has sent down ten commandments that we all must follow. Listen well. Remember them. Study them. Repeat them to your children. Live by them as examples.

And if we all abide by them, then, and only then, will we be a great nation." Then Moses began to read.

I am Adon, your God, who brought you out of the land of Kem, out of the house of bondage.

You shall have no other Gods before me.

You shall not make for yourself a graven image, or any likeness of anything that is in heaven above, or that is in the earth beneath, or that is in the water under the earth; you shall not bow down to them or serve them; for I am a jealous God, but showing steadfast love to thousands of those who love me and keep my commandments.

You shall not take the name of the Lord your God in vain; for I will not hold him guiltless who takes my name in vain.

Remember the sabbath day, to keep it holy. Six days you shall labor, and do all your work; but the seventh day is a sabbath to me; in it you shall not do any work, you, or your son, or your daughter, your manservant, or your maidservant, or your cattle, or the sojourner who is within your gates; for in six ages I made heaven and earth, the sea, and all that is in them, and rested the seventh; therefore Adon blessed the sabbath day and hallowed it.

Honor your father and your mother, that your days may be long in the land which I give you.

You shall not kill.

You shall not commit adultery.

You shall not steal.

You shall not bear false witness against your neighbor.

You shall not covet your neighbor's wife, or his manservant, or his maidservant, or his ox, or his ass, or anything that is your neighbor's.

"Hear this, my people, for Adon is our God, Adon is the One!" Then the entire assemblage repeated these same words.

I called a meeting of all priests once Moses was done. Every scribe in the camp was called to make copies of the Ten Commandments, as they became known, enough so that every family would have one. Moses and I held sessions with the High Priests, who then disseminated our teachings about the

Commandments to all our people.

We next brought in artisans in wood to create the tabernacle, which would be located in the Holy of Holies, within the tent of God, a place where sacrifices could be made and prayers to Adon offered by the High Priests. Moses was against sacrificing animals to appease Adon, just as he forbade the practice when he was Akhenadon, King of the Two Lands. But the Yahvehites and the Council thought differently, and since Moses did not have direction given to him by Adon on this matter, he relented. But I know that until his death, he abhorred the sacrifice of animals in the name of Adon.

With the addition of the Commandments and the tabernacle, the comfort level of the people increased. Now there was a normal rhythm to each day. People prayed, they came to the tabernacle to seek intercessions to Adon, and they had a set of behaviors that they had to emulate. Suddenly, we were not wild beasts but respectable people living a higher purpose.

As with all matters of life, rarely do things go smoothly, and though we now moved on, there was one matter that proved the point. That matter was circumcision. I did not know that Moses had asked Adon for counsel on this matter during his forty days on the mountain. I was concerned when Moses told me that Adon's answer was that all men had to be circumcised. I learned of Adon's reasoning when Moses spoke to the camp, only now his feeble voice could not carry. He whispered the words to me, and I spoke them for him.

"People of Adon, please gather closer so you may hear my words, as told to me by Adon. You have all made the choice to follow Adon, and you are the chosen people of Adon. He... has... chosen... you!

"But, I tell you now, if you think it is an easy path you choose, you are surely mistaken. Believing in a One and Only God makes you different from all others. Following the Ten Commandments makes you different. And there is one more thing that will make you different.

"From this day forward, all men must be circumcised." A gasp arose from the crowd. I saw many men put their hands to their groins. Wives and girlfriends looked toward their men, who stared back in disbelief.

"As I said, our God is a demanding God. He requires this as proof of belonging to this miraculous faith. It will show Adon that you are faithful and trust in His word. I, myself, am circumcised, as are all of our priests. In Kem, it was a sign of purity, as it was for two thousand years.

"Our physician priests will begin doing the circumcisions tomorrow, starting with the oldest men and working backward to the youngest. From now on, all male children will be circumcised on the eighth day following their birth to ensure that they have survived the birth experience.

"Only men?" a man shouted from amidst the crowd.

"Yes, only men and boys. It will not change a man's ability to procreate and enjoy relations with his wife. But for a woman to be circumcised would destroy her pleasure in the act. It is in the pleasure of this holy union that we shall be fruitful, and our faith will multiply."

The next few ten days were not the most pleasant of our journey. I thank Adon's mercy for giving us Adjo, who found a deep mountain spring with cooling waters to temper the moans of the men in camp.

Scroll Forty-Six

The Son I Never Knew

It is now the end of the third year of our journey. Who could have imagined this? We have passed through the mountains and are now camped across the Dashret Sea from Midian. We have lost over a thousand of the people who began our journey. Old age, illness, falls from cliffs, and other mishaps have all contributed to these losses. Yet we also gained more than three hundred newborn adherents, a blessing that we all appreciate and celebrate. Never have babies received such love, attention, and caring.

I no longer write my own narrative, for my hands suffer greatly from bone aches, and my heart and stomach now pain me. Instead, my scribe for these many years does the writing for me as I narrate my thoughts and observations to him. He is a smart lad and very devoted. He also studies for the priesthood under High Priest Eleazar.

It is impossible to describe how this journey has affected each of us, but I will start with Moses, for all eyes are upon him every moment of every day. If Horemheb were alive to see him, he would not recognize Moses as Akhenadon. The journey has robbed him of years. That is not entirely true. Perhaps Akhenadon's chosen path, now Moses' path, is what has transformed him into who he is today.

It is not his diminished physical appearance I speak of,

although that is profound. Moses eats little. His body is nearly as thin as his staff, which he must grasp onto when he stands for fear of falling. He is so bent he stares at the ground as he walks. His paunch hangs limp.

His face is what causes people great pain to look upon. His skin is blistered from the desert dryness. His eyes are encircled by black rings. He has even taken to wearing a face covering, showing only his eyes, to spare our people the sorrow of his countenance.

Yet truly, none of this matters, for from his presence emanates a penetrating light so bright that sinners must turn away from it for fear of it exposing their darkest shadows. People say he walks with Adon, and I, admittedly, am one of those. Some say he is truly the son of an ageless God. There are those who claim to have been healed by his mere presence. For me, just breathing in his presence infuses my very soul. He is hardly of this world. I do not think he walks with God. God dwells within him.

Even so, this Man-God is not always a loving, benevolent spirit. I must relate an incident that proves this point. After the Ten Commandments were given and studied, and after we had built the Tabernacle, we developed a daily routine. Not that it was easy, for, amongst other things, we had to adjust to a seven-day cycle rather than the ten-day cycle we had all been raised with. But that ultimately helped since our daily religious practices culminated in the Sabbath observance each week, when the camp rested, and families restored themselves.

It was eight months ago when an incident occurred that left a mark on our people, never to be forgotten. I still dwell on it today, wondering and questioning. We had established a religious routine whereby the people would approach the Tabernacle with offerings. These items would be burned on the alter within the Holy of Holies by me and, due to my frailty, assisted by one of the High Priests. No one other than I could do these offerings, for Adon had given precise instructions to Moses concerning this.

As would happen, Moses and I decided to retreat to a hill

far from the camp to meditate and discuss the delicate issue of succession, for we both knew that our days were numbered. High Priests Eleazar and Ithamar took us by chariot to the site.

For two days and nights, we meditated, seeking Adon's guidance. We talked for hours on end about our people and their future. And when we were done with our plans, we rode back to camp. When we entered the inner circle where the Tabernacle was located, we noticed something strange. There was smoke from an offering coming from the Holy of Holies. My heart sank. In addition, dozens of people milled about inside the Tabernacle, a sin that caused me to gasp.

Moses was enraged. He was helped out of the wagon and hobbled to the Tabernacle. Eleazar noticed Joshua and his guards nearby and frantically called to him.

"Get those people out of the Tabernacle and hold them separate," he had the presence of mind to order. "Put a cordon around Moses. And push the rest of the people back… far back from the Tabernacle." Joshua rushed to do as Eleazar requested.

"How dare you transgress against God's word!" Moses whispered angrily at High Priests Nadab and Abihu, for his voice was weak. "Even I am not allowed into the Tabernacle. You made offerings. You allowed people into the Tabernacle. You must be made an example, for this is a high crime in Adon's eyes. You… and those you allowed into the Tabernacle must be punished."

"I… we are sorry, Moses, but there was an emergency. A family… we could not wait for Aharon to return… they are dying…"

"There are no exceptions," Moses said. "The words of Adon are absolute. I will seek Adon's word on your punishment. Now remove yourselves and beg forgiveness of Adon."

Moses was so weak after this confrontation he had to be helped to his tent. There he sat for two more days before Adon's answer came to him. He called Joshua and me into his tent.

"It is with a heavy heart that I must place a terrible burden upon you, Joshua. Adon has spoken to me. What happened was a terrible transgression. The Tabernacle is now polluted and must be cleansed, a difficult task, for our God is exacting.

"This must serve as an example to the people. If they obey God's will, then He will protect them and heap blessings upon them. But if they violate His most precious laws, the penalty is death. I instruct you to put Nadab and Abihu to death, along with all those who entered the Tabernacle. They have polluted Adon himself!"

Joshua fell back against his chair's back. "Surely. Moses... surely there must be another way..."

"Surely not, Joshua. Do not dare to question the word of God! That is His order. My heart aches, too. I must leave it to you to carry it out. And it must be done quickly, for all to see." Joshua left, burdened with the terrible task he faced.

This event, and Moses' response to it, weighed heavily on my soul. Why was Moses so terribly angry by this all too human transgression? Where did this anger come from? Was this truly Adon's judgment? I will admit that the answers that I came up with that fit uncomfortably as truth in my heart were troubling, for I came to believe that Moses' decision came more from him than Adon.

Moses always carried within him the burdens of his past. He was cast aside, tortured in his heart, for his physical appearance, something that he could not change. He was rejected by a priesthood that should rightfully have embraced him. He was driven from Kem by sinister forces. But most of all, most painful to his heart and soul, was his forced separation from Nefertiti. She grounded him, gave him direction, shared with him her bodily pleasures, supported his vision, and gave him children that were torn from him.

I love my brother, but I know that he carried within him terrible anger for the torments that were thrust upon him. He hid that anger well. He built walls around it. By sheer force of will, he kept it imprisoned within. But, such prisoners can never be contained forever. Like a suppurated boil, it must eventually burst out. In my heart, I believe that is what happened with the Tabernacle incident.

I soon paid a visit to Nadab's tent, where he and Abihu were guarded. My heart was filled with pain.

"I do not profess to know why your punishment is so severe," I began, "but I do know that Moses has prayed long for an answer from Adon. He has received it. You shall be put to death." I hung my head. They said not a word to object.

"You two are like sons to me. I know that despite this transgression, which you will make amends for with your death, you will earn a place beside Adon in the hereafter. I wish your deaths to be painless. I suspect I will see you sooner than we can imagine." With that, I hugged each of them to my breast. Their bodies shook with fear.

All that day, Joshua's men dug a pit atop a high sand dune. When it was completed, they marched the transgressors to the base of the dune, many of them struggling against the soldiers grasps. Women cried, clutching their children to them tightly as the soldiers pried them apart, handing the children to relatives. Those adherents who wished to observe God's wrath gathered around the base, a few hundred men, women, and children. One by one, the transgressors were put to the sword and laid in the pit in a terrible, bloody spectacle. I was helped to the top before Nadab, and Abihu received their punishment. Tears flowed down my cheeks as I blessed them and turned to all the others who lay in the pit. I turned to Joshua and nodded. He gave the signal, and with swift sword strokes, the bodies of the two High Priests toppled into the pit, their heads rolling before them.

The camp was strangely silent as the task of purifying the Tabernacle went on for the next thirty days. The entire tent was dismantled. Each board was scrubbed, and a smokey offering was made to purify them. The same was done for the fabric that covered the Tabernacle. The gold chains and ornate drapes were cleaned, and finally, the Tabernacle was reconstructed. Prayers outside were conducted, blessing the ground upon which it stood, and I offered prayers inside, with Eleazar and Ithamar assisting me. It was a somber experience, and one that left a mark on our hearts, for each person had to reconcile for himself the contradiction of our loving yet angry God.

Eleazar and Ithamar were especially affected by the execution of their colleagues, for they had trained with them and served with them for the longest time. Following the event, they were somber and subdued. They went about their work, but I saw them struggling with the implications of God's will. They avoided Moses whenever possible.

As for the people's sobering reaction, Moses felt it was a sad but important example. That became clear when we met a few days later with Joshua to explain our plans. As soon as he entered Moses' tent, I could see he was uncomfortable, avoiding our eyes.

"Joshua, you are the son I never knew," Moses started. "I am sorry I had to place you in this role. It could not be avoided, or else I would have." Joshua sat silently.

"We have..." Moses started, moving to our business, but I sensed that Joshua needed to speak.

"Joshua, is there something you feel you must say?"

He shifted in his seat. "There is. Moses, you say there was no other choice, and you know how much I respect you and would give my life for you. But still, I wonder if there was a better way."

Moses closed his eyes for a moment before he spoke. "Yes, there were other ways that I thought better, Joshua, other forms of punishment not so severe. I argued, and I wrestled with Adon over them. But who am I to decide? I am but a speck of dust in the universe that Adon has created from nothingness. I do not comprehend this... this decision, but there must be a greater reason for it that we do not yet understand."

Joshua shook his head, looking down at the floor. "I will say this, Moses... and Aharon. I have seen the power of our God. I have seen both His creation and His destruction and feel my… insignificance. I will be the obedient servant I have trained to be and await understanding later." He hesitated. "Now, what is it you wish to speak with me about?"

"Joshua, your pain rests in my heart. Truly, I feel it." Moses continued. "Have faith that it will all become clear to you… to all of us, later. What we must discuss with you is more pressing." He gave Joshua a chance to collect himself.

"Both Aharon and I are advanced in years, far more than either of us thought possible. We played together as children when I was barely able to walk. Isn't life funny, for we are still friends, and now neither of us can walk well?" We smiled at Moses' words.

"I fear that one or both of us will pass into Adon's arms soon," he said, reaching over to pat my hand. "Our people must have continuity, a strong leader who will take them the rest of the way to the land we will soon settle, wherever that is. I have been told by Him that we are close to the end of our journey.

"We have discussed and debated this for months now. We have called you in to tell you that we have chosen you to be the leader of our people."

Joshua's face paled. He drew a breath, and his hands fell to his side, his strength drained from him. It took him moments of silence before he was able to speak. "I know you do not joke, Moses, but I fear you… you and Aharon are sorely mistaken. I am not a leader of people, I am a leader of soldiers. There is a big difference, for a soldier is sworn to obey without question, without complaint."

"You are right about that," I started to say.

"And besides, I have no religious training in the ways of Adon. I only listen to what the two of you and the High Priests tell me. How can I, not even a trained priest, lead our people?"

"Listen, you must listen carefully," Moses replied. "This is the way it is supposed to be. I will help you to see the light. Look at Kem. It has been a great nation for more than two thousand years. And how did that happen? The High Priests study such things as they seek higher truths. What has made Kem successful is that they devised a way to divide responsibilities. Generals waged war, and priests administered religion. When I was a younger man, I often said they waged religion." I smiled at the recollection.

"Now our young nation is ready to divide leadership, too. We must have a strong leader for the people. Leave the religious aspects to the High Priests and future High Priests. Work together.

"Your soldiers adore you. They respect you. I have seen you be fair but firm with them. You recognize that discipline is important, especially self-discipline. Our people need the same, although they often act more like children than experienced soldiers. Be patient, but hold high expectations of them, and you will all prosper."

With that, we all sat quietly, absorbing Moses' words. We could see the battle going on in Joshua's heart. It took a while before he spoke.

"I am honored to be asked that you both think so highly of me. Adon, too, from what you have said. But I have doubts as to my ability to take on such a task. I am humbled beyond imagining. Allow me a few days to think on this, and I will come back with an answer."

"There is no need," Moses whispered, "for I already know your answer. You will lead our people into the land we will settle. Adon has already shown me this."

Scroll Forty-Seven

My Right Arm Has Been Severed

The Sabbath. If there is one gift that Adon had given to us, it is the Sabbath. From the setting of Adon's disk on the sixth day to its setting on the seventh, we pause to give thanks for the blessings we have, to pray for help and guidance for the days to come, and to reflect on Adon and our relationship to Him and to our fellow humans. It is time we honor both the masculine and feminine sides of Adon. It is a sweet day, the Sabbath.

I lay here, trying to narrate to my scribe, but my energy drains quickly, and I alternate between waking and sleeping. One of my blessings is having such a patient scribe who sits quietly and reminds me where we left off when I awaken. Yet even then, I find it difficult to remember what I wanted to say.

The pain in my heart increases, and sometimes feels as if an elephant is sitting on my chest. I can no longer walk even fifty steps without my breath leaving me. So, I spend most of my time resting in my tent, thinking all the time about what my life has meant. Have I done anything worthwhile? Is Moses pleased with me? But, most of all, I think of Adon.

I wonder, is Adon truly the One and Only God? We certainly believe so, but what of the multitudes of humans? Are they wrong to worship their Gods? Or are they really worshipping Adon by another name? Are we so petty as to argue over what Master created the universe? Does He, or possibly She, look down upon us, laughing at our foolishness?

I think back to my training in Kem and their beliefs in the creation of Kem from Nun, nothingness, the ethereal realm. How did Adon create the rocks we stand on, the flowers, trees, animals, mountains, and deserts from nothingness? I can only think for so long before sleep takes me. And then I wonder, is that what the Afterlife is, a long, dream-filled sleep?

It has been a few days since Moses visited me, even though our tents are next to one another. He has his own infirmities. Now he spends his time instructing Joshua, who has his own ideas about leadership. To his credit, Moses does not attempt to influence that, only his religious training so he will better understand the boundaries between everyday leadership and spiritual leadership.

We are now camped at the farthest inland reach of the Dashret Sea. We have rested here for three Sabbaths as we regain our strength. We are, but a stone's throw from Midian land and Joshua has sent his emissaries to request permission to transit their land on the way to Canaan. The negotiations have been difficult, for the Midian king does not wish to antagonize his neighbors, nor Kem either. But Joshua's emissaries have told him the story of the Kemian army's drowning, showing him the swords they salvaged. In the end, we were allowed to go through, but we needed to stay close to the border between Midian and Edom.

"We need to get permission now to go through the lands of Edom and Moab in order to get to the Salt Sea and into Canaan," Joshua told us. "The people are eager to go." Both Moses and I sat in our chairs, hardly moving, trying to stay awake.

"Is there a problem with that?" I asked.

"We have heard that neither country wishes to have us on their land. They fear we might stay. They have also heard rumors that our army defeated the Kemians, so they are wary of us."

"And you offered them a promise of peace?" Moses asked.

"Of course, as you wished. I think I can argue for permission to detour across the northeastern part of their lands, then head straight west to Canaan. It will lengthen our time, but we are so close I feel our people will be agreeable to the delay."

"If you are asking for our permission, I believe I speak for us both in saying to go ahead," Moses assured him.

And so we proceeded to enter the lands of our future neighbors. We had finally completed our perilous journey through the Mafkat, a journey that no one who participated would ever forget and one that I felt sure our future generations would recall.

We were not exactly treated well as we passed through Midian. Soldiers watched us from every hilltop, and Joshua had to be sure to protect our flanks with an adequate show of force. We were pleased when we left Midianite land.

Edom and Moab proved to be the greater problem. Their people eyed us with suspicions, and not a friendly look or kind word passed their lips. Mothers gathered their children as our long caravan passed through, pointing to our ragged, dirty group with obvious disdain.

As we passed Edom and entered the easternmost portion of Moab, Joshua sent scouts ahead to see what we might face when we entered Canaan. In two days, they returned, their horses slathered in sweat.

"We never reached Canaan or even near it," they reported. "There is trouble brewing at the northeastern edge of Moab. The Ai people are massing as if for war."

Joshua took in all the information they could provide. "It does not sound as if they are a well-trained force. Would you agree?"

"From what we could see, they were mostly farmers," one of the scouts responded. "But there were regular soldiers nearby. Not sure whether they have a strong army. It was impossible for us to judge."

Joshua immediately called a meeting of his captains. "It appears we have a fight coming up. Do any of you know anything about the Ai people north of Moab?" His captains looked at each other and shrugged their shoulders.

"Our scouts report that they are massing people to attack us as we pass through. I am not going to wait until they decide a good time to attack. I prefer to attack them first. We will draw up a battle plan based on what the scouts have told us about the land. We have fewer than one thousand men ready to fight, many with inferior weapons. That means that our soldiers from Kem and those that we trained on our journey will have to do the majority of the fighting." The captains shook their heads in agreement.

The next morning, after prayer services, Joshua met with Moses and me to explain his strategy. "I see no reason to put our women, children, and elderly in harm's way," he said. "I will lead an army of five hundred of our soldiers to challenge them. I will leave another five hundred here for protection in case this is a ruse to leave you unprotected. I would like your blessings to proceed." We gave them and said a prayer for a sure and quick victory.

Joshua led his army to the hills and valleys of northeastern Moab, and on the second day, they met the enemy. From their vantage point on a small hill, they determined that the ragtag enemy numbered perhaps two hundred soldiers and an equal number of farmers and peasants probably forced into the fight and armed with pitchforks and staffs.

"We will camp here and wait for just before Adon's rising," he told his Captains. "Here is what we will do," he said, drawing his battle plan in the dusty earth.

While it was yet dark, Joshua's army rose and quietly readied for the battle ahead. "The scouts say all is ready. Remember, we fight for Adon and for the right of our people to live together in a land where we can worship as we please. Be brave. Be merciless."

The footmen crested the hill, crouching to avoid detection. When they were all in position, the horsemen rode up. Once all were in place, Joshua dropped his arm, and the men charged down the slope toward the encampment. As they shouted their battle cries, the enemy camp awoke and, in their confusion, were pathetic in their defense. Too late, Joshua realized his mistake.

What his men were confronting was not the enemy army but poor peasants given no warning or training in battle. Joshua's men slaughtered those that stayed to fight, but most ran. It was then that Joshua looked around at the hills that surrounded them. As he feared, the crests suddenly grew hair, the outlines of soldiers carrying spears and swords. With Adon's disk rising, they charged down upon Joshua's men.

"Rally around!" he screamed, but before his men could figure out his meaning, the enemy began throwing wave after wave of spears. Scattered around the field, Joshua's men fell.

"Circle around!" he yelled, and this time the men came to their senses. "Archers to the outside!" he shouted. "Shield bearers and spearmen, protect them!" As the enemy charged, they began to fall to well-aimed Adonite arrows. "Swordsmen, ready!" Joshua called out and dismounted. He led them to the rear in a flanking maneuver.

As the enemy concentrated on the core of Joshua's defense, his swordsmen, with Joshua in the lead, created a pincer that trapped many of the Ai soldiers in a vise. In an hour, it was all over. The enemy retreated. Yet there was no cheer of victory.

"I was a fool!" Joshua said, kicking a rock. "I should have anticipated this." As he walked the battlefield, his men took up their dead and wounded. Thirty-four of his soldiers were killed and twenty-eight wounded. Ai lost seventy-three soldiers. Any wounded enemy was summarily killed by Joshua's men. Joshua forbade his men from counting the dead peasants.

In the aftermath of the battle, a skirmish really, Joshua met with his Captains, and together they assessed the fight. To engage an enemy in its territory, turn the tide of battle, and have the enemy withdraw was probably the best they could have expected. They learned important lessons about this enemy and would assume that all of the local armies would be similarly equipped and trained, for local tribes usually fought each other. They now knew how they needed to train. This gave them hope for the future.

Before they left the battlefield, Joshua called two of his best scouts to him. "We are close to Canaan where we sit right now. I want you to dress in the clothes of two of these dead peasants and go into Canaan and spy on the people and the army there. We will be at this spot with our entire people in about ten days, so meet us here. We must be prepared for what we will face when we cross the river into Canaan. Go!"

Back in camp, Joshua met in my tent with me Moses, Eleazar, and Ithamar. I found it hard to breathe, and even walking from my bed to my chair was difficult.

"I am ashamed to say that we did not do as well as I had hoped against the Ai," Joshua began. "I made a foolish mistake, one that I will never again repeat. Yet we managed to fight to a draw, I would say. The enemy withdrew."

"What turned the tide of battle?" Ithamar asked.

"I think it was the accuracy of our archers and our swordsmen," Joshua responded. "Every arrow, every thrust met its mark."

"Due to the constant training that you insisted on throughout our journey," Moses pointed out. "While we all rested, you were out in the desert making your archers train until their fingers bled." Joshua bowed his head.

"I suspect it was also the work of Adon, who will always be at our side. We may suffer defeat here or there, but ultimately righteousness will prevail." That was all my voice could say.

After the group left, I lay down, narrating my impressions to my scribe. When he left, I felt my heart pumping, mixing my thoughts together, blending them into an ether that parted to reveal a bright light. The most pleasant sound I had ever heard played in my ears. I felt a strange peace descend into my heart, and I alternated between sleep and wakefulness. I no longer felt pain. My heart felt light.

I found wakefulness no longer desirable. The diffuse light that illuminated my sleep beckoned me toward it. I smiled to myself. It was suddenly so clear to me that all was finally revealed, and my heart filled with joy. No more darkness, no more pain, no more wars. Only love.

"How?… How did you know?" Joshua asked when he entered the tent.

"I sensed something was wrong when he gave me his narration," I said. "I could not understand some of his words. He kept drifting off to sleep."

Tears ran from Joshua's eyes. He wiped them with the back of his hands. "How can I tell this to Moses?" he cried. Aharon lay on his bed, and I swear there was a slight smile on his lips.

Joshua turned to me. "You will accompany me to Moses' tent. You must continue to record all that you see. Future generations will wonder how this all came about, how it ended, whether in glory or failure." I nodded and grabbed my tools.

When we entered the tent, Moses was standing, leaning heavily on his staff. His eyes were red, and his breaths came as great heaves.

"Take me to him," he whispered. Neither Joshua nor I said a word. Joshua held his arm as we walked.

Moses walked unsteadily to Aharon's side. "Help me," he said, motioning us to him, and we helped him kneel by the bed. He took Aharon's hand in his, bent his head to it, and kissed it gently.

"Oh, my brother, go gently, go peacefully to Adon's side." He stayed by the bed, deep in prayer for the longest time. Finally, he asked us to help him stand. He trembled as he held his staff and looked into Joshua's eyes. Tears rolled down his cheeks.

"My right arm has been severed," he whispered.

Scroll Forty-Eight

What Will We Do?

I do not come to this role easily. Up to now, I have been taught by Aharon the art of recording what is important. It is an entirely different matter when making my own decisions on what should be preserved for future generations. Still, Eleazar, who also trains me to be a priest, helps by offering suggestions. I also tend to write fast and do not describe events well enough, he says. I will try to do better.

We are now camped across from Canaan, at the base of Mount Nebo, north of the plains of Moab, and I've just left a meeting between Joshua and the two spies he sent into Canaan. To be truthful, I wish I had not been asked to attend.

"What did you find out?" Joshua asked, "aside from the land being very fertile and well suited for our needs. What I need are details on the army." His Captains were also eager for military news.

The two men looked at each other, but neither spoke. "Well?" asked Joshua.

"The news is not good," the older one said, taking charge. "The people there are far taller than the average Kemian."

"So?" one of the Captains said.

"So, the problem is not with them, it is with their army. The soldiers we saw were huge, almost like giants."

"Like giants? What does that mean?"

"I mean, they were big men, probably picked for their size."

"Were they fast? Did you see them fight?"

"We did see one training session for new recruits. We are both thinking they are recruiting more soldiers, knowing that we plan to settle in Canaan. Anyway, their swords and spears befit their size. They also have chariots… many of them."

"Would you say they are agile?" another Captain asked.

"No, I would say they were definitely not agile. They relied on their strength more." The Captains continued asking more detailed questions.

Joshua mulled over the report. "Thank you both for the good job you have done. I need you and several others to go back into Canaan and gather more information, especially about neighboring tribes. Will they ally with Jericho or the Amorites? Do they plan to attack us first? Find out as much as you can and hurry back. You are excused." The men did not move. "Is there more?"

"There is, Joshua. We picked up much distaste for us, for Yahvehites especially, due to their history with them. They will not welcome us, that is for sure. They are preparing for war."

Once the meeting was over, Joshua and his Captains met privately, and I was excused. It took my entire effort to stop my hand from shaking. Giants! How would our small army be able to defeat them? Would we all be massacred?

Two days later, Joshua requested a meeting with Moses, planned for right after morning prayers, when Moses would be most alert. Once again, I was asked to attend.

"Moses, I wish to show you our strategy for entering Canaan. As you know, the King of Jericho has refused to give us permission to enter his territory. The answers are the same from surrounding areas. We have tried to settle in peace, but unfortunately, we will need to fight our way in. That is the only possible way I know to find a suitable place for our people to settle."

"Is it worth it?"

"My spies report that the land is very fertile, flowing with milk and honey, they say. This will not be easy."

"Joshua, my son, always remember that our people were born and raised in hardship. We journeyed through hardship to be here. Nothing has come easy for us, but because of those hardships, we will prevail. So, go in confidence, Joshua, for Adon has told me that we will have our own land there, across that little river in the distance."

Joshua laid out a map of the area that his spies had drawn. "Here is my strategy." When he was done, Moses spoke.

"I ask you to wait for two or three Sabbaths before making a final decision. Adon has told me that changes are coming, and I want to be more certain of what I face before I embark on a military mission. Wait until your spies return." Joshua nodded and bowed his head before leaving.

During our wait, the mood in the camp was buoyant. No one but those of us in the meeting knew of the spies' report, and so the people were eager to cross the river to their new home. There was much singing, dancing, and merriment almost every evening. Offerings from our adherents for good fortune, fertile land, and healthy children kept Eleazar and Ithamar busy.

It was just before the third Sabbath that the spies returned. Joshua instructed his Captains to have them all report together. That happened the next morning.

"Jericho is definitely staging for war," one of the spies stated. "They have positioned soldiers near the border on the other side of the river."

"Worse yet," another reported, "there is now an Amorite confederacy of Jerusalem, Hebron, Jarmuth, Lachish, and Eglon united against us should we enter their territory."

"Also a northern confederacy," a pair of spies reported. "The Ai commander has reported to them on our strength from the soldiers they saw. Fortunately, he felt he faced our entire army, so they would not expect our full strength."

When all had reported, Joshua demanded secrecy and asked everyone to leave and to report back to him that evening after prayers. His brow was creased, and he paced nervously as I gathered my tools.

Joshua did not appear for prayers that evening, but by the time of the meeting, he had already formed his strategy for entering Canaan. His Captains made suggestions, and by the end of the evening, Joshua felt ready to explain all to Moses. This would be the final push to claim our land.

"I cannot look at another map, Joshua," Moses said the following morning. "Instead, have your soldiers carry me part of the way up this mountain. Let me see the land we shall settle in and what your grand plan is to conquer it."

"But why? You will see it in due course. Let me just explain it here so as not to burden you with such a climb."

"I will explain later. For now, I ask you to abide by my request." And so Joshua called eight of his strongest soldiers, and they prepared a carry chair for Moses and hiked up the mountain. When they reached a good lookout, they stopped and helped Moses to stand. He held to his staff with one hand and Joshua's arm with the other, yet he still swayed unsteadily. I stood within hearing distance. The soldiers stood a distance away.

"You look out upon the land of Canaan," Joshua said, sweeping his arm over the entire expanse before them. Moses looked in silence for a long time.

"You are right, it is fertile. The greens comfort my failing eyes after so much desert. And so many animals and trees. It is beautiful. Adon's promise is real, Joshua. You shall soon have it. Our people shall soon have it."

"And so shall you, Moses. You have been our guiding light, our inspiration. Without you, none of this could have happened."

"Oh, I am not so sure of that, my son. It has been a long journey for me. To think I was once King of the mightiest nation, commander of an army of tens of thousands, builder of monumental works. None of that mattered. What all of us have created, you, me, Aharon, the priests, and our followers, that is the greatest achievement of my life.

"Joshua, I will not walk this final step with you. I will not enter Canaan…"

"What… what are you saying, Moses? You cannot…"

"Allow me to finish… please, for I am weak, and it is an effort even to speak." He turned halfway and tried hard to stand, so he could look Joshua in the eye. "Do not have any regrets about what I say. My role in this life was to bring you here to this new beginning. We are a people unique in this world, believing in Adon, the One and Only God, a power so mighty, so all-encompassing no human can imagine Him. But, I am of the old world, one of too many small Gods. Adon has told me I must send this younger generation into the new land, fresh, with ideas as big as Adon's universe.

"I wish you to be fruitful and to multiply and to live in freedom and, eventually, in peace. Always remember where we came from and tell your children and grandchildren the story of Kem and our exodus. Be not afraid of where you are headed, for Adon will be with you forever and ever." With that, he opened his arms and pulled Joshua in for a long embrace.

In the space of two Sabbaths, Joshua immersed himself in training his soldiers for what lay ahead. They practiced being nimble, able to counteract any strengths the enemy might have with speed and cunning. Day and night, they practiced maneuvers.

Moses was in his best form when he blessed Joshua and his army before their first strike into Canaan. Joshua's plan was to take Jericho, immediately on the other side of the river, in a mighty battle, then head north and south to defeat the confederacies that had formed to destroy us.

Joshua was correct. The battle of Jericho was a mighty one and lasted for days. When the king's soldiers retreated to their fortress, Joshua and his men had to devise a way to break down the wall in a vulnerable spot so they could enter and finish the job. By the end, it was a clear victory for us, and ram horns were sounded around the walled fortress. Word of our victory spread quickly to the enemy confederacies.

Joshua left the army in Jericho and rushed back to speak

with Moses, who was heartened by the news. Joshua decided to split the army and send them both north and south to confront the Amorites and the northern tribes, both of which had lost much of their enthusiasm for battle. In a matter of a month, the land was subdued, either in battle or in a treaty. Joshua and his soldiers returned triumphantly to days of celebrations.

On the second Sabbath after their return, Moses called Joshua into his tent. "I feel Adon calling me," he whispered so softly Joshua had to lean closer to his chair to hear. "You must once again carry me up Mount Nebo and leave me for two days. When you return, you and two others who you trust must bury my body…"

"I will not hear of this! In just a few days, we will enter…"

"You must listen, Joshua, for our God has spoken. You will bury me in secret, so none will ever know where I rest. So Adon has instructed." Joshua had to restrain himself from crying, but tears still flowed freely down his cheeks.

"Do not fear, Joshua, for I am filled with joy to finally meet my God. I will again embrace Aharon, for I sorely miss his companionship. I hope I have earned a place beside Nefertiti, for her sweet countenance always buoyed my spirits. And I ache for comforting words from my dear Tiye. My body is spent. It is time for me to go. I leave knowing that the future of my people is in capable hands. Come." Moses then laid his hands on Joshua's bowed head and offered a holy blessing.

The procession up Mount Nebo was solemn. Many tears were shed as we carried our leader to meet our God. For two days, we waited, and on the second day, a fog enveloped the mountain, a fog so dense even the fingers of our outstretched hands were hidden from view. On the eve of that day, the fog lifted, and Joshua and his men hiked back up. Several of the soldiers swore upon death that they had witnessed Moses ascending to heaven toward Adon's outstretched hand. They sank to the ground in tribute and prayerful sobbing.

We cried as Joshua, and two of his most trusted Captains carried Moses' body to its final resting place, all sworn to secrecy about its location. At Moses' instruction, there were no offerings left, not even a marker of his burial within the mountain. We waited for them at the base of the mountain. A ram's horn sounded, and the people all gathered to hear the news.

People cried, some screamed, and all ripped their garments in grief. No work was done for thirty days. We all prayed and reminisced, giving solace to one another for our loss. Adon's presence was thick in the camp.

Toward the end of the month of mourning, people started expressing their fears of what was to come without our spiritual leader. The High Priests did their best to calm those fears. They explained to all the people why Moses could not join us in Canaan. The rituals they had worked hard to develop or adapt from Kem served the people well. It brought calm and stability to our lives. It was at that time that I was officially ordained as a priest.

Now it was time for us to fulfill Moses' dream for our people, to have our own land, freedom to determine our destinies, and freedom to worship the One and Only God. We were one people, but we were still adrift, an emptiness in our souls.

Joshua gave the word that we should all start packing for our entry into Canaan, but we performed the task with heavy hearts. After a few days of helping each other, Joshua called a meeting for the next morning, even before prayers. He climbed atop a boulder and spoke from his heart.

We have mourned the passing of two great men, but we shall not mourn them today. We have fear for what tomorrow will bring, but we shall have no fear today. In our fear and weakness we harbor doubts about our God, but surely we cannot doubt Him today. For today He fulfills His promise. We enter Canaan triumphant, our hearts filled with pride and joy.

Moses and Aharon led us this far. With Adon's help they

rescued us from misery. Their faith, their devotion, convinced Adon to toss the mightiest army into the sea, even while many of us shook and whined in fear and doubt. We overcame the trials of the desert and fought and conquered our new land.

But we are here now, overlooking a fertile land that we will make even more fertile. It is now our job to complete what Moses and Aharon began. Be not afraid, for Adon will protect us. And so, as we we enter Canaan now, I say...

Listen, believers, Adon is our God, our Adon is the One and Only God!

And the people, as one, repeated:

Listen, believers, Adon is our God, our Adon is the One and Only God!

About the Author

Lester Picker has more than 650 writing and photo credits in National Geographic Society publications, Better Homes & Gardens, Forbes, Time, Inc. Publications, Money, Fortune Small Business, Bloomberg Personal Finance, National Parks Magazine, and dozens of other publications. He is a former newspaper reporter, photographer and editor. Les was a weekly columnist for The Baltimore Sun and was a regular commentator on National Public Radio's Marketplace.

As a journalist, Les has cruised on a nuclear submarine deep in the Pacific Ocean and has climbed the highest peak in the Pyrenees. He has withstood minus 50-degree temperatures photographing in the Arctic and survived 120-degree temperatures with a Bedouin tribe in Egypt's desert. He was nearly bitten by a sea lion in the Galapagos (never stand between a mother and her pup!) and was chased by a 16-foot crocodile in South Africa. His camera and tripod were carried off into the Arctic tundra by a curious Grizzly.

Les has published six major novels. All are available through his Amazon Author's Page. **To contact Les, please go to his website: Lesterpicker.com**

Afterward

Those who take on the mantle of Biblical literalists must, at some point, come to grips with the fact that there is no evidence that a mass exodus ever occurred. Despite the Egyptians being meticulous record keepers, there are no known accounts of an exodus as the Old Testament describes. Also, despite archaeological research and excavations going back more than 200 years, there has been no evidence uncovered of thousands of people, let alone 600,000, according to the Bible, tramping through the Sinai. If it had taken 40 years to make that comparatively short trip, then the people would have had to camp in various places for extended periods of time. There is no evidence of this. None.

We know definitively that the Old Testament was written by many authors, and redacted several times, beginning around 400 years after the time of Akhenaten/Moses. There is simply no credible way to treat it as historically accurate. However, the Bible spins a compelling tale of creation and the rise of a people committed to monotheism, a strong moral code, and the rule of law. In that, and not for its scientific accuracy, lies its value.

The introduction of the Creation story and its subsequent seven-day week created a problem for me in Book Three. The Egyptians used a ten-day week throughout their history. A month was 30 days, and a year was 360 days. That left a shortfall of five days which were the Heriu-Renpet days of solemnity and which formed the basis of future Judaism's High Holy Days. In fact, the seven-day week did not come into Judaic practice for several hundred years after the time of the Exodus. However, to provide continuity with the biblical account, I decided to deal with the conflicting calendars within the narrative.

All the poetry and songs of Akhenaten that I included in

the story were actually written by Akhenaten or, in one case, by Nefertiti. I only changed a few words for readability.

I did not include details of the laws of Moses because there is no evidence that he created them. In fact, scholars have shown that they were written down and expanded upon many times, starting hundreds of years after the supposed Exodus. Again, the details of the laws are somewhat irrelevant, except to biblical literalists. Their gift is in forming the structure of a moral and legal code that would serve a people for thousands of years.

To date, despite exhaustive archaeological digs, Akhenaten's remains have not been found. There have been claims to that effect, but DNA evidence has not been conclusive, in part because inbreeding among the royal family complicates the picture. Various scholars over the past century have suggested that Moses was actually Akhenaten and have presented arguments and support for that view. This is especially interesting because there is no record of someone known as the biblical Moses nor of any mass exodus from Egypt. Yet Mose/Moses was a common Egyptian name, especially for Kings. It would appear to be as reasonable to assume a correlation between Akhenaten and Moses as it would be to assume they were entirely different people.

Practices in Judaism, Christianity and Islam that derive directly from ancient Egypt

While those of us raised in one of the three Abrahamic religions like to think ours is unique, that is far from true. They all had their origins in Ancient Egypt. Let's look at some examples.

This is a partial list, but it should give readers an indication of the lineage of religious beliefs and practice. Some ancient Egyptian practices inform one, two, or all three of the Abrahamic religions.

Bodies Must Be Whole for Burial. This Jewish and Muslim practice derives directly from Egyptian practice for thousands of years.

Sitting all night with corpse, praying. This ritual derives from Egyptian practice. In ancient Egypt, people were paid to do so, as is done today in Orthodox Jewish practice.

Naming of the Baby after 8 Days. Since childbirth was dangerous to both mother and baby (Egyptian women were tiny by today's Western standards, and in some villages, up to 50% of women died in childbirth), Egyptians waited to name a baby until he survived an initial time period.

Circumcision. Circumcision did not originate with Judaism. Egyptians had been circumcising for at least 2,000 years prior to it becoming a part of Jewish tradition. Not all ancient Egyptian males were circumcised, but the practice was common, especially among the King, priests, and nobility.

Moses' Name. Mose, Moses, or Moshe, was a common name in Egypt. Think of Thutmose I, II, III, and IV, Ahmose, Ramose, Ramesses... the list goes on. Mose is simply a descriptor. It is variously translated as "one who is given," "one who has come from," or "one who was delivered." The mythology that it means "drawn from the water" in the Hebrew language is incorrect.

Importance of the number 7. Egyptians had reverence for the number 7. In the Bible, we also see many references to this number. Here is an example.

Looking up, Jacob saw Esau coming, accompanied by four hundred men.

He divided the children among Leah, Rachel, and the two maids putting the maids and their children first, Leah and her children next, and Rachel and Joseph last. He himself went on ahead and bowed low to the ground seven times until he was near his brother. Esau ran to greet him. He embraced him and falling on his neck, he kissed him; and they wept. (Genesis 33:1-4)

Days of Atonement. According to Jewish tradition, between the High Holy Days of Rosh Hashanah and Yom Kippur is a 10-day window of opportunity to change your fate. This is strikingly similar to Wepet Renpet in ancient Egypt at the start of the new year. Heriu-Renpet started the 5-day countdown to Wepet-Renpet, which was the celebration of the New Year. The Heriu-Renpet period was one of atonement, prayers, and fasting. No business was transacted. Since the Egyptians used a 360-day calendar, these 5 days were "off the calendar" and hence imitated the time of Nun, the chaos before creation. People were anxious and prayed and reflected during that period, as Jews do today during the High Holy Days.

May his name be stricken. This phrase is recited repeatedly during the Jewish celebration of Passover. The Hebrew translation, Yimach Shemo, comes from Egypt. Kings would literally strike the name of predecessors from monuments and temples. This was most pronounced during the reign of Horemheb when he tried to erase all mention of the Amarna Kings, especially Akhenaten.

Pigs. In ancient Egypt, pigs were not acceptable as a food source by the priestly or upper classes and even most lower-class people. That prohibition was understandably violated by some poor people during times of famine. (See Daughters of

Isis by Joyce Tyldesley, p.107)

Menstruation. Menstruating women are considered ritually unclean in Ultra-Orthodox Judaism. In ancient Egypt, menstruation was considered a normal function, but a time when sexual relations were best avoided.

Worship of the Golden Calf. The 'Hebrews' of the Exodus worshipped Ba'al in the desert, according to the Bible, incurring Moses' wrath. Ba'al would have been the Apis bull, a staple of Egyptian religious belief.

Linen and Wool. Egyptians did not use wool much, but almost exclusively linen (made from flax), and they felt that mixing the two was crass since sheep were considered dirty animals. This is directly related to the Jewish law of Shatnitz (prohibition of wearing clothes containing linen and wool mixed together). However, wearing one piece of clothing that is linen and another that is wool at the same time is permitted. This prohibition against Shatnez is found in Deuteronomy 22:11 and Leviticus 19:19.

Ram's Horn. The use of the ram's horn to herald significant events was common in ancient Egypt. It is used to this day during the Jewish New Year services.

The Evil Eye. This once common belief in Judaism (Eyin Horah) stems from the eye of Horus.

Sexual pleasure. The expectation to please your wife sexually was an ancient Egyptian innovation and was radically different from surrounding cultures. This element was incorporated into Jewish practice.

The Shemah. The Shemah is arguably the holiest pledge in Judaism. It is recited every day in Jewish prayer services. "Listen, Israel. Adonai is our God, Adonai is One." This phrase is strikingly similar to an ancient Egyptian proverb: "God is One and alone, and none other existeth with Him; God is the One, the One Who hath made all things." Akhenaten elevated this to a high art form, as noted in the excerpts from his poems I used in the novel.

One God. This is considered the most important link between ancient Egypt and Judaism, Christianity, and Islam. During his reign, Akhenaten elevated Aten (Adon) to the highest God and then to the only God. However, Akhenaten was not the first king of Egypt to raise one God to prominence. When reading his poems, one is struck by how closely they parallel later Jewish thought and practice.

Son of God. The majority of Christians seem to be unaware that Jesus was not the first to refer to himself as the Son of God. Nor was Akhenaten. There were several kings of Egypt that considered themselves the Son or Brother of whatever God they currently elevated to the highest status, stretching back hundreds of years prior to Akhenaten.

42 Negative Confessions. Most scholars today agree that the Ten Commandments were derived from or heavily influenced by this list of confessions, which the dead were expected to pledge before Anubis before being admitted to the Afterworld. This list preceded the appearance of Judaism for hundreds of years.

Glossary

Akhet: the season of the Nile flooding its banks.

Ba: the concept of the personality.

Dashret Sea: now call the Red Sea.

Forty-two Negative Confessions: scholars assume this is the derivation of the Ten Commandments. They were to be memorized from childhood by ancient Egyptians, so they could be recited to Anubis upon death in order to gain entry to the Afterworld.

Great Green: the Mediterranean Sea

Heart: ancient Egyptians believed that all thought, emotions, and spiritual connections originated from the heart. They did not recognize the importance of the brain.

Ka: the concept of the soul

Kem: the original name that the ancient Egyptians called their country. Also called Kemet.

Ma'at: the basis for all of ancient Egypt's theology. It is needed for balance, prosperity and to keep evil spirits at bay.

Mafkat: the Sinai peninsula.

Nome: A government administrative unit, similar to county, province or prefecture. Egypt was divided into 42 nomes at the time of the 18ᵗʰ Dynasty.

Nun: The world just prior to Creation.

Proyet or **Peret**: the season of planting.

Shemu: harvest time.

Ta-Tjehenus: Libyans; constant raiders of Egypt.

Waset: the capital of Upper Egypt and the center of worship to Amun.

Wat-Hor: the important trade route between Egypt and points northeast, such as Babylon, Lebanon, and Canaan. It originated in the northeast corner of Egypt.

* * *